W9-DFQ-089

SCARE CARE

This illustration was especially drawn for *Scare Care* by my good friend Ronald Embleton, 1931–1988, in whose memory it is reproduced here.

—Graham Masterton

SCARE CARE

Edited by Graham Masterton
for the Scare Care Trust

A TOM DOHERTY ASSOCIATES BOOK
NEW YORK

This is a work of fiction. All the characters and events portrayed in this book are fictional, and any resemblance to real people or incidents is purely coincidental.

SCARE CARE

A TOR Book
Published by Tom Doherty Associates, Inc.
49 West 24th Street
New York, N.Y. 10010

First edition: June 1989

0 9 8 7 6 5 4 3 2 1

Acknowledgments

"Mommy" © 1989 by Kit Reed.

"Things Not Seen" © 1987 by James Robert Smith. First published in *2AM,* Spring 1987 issue. Reprinted by permission of the author.

"The Ferries" © 1982 by Ramsey Campbell. Reprinted by permission of the author.

"Good Night, Sweet Prince" © 1989 by D. W. Taylor.

"Printer's Devil" © 1989 by Celeste Paul Sefranek.

"Mammy and the Flies" © 1989 by Bruce Boston.

"The Tourists" © 1969, 1989 by John Burke. Reprinted by permission of the author.

"The Wish" © by Roald Dahl. Reprinted by permission of the author.

"Monstrum" © 1989 by J. N. Williamson.

"Breakfast" © by James Herbert. Reprinted by permission of the author.

"Clocks" © 1989 by Darrell Schweitzer. Published by arrangement with the author.

"The Strangers" © 1989 by Steve Rasnic Tem.

"Table for None" © 1989 by William Relling Jr.

"Little Miss Muffett" © 1989 by Peter Valentine Timlett.

"Night Watch" © 1989 by C. Dean Andersson. Published by arrangement with the author.

"The Last Gift" © 1989 by Peter Tremayne.

"Manny Agonistes" © 1989 by James Kisner.

"Family Man" © 1989 by Jeff Gelb.

"A Towpath Tale" © 1989 by Giles Gordon.

"Mars Will Have Blood" © 1989 by Marc Laidlaw.

Contents

Contents

FOREWORD

By Graham Masterton

All horror writers are children at heart. While their classmates grew up to be rational, useful members of the community—accountants and real-estate agents and housewives and social workers—horror writers remained preoccupied by the imaginary terrors of their childhood, and grew up to be—horror writers.

To be able to write horror stories, and to *want* to write horror stories, an author has to be able to conjure up those childhood fears as vividly as when he or she was six years old.

Fear of the dark. Fear of peculiar noises. Fear of what might be hiding in the closet. Fear of dwarfish trolls with razor-sharp teeth which every sensible six-year-old knows *without question* assemble under the bed every night and try to bite your toes if you dare to stick them out of the covers.

It was this strong empathy that horror writers have with childhood and all its frights that was the genesis of this new anthology of chilling short stories—the profits from which will go entirely to children's charities. The very best horror writers make their living out of their deep understanding of what it is to feel defenseless—what it is to feel threatened by forces which you can neither understand nor control.

For most of us, frightening ourselves is something we do for fun, for entertainment. We enjoy the prickles up the back of the neck, and the heightened flow of adrenaline. That is why horror stories and horror movies are so popular these days; always have been, and always will be.

But for thousands and thousands of children, being frightened is a daily and nightly reality. And while you and I can close the book, switch off the video, and put an instantaneous end to our feelings of fear, those children can never escape from the nightmare in which they live.

Every day, every night, even while you're reading this, children all across Britain and the United States are dreading the sound of approaching footsteps, the key in the lock, the door handle turning. Not because of ghosts, or vampires, or monsters from hell, but because of their own parents or guardians. Because of beatings, because of cigarette burns, because of relentless mental persecution, because of starvation, because of sexual abuse.

Those children experience unending terror that makes *The Exorcist* seem cozy by comparison.

One morning in the summer of 1986, woken by the dawn chorus, it occurred to me that the talent and the understanding of today's horror writers could be directed toward the relief of some of those abused children.

By the brighter light of nine o'clock, however, the idea of selling stories of supernatural fear for the sake of protecting children seemed to be extremely eccentric—perverse, even.

But tales of supernatural horror have an historic association with childhood: from the grisly fairy tales of the Brothers Grimm, to the tenderness which Frankenstein's monster tried to show to children, to modern-day stories like *Audrey Rose* and *The Shining.*

Children are creatures of magic. They know all about darkness and imaginary terrors.

And in the end, I couldn't resist the notion of selling imaginary nightmares for the sake of relieving real ones.

When I discussed *Scare Care* with publishers and fellow horror writers and the directors of several children's charities, their response was so welcoming and so immediate that I knew I would have to turn it into a reality.

The purpose of *Scare Care* is to give you a vivid and terrifying collection of stories from some of the most exciting authors writing today—to show you what coruscating talents are working in the horror genre—and to leave you with your hair standing on end.

At the same time, I wanted you to have the satisfaction of knowing that by buying this book you have helped to ease the fear and the misery that so many children have to face today, tomorrow, and every day.

All the profits that this anthology makes are going directly to the children who need it.

Having decided to put *Scare Care* together, I was then faced with what I thought would be the Herculean task of asking British and American horror writers to contribute stories. Even when you're *paying* authors to write for you, collecting anthologies of short stories is notoriously hard work. I was asking each author to give up hours and hours of work for nothing.

Very few horror writers make very much money. They depend on short stories which they sell to a small number of horror and mystery magazines, and on novels, which have a comparatively limited sale.

So for the contributors to this anthology, donating a story represented not just a donation of their talent, but a considerable financial donation, too.

In spite of that, the warmth and the immediacy of the response I received from horror writers on both sides of the Atlantic were remarkable. I needed twenty stories to put together a viable anthology—I was sent three times that many. Even those writers who were unable to contribute because of illness or pressing deadlines sent messages of support and enthusiasm.

I felt that I had reached out and found an extraordinary community of caring and generous people—even more extraordinary because all of them had built their reputations on stories of ghouls and werewolves and graveyards.

Many of the stories touch on childhood experiences (although my editorial policy was strict—no children to be chopped up). Some touch the subject of child abuse, and come very close to the raw nerve of the real problem that we are trying to deal with. You will see in *Scare Care* just how deep the horror writer's feeling for childhood terror can be.

Some of the stories are classic frighteners. Others are wickedly amusing. One or two of them, I have to admit, are out-and-out stomach-churners.

With two or three exceptions, all of the stories are new and were written especially for this anthology. Some of them are quite exceptional, and take the reader right to the leading edge of modern horror writing.

Others are more conventional, but still wonderfully scary. I selected them all because of their vividness, their skill, and as far as possible to give new readers a picture of today's horror writing in the round.

It is quite impossible for me to give enough thanks to all of those who made *Scare Care* a first-thing-in-the-morning daydream that so rapidly and so convincingly came true. My appreciation above all to the charities themselves, for having the imagination to see right from the beginning that *Scare Care* could benefit so many needy children; and a particular thank-you to Jerry Williamson, who unofficially appointed himself my U.S. bureau, and who radiated energy, enthusiasm, and sheer hard work like a one-man power station.

To Timothy J. L. Cox, my good friend for so many years, and to Michael Hudson, for cheerfully helping with the legal side. To Jean Manning and her ladies at her Print Centre in Epsom, for contributing so much duplicating work.

To my wife, Wiescka, who is the inspiration for everything I do. To the trustees of the Scare Care Trust, Julie Cox and Simon Carpenter.

To my three sons, magical creatures themselves.

And last, a thank-you to *you*, for buying *Scare Care*. Every penny you've spent on being scared will go to show how much you've cared.

If you wish to make a further donation to *Scare Care*, please mail your check or money order to Scare Care Trust (U.S.), Account number 103/0036189, Irving Trust Company, 51 West 51st St., New York, NY 10019.

MOMMY

Kit Reed

Kit Reed is one of the finest and most vivid writers of horror fiction I know; and here she demonstrates her skill with a matchless portrayal of what it is like to be a child in the queasy and terrifying world of adult irrationality. Kit began work as a reporter for the St. Petersburg, Florida, *Times,* and later for the New Haven *Register.* Currently she writes novels and works with student writers at Wesleyan University. She's written eleven novels, including *Captain Grownup, The Better Part,* and *The Ballad of T. Rantula.* A former Guggenheim fellow, she is the first American recipient of a five-year literary grant from the Abraham Woursell Foundation. Her newest novel is *Catholic Girls,* from Donald I. Fine. Her newest short story: this unforgettably claustrophobic meeting with "Mommy."

How she thundered through the house when she was in one of those moods. How she railed at them and hit sometimes, always hugging Penny and Sally afterward, holding them close and sobbing: "Oh, girls, I didn't mean it. You know how Mommy gets when she's on a diet."

The trouble was that Mommy was always on a diet. She lost three pounds a week. Every week. She had been doing this ever since the girls were born, because only a fool expects the weight gained in pregnancy to disappear with the birth of the baby.

Penny and Sally had heard this story so often that it made their hair stiffen and their teeth crack. It came at tea, right after Mommy had daintily pushed aside her pretty cake, uneaten, saying, with an exquisite superiority, "Oh, no thank you, I don't dare."

It was at this point that some envious girlfriend usually wiped the icing from her own mouth and said, "But you don't have to worry about your weight."

Mommy always rolled her eyes and groaned. "It's all I ever think about."

The friend, whom Mommy would choose because her clothes were a little too tight and her midsection seemed to be padded with bolsters, was always gratifying in her incredulity. "You?"

"Me," Mommy would say, running her hands down her narrow hips. "You should have seen me," she would say, shuddering with disgust, and underneath the table or behind the sofa where they were hiding, the girls would shiver because they knew what was coming. "Fat as a toad."

After a pause into which huge implications fell, Mommy would say, perhaps too grimly, "I could eat anything I wanted and never gain an ounce until I had those wretched babies."

Mommy's upholstered friends always made the girls' throats ache because they seemed so sweet, so careless of their figures and, well, so *motherly*. These friends would say at once, "But your girls are so adorable."

"Well, they cause a lot of trouble."

Under the table or behind the sofa where they were hiding, the girls would tremble because they were thin as whips and they knew how this infuriated Mommy. Without having to consult a calendar they knew where in the week they were by the way their bellies felt, and depending on how full they were, or how empty, they knew what was coming.

Mommy was rigid with dislike. "They made me gain a hundred pounds. One hundred pounds. I went through hell to lose it."

(Under the table Penny would try to think about Mommy weighing a hundred pounds more, to think what a hundred extra pounds looked like if they were cut off a person, but of course Mommy had destroyed all the old pictures, so she didn't have a clue. As near as she could come was to think about herself and Sally, mooshed together, but that was only ninety, and there was no way you could detach that from a person.) "Sally?"

"Shh. What?" said Sally, who was older.

"Where do you think it went after she lost it?"

"Where do I think *what* went?"

"The weight. The hundred pounds?"

"Oh Lord," Sally whispered. "Do you think they're still out there?"

Cramped from staying hidden so Mommy wouldn't see her and get mad, Penny considered. She envisioned the hundred pounds as a brownish amorphous vapor, shucked for the time being, but hovering . . . "They didn't just disappear. They had to go somewhere."

Now that Penny had raised the question, Sally could not let it drop. "Wow, what if they're still around? What if they're out there somewhere? What do you think they look like?"

Then Penny made things worse. "And what about the three pounds she loses every week?"

"Oh, that," Sally said, as if for reassurance. "She gains those back."

"Oh no, she doesn't," said Penny, opening a door they could never quite close again. "The three pounds go wherever the hundred went. Then she gains three new ones."

"They made me get fat and I lost Chester." Mommy was not bitter, exactly, but something in her tone silenced her whispering daughters. "So here I am, and it isn't easy. If you've ever been fat," Mommy would say to the fat friend, "you'll do anything to prevent it."

She always described the year of privation: the gruelling exercises, the agony of having her jaws wired shut, the liquid diet she subsisted on. Then came the scariest part of all. "Now I'm on maintenance."

It was maintenance that was killing them: grim meals of boiled vegetables and groats in a thin sauce three times a day, Monday through Friday, meals that depressed the girls and made Mommy increasingly edgy because, Monday to Friday, she was never not starving. No wonder the girls were thin as whips and getting thinner; no wonder they trembled. Privation made them weak, but it made Mommy furious.

Still, Monday to Friday, she weighed three times a day and again at bedtime, and Monday to Friday, she managed. She would emerge from the bathroom on Friday nights, pretty and beaming. "A hundred and five, darlings. A hundred and five."

Oh, how they would celebrate, the girls would open three bottles of Perrier and watch admiringly as Mommy circled before the mirror in that week's new purchases, after which Mommy would add a few drops of Rose's lime juice to the Perrier and they would drink. How the girls would murmur and giggle, trying desperately to make the right admiring sounds while Mommy preened, and how they hoped that this time the diet had *really worked* and everything would be different.

"If she's really thin enough this time, then maybe she can finally get married," Penny would say. "Then we can have a nice father after all."

Sally said, wisely, "Not yet. Ninety-eight, maybe. She says she doesn't want anybody to see her this way."

In her peach peignoir, Mommy looked adorable, so that Penny would say to Sally, "But she looks all right to me."

"Ah," said Sally, who was older, "but when she says see her this way, fat isn't what she means. She's talking about . . ." Her voice dropped. "You know."

In our gladdest moments come intimations of disaster, and so it was with Penny and Sally, tossing off their Perrier with abandon, and at the same time, worrying . . .

Because it was on Friday nights that the girls had to huddle in their bed, talking late until it got light about how they could change Saturday. The problem, of course, was that the matter with Saturday, if you could pin it down and make sense of it, was Fridays. It started happening Fridays, but they could never stay up late enough to forestall it.

No matter how late they stayed up, exhausted and yawning, Mommy would remain firm, staunch and unshakeable. Her only observable excess might be another Perrier. Yet if they should look up from the TV, they would find her studying them over the rim of her glass, fevered and beady-eyed, and they knew that whether it was midnight or three A.M. before they left her alone, the end would be the same. Although she pretended to be enjoying the TV, giggling into her Perrier, they knew Mommy was waiting. Just as they finished brushing their teeth and trooped into the bedroom they could hear Mommy's furry little voice, directed at Mommy alone, murmuring: "*This* calls for a little celebration."

And no matter what they planned for Saturday, there were not really any possibilities. Until she met Barry, Mommy never had much luck with men, which meant they had slim hopes for a father with a better temper. They were afraid she was never going to catch Barry, because when Mommy did go out on Saturday nights she always got home in time for a little celebration, which was always followed by Sunday, which was the best and the worst for Penny and Sally.

When they woke on Saturday mornings, Mommy would be sleeping. Sometimes she slept sitting up on the sofa with her hand trailing in the empty fudge pot, delicate pink fingers curled around the partially licked spoon. At other times she would be in her bed and the girls would find vestiges of a chocolate layer cake on the kitchen table with a loving note. Vestiges meant the layer cake had been reduced to the thinnest slice that could be left standing: "Here is the cake I made for you. Please let Mommy sleep."

So Saturdays and Sundays would be both wonderful and terrible—wonderful because of the steaks and pastas, the gallons of ice cream, the cookies, the cakes, cheeses and chocolates, food in abundance, goodies which had to be finished before Monday, or else. With the fragile cheer of an alcoholic, Mommy took the girls on outings, met potential men for long luncheons, flirted and smiled, smiled and went home to a sodden evening of food . . .

The girls decided the man they liked best was Barry, and they thought Mommy did too. On her behalf they flirted with him, thought, Oh! If they could only collect a father, a father they could keep. Barry seemed to like them too, which was both a good thing and a bad thing. It was nice to have a friend to turn to, but if Mommy found out he loved the girls, whom she didn't much like even though she swore otherwise, naturally she would drop him just to spite them.

Weekends always found her too busy to weigh so that it would be Monday morning before the girls clung and cringed; the alarm clock on Monday mornings was always superseded by Mommy's outraged shriek:

"A hundred and eight!"

After which she would appear at the door to their bedroom, shouting in a huge voice: "How could you! How could you let me? You rotten children, look what you made me do!"

It did them no good to explain or apologize then. If she had gained three pounds it was their fault, for making her bake cakes and boil fudge, for forcing her to bring in steaks and puddings, for putting her in harm's way, for her miserable life, it seemed, and for the hundred pounds, for which she had never forgiven them. In anger, Mommy was terrible.

As Mommy became more interested in Barry it got worse. Every Monday she was determined to succeed, and every Friday she toppled. As the weekend orgies got more intense, the weekday meals got even sparser. On the premise that ugly food was easier to resist, Mommy began mashing boiled turnips and serving even the green beans pureed. She hated eggplant, which the girls could not eat without gagging, and therefore she had to beat them to make them eat because even more than fat, Mommy hated waste.

To keep from starving, they began to squirrel away food—bits of chocolate and cheese and cake from the weekends, when Mommy was too far gone in food to make sense. If they rationed goodies, eating a little each day, they could almost subsist on Mommy's Slenderella meals and survive until the next feast.

They might have managed, too, if they hadn't come home one day to discover her painting their room. They should have known as they came in the front door that there was going to be trouble. The house smelled of dust turned out by a relentless taking down of curtains and moving of furniture. The house smelled of dust and was pervaded by a sound they only recognized too late as sobbing: Mommy. They found her sitting in lotus position on the bare floor of the bedroom, surrounded by the shredded paper napkins and plastic bags in which they had hidden their week's provisions. Rigid with fury, she was smirched by smeared food, surrounded by crumbs.

"Look what you did!" she screamed. "Look what you made me do. Look what you made me do and it's only Wednesday!"

The beatings were so awful that they decided to tell Barry. While

Mommy was sleeping off her Friday night layer cake that week they made a hasty phone call and sneaked out front to sob out their stories. He hugged them, he sympathized, and then he came into the house with every intention of accusing their mother.

"Where is she?" he asked. "Tilda! Tilda?"

When they went into her bedroom she was sleeping, with the peach peignoir gathered about her like a gossamer cocoon. There was not a chocolate stain on her gown, nor a crumb in her bosom. She was curled on her side, one hundred and five pounds going on one hundred and six after this evening, with her hand curved under her cheek, and she was smiling.

"Oh, kids," said Barry, "you must be mistaken."

Because they were both crying, he waked Mommy gently, and just as gently put the question to Mommy, who looked like a bewildered child herself, all sleepy and rosy from the chocolate. "You wouldn't ever hurt the girls, would you?"

"Oh, Barry," she said, and the tears on her eyelashes were like diamonds on velvet, "how could I hurt them? You know I wouldn't."

He turned to them as if he had proved it. "See? How could this sweet little lady possibly hurt anybody? Maybe you'd better apologize."

Given that he would be gone well before the retaliations, the girls decided maybe they'd better.

It was, therefore, their circumstances that made them desperate. They would not have done what they did if Mommy hadn't come to their room after she kissed Barry goodbye and turned on them. Their punishment ended some hours later with the two little girls sobbing and exhausted but determined to do something about it.

Penny said, dispiritedly, "He didn't believe us because Mommy is so tiny."

So it was Sally who put her finger on it. "It's because he doesn't know what she really, really looks like."

Penny said, "He doesn't know what she really looks like because she's always on a diet."

"The hundred pounds!" Sally said.

"And all the rest of them!"

Sally said, in a hushed voice, "Do you really think they're out there?"

"I know it!"

How do you summon a hundred pounds? How do you summon three pounds a week for fifty-two weeks over the eight years since Mommy had her jaws unwired and Penny passed her first birthday? Faith has a lot to do with it—faith and the fact that whether or not Penny and Sally knew, scientists know that fat hides in brown cells that shrink but never go away, thousands of brown cells, waiting to inflate . . .

The girls thought it would be appropriate to devise a ritual. They took the birthday money that Barry had given them and began with an orgy, something they'd never done without her. While Mommy was away at the Health Club, burning calories in the weight room so she could take in more, they brought in pizza and pies, fried chicken and candy, cans of Betty Crocker Instant Frosting; dog food, Cheez Doodles, Ring Dings, they didn't care.

They did not so much *eat* the food as *arrange* it around an effigy they had created by merging Sally's Barbie doll with a recent photograph of Mommy. Using the bathroom scales as a base, they set up the Mommy doll and then, chanting, they heaped, piled, festooned it with food as if that as much as anything would lure their mother's lost pounds, summon, command them: Be here.

Penny still thought of the lost pounds as swarming in a brown cloud that hovered—over the rooftree, or over their skinny mother, waiting to descend? She closed her eyes and squinted hard, clenching her fists and muttering, "Mommy, Mommy, come to Mommy."

Sally imagined the pounds as pink fluffy puffs of nothing that spotted the landscape until the right person passed through and they bounced over tufts of grass, magnetized by the person, so that they collected. Moved by Penny's invocation, she called, in counterpoint, "Thirty, forty, fifty, eighty, three hundred and twenty . . ."

Even though they both thought the ritual wasn't really going to bring back lost weight, it made them feel better. They might not be able to stop their mother's cruelty, but at least they were doing something about it. The world was going to know how they felt.

Neither of them imagined for a minute that through a strange conflation of events—humors, phases of the moon, the mysterious workings of justice—they were going to get what they wanted, that if pounds didn't travel in clouds or puffs they did hide in brown cells that could be re-inflated, that lost weight crouches inside the loser, waiting to spring . . .

They were, therefore, surprised when they heard the front door open and their mother's footsteps sounded heavier than usual. Caught, as it were, with their hands in the cookie jar, the girls scrambled madly, disassembling their totem, hiding food.

"When she finds out, she's going to kill us," Penny said.

Sally said, "Sometimes I wish she would."

But instead of stopping at the girls' door, the huge, thumping footsteps plopped on down the hall, and from behind their mother's closed door they could hear her pacing thunderously, puffing, groaning, screaming . . .

"Oh no! My clothes! They're splitting!" They heard a terrible thud.

Listening at the door, Sally said, "What if it worked?"

Penny whispered, "I think we'd better get Barry."

"You think he can make it stop?"

"No, dummy. I want him to believe us. He has to *see*."

So it was that during the worst of what happened next, the girls were far away from the house, which meant that when they returned with Barry they were as surprised as Barry was to find the front door hard to open. It stuck partway because the front hall was filled with something huge and awful, pink and quivering.

"We've got to get in there," Barry cried, grappling with the door, which was jounced as if by foam rubber. "Something's happened to Tilda."

Without listening to the girls' hurried warnings, he hurled himself against the door, pushing inward until it yielded, and then he entered, dragging the protesting girls after him.

"Tilda!" Barry cried, alarmed, "Tilda, dear!"

The part that had been obstructing the door was large, pink and quivering. At first Penny thought it was an enormous breast, but the absence of a nipple made it clear that it was something else—a knee, she thought, before she realized that the item, bloated beyond recognition and buried in flesh, was indeed her mother's elbow. The rest of the body ballooned to fill the hall and the living-dining room behind, but they would not want to get close enough to see the rest—how big it was, how pendulous and mottled. It was bad enough to see the face resting in the crook of the elbow, its monstrous cheeks and inflated lips, hanging flesh obscuring the eyes, the eyes! At the sound of Barry's anguished outcry, the thing that was in fact not a thing but Mommy, raised an appendage from the surging mound of flesh, and with two fingers, parted the folds where the eyes should be. As the eye reappeared and she recognized him she cried out, "Barry, oh no!" Then just before the fingers gave way and the rolling flesh thundered into other flesh, covering the eye forever, she spied the girls and from somewhere inside that huge, uncontrollable, heaving pink monstrosity she had become, Mommy brought the awful, familiar words, "Now you're going to get it."

Penny shrieked and pulled back but Sally closed firm hands on her. "Wait," the older sister said, "this is how it happens."

And it was. As the two children stood before their mother's last and greatest rages, the huge body rolled and heaved, squeaked and rumbled with Mommy's efforts to break free of the hall and the archways that girdled her waist and hips so she could get at them. Her thorax heaved and her heart inflated with her attempt to move her buttocks away from the fireplace that constrained her. Then the last three pounds—yesterday's pounds!—came out from wherever they had been hiding and swamped her.

"You did it," she groaned, thin last words coming out of her like puffs right before she deflated and it was over.

Then the orphan girls, who would be adopted by Barry, looked over the puffy pink mass of empty skin at the ravaged turkey carcass and the skeletal layer cake in the kitchen and it was Penny who said the last words before they left the house forever. "No, Mommy. *You* did."

This story is written with special thanks to Lois Gould, who first raised the question about the hundred pounds a friend had lost. Where did they go? I said she'd better look carefully before she went out because I thought he'd left them outside her front door. —K.R.

THINGS NOT SEEN

James Robert Smith

Bob Smith's participation in *Scare Care,* appropriately, got all tangled up with the birth of his first child William Andrew, so I received slightly more news from him about his wife Carole's labor pains than I did about the availability of rights for "Things Not Seen." Bob is one of those horror writers who keeps the standards of the small press sector as high as they are: this story originally appeared in *2AM* magazine but its hair-raising view of childhood sensitivity makes it especially apt for far wider appreciation. Born in Brunswick, Georgia, in 1957, Bob lives in Charlotte, North Carolina, where he owns and runs the comic specialty shops 'Nuff Said! He writes in his spare time, managing to produce several thousand words of fiction each week, and has developed a stark black style which (one day, we hope, Bob, when you've *quite* finished producing more Smiths!) we're going to see in a full-length novel.

The little boy stood in the corner—out of the couple's way—and stared in wide-eyed horror at the growing stain upon the kitchen floor. While the two busied themselves in preparing their supper, he watched as the black-red splotch welled up from the cracks between the shiny tiles. Why didn't they see? Why didn't they take note of the obscene puddle that continued to spread as they went about their pleasure?

It was obvious that they were too involved with what they were doing to notice. He just retreated even further into his corner, obeying that quote so often spoken at him: "Children should be seen and not heard." The child remained in the shadow near the pantry door and watched.

"Honey." The man straightened from his task of searching for a dish beneath the counter. "You'd better check the rolls. I think they should be done now."

"Oh. Okay." The young wife hurried across the kitchen floor to the oven. Child's eyes stared fixedly as she stepped directly into the crimson wet and made left-footed tracks wherever she moved. "You're right," she said, not seeing. She retrieved the fresh, warm bread and brought it in her mittened hands to the table. This time, her right foot was planted in the pooling stuff and she made another bloody trail across the kitchen.

Then the two were all a-flurry as they made their table ready. They moved from stove to sink to table, each time navigating the puddle. The child gazed in horrified wonder at the maze of tacky, red shoe prints that the others left behind them. The floor was a gory mess. And still, only he acknowledged it.

Finally, they were finished with their preparations and had seated themselves. The boy watched them from his hiding spot.

The woman's eyes played over the kitchen and dining area. "Where's Sonny?" she asked.

"Oh, I fed him something earlier and he went out. I expect he's outside playing." He smiled and looked hungrily at the meal before them. "Dig in," he said.

Together they ate, halting from time to time to comment on how good the food tasted or how nice the weather had been for their first, full day in their new home. They ate, cleared the table and washed the dishes together. They always shared the housework. Inside the pantry, one pair of eyes watched sickly as the creeping pool began to cool and thicken. In places, it had dried completely and was not affected as they strode upon it. In other spots, it squished under their tread.

In the middle of the floor they met on their ways to finishing their tasks of tidying up. They smiled and embraced.

"Oh, Bill, I love our new house! We were so lucky to find it!"

Bill squeezed his wife tightly. "Well, I want you to be happy. We need a nice home to raise our family in." He lifted his right arm and glanced at his watch. "We'd better get ready for the Sims couple. They're supposed to be here in a few minutes."

They went into the den. The child watched them go; their shoes were gooey with the stuff and their shins were speckled with droplets. They tracked across the neat, shag carpet. Bill went to the door and Annie set out a candy dish full of caramels and a shiny, unused ashtray. She hoped that neither of their new neighbors smoked; she hated the smell of cigarettes. Still, she felt that she must be hospitable to them.

"Do you think that they'll like Sonny?" Annie watched her husband at the door.

He half turned to her. "Sure. Sure, they'll like Sonny. Why not?"

"Well, you know how some people are." But she had to stop as their visitors came clattering up the front step to the porch. She'd have to remind Bill to fix that loose board.

For an hour, the four sat and socialized. Bill made an effort to steer the conversation away from politics and religion and did his best to find out about their new neighborhood. The evening was pleasant with talk of local shopping centers, car pools and other mundane affairs. The two men found a common fondness of duck hunting and the women shared an interest in country crafts. No one mentioned how the blood dried and flaked off their shoes.

A bottle of wine was brought out and the talk began to flow more freely and casually. Eventually, someone mentioned the house's former tenants.

"Y'know," Mr. Sims said, "we thought they were never going to put this place on the market." He paused and gave the new neighbors a serious, squint-eyed stare. "You *do* know about what happened here?" The women fell silent.

Bill fidgeted. The topic made him feel uncomfortable. "Well, yes. We know a little. Though not as much as you do, I suppose."

"The guy's name was Andersen. Al Andersen. Violent bastard. I reckon they had to wait until his sentence was carried out before they could put his house up for sale."

"And his wife was such a sweet woman . . ." Mrs. Sims was interrupted by a whining and a scratching at the front door.

Bill stood and strode across the den. "And this," he announced, "is Sonny." He opened the screen and the big, blond dog trotted in, tongue hanging and tail wagging. There was a sniff for each of the guests before he plopped himself down at Annie's feet.

They all stared blankly for a moment, out of words.

"Was there anyone else?" Annie asked.

"What do you mean?" It was Mr. Sims.

"The Andersens. Besides Al Andersen and his wife. Was there anyone else?"

"Yes," Mrs. Sims answered, her words very low and hard to hear. She was remembering a playful young voice and appreciated gifts of homemade cookies. "They had a sweet, little child. A little boy."

Inside the pantry, beneath the low shelves where he was trying to hide, the boy crouched and waited for the brute.

THE FERRIES

Ramsey Campbell

Ramsey Campbell has singlehandedly done more to promote the cause of British horror fiction than any other writer. Apart from giving us scores of finely crafted stories of depth and quality, his enthusiasm for good horror and his personal affability have helped to make countless fantasy conventions both cohesive and successful. His assistance with *Scare Care* was signal. Ramsey's work has a luminous Liverpudlianism about it: his earlier novels *The Parasite* and *The Doll Who Ate His Mother* have been reissued lately, and a new novel, *Ancient Images*, has just emerged, as well as stories for more horror magazines and anthologies than I have fingers to count. He is an anthologist in his own right: *Fine Frights* for Tor and, shortly, *Scared Stiff* as an illustrated trade-sized paperback. "The Ferries" has all the chilling atmosphere of classic Campbell.

When Berry reached Parkgate promenade he heard the waves. He couldn't recall having heard them during his stroll down the winding road from Neston village, between banks whispering with grass, past the guarded lights of infrequently curtained windows. Beneath clouds diluted by moonlight, the movement of the waves looked indefinably strange. They sounded faint, not quite like water.

The promenade was scarcely two cars wide. Thin lanterns stood on concrete stalks above the sea wall, which was overlooked by an assortment of early Victorian buildings: antique shops, cafés that in the afternoons must be full of ladies taking tea and cakes, a nursing home, a private school that looked as though it had been built as something else. In the faltering moonlight all of them looked black and white. Some were Tudor-striped.

As he strolled—the June night was mild, he might as well enjoy himself as best he could now he was here—he passed the Marie Celeste Hotel. That must have appealed to his uncle. He was still grinning wryly when he reached his uncle's address.

Just then the moon emerged from the clouds, and he saw what was wrong with the waves. There was no water beyond the sea wall, only an expanse of swaying grass that stretched as far as he could see. The sight of the grass, overlooked by the promenade buildings as though it was still the River Dee, made him feel vaguely but intensely expectant, as though about to glimpse something on the pale parched waves.

Perhaps his uncle felt this too, for he was sitting at the black bow window on the first floor of the white house, gazing out beyond the sea wall. His eyes looked colourless as moonlight. It took three rings of the bell to move him.

Berry shouldn't feel resentful. After all, he was probably his uncle's only living relative. Nevertheless there were decisions to be made in London, at the publishers: books to be bought or rejected—several were likely to be auctioned. He'd come a long way hurriedly, by several trains; his uncle's call had sounded urgent enough for that, as urgent as the pips that had cut him off. Berry only wished he knew why he was here.

When at last his uncle opened the door, he looked unexpectedly old. Perhaps living ashore had aged him. He had always been small, but now he looked dwindled, though still tanned and leathery. In his spotless black blazer with its shining silvery buttons, and his tiny gleaming shoes, he resembled a doll of himself.

"Here we are again." Though he sounded gruff, his handshake was firm, and felt grateful for company. When he'd toiled upstairs, using the banisters as a series of walking-sticks, he growled, "Sit you down."

There was no sense of the sea in the flat, not even maritime prints to enliven the timidly patterned wallpaper. Apart from a couple of large old trunks, the flat seemed to have nothing to do with his uncle. It felt like a waiting-room.

"Get that down you, James." His uncle's heartiness seemed faded; even the rum was a brand you could buy in supermarkets, not one of the prizes he'd used to bring back from voyages. He sat gazing beyond the promenade, sipping the rum as though it was as good as any other.

"How are you, uncle? It's good to see you." They hadn't seen each other for ten years, and Berry felt inhibited; besides, his uncle detested effusiveness. When he'd finished his rum he said, "You sounded urgent on the phone."

"Aye." The years had made him even more taciturn. He seemed to resent being reminded of his call.

"I wouldn't have expected you to live so far from everything," Berry said, trying a different approach.

"It went away." Apparently he was talking about the sea, for he continued: "There used to be thirteen hotels and a pier. All the best people came here to bathe. They said the streets were as elegant as Bath. The private school you passed, that was the old Assembly Rooms."

Though he was gazing across the sea wall, he didn't sound nostalgic. He sat absolutely still, as though relishing the stability of the room. He'd used to pace restlessly when talking, impatient to return to the sea.

"Then the Dee silted up," he was saying. "It doesn't reach here now, except at spring tides and in storms. That's when the rats and voles flee onto the promenade—hordes of them, they say. I haven't seen it, and I don't mean to."

"You're thinking of moving?"

"Aye." Frowning at his clenched fists, he muttered, "Will you take me back with you tomorrow and let me stay until I find somewhere? I'll have my boxes sent on."

He mustn't want to make the journey alone in case he was taken ill. Still, Berry couldn't help sounding a little impatient. "I don't live near the sea, you know."

"I know that." Reluctantly he added, "I wish I lived farther away."

Perhaps now that he'd had to leave the sea, his first love, he wanted to forget about it quickly. Berry could tell he'd been embarrassed to ask for help—a captain needing help from a nephew who was seasick on hovercraft! But he was a little old man now, and his tan was only a patina; all at once Berry saw how frail he was. "All right, uncle," he said gently. "It won't be any trouble."

His uncle was nodding, not looking at him, but Berry could see he was moved. Perhaps now was the time to broach the idea Berry had had on the train. "On my way here," he said carefully, "I was remembering some of the tales you used to tell."

"You remember them, do you?" The old man didn't sound as though he wanted to. He drained a mouthful of rum in order to refill his glass. Had the salt smell that was wafting across the grass reminded him too vividly?

Berry had meant to suggest the idea of a book of his uncle's yarns, for quite a few had haunted him: the pigmies who could carry ten times their own weight, the flocks of birds that buried in guano any ships that ventured into their territory, the light whose source was neither sun nor moon but that outlined an island on the horizon, which receded if ships made for it. Would it be a children's book or a book that tried to trace the sources? Perhaps this wasn't the time to discuss it, for the smell that was drifting through the window was stagnant, very old.

"There was one story I never told you."

Berry's head jerked up; he had been nodding off. Even his uncle had never begun stories as abruptly—as reluctantly—as this.

"Some of the men used to say it didn't matter if you saw it so long as you protected yourself." Was the old man talking to himself, to take his mind off the desiccated river, the stagnant smell? "One night we all saw it. One minute the sea was empty, the next that thing was there, close enough to swim to. Some of the men would almost have done that, to get it over with." He gulped a mouthful of rum and stared sharply out across the pale dry waves. "Only they could see the faces watching. None of us forgot that, ever. As soon as we got ashore all of us bought ourselves protection. Even I did,'' he said bitterly, ''when I'd used to say civilized men kept pictures on walls.''

Having struggled out of his blazer, which he'd unbuttoned carefully and tediously, he displayed his left forearm. Blinking sleepily, Berry made out a tattoo, a graceful sailing ship surrounded by a burst of light. Its masts resembled almost recognizable symbols.

''The younger fellows thought that was all we needed. We all wanted to believe that would keep us safe. I wonder how they feel now they're older.'' The old man turned quickly toward the window; he seemed angry that he'd been distracted. Something had changed his attitudes drastically, for he had hated tattoos. It occurred to Berry, too late to prevent him from dozing, that his uncle had called him because he was afraid to be alone.

Berry's sleep was dark and profound. Half-submerged images floated by, so changed as to be unrecognizable. Sounds reached him rather as noise from the surface might try to reach the depths of the sea. It was impossible to tell how many times his uncle had cried out before the calls woke him.

''James . . .'' The voice was receding, but at first Berry failed to notice this; he was too aware of the smell that filled the room. Something that smelled drowned in stagnant water was near him, so near that he could hear its creaking. At once he was awake, and so afraid that he thought he was about to be sick.

''James . . .'' Both the creaking and the voice were fading. Eventually he managed to persuade himself that despite the stench, he was alone in the room. Forcing his eyes open, he stumbled to the window. Though it was hard to focus his eyes and see what was out there, his heart was already jolting.

The promenade was deserted; the buildings gleamed like bone. Above the sea wall the lanterns glowed thinly. The wide dry river was flooded with grass, which swayed in the moonlight, rustling and glinting. Over the silted river, leaving a wake of grass that looked whiter than the rest, a ship was receding.

It seemed to be the colour and the texture of the moon. Its sails looked stained patchily by mould. It was full of holes, all of which were misshapen by glistening vegetation. Were its decks crowded with figures? If so, he was grateful that he couldn't see their faces, for their movements made him think of drowned things lolling underwater, dragged back and forth by currents.

Sweat streamed into his eyes. When he'd blinked them clear, the moon was darkening. Now the ship looked more like a mound from which a few trees sprouted, and perhaps the crowd was only swaying bushes. Clouds closed over the moon, but he thought he could see a pale mass sailing away, overtopped by lurid sketches that might be masts. Was that his uncle's voice, its desperation overwhelmed by despair? When moonlight flooded the landscape a few moments later, there was nothing but the waves of grass, from which a whiter swathe was fading.

He came to himself when he began shivering. An unseasonably chill wind was clearing away the stench of stagnant water. He gazed in dismay at his uncle's blazer, draped neatly over the empty chair.

. . .

There wasn't much that he could tell the police. He had been visiting his uncle, whom he hadn't seen for years. They had both had a good deal to drink, and his uncle, who had seemed prematurely aged, had begun talking incoherently and incomprehensibly. He'd woken to find that his uncle had wandered away, leaving his blazer, though it had been a cold night.

Did they believe him? They were slow and thorough, these policemen; their thoughts were as invisible as he meant his to be. Surely his guilt must be apparent, the shame of hiding the truth about his uncle, of virtually blackening his character. In one sense, though, that seemed hardly to matter: he was sure they wouldn't find his uncle alive. Eventually, since Berry could prove that he was needed in London, they let him go.

He trudged along the sweltering promenade. Children were scrambling up and down the sea wall, old people on sticks were being promenaded by relatives. In the hazy sunshine, most of the buildings were still black and white. Everywhere signs said FRESH SHRIMPS. In a shop that offered "Gifts and Bygones," ships were stiff in bottles. Waves of yellowing grass advanced, but never very far.

He ought to leave, and be grateful that he lived inland. If what he'd seen last night had been real, the threat was far larger than he was. There was nothing he could do.

But suppose he had only heard his uncle's voice on the silted river, and had hallucinated the rest? He'd been overtired, and confused by his uncle's ramblings; how soon had he wakened fully? He wanted to believe that the old man had wandered out beyond the promenade and had collapsed, or even that he was alive out there, still wandering.

There was only one way to find out. He would be in sight of the crowded promenade. Holding his briefcase above his head as though he was submerging, he clambered down the sea wall.

The grass was tougher than it looked. Large patches had to be struggled through. After five hundred yards he was sweating, yet he seemed to be no closer to the far bank, nor to anything else. Ahead through the haze he could just distinguish the colours of fields in their frames of trees and hedges. Factory chimneys resembled grey pencils. All this appeared to be receding.

He struggled onward. Grass snagged him, birds flew up on shrill wings, complaining. He could see no evidence of the wake he'd seen last night: nothing but the interminable grass, the screeching birds, the haze. Behind him the thick heat had blurred the promenade, the crowds were pale shadows. Their sounds had been swallowed by the hissing of grass.

He'd been tempted several times to turn back, and was on the point of doing so, when he saw a gleam in the dense grass ahead. It was near the place where he'd last glimpsed the ship, if he had done so. The gleaming object looked like a small shoe.

He had to persuade himself to go forward. He remembered the swaying figures on the decks, whose faces he'd dreaded to see. Nevertheless he advanced furiously, tearing a path through the grass with his briefcase. He was almost there before he saw that the object wasn't a shoe. It was a bottle.

When inertia carried him forward, he realized that the bottle wasn't empty. For an unpleasant moment he thought it contained the skeleton of a small animal. Peering through the grime that coated the glass, he made out a whitish model ship with tattered sails. Tiny overgrown holes gaped in it. Though its decks were empty, he had seen it before.

He stood up too quickly, and almost fell. The heat seemed to flood his skull. The ground underfoot felt unstable; a buzzing of insects attacked him; there was a hint of a stagnant smell. He was ready to run, dizzy as he was, to prevent himself from thinking.

Then he remembered his uncle's despairing cry: "James, James . . ." Even then, if he had been able to run, he might have done nothing—but his dizziness both hindered him and gave him time to feel ashamed. If there was a chance of helping his uncle, however impossible it seemed— He snatched up the bottle and threw it into his briefcase. Then, trying to forget about it, he stumbled back toward the crowds.

. . .

His uncle was calling him. He woke to the sound of a shriek. Faces were sailing past him, close enough to touch if he could have reached through the glass. It was only a train on the opposite line, rushing away from London. Nevertheless he couldn't sleep after that. He finished reading the typescript he'd brought with him, though he knew by now he didn't want to buy the book.

The state of his desk was worse than he'd feared. His secretary had answered most of his letters, but several books had piled up, demanding to be read. He was stuffing two of them into his briefcase, to be read on the bus and, if he wasn't too tired, at home, when he found he was holding the grimy bottle. At once he locked it in a drawer. Though he wasn't prepared to throw it away until he understood its purpose, he was equally reluctant to take it home.

That night he could neither sleep nor read. He tried strolling in Holland Park, but while that tired him further, it failed to calm him. The moonlit clouds that were streaming headlong across the sky made everything beneath them look unstable. Though he knew that the lit houses beyond the swaying trees were absolutely still, he kept feeling that the houses were rocking slyly, at anchor.

He lay trying to relax. Beyond the windows of his flat, Kensington High Street seemed louder than ever. Nervous speculations kept him awake. He felt he'd been meant to find the bottle, but for what purpose? Surely it couldn't harm him; after all, he had only once been to sea. How could he help his uncle? His idea of a book of stories was nagging him; perhaps he could write it himself, as a kind of monument to his uncle—except that the stories seemed to be drifting away into the dark, beyond his reach, just like the old man. When eventually he dozed, he thought he heard the old man calling.

In the morning his desk looked even worse; the pile of books had almost doubled. He managed to sort out a few that could be trusted to readers for reports. Of course, a drain must have overflowed outside the publishers; that was why only a patch of pavement had been wet this morning—he knew it hadn't rained. He consulted his diary for distractions.

Sales conference 11 A.M.: he succeeded in being coherent, and even in suggesting ideas, but his thoughts were elsewhere. The sky resembled sluggish smoke, as though the oppressive day was smouldering. His mind felt packed in grey stuffing. The sound of cars outside seemed unnaturally rhythmic, almost like waves.

Back at his desk he sat trying to think. Lack of sleep had isolated him in a no-man's-land of consciousness, close to hallucination. He felt cut off from whatever he was supposed to be doing. Though his hand kept reaching out impulsively, he left the drawer locked. There was no point in brooding over the model ship until he'd decided what to do.

Beyond the window his uncle cried out. No, someone was shouting to guide a lorry; the word wasn't "James" at all. But he still didn't know how to help his uncle, assuming that he could, assuming that it wasn't too late. Would removing the ship from the bottle achieve something? In any case, could one remove the ship at all? Perhaps he could consult an expert in such matters. "I know exactly whom you want," his secretary said, and arranged for them to meet tomorrow.

Dave Peeples lunch 12:30: ordinarily he would have enjoyed the game, especially since Peeples liked to discuss books in pubs, where he tended to drink himself into an agreeable state. Today's prize was attractive: a best-selling series that Peeples wanted to take to a new publisher. But today he found Peeples irritating—not only his satyr's expressions and postures, which were belied by his paunch, but also the faint smirk with which he constantly approved of himself. Still, if Berry managed to acquire the books, the strain would have been worthwhile.

They ate in the pub just round the corner from the publishers. Before long Berry grew frustrated; he was too enervated by lack of sleep to risk drinking much. Nor could he eat much, for the food tasted unpleasantly salty. Peeples seemed to notice nothing, and ate most of Berry's helping before he leaned back, patting his paunch.

"Well now," he said when Berry raised the subject of the books.

"What about another drink?" Berry was glad to stand up, to feel the floor stable underfoot, for the drinkers at the edge of his vision had seemed to be swaying extravagantly.

"I'm not happy with the way my mob are promoting the books," Peeples admitted. "They seem to be letting them just lie there." Berry's response might have been more forceful if he hadn't been distracted by the chair that someone was rocking back and forth with a steady rhythmic creaking.

When Berry had finished making offers Peeples said, "That doesn't sound bad. Still, I ought to tell you that several other people are interested." Berry wondered angrily whether he was simply touring publishers in search of free meals. The pub felt damp, the dimness appeared to be glistening. No doubt it was very humid.

Though the street was crowded, he was glad to emerge. "I'll be in touch," Peeples promised grudgingly, but at that moment Berry didn't care, for on the opposite pavement the old man's voice was crying, "James!" It was only a newspaper-seller naming his wares, which didn't sound much like James. Surely a drain must have overflowed where the wet patch had been, for there was a stagnant smell.

Editors meeting 3 P.M.: he scarcely had time to gulp a mug of coffee beforehand, almost scalding his throat. Why did they have to schedule two meetings in one day? When there were silences in which people expected him to speak, he managed to say things that sounded positive and convincing. Nevertheless he heard little except for the waves of traffic, advancing and withdrawing, and the desperate cries in the street. What was that crossing the intersection, a long pale shape bearing objects like poles? It had gone before he could jerk his head round, and his colleagues were staring only at him.

It didn't matter. If any of these glimpses weren't hallucinations, surely they couldn't harm him. Otherwise, why hadn't he been harmed that night in Parkgate? It was rather a question of what he could do to the glimpses. "Yes, that's right," he said to a silence. "Of course it is."

Once he'd slept he would be better able to cope with everything. Tomorrow he would consult the expert. After the meeting he slumped at his desk, trying to find the energy to gather books together and head for home.

His secretary woke him. "OK," he mumbled, "you go on." He'd

follow her in a moment, when he was more awake. It occurred to him that if he hadn't dozed off in Parkgate, his uncle might have been safe. That was another reason to try to do something. He'd get up in a few moments. It wasn't dark yet.

When he woke again, it was.

He had to struggle to raise his head. His elbows had shoved piles of books to the edge of the desk. Outside, the street was quiet except for the whisper of an occasional car. Sodium lamps craned their necks toward his window. Beyond the frosted glass of his office cubicle, the maze of the open-plan office looked even more crowded with darkness than the space around his desk. When he switched on his desk-lamp, it showed him a blurred reflection of himself trapped in a small pool of brightness. Hurriedly he switched on the cubicle's main light.

Though he was by no means awake, he didn't intend to wait. He wanted to be out of the building, away from the locked drawer. Insomnia had left him feeling vulnerable, on edge. He swept a handful of books into the briefcase—God, they were becoming a bad joke—and emerged from his cubicle.

He felt uncomfortably isolated. The long angular room was lifeless; none of the desks seemed to retain any sense of the person who sat there. The desertion must be swallowing his sounds, which seemed not only dwarfed but robbed of resonance, as though surrounded by an emptiness that was very large.

His perceptions must be playing tricks. Underfoot the floor felt less stable than it ought to. At the edge of his vision the shadows of desks and cabinets appeared to be swaying, and he couldn't convince himself that the lights were still. He mustn't let any of this distract him. Time enough to think when he was home.

It took him far too long to cross the office, for he kept teetering against desks. Perhaps he should have taken time to waken fully, after all. When eventually he reached the lifts, he couldn't bring himself to use one; at least the stairs were open, though they were very dark. He groped, swaying, for the light-switch. Before he'd found it, he recoiled. The wall he had touched felt as though it were streaming with water.

A stagnant stench welled up out of the dark. When he grabbed the banister for support, that felt wet too. He mustn't panic: a door or window was open somewhere in the building, that was all he could hear creaking; its draught was making things feel cold—not wet—and was swinging the lights back and forth. Yes, he could feel the draught blustering at him, and smell what must be a drain.

He forced himself to step onto the stairs. Even the darkness was preferable to groping for the light-switch, when he no longer knew what he might touch. Nevertheless, by the time he reached the half-landing he was wishing for light. His vertigo seemed to have worsened, for he was reeling from side to side of the staircase. Was the creaking closer? He mustn't pause, plenty of time to feel ill once he was outside in a taxi; he ought to be able to hold off panic so long as he didn't glimpse the ship again—

He halted so abruptly that he almost fell. Without warning he'd remembered his uncle's monologue. Berry had been as dopey then as he was now, but one point was all at once terribly clear. Your first glimpse of the ship meant only that you would see it again. The second time, it came for you.

He hadn't yet seen it again. Surely he still had a chance. There were two exits from the building; the creaking and the growing stench would tell him which exit to avoid. He was stumbling downstairs because that was the alternative to falling. His mind was a grey void that hardly even registered the wetness of the banisters. The foyer was in sight now at the foot of the stairs, its linoleum gleaming; less than a flight of stairs now, less than a minute's stumbling—

But it was not linoleum. The floorboards were bare, when there ought not even to be boards, only concrete. Shadows swayed on them, cast by objects that, though out of sight for the moment, seemed to have bloated limbs. Water sloshed from side to side of the boards, which were the planks of a deck.

He almost let himself fall, in despair. Then he began to drag himself frantically up the stairs, which perhaps were swaying, after all. Through the windows he thought he saw the cityscape rising and falling. There seemed to be no refuge upstairs, for the stagnant stench was everywhere—but refuge wasn't what he was seeking.

He reeled across the office, which he'd darkened when leaving, into his cubicle. Perhaps papers were falling from desks only because he had staggered against them. His key felt ready to snap in half before the drawer opened.

He snatched out the bottle, in which something rattled insect-like, and stumbled to the window. Yes, he had been meant to find the bottle—but by whom, or by what? Wrenching open the lock of the window, he flung the bottle into the night.

He heard it smash a moment later. Whatever was inside it must certainly have smashed too. At once everything felt stable, so abruptly that he grew dizzier. He felt as though he'd just stepped onto land after a stormy voyage.

There was silence except for the murmur of the city, which sounded quite normal—or perhaps there was another sound, faint and receding fast. It might have been a gust of wind, but he thought it resembled a chorus of cries of relief so profound it was appalling. Was one of them his uncle's voice?

Berry slumped against the window, which felt like ice against his forehead. There was no reason to flee now, nor did he think he would be capable of moving for some time. Perhaps they would find him here in the morning. It hardly mattered, if he could get some sleep—

All at once he tried to hold himself absolutely still, in order to listen. Surely he needn't be nervous any longer, just because the ship in the bottle had been deserted, surely that didn't mean— But his legs were trembling, and infected the rest of his body until he couldn't even strain his ears. By then, however, he could hear far better than he would have liked.

Perhaps he had destroyed the ship, and set free its captives; but if it had had a captain, what else might Berry have set loose? The smell had grown worse than stagnant—and up the stairs, and now across the dark office, irregular but purposeful footsteps were sloshing.

• • •

Early next morning several people reported glimpses of a light, supposedly moving out from the Thames into the open sea. Some claimed the light had been accompanied by sounds like singing. One old man tried to insist that the light had contained the outline of a ship. The reports seemed little different from tales of objects in the skies, and were quickly dismissed, for London had a more spectacular mystery to solve: how a publisher's editor could be found in a first-floor office, not merely dead but drowned.

GOOD NIGHT, SWEET PRINCE

D. W. Taylor

Of all the horror writers with whom I discussed the notion of a charity anthology to help abused children, David Taylor was the most expert and the most committed, and he sent not one but several outstanding stories. My choice just had to be "Goodnight, Sweet Prince," which climaxes with a stunning comprehension of a child's imaginary terror. David is an assistant professor of English at Moravian College in Bethlehem, Pennsylvania. He has contributed horror stories to *Fantasy Tales, Footsteps, Grue,* and other magazines. A former co-editor of the *Hampden-Sydney Poetry Review,* he has also written books and articles on dyslexia, parents and the reading process, and the teaching of college writing. His wife Diane is a children's author, and as enthusiastic as David about helping children in need. But the young protagonist of "Good Night, Sweet Prince" is beyond anybody's help . . .

Nicholas is scared. He lies in the dark bed, fuzzy yellow Snoopy blanket against his cheek. He has been very bad. And now in his room without any supper, he waits for his mother. She might bring the willow switch that's thin and green as a snake's tongue.

Filling the sugar bowl with salt had sounded like fun to Nick. A big third-grader named Roger told him about the trick and how much fun it would be to watch what happened. Sure enough, when his mother's friend Alice took a sip of coffee she made a face just like she'd tasted some dog do-do. But Roger didn't say anything about how Nick's mother would grab Nick by the hair, drag him to his room and lock the door!

Nick hears the key rattle in the lock, pulls Snoopy tighter around him and shuts his eyes. If he's asleep maybe she won't— The bed sinks beside him, a hand strokes his forehead. He's safe. Safe from the switch that makes your legs dance.

''Nicholas? Nicholas, I know you're not asleep.'' Her voice isn't angry but it's not her lovey voice either.

Nicholas crawls into her arms and suddenly the sobs well up from his empty stomach.

''I'm sor-ry, Mom-my!'' he cries.

''It's okay, son. It's okay.'' She rocks him back and forth. ''Mommy loves you. Mommy loves you.'' Now her voice is soft as his blanket.

Nick can hardly catch his breath betweeen sobs. ''Will you leave . . . like Daddy did . . . 'cause I was bad?''

''No, Mommy won't leave you.''

They rock back and forth until Nick's sobs are little sniffles, then she gently wipes his tears with Snoopy.

''Do you know why Mommy punished you?''

Nick nods and sniffs.

''Will you do it again?''

Nick shakes his head and sniffs.

''Do you know what happens to little boys who can't learn to be good?''

''No, ma'am. What?''

''Well, Mommy knows a story about a little boy who never learned to be good. Do you want me to tell it to you?''

Nick nods again.

''It's called 'Prince—The Boy Who Went Away' and it goes like this.''

Nicholas slips back under the covers. He's all the way in first grade now, but he can still listen to bedtime stories. And a story is so much better than Mr. Switch. As his mother pulls the blanket up around him, her voice begins . . .

"Once upon a time, there was a little boy named Prentice. Right away his mommy and daddy started calling him 'Prince' because they hoped he would be a prince among men. But soon Prince's mommy knew something was wrong with her little boy. You see, Prince always tried to do a number one right in her face whenever she changed his diaper."

Nicholas giggles. Imagine getting some wee-wee right in your eyes or nose. Or mouth!

"Once or twice would have just been accidents. But every time she would pull that diaper down past Prince's little tally-wacker, he would lie real still—I guess he was getting a good aim—and then let her have it right between the eyes!

"Of course Prince's mommy knew this was very unusual behavior, but told herself that perhaps her little boy had been frightened terribly in the hospital; 'infant trauma' they call it. And now he did this as a reflex to protect himself. Like when a skunk sprays you with stinky, Nicholas, if you get too close, or a porcupine aiming its quills. Needless to say, it was a relief when Prince was finally potty trained. Some people had started to say bad things about Prince, about how some children are just born with evil in them.

"When Prince began his next trick, she knew it wasn't 'infant trauma' any more. But even if she had known what it was, she couldn't have done anything about it, not then, not to her sweet, precious son.

"And Prince could be so sweet. He would waddle over with one of his toys, wrinkle his nose and smile as he offered it you. 'Play?' or 'Car go!' he would say, then reach out his arms for you to hold him. Who could resist a child asking to be loved? Wrapping his arms around you, Prince would snuggle his little face against this tender spot right here."

His mother rests her fingers on Nicholas' neck.

"And then Prince would sink his sharp little teeth into you like a vampire bat!" When she pinches him lightly, Nicholas jumps but then lies very still. This is a scary story!

"At first the person just stood there, surprised by the pain shooting through them, almost nailing their feet to the floor. Then they cried out and tried to pull Prince away. That's when they realized Prince wasn't letting go, and if they jerked him away, part of their neck was coming, too.

"After Prince finally let go, he would begin bawling right away—screaming and crying as if *he* had been hurt, as if *he* were the victim. And what's the use of spanking a bawling child? Soon very few relatives or neighbors came near their house, and no children were ever allowed around Prince without adult supervision, which was a good idea.

"So Prince turned against animals, and soon his mommy and daddy had no pets *or* friends. It started with a blond-haired cocker spaniel puppy named 'Sandy.' Sandy looked just like your puppy, Nicholas. She's a cocker spaniel, too. Well, one day Prince was outside playing tug-of-war with Sandy and a piece of garden hose. Once when Sandy wouldn't do just right, Prince hit Sandy over the head with the hard rubber hose. Sandy staggered a little bit, of course. Wouldn't you? Then Prince said, 'You're drunk! Just like Daddy.' Prince made a game out of it. He would hit Sandy and make her stagger, then he would chant, 'Just-like-Dad-dy! Just-like-Dad-dy!'

"Prince followed the puppy around the backyard, knocking it down with the hose and chanting as it staggered to get away from him. Then Sandy couldn't get up any more. Prince poked at the dog's head, which was rather mushy by now, but Sandy wouldn't move. The puppy was dead. Prince tossed the hose aside and went to look for more fun.

"It was that day Prince's mother said the horrible words for the first time. When she went into the backyard to call Prince for supper and saw the puppy lying so still, its bloody head flattened on the ground, something inside of her finally broke. She had chosen Sandy at the pet shop. There was something so innocent in the puppy face, such joy and trust in that puppy smile. Sandy was everything good and sweet that Prince wasn't, everything Prince's mommy had never known in a child. And Prince had killed it. Not just killed it, but tortured the life out of it bit by bit, just as he was doing to her.

"She found Prince easily by following the frantic mewing of a neighborhood cat in a vacant lot next to their house. She waded through the coarse weeds, and found Prince holding down the cat with one foot while tying a kerosene-soaked rag to its tail. Matches were sticking out of his pocket. She grabbed Prince by his shiny black hair and dragged him to the house. Oh, he fought all the way, beating at her hand and trying to kick her. But his mommy was very determined and she just jerked on him that much harder.

"Once inside, she threw Prince into his room and slammed the door. She had sent him to his room as punishment before, but this time she said, and she'll never forget how the words just came out of nowhere, as if someone else were saying them, she said, 'One of these days I'm going to put you in this room, lock the door and throw away the room!' She tried to control her anger and spoke in a low, level voice. 'Do you hear me, Prince? *Throw away the room.*' Then she locked the door.

"After that, Prince seemed to be a good boy for a while. His mommy was so glad because by now she had another baby boy and Prince's daddy had left them. But Prince wasn't good. She soon learned that there was something in him that would never let him be good, something evil that was beyond her control.

"It happened at an important dinner she was having for the East Coast manager of Avalon Cosmetics. Prince's mother had worked for days cleaning house and cooking so that everything would go just right. Prince's mother had to look like someone who could manage kids, a house, and the new position of sales manager for all of New York—that's our state, too, Nicholas.

"The chilled gazpacho soup was perfect for a summer's evening, complemented by an Alsatian cheese salad—cool and creamy on the palate after the tangy soup. The main course was *pasta al pesto*—noodles with a special green sauce made from the fresh basil leaves that are in season for only two weeks here in New York. But there the meal ended.

"Mrs. Costello, a big-boned woman with a painted face and diamonds on nearly every finger, was telling about her recent visit to Renee Avalon's mansion in California when a green noodle dangled suspiciously from her fork and dropped to her plate—an unusual mistake in table manners that everyone politely ignored. But Prince's mother watched that noodle fall and then *burrow* down into the mound of pasta.

"She checked her own plate and the plates of her guests, who were all listening very respectfully to Mrs. Costello. And by staring long enough she could see it happening in each plate—a few noodles wriggling just slightly.

"She glanced to the kitchen and saw Prince peeking around the corner. His eyes were lit up like a child's on Christmas morning, and a smile was starting to crease his evil little mouth. She knew then that she had lost. She would never get that promotion or anything else because HE would always be there to take it away from her, just as he had taken away the puppy Sandy, just as he would corrupt her other son.

"Poor Louise Bryan. Just then one of the green noodles found its way out of her mound of pasta and began to worm its way back home. It squirmed over the edge of her plate and fell on to the Irish linen tablecloth. Louise dropped her fork with a clang and jerked back in surprise. 'It's a. . . !' She choked and couldn't finish. Now the other guests saw it, too. One whispered 'Good Lord!' Another just 'Arrragh!' and a third almost lost her dinner right on the spot.

"At the other end of the table Mrs. Costello was chatting away in her nasal, put-on voice about the gold-plated fixtures in the Avalons' master bathroom. She paused for a small bite, saying to Prince's mother, 'Absolutely exquisite pasta, my dear.' And as she started to chew, her penciled eyebrows (Shadow of the Night) knitted together when she felt something wriggling in her mouth, yearning to be free. Then Mrs. Costello emptied her mouth right on to the table, vomiting out the green noodles in a most indelicate fashion. One crawled happily away.

"Prince was rolling on the kitchen floor, laughing so hard he couldn't breathe. His mother flew up from the table, tears of rage—all eleven years' worth—screaming in her eyes. Her hands hungered for his shiny black hair, to pull it from its black roots. And with her dinner guests gagging all around her, she dragged that evil thing with arms and legs pretending to be a son straight to 'its' bedroom. She kicked open the door and threw Prince on to the floor. He was still laughing when she slammed the door and locked it. She closed her eyes and, summoning every ounce of will, she was finally able to say in a strangely quiet voice, 'Good night, Prince, my sweet Prince. And *good-bye*.'

"As she turned and walked away, she was stricken in her heart by the deep emptiness of loss that only a mother can feel. But in her mind she knew just as deeply and just as surely that she could no longer abide his evil—an evil which comes from another world, Nicholas, to live in little boys like Prince who cannot learn to be good.

"We must now imagine Prince in his bedroom that night, lying in bed just like you are now, Nicholas, in a room exactly like this one. Why, this could be that very room! It is long after his laughter has finally stopped, long after the hunger pains from his missed supper have faded. He awakens to silence—the guests gone, his mother and infant brother fast asleep. Prince must go to the bathroom. He swings his feet out of bed and on to the floor, then chuckles quietly as he remembers the green worms flowing from the painted lady's red mouth.

"Prince moves carefully to the door, running his hand along the bed to guide himself. There is no night-light; Prince must have total darkness. He finds the dresser with one hand, reaches for the doorknob with the other. His mother would have unlocked the door later, as she always did.

"But there is no doorknob. He moves his little hand to the left. Down. Up. Back to the right. Still no knob. Now he searches desperately with both little hands. There is no door. Only a blank wall. He feels coldness on the other side, an absolute silence. Prince punches the Bozo light switch right on the nose—nothing. Only a quiet blackness that seems deep as forever.

"At the window he flips up the shade. The sky is pocked with stars, the moon bright as the end of a flashlight. But gone is the vacant lot with its hairy weeds, gone the neighborhood houses. There is only the emptiness of space above and below him, and the millions of stars like sad eyes. He is alone in the dark. No mother, no friends—all alone, Nicholas, forever. His mother has finally kept her word. And no one ever saw the boy named Prince again.

"That's the end, Nicholas. Did you like that story? Now I want you to say your prayers and go to sleep like a good boy. Okay? Give Mommy a kiss."

At the door she says, "Good night, sweetie," then pulls it closed softly, locks it. Nicholas lies perfectly still, his little fists clutching the Snoopy blanket. Eyes closed tight, he mumbles his nighty-night prayer over and over: ''God bless Mommy. And please, God, make me a good boy. I *want* to be a good boy. Don't let me go away! Please!''

Outside his room, Nick's mother listens to her son's urgent prayers. She closes her eyes, rests her head against the door and prays, too. She wants so much to keep this one. Only time will tell.

PRINTER'S DEVIL

Celeste Paul Sefranek

Celeste complains that her "cantankerous" word processor only works when it's in the mood. But the gremlins left her alone long enough for her to compose this wonderfully folksy small-town tale of horror and sheer embarrassment. Celeste is a new writer and "Printer's Devil" is her first published work. She lives in Portsmouth, Rhode Island, with her husband, four boys, and two cats (or was it two boys and four cats? or four husbands and one cat? I forget). She is one of scores of new writers I encountered who are enthusiastically turning their talents to horror fiction, so the prospects for the future of the dark genre can't be anything but bright. One small thing: despite the fact that this is Celeste's first story in print, she happily contributed it, like every other author in *Scare Care,* for free. She deserves appreciation as well as congratulation.

I used to like working at the *Clarion*. It never rivaled the *Boston Globe* or *The New York Times* or even the *National Enquirer*. Its circulation ran seventeen, eighteen thousand at best. Still, I was kind of proud of it. They maintained a high standard. You wouldn't find headlines about Martians kidnapping local housewives or pictures of two-headed babies in the *Clarion*. No. Just good, solid news, the kind that's fit to read with your evening coffee and dessert.

That is, until March 26.

March 26 was a dark day for the *Clarion* in more ways than one. The night before, Bill Preeny, the senior editor, was to have been the guest speaker at the Annual Junior Achievement Awards Banquet. Sometime between the salad and the main course, however, Bill's heart simply decided it'd had enough. He keeled over right in front of all those little Junior Achievers and their parents. Those familiar with Bill's caustic editorials considered it a rather fitting end.

Besides his scathing attacks on censorship, the Papacy, and the ERA, Bill will be most remembered for his skill as a practical joker. If old Bill managed to make it through those Pearly Gates, it was a sure bet that he was probably giving St. Peter a hot foot or an exploding cigar. Everyone at the *Clarion* had been the butt of his humor at one time or another, myself included. Still, with Bill taking up space in a spanking new coffin at Morrison's Funeral Home, he was the last one we suspected when the troubles of March 26 began.

It started like any other day. I came to work at noon, took a quick look-see at the insert I was assigned that day. Name's Platt Farris. Inserts. That was my job. You know—those slick, brightly colored circulars for Furniture World and Foodland that are always falling out of the back of your newspaper. I put them in there in the first place.

I worked on the Smithfield 24P Inserter, a big mother of a machine that looks like a cross between a child's carousel and a monster octopus. It runs on vacuum and compressed air and you can hear its *ca-chunk-ca-chunk* all the way up in the editorial department when it's working.

The papers come off the press and are fed to a main hopper that drops them into the carousel, where the fold is opened up by a jet of air. Around the outside of the machine are five hopper stations, each with its own operator. That's what I did. As the papers come around on the carousel, you feed the inserts into your hopper and they drop, one by one, into the main fold of the paper. You have to be fast. When the Smithfield's going full steam we process 250 papers a minute. I may be sixty-seven, but my hands are still nimble. It was good, honest work. I liked it.

Everything went smooth as silk on March 26. In three hours, we were done and I was on my way home with a free paper tucked under my arm, one of the few fringe benefits the job had to offer. Soon I was lying on the couch with a brew, ready to sample the day's news.

A newspaper is a strange animal. It's a brand-new product every day and because of that, it's subject to mistakes. Proofreaders catch most of them and the rest we just hope the public will forgive. But as I started to leaf through the paper that day, I knew that the *Clarion* was in deep trouble.

The President had given a speech on TV the night before and it'd made the front page, along with his picture. That was all well and good, but someone had added a huge handlebar moustache to his upper lip that was certainly not part of his usual makeup. It didn't occur to me then that Bill Preeny had been a Democrat.

Page two should have contained police and fire clips. Instead, it was a full-page reprint of "The Walrus and the Carpenter," complete with a border of stylized oyster shells. I began to feel a little uneasy. That'd been a favorite of Bill's. He was fond of reciting it from memory just to show off how much he knew.

The obituary page was a revelation. In a small town, friendships are often lifelong . . . hatreds more so. Bill's editorials and opinions had made him many enemies over the years. On the obit page that day was a death notice on everyone who'd ever crossed him. Bill had killed them off in print. The mayor's name was there, along with the chief of police, the head of the Town Council, and Miss Margaret Trewhistle, the chairwoman of the Citizens' Decency League. Once, years ago, Bill had used a four-letter word to make a point in one of his columns and Miss Trewhistle had been on his case ever since.

If anyone still had any doubt that Bill was having a ghostly laugh at the town's expense, the Lifestyle Section surely convinced them. In his youth, poor Bill had had the misfortune to marry money. Oh, Amanda Preeny wasn't a bad sort and she'd been a good wife to Bill. No. It was her mother, Althea Brognan Spencer, matron of the town's oldest family, who'd made Bill's life hell for twenty-five years. She felt her only daughter had married beneath her station and she'd never let Bill forget it. Now he had his revenge.

The Lifestyle Section was devoted to fashion and food and on March 26 Althea Brognan Spencer was its star. She was resplendent on a double page . . . totally nude. That might not have been so bad, except that Althea was seventy-four years old and had a body like a hot-air balloon gone flaccid. The sight left little appetite for the recipes that made up the remainder of the section.

When I came to work the next day, the front of the *Clarion* building was blocked by picketers from the Citizens' Decency League, a red-faced and very much alive Miss Margaret Trewhistle at the head of the line. Passing the editor in chief's office, I could hear Althea Brognan Spencer's patrician voice haranguing the poor secretary with threats of a lawsuit. I reported to circulation, but for the first time in over a century of publication, the *Clarion* didn't roll off the press at 12:30.

Oh, a few papers came through, but it was more of the same—pages of elephant jokes, reprints of Bill's favorite editorials, ads for whoopee cushions and joy buzzers. The second section began with a six-column, half-page display ad that read "Call Margaret for a Good Time," and below that, Margaret Trewhistle's unlisted phone number in big, bold type. On the front page, a bigger-than-life photo of Bill Preeny, grinning like a Cheshire cat.

Things remained at a standstill for a week. By that time Bill had tinkered with the food and beverage machines in the Employees' Lounge. All they'd give were black coffee and Choc-o-Fluff bars—Bill's favorite snack.

I don't know what went on behind the closed doors of the editor's office, but they must have finally admitted to themselves that Bill really was responsible for what was happening. I could have told them that a week ago. At any rate, that Friday, Father Brennan, the pastor from St. Philomena's on Spring Street, showed up in full regalia, complete with altar boy and incense burner. He went through the whole building, from top to bottom, mumbling prayers and sprinkling holy water like rain.

I'm a Baptist, myself, and I don't believe in all that Catholic mumbo jumbo. Still, it seemed to work. The next day, things at the *Clarion* went back to normal. Father Brennan went back to his 9 A.M. mass and 5 P.M. pot roast, Margaret Trewhistle went back to her crusade to take *The Carpetbaggers* off the shelves of the town library, and Althea Brognan Spencer went into seclusion. Everything settled down for about a week.

Then all hell broke loose.

It started with the Smithfield inserter. Like all big machines, there's a danger factor to the Smithfield. Cams and gears can make short work of a finger or catch a loose sleeve. The lever arm that pulls each insert out of its hopper is tipped with a steel needle. Because of this, safety is a big concern and it's drilled into you right from the first day on the job. The machine itself has built-in safety features that are foolproof. If everyone is careful and follows the rules, there's no reason for anyone to get hurt. In the seven years I worked at the *Clarion,* there'd never been an injury.

That afternoon, Sherri Thomas was working insert station no. 3. Sherri was a nice kid, newly married to Jake Thomas, one of the truck drivers. She knew her job well. Her hopper jammed, a common occurrence, and she stopped the machine and reached in to clear it. When a red light is on, at any of the six hopper stations, it's impossible to start the machine. Now, they tried to say later that Sherri forgot to push the safety stop, but I know better. The red light was on. I saw it. There was no way that machine could have started running, even if someone had deliberately thrown the switch.

But it did.

The Smithfield pulled her hand in before she even had a chance to scream and the *ca-chunk-ca-chunk* sounded like some great beast gnashing its teeth. When she did start to scream the sounds made a strange duet, and it seemed to me that there was a third sound there, strangely like laughter. We all tried to help, of course. Everybody pressed their stop button, but it didn't work. Keith Bates, who ran the main hopper, had the presence of mind to pull the plug on the thing and at last it stopped.

I've been in the war—the Big One, WW II—and I've seen a lot of nasty things, but nothing like what that machine did to her hand. They shut the paper down for the day and we all went home. We had no way of knowing that this was only the beginning.

The next day, the papers came off the press printed in red ink. You've got to understand; we're too small an operation to print in color—there's no red ink even kept on the premises. That was strange enough, but they *stank,* like something out of a charnel house. One of the smart, young reporters had some tests done and they found it was blood, AB negative to be exact. When you handled the papers, its stickiness rubbed off on your hands.

The content was little better. There were stories of ax murders, of devil worship, of tortures and atrocities. Nothing like this had come in over the UPI wire. Not even the classified page was spared. The Notices and Personals column contained some of the most obscene material I've ever seen.

On the third day Ed Medeiros was killed.

Ed was a father of six, a member of the Knights of Columbus, a hell of a good press operator, and one of the nicest guys I've ever had the privilege to know. He was short and, without the height to accommodate it, every ounce of food he ate went to his middle. He played Santa Claus every year at the company Christmas party.

At noon, Ed was making the last preparations before switching on the huge press. I was sitting on the sidelines, having a sandwich. We were friends, Ed and I. I knew his folks and we often got together before presstime to trade our own sort of small town news. He was telling me about his newest addition to the family, a 7 lb. 12 oz. boy, when the big press suddenly came to life.

The huge rollers began to turn and the conveyer came on with a loud whine. Ed hit the main switch, then the emergency cutoff. Nothing worked. His leg was close to the first roller, but not close enough for him to be in any danger. We were both puzzling over what could be wrong, when I saw it.

Except for a beer or two after work, I'm not a drinking man and old Doc Horton, who's been my family doctor for years, can testify that I've never been prone to hallucinations. Still, what I saw had to have been my imagination.

A hand came out of the press. Came out as just sort of a glow at first, but then became solid. It grabbed Ed by the ankle and hauled him into the rollers. At night, when I sit alone with a can of beer, I can still hear him screaming, begging . . . pleading.

I was paralyzed at first and I still blame myself for that. It was the sight of that hand, forming out of thin air and grabbing him—it made my knees go soft and kept me just staring at the press for too many precious seconds. The main power switch was at the other end of the room. By the time I reached it, it was too late.

Ed's body and head had gone under the rollers. Only one hand remained outside the machinery, the finger pointing accusingly toward me.

They shut the paper down for two weeks to give the higher-ups time to figure out what to do. The *Clarion* had been in business for 123 years and they were not about to let it go down without a fight. I guess they were getting ready to call in Father Brennan for a repeat performance or something, when suddenly, everything settled down to normal.

On April 30, the paper went out as usual. Things worked without a hitch, in fact we set a record and had the last truck on the road within two hours and ten minutes.

I don't work at the *Clarion* any more. Not since that last day. You see, with all the troubles the paper was having, some of the advertisers dropped off. On April 30, there were only two inserts to go into the paper. Now normally, when a hopper isn't used, it's disengaged from the machine. Only two hoppers were full that day, but three ran.

Hopper no. 6 operated by itself through the entire run. I saw it. *Ca-chunk-ca-chunk,* it dropped an invisible insert into every paper as the carousel whirled beneath it.

I don't know what we sent out with the papers that day, but the town's been different since then. The murder and suicide rates are up. Rape, child abuse, violent crime are all on the increase. It's not a nice place to live, any more. Still, I was born here and I don't intend to leave.

I have my own theories on what happened. In the Good Book, Jesus says that when an evil spirit goes out of a man, it travels for a while and then comes back, bringing along seven of its buddies, all worse than itself. I figure something like that happened at the *Clarion*. Rather than get exorcised a second time, Ed and his cronies decided to take matters into their own hands and used the papers to infiltrate the town.

I still go to the Baptist church on Sunday, but I stop in every day in the late afternoon at St. Philomena's. Father Brennan and I light a candle and we pray for our little town . . . and for the world. Father Brennan understands.

You see, the *Clarion* is a small paper, but it has a wide circulation. We mail to sons and daughters away at college, to hometown boys in the service overseas. The papers go to just about every state in the union and a lot of foreign countries. And I'm scared.

Have you read the headlines lately?

MAMMY AND THE FLIES

Bruce Boston

Bruce Boston's first letters to me were supportive and polite, but not particularly forthcoming. They certainly didn't prepare me for the chillingly original voice which tells the tale of "Mammy and the Flies." A resident of Albany, California, Bruce has written stories for an impressive array of the best fantasy and sci-fi magazines, including *Twilight Zone, Isaac Asimov's SF Magazine, Amazing, Night Cry,* and *Nebula Awards 21.* He also writes outstanding fantasy poetry, including a collection called *Nuclear Futures,* all proceeds from which Bruce donated to the cause of nuclear disarmament, and *The Nightmare Collector,* published last fall by 2AM Press. Those of you who want further proof of Bruce's skills should seek out *A Bruce Boston Omnibus* from Ocean View Press. Meanwhile, relish one of those truly distinctive horror stories which sticks in your mind like something black and glistening and nasty, and which you can never quite dislodge . . .

"You a smart boy, all right, too darn smart for your own good. Now get down in that cellar!"

Mammy Jordon came across the kitchen and he moved back toward the cellar door. He knew she wasn't really mad, 'cause when she was mad she sent him down to the cellar dark, and here she was holding out the flashlight. And she wasn't looking at him like she was mad, but somewhere over his head, her bulk crowding him back, her perfume and party dress, even bigger now in her heels and towering over him.

How he hated her bigness, just as he loved it when she held him against her soft in the bedroom upstairs.

He went down the wood steps to the dirt floor with the ceiling so low no man could stand, for he was no man yet and he couldn't stand all the way, and he could hear the door closing and Mammy Jordon sliding the bolt into place. He could hear her moving about the house. And later her heels on the front porch and the old car coughing, and he knew she had gone into town to bring back one of her gentlemen.

He didn't turn on the flashlight.

It was still light outside and the light came through the chinks in the cinder blocks along three walls of the cellar and the flies hadn't come yet. If he looked through the chinks on one side he could see plowed fields and burnt-off hillsides and at night the lights of cars as they passed on the highway. On the other side, only fields and hills. But if he knelt down and looked through the chinks at the rear of the cellar, he could see their yard and the garden Mammy had planted and through the trees and beyond to Mr. Skinner's house in the distance. Mr. Skinner was their landlord. His house was white, whiter than theirs which was once white and Mammy called it dirt-white.

He didn't know how she had found this Skinner place. When they left the other place they drove for days, sleeping in the car, Mammy making him stay on the floor in back so no one would see. Then they had come to this place and she started locking him in the cellar. He had been with Mammy since before the other place, but down in the cellar with nothing to do but sit and think and listen, he had begun to remember his real mother.

The cellar had been cold at first with the wind racing through the chinks. He'd found an old mattress and tried to lie on it with the blankets Mammy Jordon had given him, but the mattress was wet and smelled bad. When he pushed up one corner he could see worms and dark crawlies underneath. So he found a dry place on the dirt floor and curled up there with the covers and thought about his mother.

Mammy Jordon was his mother's mother, but she wouldn't let him call her that. She said she was too young to be anyone's grandma, leastwise someone grown up as he was getting to be. His real mother was smaller than Mammy Jordon and she didn't smell like Mammy, always sweet or flowery, still she smelled good, only he couldn't remember just how 'cause the cellar smelled and the mattress even when he wasn't near it. He'd get this all mixed up with his mother's smell and Mammy Jordon's. And sometimes he'd remember her and she was brown like Mammy Jordon or yellow like he was, and sometimes she was a white lady and once she was soft all over like a kitten. The more different ways he thought about her the less he remembered so she became less and less until finally there was nothing left to her at all. And then he couldn't think about her anymore or pretend he wasn't in the cellar.

So he began to sing to himself in the dark, tuneless nonsense songs which never repeated yet always sounded the same. He kept his voice low so Mammy wouldn't hear. She said he was strange enough already without doing no singing, and she only let him listen to music on Sundays when she read from the book. He loved the music and he could feel it trying to move inside him, but he had to sit still while the record turned on the player. Sometimes when he sang to himself in the cellar he didn't sit still. He rocked with the nonsense words. Hunched there in the dark, he beat the heels of his palms against his thighs until they were sore.

And that was when the seeing started.

He didn't tell Mammy about the singing or the seeing. He knew she wouldn't like any of it.

. . .

Mr. Skinner's dog was chained in its yard barking to be fed and the sun was going down. He couldn't see the dog 'cause of the fence and the trees. He couldn't see the sun 'cause that side of the cellar was boarded over, but he could see what it was doing to the land, turning the trees and fence posts golden, the white of Mr. Skinner's house pink and grey, the tomatoes by the back porch as if they were about to catch on fire. It was hotter under the house now, the hottest time of all each day at dusk. As the land cooled it gave up its warmth to the cellar which would hold it long into the night. He could feel the warm air flowing in through the chinks in the cinder blocks. And soon the flies would follow.

Each time Mammy sent him to the cellar it was warmer and there were more flies. He could listen to their buzzing in the dark, he could feel them landing and crawling on his skin, sucking his sweat, their hairy legs itching him. He could turn on the flashlight and see them moving in its beam: black and gold-green in the yellow circle of light.

He knew that if Mammy Jordan came back and she didn't have a gentleman with her, he wouldn't have to stay with the flies. If she came back alone she'd unlock the cellar door. She'd come partway down the steps and she'd call, ''Baby, baby, come up,'' and when he did she'd take him upstairs and hold him against her in bed and tell him stories—about the animals back home or about his daddy, Pappy Jordon, who was *mojo* and Creole and something special, and since he was part Pappy Jordon that was why his skin was yellow and that made him special, too.

But if Mammy brought any gentlemen with her, he might have to stay in the cellar all night. In the morning there would be red bites on his arms, his face and neck. In the morning Mammy would unlock the cellar door and come partway down the steps and she'd call, ''Baby, baby, come up.'' Then she'd have him sit at the kitchen table and she'd cook breakfast for him, special to make up for the cellar, muffins and bacon ends and the eggs which were gooey and ran yellow over the plate. Mammy would hum to herself while she cooked, just like he did when he was in the cellar. And sometimes he could look at her eyes while she hummed and cooked and see the thoughts slowly turning in her head. And he could tell that she didn't know she was doing the humming.

After breakfast she'd let him play in the yard behind the house. He could play there almost every day now that Mr. Skinner knew about him. At first Mammy only let him play a little at a time and he had to promise to stay close by and run back inside if anyone came. Then one day he had been squatting in the dirt watching the ants. Taking little steps on his heels, he had followed one too far from the house. He watched it crawling over pebbles and twigs across the baked earth away from the other ants and further and he decided it must be running away from home. When he killed it with his thumb its body crushed down like it was empty and there was nothing inside. And then he looked up and saw Mr. Skinner.

Mr. Skinner was a white man and he was big, not big like Mammy Jordon, but tall. He had dark hair on his arms like the flies when they crawled on the light, but the hair on his head was white, dirt-white like their house, not like his. Mr. Skinner was climbing the steps to their back porch. There was no way he could run inside without being seen so he ran into the bushes and hid there.

After a while Mammy came to the screen door and she and Mr. Skinner started to talk, so he crawled closer so he could hear. Mr. Skinner was pointing to the yard and saying, ''Strange-looking boy you got there, strange-looking,'' and he knew Mammy would be mad at him for letting Mr. Skinner see him, but Mammy just said, ''He ain't my boy. He's my sister's boy,'' and he didn't know why Mammy was lying 'cause she told him it was bad to lie. Mr. Skinner kept saying ''strange-looking, strange-looking,'' like those were the only words he knew, with his hand on the screen, and Mammy shrugged and said he was ''just a boy,'' and Mr. Skinner said he'd never seen no boy with eyes like that. And then Mammy opened the door. Mr. Skinner looked around the yard once and went inside.

After that Mr. Skinner became one of Mammy's gentlemen. And he could play in the yard as much as he wanted 'cause Mr. Skinner never came near him anyway.

. . .

It was almost dark, but he could see the shapes of the trees and the way the breeze was moving them. There was no breeze in the cellar. It was just as hot and the flies had started to come. He could hear the buzzing of one and then two and then three, so he went over to the crumpled blankets, which he never used anymore 'cause it was too hot, and he reached under the blankets and took out the fly swatter he had stolen from the hook in the kitchen. It was the same swatter Mammy sometimes hit him with when she was mad.

He went back to where he had been sitting and he watched the trees go away in the dark. Mr. Skinner's dog had stopped barking and that was good 'cause when the barking went on and on he could sometimes feel the dog's hunger gnawing in his belly and that was bad. He held the swatter between his legs and pressed the metal loop of its handle against his cheeks and forehead 'cause it felt cooler than the air in the cellar. He listened to the flies coming one by one until their buzzing was together and he couldn't tell how many there were. They began to land on his arms and face in the dark and he brushed them away.

He didn't turn on the flashlight.

He wasn't going to kill the flies yet. He was waiting until Mammy Jordon came back. If she had a gentleman with her he would kill the flies so he wouldn't have to listen to them upstairs. He didn't want to hear their heels on the porch together. He didn't want to hear the talking and the laughter. Most of all he didn't want to do the seeing when Mammy took the gentleman to bed. If he waited to kill the flies, that would be good.

Every Sunday Mammy taught him about the good and the bad. Sometimes he understood and sometimes he'd get mixed up. He knew the music was good, but singing and dancing were bad. The book was good 'cause it told about the good and the bad. The gentlemen were bad and he hated them, but he knew Mammy had to see them anyway. The cellar was bad and he hated it and knew that. The flies were bad and he hated them. But with Mammy Jordon, sometimes she was good and he loved her and sometimes she was bad and he hated her. Some nights she'd do the drinking, and then she was very bad.

Mammy said the drinking was bad, but she did it anyway, just like going with the gentlemen. Sometimes it was different with the gentlemen, but with the drinking it was always the same. She'd sit at the kitchen table and the more she drank the quieter she got. After a while she'd start to cry. Then the crying would become cursing, low at first and under her breath. Pretty soon the cursing got louder and next she'd be yelling at the top of her voice, at no one but like there was someone there, saying how she should of never got mixed up with no *mojo* swamp man, singing and changing all the time like he did, chasing after his own daughter and the two of them flying off in the sky and leaving her with the sin of it all. And then she'd see him watching her and she'd curse at him and start hitting him for no good reason. He'd crouch in the corner or under the table and Mammy would hit and kick at him until she got tired. Then she'd go back to the cursing and the crying. Until finally she'd get quiet again and want to hold him to make his hurts go away. But he didn't like her softness then 'cause it smelled like the drink.

Sometimes he thought all good things had something bad in them, like the tomatoes going bad when they got old, and he wondered if all old things went bad. Mr. Skinner was old and he didn't seem that bad. But Mammy said that since he was a white man, that made him bad enough.

. . .

By the time he heard Mammy's car and the car that followed it, the gentleman's car, the flies had clustered upon him, the closed space of the cellar filled with their buzzing. He did not wait for the sound of heels on the porch. He clicked on the flashlight and stood, his knees bent and his neck forward so he wouldn't bump his head on the ceiling. With this movement the flies rose from his body, and some settled back. His shirt was soaked through with sweat so he stripped it off and the flies rose from him again.

In the heat and dark he moved toward the mattress and leveled the flashlight across its expanse. In the dim cone of light he could see its stained ticking and the rips where springs and stuffing were exposed. Its entire surface was alive with the crawling black dots of the flies.

He began to kill them.

He raised the swatter and brought it down—slap!—on the mattress. With the force of the blow the flies rose as a cloud, their buzzing angry, and he brought the light closer and he could see one dead fly and one crushed but still moving, its buzzing broken. He could see they were not hollow like the ants, but filled with goo like the eggs on his plate. And then he went back to the killing.

He put the flashlight at one end of the mattress so that its beam spread in a "V" across the surface and he waited until the flies settled back on to the ticking and started their crawling, and then he aimed and struck—slap!—and the flies which did not die rose up and he waited for them to settle again. He crouched at the other end of the mattress, rocking his body, moving his shoulders so the flies wouldn't settle on him. But each time he waited, he could hear the noises from upstairs. He knew Mammy's voice too well to pretend it wasn't hers. And the gentleman's voice, he knew that for a white man's voice. So he picked up the flashlight and began shining it around the cellar.

The flies were everywhere, on the walls, the posts, some even crawling in the dirt. He moved about killing them—slap!—and he pretended this one was Mammy's gentleman and this was another gentleman—slap!—and this was Mr. Skinner's dog and this was Mr. Skinner—slap!—and this was Mammy when he hated her—slap!—and this was Mammy when he loved her so he let it go.

His breath heavy, his body bare to the waist, the flies striking him as he moved through them, their buzzing louder and angrier the more he killed, and still they came in through the chinks so he killed them there. As he waved the flashlight about in his hand it began to fade. In the thickening darkness he could sense the life and death and dying all about him. He no longer needed the light so he hurled it against the cinder blocks and it shattered. Moving to and fro, twisting and turning, he killed and killed—slap!—and still they came. He could hear the buzzing all about him as a music fierce and filling. He could feel his feet pounding the packed dirt floor. He could hear his voice rising from within his chest. He was singing. He was dancing. He was changing.

By the time Mammy Jordon unlocked the cellar door and came partway down the steps and called, ''Baby, baby, come up,'' all of the flies were dead but one. A huge and hairy flapping rose from the darkness of the stairs.

THE TOURISTS

John Burke

Is there no end to John Burke's ability? Apparently not. Apart from having penned "about" 120 books, including Victorian gothics and thrillers and having edited three volumes of *Tales of Unease,* he has recently compiled a 200,000-word dictionary of music, plays Schumann, Brahms, Finzi and Vaughan Williams on the piano, and translates books from the Danish. John scored full marks and no passes when he appeared on the horrifyingly difficult British quiz show *Mastermind* to answer questions on the life and music of Carl Nielsen. Born in Sussex in 1922, John Burke now lives in Southwold, Suffolk, where he continues to be as enragingly prolific and talented as ever. While "The Tourists" has a stronger science fiction flavor to it than most of the stories in this collection, I particularly relished its stark black-and-white-TV quality, and its description of pain that reaches a pitch that I can only describe as dental.

He knew he was not welcome. He also knew that unless he got drunk or quarrelsome he would not be thrown out. And he never got drunk; and his bleak pleasure in intellectual discussion could never be called quarrelsome. The landlord didn't like him, but was a fair man who fretfully knew there was no real excuse for disliking him.

Dr. Spexhall ordered his usual light ale, and leaned on the bar.

It was warm in here after the dark chill outside. The landlord's wife stooped over the fire and put two pieces of coal and one log symmetrically on the bright glow.

"Good evening, Mrs. Carson," said Spexhall.

She gave him a sharp, apprehensive glance and scurried towards the flap in the bar. "Good evening, Doctor." She looked relieved to be back on the other side of the counter.

A sudden breeze shook the window behind two strangers sitting on the red padded bench.

"Airy," said one of the locals.

"Reck'n it'll blow tonight."

"Mebbe. No frost, though."

"No. Airy, but no frost."

The same petty variations on the same predictable themes—every night the same, every drawling voice the same. Spexhall found it exasperating yet reassuring: it did him good to come in here, to sense their dislike, and to feel without any conceit whatsoever his own superiority.

Another regular came in through the door from the yard. Always the same there, too: Charlie would never have dreamed of using either of the other two doors. Creatures of habit, all of them, with dull minds and dulled reflexes.

Charlie was greeted by a shrill yapping. The Carsons' corgi, of pedigree as uncertain as that of so many Welsh bitches, came scampering after him into the bar. Then she stopped, knowing at once that Spexhall was there. The shrieking adulation with which she greeted her favourites was almost as unpleasant as the hatred she bestowed on Spexhall. Now she edged along the floor, while Carson said, "That's enough, Daisy," and Mrs. Carson came fussing out again to scoop up the animal and carry it away.

"Sorry, Doctor."

But she was stroking Daisy, and both of them blamed Dr. Spexhall for being what he was.

He wondered what reaction he would get from the creature if he had it in his laboratory. Daisy, he meant, not Mrs. Carson . . . but at the thought of dissecting fat, flabby Mrs. Carson he couldn't restrain a secret little grin. Opening up, keeping the creature alive while he probed and sliced, connected and disconnected—all for the eventual good of mankind, of course.

Charlie looked along the bar. "Nasty smell from your place last night, Doc." He had been drinking before he got here. His voice was slurred and aggressive. "Burning some of your failures, eh?"

"We never have what you could call a failure," said Spexhall smoothly. "There's something valuable to be learnt from everything we do."

"Like how to make it hurt a bit more next time?"

"Come off it, Charlie," said Carson, still correct and reasonable.

Spexhall looked round the smoke-wreathed room, studying the occupants with clinical detachment. Invariably after a few seconds they avoided his gaze. He hadn't touched them and would never have the chance of touching them, but they squirmed in vicarious terror. It would be so fascinating—in a purely analytical way, naturally—to watch their reactions under the reality. So much more valuable than all the dogs and cats and rabbits which couldn't express their symptoms and pain in words. A human being could contribute so much more than a dumb animal—an animal dumb, that is, save for all those uncommunicative squeals and yelps. A human being would be able to tell him where it hurt, how much it hurt, how much was endurable and for how long . . . and where the breaking point came.

A pity there were no volunteers.

He realized abruptly that two people, unlike the rest, were not averting their eyes. The strangers under the window seemed to be returning his casual appraisal with a more than casual interest.

The man wore a dark green tweed, the woman a dove-grey dress and a piebald coat. They looked poised and self-assured, with all the enviable confidence of good taste and prosperity. They did not quite nod at Dr. Spexhall, but somehow he knew they had accepted him.

"Stinking," said Charlie suddenly. "It ought to be stopped, that stink. When the wind blows east we get it something shocking. Makes the wife sick, it does. What I say is—"

"That's enough, Charlie."

Charlie growled and ordered another pint of brown and mild.

Dr. Spexhall said across the room: "Taking a late holiday?" He wanted to make it clear that he was allying himself with these strangers against the doltish regulars. "Or are you looking for property in the district?"

"We are just travelling," said the man.

"Not the best time of year." The landlord joined in. He liked to make people feel at home, and to keep the bar buzzing with uncomplicated talk. "We get most of our tourists between June and early September."

The couple did not turn towards him but went on staring at Dr. Spexhall.

The woman had tawny yet lustreless eyes. She said: "We find this as good a time as any for our purposes." She spoke with an odd lack of resonance. There was something in her intonation which could not be called an accent yet was somehow, indefinably, foreign.

With the same flatness the man said: "You live here?"

"And work here," said Spexhall. "At the Plant Toxicity Research Centre, across the heath."

"Poisoning animals," Charlie contributed. "And then frizzling 'em. Making a stink half the night."

"Scientific research." Dr. Spexhall made another weary attempt to state his credentials and have them acknowledged by these wilfully obscurantist idiots. "For the benefit of mankind. To save us from disease, infection, poisoning by sprays, the distortion of our ecological balance . . . from a hundred dangers."

The two strangers nodded. Quite unmistakable this time: quite definite nods.

Encouraged, Spexhall went on: "Experiment is essential. We have to see how poisons and irritants work before we can see how to *stop* them working."

"Without anaesthetics," said Mrs. Carson, staring at Spexhall with undisguised loathing. "It's horrible."

"Our establishment is inspected regularly by the appropriate authorities."

"And I bet they don't see the half of it."

The man smiled the faintest of sympathetic smiles at Spexhall, who moved round the bar.

"Would you care for a drink?"

"Thank you, we have enough."

Close to, the woman's face was remarkably unlined: a perfectly moulded prototype of a face. The man, too, had an almost feminine skin. You could hardly believe that he ever needed to shave.

Spexhall said: "I'm afraid it's not very lively here in the winter."

"Tell me . . ." The man leaned forward, his voice muffled by the noisy beginnings of a dirty joke at the bar. "What would your reaction be if, for the sake of a superior species, human beings had to be treated as I understand you treat your animals?"

"What superior species?"

"Supposing the existence of one."

"Well, I'd approve. Naturally. But it's rather a fanciful idea, isn't it?"

"You think so?"

Spexhall had begun to hope this might turn into an interesting discussion between equals, but he became aware that the story at the bar had come to its clumsy end and the dolts were now listening.

"Supposing the existence of such a race," he said brusquely, "I see no reason why human beings shouldn't make a contribution to its store of essential scientific knowledge."

"Vivisection?" said the landlord's wife, pale beneath her mop of black curls. "On human beings?" Then she sniffed. "Well, no worse than on animals, I suppose. And there's some I wouldn't mind seeing—"

"Watch it, love," said her husband.

Charlie thumped his tankard down. "Reck'n I'd sooner have a pint in The Crown." He lurched towards the yard door. A scythe of cold air cut a swathe along the passage as he went out.

"Superior race?" The landlord was over-eagerly trying to make up for his wife's antagonism. "You mean Martians or something?"

The man and woman exchanged glances and produced identical smiles. Spexhall had thought of them as husband and wife but now felt they must surely be brother and sister. "Hardly Martians," said the woman.

"Well, superior, anyway. From somewhere else."

"Just so. From somewhere else."

"If they were that superior," said Carson, "they'd know *we* were intelligent, too. Sensitive, I mean. I mean, they'd see it wasn't right to treat us like animals."

"My Daisy's an animal," said his wife, "and *she's* sensitive."

The warmth of the fire had swallowed up the brief draught from the passage, yet Spexhall was conscious of a chill. The man was looking at him with a fixed, contemplative expression—looking at him, Spexhall abruptly realized, the way he himself had so recently been looking at other people in the bar. But who had the right to study him like that, look down on him like that? Sheer impertinence.

He had been mistaken. These were not people he wished to talk to. He said a terse goodnight and left the pub.

. . .

There was no moon. The path across the heath was little more than a pallid scar upon the darkness. As he walked, the sky became faintly lighter, chopped up by the jagged rooftops of the village. Then the far rim of the heath became his only horizon. A plume of cloud drifted like lazy smoke, as though from the distant incinerator of the Research Centre.

His house lay in a dip below a windbreak of trees. There was a rough track to the main road a mile away, but he preferred the walk across the heath itself. Its atmosphere suited him. He had never been afraid of being alone.

Alone?

Tonight he had a peculiar feeling, not of being followed, but of being *accompanied*.

Superior beings . . . ?

Nonsense.

He quickened his pace. Not because he was frightened: just that it was cold and he wanted to get home.

He lived alone and liked that, too. Mrs. Leggett came in and cleaned three mornings a week. She cleaned everywhere, even in his small workroom. It didn't really need much doing to it: he himself tidied up and removed all traces of his little private experiments before she arrived; but if he hadn't let her in there, she would inevitably have gossiped in the village. Once or twice he had been tempted to leave the remnants of one of his experiments for Mrs. Leggett to find. What a field day that would be for them! But he was too much devoted to his work to endanger it by flippant gestures.

The path forked. He turned right and went down towards his own front door.

As he put the key in the lock there was a faint rustle under the shadow of the trees. He opened the door and flicked on the switch immediately inside so that light spilled out over the step.

"Doctor . . ."

Ben Doy moved into the pool of brightness, a small sack dangling from his fingers.

"Two for you, Doctor," he said.

The shambling young man came from miles away, beyond the heath and the river. Folk from that part of the world rarely mixed with folk on this side. "Turnip country" was the contemptuous name bestowed by the locals on Ben's neighbourhood.

It was useful. For Dr. Spexhall, a very useful source of supply.

He took the sack. As he put it down on the table at the foot of the narrow staircase, the sack stirred. Spexhall opened it and looked in. Two fine specimens—two healthy, very well cared for cats. "Good." He fastened the neck again so that they could not fight their way out.

Ben stood awkwardly in the doorway. Once the money was in his pocket he would plod off at a steady pace along the five miles to home.

"Come in. I think I've got some silver in my desk drawer."

Spexhall opened the door into the sitting-room which also served as his study. Ben shuffled after him as he snapped on the light.

The man and woman were sitting by the fireplace. The man did not even blink as the light went on. He said levelly: "We have been waiting for you."

. . .

They couldn't be here. Couldn't possibly have passed him on the heath and got here first.

"I'll be off then, Doctor," said Ben hoarsely.

He radiated an animal fear that reeked almost as strongly as the stench of his body and his clothes. Not waiting for the money, he turned back towards the door.

And stayed there, motionless.

Spexhall felt the struggle. It was a physical tension, a thrumming and a thrashing inside his head. But that was only the echo of what was going on inside Ben's head. He heard Ben groan, though his lips were tightly shut. The man and the woman, not moving a muscle, exerted themselves until there was one last wordless protest from Ben. A silent shout—how could there be such a thing?—followed by a silent howl.

Spexhall tried to clear his mind of irrational terror. This could prove most interesting. With his own fine analytical mind he could surely contribute. He would help these remarkable visitors to evaluate whatever it was they were after. It would have to be understood, of course, that they worked as equals. This was, after all, his house. They owed him respect—and an explanation.

He said: ''I'm afraid you haven't made clear what you are doing in my house.'' It sounded firm and decisive. ''You have still not told me where you come from, or what you want.''

A fleeting thought brushed his mind and was lost in a tangle of muddled concepts which he thought he could grasp but which then eluded him. Half-finished phrases slid off into a dizzying maelstrom. In a fraction of a second he experienced all the sick humiliations of nightmare, when nothing will respond, nothing is coherent.

The man said aloud: ''If we explained, you would not understand. Let us not waste time.''

Ben began to move away from the doorway. His legs did the walking, but Spexhall sensed down every fibre of his own nerves that the man and woman were controlling the motion. In some way they had reached in and taken hold, applying . . . applying what?

He caught the contemptuous flick of a passing thought in the man's mind. Or perhaps it was the woman's. He wasn't conscious any longer of any separateness.

The thought was clear enough, though. *Doesn't understand . . . crude material . . . do the best we can . . .*

Crude? They must mean Ben and the quality of Ben's mind.

Indignantly he knew they didn't mean Ben.

He had to reassert himself. ''If you want to use my workroom . . . instruments, equipment . . .''

Something scratched at his mind like a fingernail and then slid derisively away. *Crude*. The implication of the word darted in and out again.

Ben went to the couch and lay down on it. For a moment he summoned a last flicker of resistance. ''Look here, Doctor . . .''

It was all he said. All he said aloud, anyway. The woman looked at him, and he stiffened and jerked his head back as if the neck had been snapped.

Spexhall began to tremble. There was the inner tremor of a thunderstorm approaching—an earth shift, an electrical discharge, something to set the hackles up. And a jumble of distorted visions and echoes filled the room. A drunken Ben calling out, "Dad, it wasn't, honest, I didn't," and somehow a dozen older men were marching back into an irrecoverable past, or toppling off into infinity. Ben's hand groped over his face to cover his eyes, but still he could see. Spexhall tried to back away, to shut it out; but the room was full of it. And the voices, the pleas, the anguish pulsing up—the confused agonies of a simpleton unable to cope. It was like eavesdropping outside a confessional.

All at once there was the last of those silent screams. Ben crumpled.

He crumpled from within. No blood had been lost, there were no wounds. Not a mark on him. Yet he shrivelled visibly. His mouth sagged and the mind itself was dissolving. Not just brain tissue but the whole mind, the man's whole entity, flowing out of him in a viscous stream. Blood and pulp, thought and feeling, the soul . . .

Soul?

It was not a concept Spexhall had ever taken much account of. But what else was it that had failed inside Ben? Failed, dissolved, turned to obscenity and rotted away, all in a matter of seconds.

"Not sensitive enough," said the woman without moving her lips. "We need a more advanced mind."

"The resources are disappointing."

"We must do the best we can."

They turned their blankly accusing gaze upon Dr. Spexhall.

He prided himself that his reactions were faster than poor, backward Ben's. He flung himself at the door and was out in the night before they could grab him.

He ran.

Nobody pursued. He gulped for breath and headed for the distant, warm lights of the village. Still there was nobody behind him. He tried to gasp defiance into the blanket of the night, but found himself quivering with the feeling that he was on the end of a line: they were casually unreeling, but would jerk it taut when they chose.

Keep going.

Suddenly he was twitched to one side. The door opened.

What door? There couldn't be a door out here in the middle of the heath, like some grotesque surrealist painting.

I shall wake up.

Through the door. Into the impossible room. Not warm, not cold, not bright. Just a room. You knew you were in a room where no room could be, and that was all.

The woman, calm and unhurried as though she and the man had not run here but had been waiting here all the time, said: "Shall I prepare?"

"Yes. The exhaustion level may be a factor."

He was frozen into immobility. And they began to finger his mind. A hundred times worse than having the body touched and prodded—as it had once been prodded and toyed with by that tribe of little swine at school, fingering him and giggling. Slime running over his mind, soaking up his thoughts. Dimly he sensed the filthy draining of Ben's mind. Now it was dripping over him too, flowing away with him. And time had gone crazy, and there was his father, the time he had pulled a frog to pieces . . . and his mother catching him in the lavatory and screaming, "You little beast, oh, you dirty, *dirty* . . ." And the form master who loved to thrash him, and again those sniggering boys and later the girl who had mocked and said he hadn't got anything big enough to offer and would never be good enough, never . . .

"Yes." The man's voice mused from a long way off. "Now. Complete release. But the antidote is what we need. Tell me, how does *this* feel?"

Agony whipped across his mind. They flayed him and dissected him with fleshless fingers; just as he might have carved up the body of a bulldog. He screamed, and felt their displeasure.

"You said you would be willing," the man said.

He tried to shout back. Let me go. Take your hands off me. Please let go. Please. Let go. *Please*.

But there were no hands. No instruments, no incisions, no blood. Only pain. Unendurable pain.

"We shall make no progress here," said the woman. Or was it the man? He floundered in a world of red and grey pus. They were draining him.

"You were in favour of making a contribution." The manner was that of the form master—no, more like the headmaster's sternly reproachful lisp, demanding decency and application and cleanly upright manhood. *We all have our task in this world, Spexhall . . . Beware unclean thoughts . . . Spexhall, I am disgusted beyond measure . . .* "Help us," said the man clearly and directly. "Where we come from there is a plague."

Spexhall's intellectual pride fought to maintain him in the welter of filth. "Where *do* you come from?"

"I have said you would not understand." The indifference, far beyond contempt, was almost as savage as the physical and mental pain. "Does a dog understand when *you* lay it bare?"

I demand to know. Spexhall did not even say it out loud; but the answer came at once. "We need to know how to counteract a widespread mental infection in our community."

"You can't use terminology like that." Spexhall tried to steady his world in the middle of the hell that foamed over it. He clung to his own integrity, his exactness, his belief in meticulous analysis. "It's the wrong word. You can talk about a mental disturbance, but not an infection."

"It is the only word. Listen."

Only they didn't really mean *listen*. They meant something inexplicable. Fleetingly he caught a hint of what they meant by a mental infection; and his own comprehension dissolved into something more appalling yet. He felt a smell; saw hideous discord; heard the seeping silence that would destroy him.

He began to weep.

"You disappoint us," they said.

The pain, he pleaded. Please, it can't be, it can't go on, there isn't this much, there can't be . . .

"Pain?" they said. "You think this is pain? It is no more than the faintest taste of what *we* have to suffer—we, who are truly sensitive. Listen," they said again.

"No," he screeched.

But they had lost patience. They jabbed him with the tiniest dose of their pain and tossed him aside as he himself might once have hurled the pulsating remains of a dissected cat against the wall in a fury of frustration.

What was left of his mind flooded away on a tide of yellow scum, down into an eternal sewer.

"Another failure," said the man—or whatever it was.

"We must try another thousand times. One thousand fragments may still make the complete picture."

"Come, then. We travel on."

"Do we leave this where it is?"

"Discarded experiments must not be left lying around."

Spexhall made a last attempt. "Please"—it was a whisper, he was still capable of forming words—"let it stop now. Please help." He fought against the disease and against the foul ignominy of his own dissolution. He half understood now what they meant, and how a mind could be infected, contaminated. Or perhaps it was only one thousandth of an understanding. But he pleaded: "There must be help. Must be mercy. Somewhere."

"Strange," came the woman's remote voice. "I felt it responding."

"Yes," he implored. "Listen to me. You've got to . . . got to . . ."

"Yelping," said the man dispassionately. "That is all it is: merely yelping."

"Disposal, then. Fire?"

"Crude. But it appears to be the accepted custom in this world."

"Think it, then." Their minds came to bear on what was left of Spexhall. "Think it, and let us be done with it."

. . .

Charlie came blearily out of the public bar of The Crown and shuffled across the street. The wind blew up an alley and stirred a shred of newspaper in the gutter. Charlie stood on the kerb and sniffed the night air.

"Gets worse," he muttered. "Burning. That bloody doctor's burning again."

THE WISH

Roald Dahl

Roald Dahl told me that he never writes original stories for anybody, except himself; but he was more than happy to give me free use of any of his published works. I took up the offer with appreciation and relish, and took longer reading his collected stories of horror and revenge than I ought to have done. But in the end, for *Scare Care,* it was no contest: it had to be "The Wish." It is an unsurpassed conjuring-up of childhood magic and terror, one of those stories that opens the ground beneath your very feet. Roald Dahl lives in Great Missenden, Buckinghamshire, where he continues to write his monstrously successful children's stories; and to prove that—far from being harmful—horror fiction helps people of all ages to come to terms with everything in life that is frightening and painful and incomprehensible.

Under the palm of one hand the child became aware of the scab of an old cut on his kneecap. He bent forward to examine it closely. A scab was always a fascinating thing; it presented a special challenge he was never able to resist.

Yes, he thought, I will pick it off, even if it isn't ready, even if the middle of it sticks, even if it hurts like anything.

With a fingernail he began to explore cautiously around the edges of the scab. He got the nail underneath it, and when he raised it, but ever so slightly, it suddenly came off, the whole hard brown scab came off beautifully, leaving an interesting little circle of smooth red skin.

Nice. Very nice indeed. He rubbed the circle and it didn't hurt. He picked up the scab, put it on his thigh and flipped it with a finger so that it flew away and landed on the edge of the carpet, the enormous red and black and yellow carpet that stretched the whole length of the hall from the stairs on which he sat to the front door in the distance. A tremendous carpet. Bigger than the tennis lawn. Much bigger than that. He regarded it gravely, settling his eyes upon it with mild pleasure. He had never really noticed it before, but now, all of a sudden, the colours seemed to brighten mysteriously and spring out at him in a most dazzling way.

You see, he told himself, I know how it is. The red parts of the carpet are red-hot lumps of coal. What I must do is this: I must walk all the way along it to the front door without touching them. If I touch the red I will be burnt. As a matter of fact, I will be burnt up completely. And the black parts of the carpet . . . yes, the black parts are snakes, poisonous snakes, adders mostly, and cobras, thick like tree-trunks round the middle, and if I touch one of *them,* I'll be bitten and I'll die before tea time. And if I get across safely, without being burnt and without being bitten, I will be given a puppy for my birthday tomorrow.

He got to his feet and climbed higher up the stairs to obtain a better view of this vast tapestry of colour and death. Was it possible? Was there enough yellow? Yellow was the only colour he was allowed to walk on. Could it be done? This was not a journey to be undertaken lightly; the risks were too great for that. The child's face—a fringe of white-gold hair, two large blue eyes, a small pointed chin—peered down anxiously over the banisters. The yellow was a bit thin in places and there were one or two widish gaps, but it did seem to go all the way along to the other end. For someone who had only yesterday triumphantly travelled the whole length of the brick path from the stables to the summer-house without touching the cracks, this carpet thing should not be too difficult. Except for the snakes. The mere thought of snakes sent a fine electricity of fear running like pins down the backs of his legs and under the soles of his feet.

He came slowly down the stairs and advanced to the edge of the carpet. He extended one small sandalled foot and placed it cautiously upon a patch of yellow. Then he brought the other foot up, and there was just enough room for him to stand with the two feet together. There! He had started! His bright oval face was curiously intent, a shade whiter perhaps than before, and he was holding his arms out sideways to assist his balance. He took another step, lifting his foot high over a patch of black, aiming carefully with his toe for a narrow channel of yellow on the other side. When he had completed the second step he paused to rest, standing very stiff and still. The narrow channel of yellow ran forward unbroken for at least five yards and he advanced gingerly along it, bit by bit, as though walking a tightrope. Where it finally curled off sideways, he had to take another long stride, this time over a vicious-looking mixture of black and red. Half-way across he began to wobble. He waved his arms around wildly, windmill fashion, to keep his balance, and he got across safely and rested again on the other side. He was quite breathless now, and so tense he stood high on his toes all the time, arms out sideways, fists clenched. He was on a big safe island of yellow. There was lots of room on it, he couldn't possibly fall off, and he stood there resting, hesitating, waiting, wishing he could stay for ever on this big safe yellow island. But the fear of not getting the puppy compelled him to go on.

Step by step, he edged further ahead, and between each one he paused to decide exactly where next he should put his foot. Once, he had a choice of ways, either to left or right, and he chose the left because although it seemed the more difficult, there was not so much black in that direction. The black was what made him nervous. He glanced quickly over his shoulder to see how far he had come. Nearly half-way. There could be no turning back now. He was in the middle and he couldn't turn back and he couldn't jump off sideways either because it was too far, and when he looked at all the red and all the black that lay ahead of him, he felt that old sudden sickening surge of panic in his chest—like last Easter time, that afternoon when he got lost all alone in the darkest part of Piper's Wood.

He took another step, placing his foot carefully upon the only little piece of yellow within reach, and this time the point of the foot came within a centimetre of some black. It wasn't touching the black, he could see it wasn't touching, he could see the small line of yellow separating the toe of his sandal from the black; but the snake stirred as though sensing the nearness, and raised its head and gazed at the foot with bright beady eyes, watching to see if it was going to touch.

"I'm not touching you! You mustn't bite me! You know I'm not touching you!"

Another snake slid up noiselessly beside the first, raised its head, two heads now, two pairs of eyes staring at the foot, gazing at a little naked place just below the sandal strap where the skin showed through. The child went high up on his toes and stayed there, frozen stiff with terror. It was minutes before he dared to move again.

The next step would have to be a really long one. There was this deep curling river of black that ran clear across the width of the carpet, and he was forced by this position to cross it at its widest part. He thought first of trying to jump it, but decided he couldn't be sure of landing accurately on the narrow band of yellow the other side. He took a deep breath, lifted one foot, and inch by inch he pushed it out in front of him, far far out, then down and down until at last the tip of his sandal was across and resting safely on the edge of the yellow. He leaned forward, transferring his weight to his front foot. Then he tried to bring the back foot up as well. He strained and pulled and jerked his body, but the legs were too wide apart and he couldn't make it. He tried to get back again. He couldn't do that either. He was doing the splits and he was properly stuck. He glanced down and saw this deep curling river of black underneath him. Parts of it were stirring now, and uncoiling and sliding and beginning to shine with a dreadfully oily glister. He wobbled, waved his arms frantically to keep his balance, but that seemed to make it worse. He was starting to go over. He was going over to the right, quite slowly he was going over, then faster and faster, and at the last moment, instinctively he put out a hand to break the fall and the next thing he saw was this bare hand of his going right into the middle of a great glistening mass of black and he gave one piercing cry of terror as it touched.

Outside in the sunshine, far away behind the house, the mother was looking for her son.

MONSTRUM

J. N. Williamson

Jerry Williamson is a force to be reckoned with in modern American horror writing—not only for the originality of his themes and the grip of his narrative, but for his sheer unstoppable enthusiasm, which lifts up people and houses just like the twister in *The Wizard of Oz.* A pipe-smoker from Indianapolis, Jerry appointed himself unofficial U.S. bureau for *Scare Care,* and put me in touch with many writers I would not otherwise have been able to reach—particularly new writers, whom he nurtures and encourages with a devotion beyond the call of duty. His own credentials include a stack of horror novels, including *Noonspell, Brotherkind, The Offspring, Wards of Armageddon, The Banished,* and *Dead to the World,* more short stories than you can shake a stick at, and the editorship of the highly acclaimed *Masques* anthologies. "Monstrum" is Jerry at his best: thoughtful, alarming, and apt, with a disconcerting view of the way in which we treat our children.

It was never my intention to take over that miserable account for the holidays and I never did figure out why Stinwall gave it to me. Rachel Guthrie, who'd already produced two commercials using kids, knew far more about working with them than I.

Both my marriages were childless, after all—a fact I viewed as a sort of no-show Act of God. I was much too selfish and insecure a man for fatherhood. The sum total of my ambition just about then was to continue writing commercial scripts and to direct a spot now and then; just to keep my hand in.

Stinwall, however, was apparently incapable of forgetting I had directed feature films once; back before I began drinking in earnest. I guess Lew was motivated by some kind of damned healer complex. You know the way that works. Get Fred Tarkington back on his feet and in the saddle whatever it takes, onward and upward to fulfilling his once-brilliant promise.

But none of us came off looking like ministering angels to a marvelous little boy named Kin Libby.

The actual beginning of all this was an agency party when I dove off the wagon, headfirst, sidled up to Lew, and made the drunken announcement that something ''awf'ly strange'' had just happened in my life. When he wanted to know what, I said drunkenly that I'd come face-to-face with evil yesterday. At the exact moment when it had gotten a toehold on somebody I cared about.

I can see, now, that it was just like Lew Stinwall to conclude that my alcoholic sentiment indicated a deep adoration of kids, and that I had to have them around just to remain sober.

He asked me to be more precise and I blurted, ''My six-year-old niece just twisted hell out of my finger.''

''Well, I hope you shot her on the spot, Fred,'' Lew replied stoutly. ''Obviously, the child is a menace to all—''

''Lew,'' I'd said hastily, ''I *told* Pammie my finger was badly sprained. You remember. We played volleyball, and I jammed it. Remember the splint, the bandage?''

Stinwall's face screwed up in that irksome fashion he retains, trying to look less the boy genius, more a corporate man of the world. ''Let me get this straight, Fred. You showed this child Pammie, your, um, bandaged digit. No doubt expressed the intolerable agony you were experiencing. Whereupon she jumped right off the floor, to rend it. Snarling, was she?''

I sighed hugely. "I was holding her in my arms at the time." I recall wishing that we were closer to the bar. "Lew, Pammie did it from sheer meanness, she *wanted* to hurt it."

"I see."

"And when she had twisted it with all her might, she laughed. Lew, she *laughed*."

Someone gave Stinwall another drink then, and when he turned back to me his expression was carefully blank. Noncommittal. "Go on."

That was about it but he wasn't understanding. "Pammie and I were very close once. Six months before, Lew, she was the dearest little thing anyone could imagine. But Jessamyn, my sister, and her husband, Kurt . . . well, they're into hard stuff. Coke."

"I see."

Now I was sweating profusely. "They began neglecting Pammie. Constantly. And they're always bickering, or plotting ways to make more money for their damned habit."

Lew nodded. I thought he stifled a yawn. "Sins of the father—and the mother, of course. That it?"

"It is. Precisely." I'd nodded back, abruptly more sober then than when I'd been on the wagon. I needed Lew to understand my niece's problem, not try to solve mine. "If we grown-ups vanished from the planet and left the right mix of computers and robots to provide food, and a basic education, our next generation could be what God had in mind. Kids, Lew, they're so malleable, so much what we make them. But not just because of what we say, or do, but from how they *see* and quietly *observe* us. Little Pammie's face—"

"Pammie being your niece?" Stinwall's gaze was wandering.

"Her face," I nodded, "after she'd yanked my finger back—Lew, it was horrible." Surprise showed in my boss' features. "Lew, she had *changed*." Now I had his attention. "I can't be absolutely sure, Lew. But I don't think it was even the *same* face I adored when Pammie was three years old."

Lew held my gaze steadily for a moment. Then he finished his Lillet, shook his head, and our conversation was over.

• • •

The months passed and the holidays hove near and Lew Stinwall asked me to produce and direct the Christmas spot for our most important account—as well as to write and *cast* the miserable thing.

Which meant I'd been handed the monumental task of hiring a dozen boys and girls under eight, and getting them to appear overjoyed at the prospect of finding our sponsor's famous dolls beneath their Christmas tree. And never mind the fact that all the parents who could afford the ugly monstrosities had already bought 'em *last* Christmas!

I had the idea of depicting the homes of poor children as well as the easier usual kind. To play down the cost of the dolls. Lew bought it, too—but it turned out to be the worst concept I'd had in my entire stint at the agency. At thirty-nine years of age and holding—by my bruised fingertips—Fred Tarkington knew less about coping with child actors than he did about staying on the wagon.

But it still could have worked out had it not been for little Kin Libby's face.

I'm certain, in retrospect, that Kin's looks had everything to do with what happened. You see, we're all inclined to lump extraordinary handsomeness with the flag, God, motherhood, as the good things. But with children, that's only the case if he or she isn't *too* exceptional—if what we really mean is that such-and-such a child is charming, amusing, or cute. Or our own child, of course.

Because just as we're awed by a genuinely beautiful woman, gawk at her, and can't contain ourselves until she's drunk, or pregnant, we're almost terrified of a child who might have been personally designed—handmade—by the Creator. With His face.

And we can't wait until he snaps a bone playing ball in Little League. Or simply picks up enough of our snide, calloused, adult damned attitudes to reveal aggression, self-righteous anger, and wary calculation in his perfect, all-too-plastic little features.

It reassures us that he is one of us then.

Of course, I knew nothing of that until I'd written all of a rough script except the closing sequence, which wouldn't quite come together. Then I began ringing up talent agents who represented child actors. There's no problem whatever in getting kids to look at; inside an hour, one is bumping his way through well-coiffed herds of people under four feet high and bawling back at the many moms who answered the cattle call.

My budget was generous, I had just enough time to get the spot on film, but I hadn't adequately estimated the sheer numbers of the girls and boys who'd show up. Or how bloody *grilled*—rehearsed to say what I'd want to hear—they would be. Coming in early on a Monday following my driest weekend in half a year, I had the initial impression that some fool had emptied an orphanage and dispatched them to Studio C.

Then I had the notion awhile that most of these tiny people were midgets, in reality. And the only tots who appeared outwardly normal or natural at all were those whose canny mothers had been through this several times and were sharp enough to anticipate me. There was so much damnable winsome cuteness and practiced sweetness of disposition during the first ninety minutes of the day that I was beginning to contract diabetes.

It wasn't utterly fruitless, of course. A girl-boy set of twins looked promising as a more or less indeterminate social class, for the purpose of my commercial; a titanically professional kid called Ernie, actually ten years old but redheaded and small for his years, showed signs of fitting in with the twins. That made one TV "family" fairly firm. I was also smitten by a roly-poly black girl, Mavella. But the other youngsters of her hue who had come in—actually, being there was their mothers' work—were doing the moms' level best to imitate one or more of the children on the Bill Cosby program. And I didn't work with clones.

I held it to two martinis at lunch, pretending that wasn't the world's oldest cliché, then went back behind my makeshift desk in the great barn of Studio C and—when I glanced up again—saw wholly perfect human beauty for the first time in my life.

Kin was small, even for seven. So what I saw first was just his face, bobbing up over the old wood table like a natural jewel surfacing from the sea. His hair was coal black and naturally wavy; I could tell. The shape of his head was . . . this is difficult to describe . . . proportioned ideally for what turned out to be a small body. That gorgeous head wasn't oversized, cute—point of fact, nothing was "cute" about Kin, least of all his features. Goldie Hawn and Sally Field are cute; Jayne Kennedy and Kelly McGillis are beautiful.

And Kin—I'm not gay, either, you can check that—was a remarkably beautiful boy.

Look, some kids get you with their eyes or the tilt of a nose or a smile that's coy, or lopsided, bashful or brash or eager to make you laugh. I learned in that three days it took to cast the damned commercial that there's almost always a single feature about a child that wipes you out, zaps you until something clicks inside and you mutter to yourself, "That child has exactly the *right* (fill-in-the-blank)!"

Little Kin Libby had it all. Astonishingly light-colored eyes with these thick, black lashes, eyes spaced so perfectly and so very level in how they stared back—so frankly, so honestly—that they might have been engineered. His nose was neither tiny nor pugged, it merely went with the rest. And his lips, grinning, concealed nothing but said they *liked* you on sight. They didn't plead for you to like him or show him attention because they were guileless; without that quality, they'd have seemed to be adult lips. I've thought about it, hard, and the closest I can come to capturing Kin's child's beauty of face for you is to evoke a little-boy Cary Grant—but devoid of ambition, anxiety, anything whatsoever to gain or prove. And I soon found he had a warmth that Grant never conveyed his whole life.

What made him vulnerable was twofold. While Kin wasn't emaciated or anything like that, he was just thin enough to appear frail, and his skin—despite the black lashes and eyebrows—was an ivory white that virtually glowed. That was one source of Kin's vulnerability.

The other was how he dressed. This, I'm aware, is when I have to be extremely precise in the way I describe him. Because his clothing wasn't made in an earlier century, or taken from a trunk left for decades in a cobweb-strewn attic. It only *looked* that way; as if the tattered, open-down-the-front gold pullover and a label-free pair of jeans rife with holes and a pale knee poking from an especially sizable gap had been bought for another child many years earlier.

Or, I realized, still grinning back at Kin like an idiot, as if something intrinsic to Kin-Libby-the-person had been made long before this century and modern garb simply wouldn't quite fit his body. The sweater and jeans drooped; he had to keep tugging up his trousers around his slender waist and, when I saw the oversized tennis shoes Kin wore—the toe gone in one, the other heel almost completely worn away—I realized that this kid was the living embodiment of the dirt-poor child I'd envisioned for the heart-rending, get-this-child-an-ugly-doll close of the commercial.

"Where's your mother?" I asked after he'd told me his name.

"She had to leave, sir." His voice possessed none of the

squeakiness of most of the boys I'd already interviewed. It was forthright—unhesitant, and mellow—and unimpressed by his whereabouts.

"When is she coming for you?" I inquired. I was surprised and a bit annoyed to realize my heartbeat was accelerating and told myself I didn't know why.

"She's not." The dark lashes blinked once and I had a feeling that he wasn't telling me everything. "But that's all right, 'cause I can walk home."

I nearly exclaimed, "In *this* neighborhood?" Then I remembered that people, presumably with more than their supply of offspring, probably did rent the dilapidated old domiciles surrounding the station. "I'll need her to sign some papers, Kin," I said.

"I can take them to her, sir," Kin murmured, colorless eyes bright and so very earnest above the edge of my table.

And I stopped talking to think, heartbeat a hammer pounding now, trying not to get ridiculous about this. But I'd seen in my mind's eye a panorama of shadowy, youthful faces belonging to mystery-shrouded kids of the past. For one, young Casper Hauser, who had basically materialized in the center of a German town square with no real clue to his identity. A thorough search was launched but nobody ever came for poor Casper, and no one was ever found who knew his origins. Where he'd come from, and for what purpose, had been an enigma for decades.

I thought of other anomalous little ones, too, some much more famous but whose childhoods were still veiled by mystery. "What are your mommy and daddy's names?" I asked at last.

"Mary," Kin said, readily enough, answering the way children always answer that question; with Christian names. "And Joseph."

My reaction wasn't, I believe, as standard in form as the boy's.

But I assured myself it was only the lunchtime martinis that were getting to me, and made myself get down to business. Which meant calling over Rachel Guthrie and asking her to pose little Kin for a series of camera shots, Jared Wakefield manning the equipment and, while he was at it, getting the boy's sound level recorded. Jared was one of those enormously experienced cameramen who can disappear into thin air when it's time to be unobtrusive or shoot first-rate film for the evening news while scampering over bridges and up hills. The last impression I had of Jared with an expression other than boredom was nearly two years ago when a political type wigged out and flashed Rachel Guthrie, and Wakefield had almost laughed.

Now he worked his camera magic with Kin Libby in his lens and a look on his weatherbeaten face I must describe as a mixture of intent, professional attentiveness, and awe.

Rachel, of course—she's raised three boys of her own and I suspected she'd hated my guts for getting this assignment, not for the money or prestige but because it meant working with children—promptly made a new run at Mother of the Year. There was a moment or two when I feared little Kin Libby might be smothered to death by her soft, generous bosom.

''He's perfection,'' she breathed at me once when I'd called a break and treated Kin to a Coke. And I'd seen Jared Wakefield when he overheard her and, to my surprise, winked and bobbed his chin in agreement.

I was far more fascinated by the sight of the seven-year-old struggling with the Coke machine.

He'd put the change I gave him into the proper slots, but now he was simply *waiting,* it seemed, for a can or bottle to come out. Apparently, I realized, he hadn't made his selection or pushed a button.

''What do you like to drink?'' I asked when I'd gone over to him.

He screwed his head around to gaze up at me with those matchless eyes. He said, ''Milk, sir.''

I blinked, then scanned the dispenser's display. No milk; just soft drinks and coffee. ''How about a Pepsi?''

He just shrugged and managed to look mystified.

But when I'd pushed the button and taken out the can and, somehow anticipating the challenge to Kin, popped the tab and handed the Pepsi over, Kin took a long pull and I watched a delightful smile take shape.

''That's wonderfully delicious,'' he said, marveling. And gave me the empty can. He'd drunk it down without a pause. ''Is it possible, sir, I might have another?''

It was possible. He had two more cans of Pepsi before I remembered it was time to wade through another wave of small people and try to cast a few more parts. I folded up an application form and permission sheet and made sure Kin tucked them away in a pocket of those tatterdemalion jeans, then stared after him while he went soundlessly across the huge studio and dwindled out of sight. I'd elicited his promise to be back with the application filled out and the permission form signed at ten the next morning—a Tuesday—and I wondered for a moment if he really would return. *Or if he can,* I thought, half convinced that I might be entitled to only one glimpse of so handsome a human being.

But he did return, a few minutes early Tuesday, wearing exactly the same bizarrely out-of-place clothes and making me both ashamed and irked that I'd lost sleep wondering if I'd ever see him again. Determined to be grown-up, a professional, I snatched the papers from Kin's small hand and spread them out before me on my wooden table.

Somebody had scrawled the name "Mary Libby" on the right line, the writing more printing than it was script—it was in pencil, too—and I frowned down at the page without saying a word, wary.

I covered the paper with the other one, the application, and recognized the same childish scrawl. It said that Kin Libby was, indeed, seven years old, had been born there, that his parents, as advertised, were Joseph and Mary Libby. But two things—one, a blank space, the other an answer to one of the application's questions—made my heart begin its extra-duty pounding again.

Kin's dad, Joseph, was a self-employed carpenter. And the line left blank had been reserved for the applicant's school.

I let the space that was filled in be. "Why didn't Mrs. Libby indicate where you attend school?" I asked, and my voice sounded sharper, drier, than I'd intended it.

"I don't go to school," replied Kin, light-colored eyes wide and ingenuous.

"But you're seven," I pointed out. "Why don't you go to school?"

There was no evasion in his handsome face or eyes. "My Daddy needs me to help out, sir. That's why Mommy brought me here." He blinked. "To earn some money for Christmas."

"But you have to go to school," I said, rather too loudly. Rachel, who'd entered the studio with that I'm-looking-for-somebody-and-I'd-better-find-him look substituting for the maternal one I preferred, overheard me and stopped to gape appreciatively at beautiful Kin from the distant doorway. "It's the law, son."

Kin didn't even shake his head to defy me. He merely reported the facts. "I have to be about my Father's business. He said so."

. . .

I buried myself in the script that afternoon, half relieved that Rachel corraled Kin for a wardrobe fitting. But I knew, that night, I would have to meet the Libby parents, would have to drive there and see what they were like or become so neurotic I'd dive into a whisky bottle and never emerge from it sane.

But Jessamyn, my sister, phoned the way she generally did every week or so and, while we caught up with the latest family gossip, I knew suddenly that I'd come up with the ideal end for the commercial. A mean rich girl would appear, showing off her new ugly doll to a poor little boy. The latter, played by Kin, would seem heartbroken; we'd catch him alone in a pitiful hovel, observe no gifts whatsoever under a mangy tree, and then a pair of adult arms would reach down to Kin to give him an ugly boy doll of his very own. Establishing for all the parental suckers gawking at the gorgeous kid on the screen that even the poorest children had a right to expect stuffed ugliness Christmas morning.

It was sheer garbage, of course. A lie. But lies were my stock-in-trade, if they were credibly told, and everything about Kin Libby virtually shouted his honesty as well as his beauty.

And Pammie, my niece—sister Jessamyn's daughter—would be the perfect choice to play the show-off little brat I'd envisioned! It even occurred to me that having the opportunity for a change of scene and to earn some money on her own could help Pammie, might make her a nicer human being.

That Christmas season, my ideas ranked right up there with the wisdom of Attila the Hun, Adolf Hitler, and Charles Manson!

Jessmayn wasn't sure it was a great notion but Kurt, her husband, had been listening on an extension and couldn't agree fast enough. Even before I'd broken the connection—after arranging for Pammie Montgomery to be on the set at ten Wednesday morning—I had the sinking feeling that Pammie would be lucky to see a nickel of what she earned and that my brother-in-law was already figuring out how much cocaine they could buy with his daughter's earnings.

But admen at any level weren't paid to be moralists, the great ending for my script was the reward for days of agonizingly drawing a blank but hanging in there, and I spent half the night putting it on paper. By the time I'd gulped down some half a pot of black coffee and freshly turned my innards into a wasteland vast enough to compete with anything on the tube, I was starting for the first time to imagine the awards I might win for this commercial.

It didn't occur to me even fleetingly that Kin Libby had never seen the sponsor's dolls and would elect to agree with my private conviction that they were the most repulsive creations ever foisted on innocent children.

''But I don't want one for Christmas, sir,'' he said softly, not the trace of a whine, or belligerence, in his voice or features.

''This is acting, Kin,'' I explained patiently to him. Rachel and the wardrobe personnel had found a cotton shirt with patches that fitted him better than his sweater but they'd left Kin with the holey jeans, incapable of devising a pair of pants that made the seven-year-old appear more poverty-stricken. Makeup had accentuated his large, solemn eyes and added mascara to his absurdly lovely lashes but otherwise let him remain vulnerably pale. ''It doesn't matter what you say because, well, it's *play* acting.''

''Father doesn't want me to say what is untrue.'' He'd uttered the comment so softly that I had to stoop to understand him. I recalled that Kin had called his father ''Daddy'' before and there was something else odd but I couldn't remember the details. ''Isn't lying a sin?''

''Kin,'' I said, trying a new tack, speaking into his ear so that no one else could hear me, ''your mommy and daddy are depending upon you, remember? To have money for Christmas?''

He turned his head slowly to peer directly into my eyes and his breath on my face was the sweetest thing I had ever smelled. It was desperately cold outside, I'd felt chilled ever since leaving my apartment, and my proximity to Kin and his soft, sweet-smelling breath somehow warmed me. His next question did not.

''Do *you* think it's all right?'' he asked me.

I blinked, broke the gaze, quested for Rachel with a panicky glance that reminded me how hollow, how huge, how busy but artificial—how silly—the place was, and my work, and I strove to come up with an answer that didn't condemn me as much as Studio C had already done it.

Then I saw my niece Pammie entering the studio with the prettiest, most expensive little dress in town, considered once more that the way this commercial was shot could mean major awards—even the return to feature films Lew Stinwall was kind enough to want for me—and I nodded. Didn't say anything affirmative aloud; nodded.

Rachel and wardrobe couldn't top my niece's street dress and she was on the set in under an hour, drawing near us in that choppy-stepped yet unhurried manner Pammie didn't have a year ago.

"Unca Fred!" she exclaimed when she was close enough—as if surprised, or recognizing my presence for the first time—and vaulted into my arms. I noticed that she still spoke in baby talk when it suited her purposes. One chubby hand clutched my wrist, drew my hand before her eyes. "Do you still have the poor hurt finger?"

It would always hurt when the weather changed, I knew. "No," I answered Pammie, carefully putting her on feet that were encased in snow-white patent-leather shoes. "It's well now."

"I'm *so* glad." She spun in a half-circle, deigning to notice Kin. "Are you an actor too?"

Kin, smaller than Pammie the way most boys remain shorter than girls until their teen years, searched my eyes, then nodded.

"Why's he wearing those *clothes*?" my niece demanded, her cute nose wrinkling with disgust.

"Kin is playing a poor boy, Pamela," Rachel replied, smiling. I wondered how much she'd been taken in; I wondered if, for most adults of middle age, a child's outward innocent appeal and inward but obvious malice were apparent, and if the former should actually be allowed to outweigh the latter. "He's the one to whom you show your doll, and who believes he isn't going to get one for Christmas."

"Well, I don't think he is," my niece said airily. When a propman brought her the doll for use in the commercial, she gazed up at him with her vivid blue eyes. "I was going to bring my *own* doll, Esmerelda, but I can always use two."

Apparently, Rachel or someone else there had already informed Pammie that all the kids acting in the commercial would receive free dolls as a bonus. I took the children by their hands and led them to two sets where Jared and his assistants were waiting at their cameras.

I taught them about finding their subtly marked places and we tried a run-through.

Which was all it was intended to be. I swear that.

At first, it went amazingly well. Pammie was nearly letter-perfect in her role despite having half read, half listened to her simple lines but once, and my heart began to beat faster for reasons more consoling and easily understandable than it had of late.

But then Jared and George Scifres began shooting the scene with Kin alone in his let's-pretend living room, staring wistfully at a Christmas tree that was a masterpiece of broken-down flora. It had maybe four or five dully gleaming bulbs like cancers on its limbs, a few strands of dirty-looking tinsel, and was gorgeous! There was nothing in the world about the moment that could have warned me that everything was about to go terribly, irremediably wrong.

Dutifully, little Kin glanced toward the tree and sighed the way I'd asked him to. Obediently, he rose from the bare wooden floor where Jared's cameras had found him and crossed the set to the mangy tree with exactly the projected despair, and hopelessness, I'd put in the script. I had never seen anybody more touching to see than he was then and, when he slumped to his thin knees beside the tree, it shot through my mind that Kin Libby was either the most natural actor I'd come across in my career—

Or that Kin wasn't acting at all.

You could've heard the proverbial pin fall. A crowd had gathered, I was dimly aware of that, and I sensed their presences and rejoiced at the breathless sense of wonder they exuded. It occurred to me that we might complete this sequence of the commercial in record time. Delighted, I felt the silence deepen.

And when it was so deep I heard my own heart beating and that of Rachel Guthrie, who couldn't have been driven away from that set by a team of Budweiser horses, it came to me that Kin had forgotten his line. The silence turned tense; someone had opened the front door of the building and I shivered.

"Cue him," I whispered to Ruth Riley, who always worked for me in that capacity.

But before Ruth could respond, another, higher voice piped up, its pitch a virtual shriek in that encompassing quietude. "'Gosh, I wish *I* had a doll like Alice Stratton got for Christmas!'" It was, naturally, my niece Pammie—who played Alice—and she wasn't looking at either the script or the cue cards. She'd remembered the lines. She hovered on the apron of the set, just out of her own little-rich-girl playroom, small back straight as a board and curls jostling as she spoke once more. "Boy, you're *dumb*! 'Gosh, I wish *I* had a—'"

"Pamela Montgomery," I hissed, "shut up."

"But he doesn't know his lines," she cried, coiffed head bobbing from left to right. "He's stubborn, and dumb, and he's *ruining* your commercial!"

I noticed Rachel's brows rise in a familiar manner that told me she empathized with my embarrassed role as Pamela's uncle. Unsure what to say or how to proceed, I got to my feet.

And Kin said, his level voice cutting through the newly fallen and electrically charged silence, "Gosh, I wish *I* had a doll." But then he stopped speaking, kneeling before the tree, his back to me.

Relieved, I smiled and knew Kin would be able to get the rest of his dialogue out, now that he was started. I wanted to encourage him so I veered around to face him, the way the cameras and lights were centered on his small form.

"Jesus," cameraman Jared Wakefield breathed from beside me.

Kin still knelt and his fists were doubled up so tightly I saw trickles of blood oozing from his palms. With the powerful lighting trained on his perfect face, I detected globules of perspiration as it sprang out from his temples, wreathing the crown of his head until the raven-wing hair looked drenched. The anguish in his features was unforgettable.

"Wish . . . I had a doll," Kin mumbled, not looking at me, his words scarcely audible, "like Alice Stratton got . . . for . . ." Then he broke off and I realized he'd had his head partly bowed because he was raising it now and meeting my eyes with his. "—for Christmas . . ."

With the last word he uttered, Kin began spitting blood. The front door of the building slammed shut like a detonation of thunder. There wasn't a great quantity of blood but enough to be terrifyingly, brilliantly crimson in that harsh light and enough to drip down his chin and, eventually, to make him begin to cough rackingly.

But he'd said the lines I had written for him and when I stumbled forward to encircle him with my arms, in case he was ready to pitch forward on his face—that possibility horrified me—the look in Kin's colorless, night-fringed eyes begged me to tell him he had done well.

And it forgave me.

. . .

What I had expected to find at the Libby household when I went there to notify them that we'd rushed their son to the hospital, I don't know now. The single discovery that satisfied my expectations at all was a Christmas tree that could have been a duplicate for the one on our set.

Apart from that, I found Joe and Mary Libby screaming at each other from inside the sixty-year-old frame house and, for one second, I couldn't knock on the door. I just trembled with cold. When I had knocked, when Kin's mother had yanked it open and lurched before me like some jungle mother distracted from her kill, it occurred to me that Mary Libby would probably have found it impossible to recall that period of time when she had been a virgin. Big Joe Libby made a halfhearted effort to conceal a claw hammer he clutched in his fist behind his back. But when I'd identified myself they were very solicitous of my comfort, vociferously grateful that I was concerned for their youngest son. Two others—infinitely older—played rock on a radio; a fourth son, I heard later, was serving time somewhere for breaking and entering.

But soon, their excessive appreciation for my concern was replaced with threats of legal action. What had happened, they opined, improvising, was all my fault, and I was never able afterward to dispute the point with anyone. The upshot was that my boss Lew had no choice except to permit little Kin to return to work.

I pleaded for, and got, a different assignment. Rachel took over the production and the direction of the Christmas spot, and made a point of reassuring me that she "wouldn't change a word of that fabulous script, especially the last sequence." She also promised me that Kin was probably well enough to do what his parents wanted of him, and I forget the medical explanation. It remained my unrelenting conviction that the doctors at the hospital could not conceivably have accurately diagnosed the boy's problems.

The day that Rachel was wrapping it up, I found myself wandering back into Studio C, discreet about hugging the long, vertical shadows along the walls until I'd edged near enough to watch, far enough away—because of the lights shining in their eyes—to go unobserved. People were everywhere, even Lew Stinwall.

And I thought Pammie was great. Not quite seven, and typecast; but great in the role.

Then the lights flared on the second set and I saw little Kin clad in a different shirt but otherwise, apparently, the same. *Sure,* I thought; *the blood wouldn't come out of the other shirt.* He was on the opposite side of the set, too far away from me to see his features clearly. But I watched him arise, cross to the Christmas tree, and sink forlornly before it with even greater poise than before. While I did not really wish to be seen, or to talk with him or even my niece, I drifted quietly closer and heard the dull, uneven throb of my heart sounding in my ears. Almost a week had passed since the first rehearsal and I'd been off the wagon, not even attempting to throw up my arms and graze the sides of it, most of that time.

''Gosh,'' Kin said, wistfully, clearly, ''I wish *I* had a doll like"—he paused, scaring me; but all that issued from his throat was an uncannily professional sigh of boyish desire—"like Alice Stratton got for Christmas!''

And as I stared at Kin, he got it. Rachel, saving expenses by providing the maternal arms that lowered the ugly thing into Kin's eager-to-hug hands, did her thing—unrecorded by the camera—and stared down, lovingly, at the beautiful boy.

And, ''Cut!'' Rachel cried exultantly, dropping to her knees to kiss Kin.

He did it, I thought, and abruptly felt myself a voyeur. Kin had done what we all truly desired for him to do, uttered his carefully crafted lie like a cooperative little man, and become one of us.

It should've been a happy ending. Jessamyn and Kurt, mine own dear family, had enrolled my niece in show biz, and won enough spare dough to make a pusher smile for a weekend. Joe and Mary Libby had forced their youngest child into maturing, as it were, even more rapidly than he'd ordinarily have had to do it; maybe God knew what they'd do with their child's income; get a divorce, perhaps. I hoped.

And since Rachel and Lew Stinwall were good folks, according to their lights and my own, they might even ask me to take a credit for myself on the commercial. I might, even now, clamber back up on the ol' reality wagon and ride it west to Hollywood gold and glitter. Maybe God knew what would happen to Fred Tarkington then.

I had walked stiff-leggedly away from the two sets when it passed through my mind on a wobbly, wavery kind of line that kept trying to dip back into the world where I'd thought I belonged, that the young German kid who'd materialized from nowhere into the town square—poor little Casper Hauser—had never seemed to be sure who he was. His own, destined identity had been kept from him somehow and, at the end, a stranger who had also never been identified had produced a pistol and filled him full of holes. Slaughtered him in the streets, close to where he'd originally been discovered.

I threw out a hand to brace myself against the studio wall when I wondered, that instant, if it was possible Casper Hauser might have grown up to be Christ.

"Where's my doll?" The voice wasn't that of my niece Pammie. It was strident, full of command, grievance, anxiety, insecurity, and avarice, a modern boy's voice. That of a child who was a complete stranger to me. "The commercial's over and *I want* my *free doll*!"

Let him have it, Rachel, I thought, my heartbeat subsiding to its customary, turgid stroke as I hurried toward the exit at an accelerating pace. *At the very least, he's earned the ugly damned thing.*

BREAKFAST

James Herbert

One of the world's most successful horror writers, James Herbert remains one of the least affected and most approachable. His contribution to *Scare Care* is a vignette which was cut from his best-selling novel *Domain,* in which the world is taken over by the horrific rats that made James famous. *The Rats* and all of James's subsequent horror novels, such as *The Fog, The Survivor, The Dark, Moon,* and *Sepulchre,* are *tours-de-force* of hit-you-where-you-live, out-and-out terror, and his enormous popular success is well deserved. James lives in Henfield, Sussex, with his family and his S-Type Jaguar, appropriately nicknamed The Beast. His latest novel was a classic ghost story, *The Haunting.*

The cold water trickled to a halt and the woman clucked her tongue. She twisted the tap off and placed the meagerly filled kettle on the electric stove. She left it to boil on the stone-cold ring.

Walking through to the hallway, the woman picked up the telephone receiver and flicked open the book lying beside it on the narrow hallstand. She found a number and dialled.

"I've already complained twice," she said into the mouthpiece. "Now the water's gone off completely. Why should I pay my water rates when I can't have bloody water?"

She flushed, angry with herself and the noiseless receiver. ''You've made me swear now, that's how angry I am,'' she said. ''Don't give me any more excuses, I want someone round today to sort it out, otherwise I shall have to speak to your supervisor.''

Silence.

''What's that you say? You'll have to speak up.''

The phone remained dead.

''Yes, well, that's more like it. And I'll have you remember that civility costs nothing. I'll expect your man later this morning, then.''

The earpiece could have been a sea shell for all the noise it made.

''Right, thank you, and I hope it isn't necessary to call again.''

The woman allowed herself a *humph* of satisfaction as she replaced the receiver.

''I don't know what this country's coming to,'' she said, pulling her unkempt cardigan tight around her as a breeze—a warm breeze—flowed down from the stairway. She went back into the kitchen.

As she rinsed the teapot with water from the cold kettle, the woman complained to her husband seated at the pine kitchen table, newspaper propped up against the empty milk bottle before him. A fly, its body thick and black and as big as a bee, landed on the man's cheek and trekked across the pallid landscape. The man ignored it.

''. . . not even as though water's cheap nowadays,'' his wife droned. ''We have to pay rates even when it's off. Should never have been allowed to split from normal rates—it was just their way of bumping up prices. Like everything else, I suppose, money, money, it rules everything. I dread doing the monthly shop. God knows how much everything's gone up since last time. Afraid you'll have to give me more housekeeping soon, Barry. Yes, I know, but I'm sorry. If you want to eat the way you're used to, you'll have to give me more.''

She stirred the tea and quickly sucked her finger when cold water splashed and burned it. Putting the lid on the teapot, she took it over to the kitchen table and sat opposite her husband.

''Tina, are you going to eat those cornflakes or just sit and stare at them all day?''

Her daughter did not even shrug.

''You'll be late for playschool again if you don't get a move on. And how many times have I told you Cindy isn't allowed at the table? You spend more time speaking to that doll than you do eating.''

She scooped up the dolly that she, herself, had placed in her daughter's lap only minutes before and propped it up on the floor against a table leg. Tina began to slide off her chair.

The mother jumped up and pulled the child erect again, tutting as she did so. Tina's small chin rested against her chest and the woman tried vainly to lift it.

"All right, you go ahead and sulk, see where it gets you."

A small creature with many eyelash legs stirred from its nest in the little girl's ear. It crawled out and scuttled into the dry white hair of the child's scalp.

The woman poured the tea, the water colourless, black specks that were the unbrewed tea leaves collecting in the strainer to form a soggy mould. Silverfish scattered from beneath the milk jug as she lifted it and unsuccessfully tried to pour the clots of sour cream into the cups.

"Sammy, you stop that chattering and finish your toast. And will you put your school tie on straight, how many more times do I have to tell you? At ten years of age you think you'd be old enough to dress yourself properly."

Her son silently gazed at the green bread beside his bowl of cornflakes, the cereal stirring gently as small creatures fed beneath. He was grinning, a ventriloquist's dummy, cheek muscles tightened by shrinkage. A misty film clouded his eyes, a spoon balanced ungripped in his clawed hand. A length of string around his chest tied him to the chair.

The woman suddenly heaved forward, twisting her chair so that the ejected vomit did not splatter the stale food. She retched, the pain seeming to gut her insides, her stomach jerking in violent spasms as if attempting to evict its own internal organs.

The excruciating pain was in her head too, and for a brief second it forced a flash of lucidity. The moment of boundless thunder, the quietness after. The creeping sickness.

It was gone, the clearness vanquished, muddy clouds spoiling her mind's fleeting perspicuity. She wiped her mouth with the back of her hand and sat upright. The hurt was easing, but she knew it would linger in the background, never far away, waiting to pounce like Inspector Clouseau's Chinese manservant. She almost managed to smile at the memory of old, better times, but the present—her own vision of the present—closed in on her.

She sipped the tasteless tea and, with an impatient hand, flicked at the flies buzzing around Tina's head. Her husband's pupilless stare from the other side of the table irritated her, too, the whites of his eyes showing between half-closed lids a silly affectation he assumed to annoy her. A joke could be taken *too* far.

"What shall we do this morning, everyone?" she asked, forgetting it was both a work and school day. "A walk to the park? The rain's finally stopped, you know. My goodness, I thought it never would, didn't you, Barry? Must do some shopping later, but I think we could manage a little walk first, take advantage of the weather, hmn? What do you say, Sammy? You could take your roller skates. Yes, you too, Tina, I wasn't forgetting you. Perhaps the cinema later. No, don't get excited—I want you to finish your breakfast first."

She leaned across and patted her daughter's little clenched fist.

"It'll be just like old times, won't it?" Her voice became a whisper, and the words were slow. "Just like old times."

Tina slid down in her chair once more and this time disappeared beneath the table.

"That's right, dear, you look for Cindy, she can come to the park too. Anything interesting in the news today, Barry? Really, oh good gracious, people *are* funny, aren't they? Makes you wonder what the world's coming to, just what on earth you'll read next. Manners, *Samuel,* hand before mouth."

She scraped away surface mould from a drooping slice of bread and bit into it. "Don't let your tea get cold, pet," she lightly scolded her husband, Barry. "You've got all day to read the newspaper. I think I'll have a lie-down in a little while; I'm not feeling too well today. Think I've got flu coming on."

The woman glanced towards the shattered window, a warm breeze ruffling the thin hair straggling over her forehead. She saw but did not perceive the nuclear-wasted city outside.

Her attention drifted back to her family once more and she watched the black fly, which had fully explored the surface of her husband's face by now, disappearing into the gaping hole of his mouth.

She frowned, and then she sighed. "Oh, Barry," she said, "you're not just going to sit there all day again, are you?"

Tiny, glittering tear beads formed in the corners of each eye, one brimming over leaving a jerky silver trail down to her chin. Her family didn't even notice.

CLOCKS

Darrell Schweitzer

Darrell Schweitzer is a co-editor of the revived horror/fantasy magazine *Weird Tales,* but is himself a horror writer of exceptional talent. Born in 1952, he is the author of two novels, *The White Isle* and *The Shattered Goddess* and two story collections, *We Are All Legends* (a noveloid of linked stories) and *Tom O'Bedlam's Night Out.* Other stories of Darrell's have featured in *Twilight Zone, Night Cry, Amazing, Fantastic,* and *The Year's Best Horror Stories.* He has also edited numerous books of critical essays, such as *Discovering Modern Horror Fiction* and *Discovering H. P. Lovecraft.* Darrell lives in Strafford, Pennsylvania, where he continues to develop the penetrating style that makes "Clocks" one of the most haunting contributions to this collection.

He returned to the house again on an evening in November. He had been away a year, but nothing had changed. The house stood pale and dark among the trees as the twilight deepened, as the walls, trees, ground, and sky all faded into that particular autumn grey which is almost blue. He stood there in the cold, listening to the rain hiss faintly on the fallen leaves, wishing he could stand there forever, that time would cease its motion and this moment would never pass.

But, inevitably, as he did every year, he made his way along the leaf-covered path to the front porch. Again he stood procrastinating, fumbling with his keys until his fingers, by themselves, found the key he needed and his hand had turned it in the lock before he was even aware. Then he stepped into the dark house, the door sweeping aside a year's worth of junk mail he had never been able to cancel.

Behind him, the rain whispered, and when he closed the door there was another sound, a faint ticking. He stooped to gather the junk mail into a basket, and noticed the clock on the mail stand, a few inches from his face. It was a cheap, plastic thing, decorated with figures of shepherd girls, like characters out of *Heidi*.

It was one of his wife's clocks. As long as her clocks were here, she was too, in a way. All her life, Edith had collected clocks.

He wound it, and it seemed to tick louder. Then he stood up and wound a row of little golden alarm clocks that stood along the top of a bookcase to his left. They had stopped, and now they added to the faint, rhythmical ticking. He didn't set the time on any of them. That wasn't the point.

It was only after he had completed this task that he turned on the lights, surveyed the hallway, and stepped to his right, into the living room. The ticking followed him, until it was lost in the deeper sound of the grandfather clock that waited in the shadows by the fireplace. He remembered how they had found that grandfather clock in an antique shop once, long, long ago, how Edith had raved over it, begging him to buy it in her joking but earnest way, until he relented (even though they *couldn't* afford it). There had been weekends spent polishing, repairing, finishing. In the end, when they were ready, when the thing stood dark and gleaming in the living room, it had been like a birth. Or that was how he remembered it now.

He flicked on one small light, and saw in the semi-darkness another clock humped on the mantelpiece. There was a story about that one, too, and as he wound the clock, once more the memory came to him.

Then he sat down by the empty fireplace, exhausted and sad. He put his feet up on a little stool and stared into the fireplace for a while, listening to the clocks. The house was stirring, the soft tick-tick-ticking like the breathing of a great beast turning in its sleep.

He dozed off, and when he awoke it was dark outside. He heard sounds from the kitchen, dishes touching gently, a cabinet door closing, but he remained where he was, listening to those sounds and to the clocks. The grandfather clock chimed softly.

A few minutes later he did get up, his joints aching. He realized that he was still wearing his hat and coat. He left them on the chair and walked through a narrow hall, past the dark basement stairway, into the kitchen.

There was a steaming cup of tea on the counter by the sink, and two slices of warm toast on a plate, both buttered, one with jam, one without, the way she had always fixed them for him when he worked late at night. He turned and stretched to wind the clock on top of the spice cabinet. It was a smiling metal Buddha with the clock face in its belly, a ridiculous thing (again, full of memories), but she had put it there once, long, long ago, and there it remained, gazing down at him serenely as he ate his toast and drank his tea.

He was almost crying then, but he held back his tears as he went from room to room, winding clocks, until their sound was like that of a million tiny birds outside the windows, gently, very patiently pecking to get in.

Upstairs, a door closed.

In the library he found a brush with long, blond hairs in it, discarded on a desktop.

He used a key to wind an intricately carven wooden castle of a clock, where armored knights appeared on the battlements at the ringing of every hour.

The ticking was still gentle, but more insistent, unyielding, like the sound of surf on a quiet night.

When he had made a circuit of the first floor, he came to the front door again, but turned away from it and slowly climbed the front stairs. He was sobbing by then. The sounds from behind him seemed to rise, to propel him up the stairs.

He found his wife's furry slippers at the top, neatly together by the bathroom door where she often left them. He wept, and leaned his head against the wall, pounding softly with his fist.

More than anything else, he wanted just to leave, but then he heard the singing from behind the bedroom door, and he knew that, of course, he could not go away. The song was one he had taught Edith before they were married, long, long ago.

He entered the bedroom and she was there, and she was young and beautiful. She helped him undress and pulled him into the bed, whispering softly as she did, then silent, and for a while he was completely happy, suspended in a single moment of time.

A clock ticked on the nightstand.

· · ·

When he awoke it was morning and she was gone. The empty half of the bed was cold, the covers thrown back. He wept again, bitterly, deeply, cursing himself for having continued the cruel, miraculous farce, for torturing himself one more time, for doing this, somehow, to her, once again. He held up his hands before his face, and he saw how wrinkled the backs of them were, how age-spotted. He touched the top of his head, running his fingers through his thinning hair.

She had still been twenty-six and beautiful. She would always be twenty-six and beautiful.

And the memories came flooding back with horrible vividness, until he was living them again: the rainy night, the screeching tires, the car on its side by the road's edge, Edith in his arms while one set of headlights after another flared by and nobody stopped for what seemed like hours.

He turned over in the bed and pressed his face into the pillow, crying like a small child, and hoping, absurdly, that he would eventually run out of tears.

He tried to tell himself that he wouldn't come again next year, that this would finally cease, but he knew better. When he got up to dress and found a note stuck onto the telephone by the bed, it was only a confirmation.

The note said: I LOVE YOU.—EDITH.

· · ·

He was still crying, but softly, as he went down the front stairs, around and into the kitchen, and from there down the dark, creaking stairway into the basement. At the bottom he stood once more, wishing he could stand there motionless forever, that he didn't have to go forward, but, again, he knew better. He flicked on the lights, revealing the thousands upon thousands of clocks that filled the basement, crowded on shelves, standing against the walls, spread across the floor, and holding in their midst by a fantastic spiderweb of wires a closed coffin that seemed to float a few inches above the rug. It was as if the clocks had grown there, proliferating. He had long since given up wondering if there were more of them now than there had once been.

His mind could supply no explanation, but he knew that somehow, if even one clock in the whole house remained running—and somehow, in defiance of all reason, one or more would always keep running for a whole year, awaiting his return—on this one night in November time would stop, or perhaps slide backward, and Edith would be as she had been the night before her death, loving him, never aware of any future, forever young while he continued to age. He didn't know if it was real or not. There no longer seemed to be such things as real and unreal.

But he could never, never bring himself to put an end to it, and he wept as he made his way gingerly among the clocks, winding each one. Their voices grew louder and louder, resonating in the cramped basement, while he wept and trembled and worked with furious, desperate care, and in the end the sound of them was like screaming.

THE STRANGERS

Steve Rasnic Tem

There's a strange design on Steve Rasnic Tem's notepaper which looks like a man with a loaf of bread under his arm admiring a new surfboard. I haven't had the nerve to ask him what it is. Steve Rasnic Tem is the author of more than a hundred horror and mystery stories, and has been a finalist for both the World Fantasy and British Fantasy awards. His first horror novel, *Excavation,* received great acclaim from critics and horror fans alike, and rightly so. He has the ability to evoke images as clearly as if you're seeing them through Rocky Mountain spring water, and yet he can ripple that water when you're least expecting it and distort those images beyond recognition. Steve Rasnic Tem lives a mile high in Denver, Colorado.

"I hear they sell children like this to rich Arabs," one of the women in the dairy department said. Helen couldn't help overhearing, couldn't help listening in. She stood still and watched the two women, who were examining the pictures of missing children printed on the backs of milk cartons.

"They?" the other woman said.

"The kidnappers, child molesters, foreigners," the woman said.

The other woman appeared to mull over this information for a while. Finally, she said, ''Really? I've heard it's pornographers, and sometimes these private adoption agencies pay for the babies.''

''All the same, really,'' her friend replied, with a wise look.

For a moment Helen had imagined that when they said ''children like this,'' they had been looking at her own little Jennifer. She turned her attention back to the processed meats. She always felt a little guilty about buying the processed meats; there was enough reason to believe that they weren't good for Jennifer. But they were inexpensive and quick to prepare, and Jennifer loved them.

She dropped a package of bologna into the cart. Then straightened up, looked around. ''Jennifer?''

The grocery store seemed strangely silent, as if a bell jar had been dropped over the building. The women's conversation had faded to a soft whisper, a mere stirring of dead air. She could hear the metallic, uneven rattle of a single grocery cart, as if from a great distance.

''Jennifer!''

A man in a tight black shirt and a dark mustache—Italian, she thought, or Greek—walked out of one of the aisles and stared at her. He had no groceries and that made Helen suddenly, painfully, anxious. He retreated. Helen rushed after him.

By the time she reached the mouth of the aisle the dark man was nowhere to be seen. Long shelves of canned vegetables and fruits walled her in. Then at the other end of the aisle there was a flash of red. Sudden as a splash of blood. No. Like red corduroy. Like her daughter's dress.

Helen strode to the mouth of the next aisle, and again caught a fleeting glimpse of red passing by the other end. Soon she was running, trying unsuccessfully to see the fullness of the red, what body there was attached to it, the rest of her daughter.

She spun back into the meat department, her arms flapping, knocking over a pyramid of seasonings. Her head grew hot, her skin irritated, as if someone had dashed the seasoning into her face.

''Mommy?'' Jennifer stood by one of the counters, next to a woman in a long, white, canvas-looking coat. Like a meat-cutter, Helen thought. A butcher. Or maybe a nurse. She immediately found herself looking for bloodstains, other stains, on the woman's coat. She tried to look at the hands, but the woman kept them hidden. The woman stared back at Helen with a stern expression. Helen looked for contrasting splotches of red on Jennifer's bright red dress. Helen looked for knives, vaguely hidden or out on the counter for all to see. Suddenly on the verge of tears, Helen made her way awkwardly past the other customers to where the woman held her daughter.

"You shouldn't let her run around by herself like that," said the woman, the stranger in the canvas coat. "This isn't a toy store."

Now Helen couldn't look at the woman. "I know. I . . . I should have been watching her better. I'm terribly sorry."

Helen could see the woman shifting her feet. "Well . . . of course. I . . . didn't mean to criticize. It's just . . ." The woman laughed nervously. "They do get underfoot, don't they?"

Helen tried to look at Jennifer instead, but there was so much red, she had to look away. Then there was all that meat, steaks and roasts cut so precisely, so *red*—she wondered if they added dyes. She looked down at her feet. "Thank you for taking care of her," she said.

"Oh, no problem. No problem." The woman's voice faded. Helen slipped her hand around her daughter's shoulders, almost surreptitiously, and guided her toward their cart, still mumbling her apologies on the edge of inaudibility.

Now and then, as she finished her shopping with Jennifer tucked safely in the cart—just another package among all the other brightly colored packages—she would see the strange man looking over and between the shelves at her, his dark eyebrows, dark eyes, and facial shadows blending into Rorschach patterns that obscured his face.

The large unattractive girl who bagged their groceries kept tickling Jennifer under the chin. Jennifer would giggle madly, then collapse into herself trying to keep the girl's fingers away from her face, as if she were being tortured. Helen watched the girl carefully, ready for the potential snatch and run. She wondered if the girl had any boyfriends. She remembered reading somewhere that a woman who had failed at romance might try to compensate, might very well try to take a child. Even as the last bag was dropping into place, Helen was pushing the cart rapidly away from the checkout counter. The bag girl had to jump to get out of her way.

Helen stood on the sidewalk outside the grocery, her cart full of brown paper sacks and Jennifer, who now climbed in and out of the top rack as if it were a tree house. From the back she looked like Helen in those old home movies. Long strands of hair lifting in the wind, obscuring the eyes and most of the face, so that she looked like she could have been anyone's little girl.

"Are you somebody else's little girl?" her father used to say when she was bad.

Helen would shake her head a vigorous negative, thinking all the time it might be true. Her father would hold the back of her neck, move her head this way and that as if she were a puppet. And laugh. He had a wonderful laugh.

"Just like I was," her mother would say in the background. "Just like me. Always getting into things. But she's going to grow up better than me, not stuck someplace. Henry! Don't hold her neck like that! You might *hurt* her."

The parking lot had filled since they'd gone into the store. Helen couldn't remember where she'd parked the station wagon.

"Daddy," Jennifer said softly to the air.

Helen jerked around as if shot. She looked at Jennifer, followed her gaze, and saw a figure in a raincoat some fifty feet away. Sandy hair.

"Daddy," Jennifer said.

"No, no, Jennifer," Helen said, pushing the cart into the middle of all those parked cars, vaguely hoping that she'd find the station wagon once she was out there. "No, Jennifer," she said, gently trying to turn her daughter's head so that she didn't look at the man in the raincoat. The sandy-headed man. The sand man. "No, now, we've talked about your father before, Jennifer. And you said you understood. I *know* you understood. So don't do this now," Helen said, as Jennifer kept turning around, saying "Daddy," standing up dangerously in the rapidly moving cart. "Jennifer!" Helen shouted, instantly angry with herself. She felt like swatting Jennifer, just a quick, short swat, to *make* her understand, to make her remember that her father was *dead,* to make her remember just how bad things had been when he'd been around with his drinking and his violence, how *she* was the one who got custody after the divorce. How he'd tried to take Jennifer a half dozen times after the divorce, and each time almost succeeded. Judges and policemen, no one could stop him. No one could see what she was so worried about. How their life had been a nightmare until he'd killed himself in that ancient red car of his, stinking of alcohol.

Out of the corner of her eye she saw the raincoat, shredded and stained with blood. She had never understood him. He'd always been a stranger.

Suddenly Jennifer reached out and grabbed at a car. "Jennifer!"

"Car . . ."

Helen stopped and held herself. They were at the station wagon. Its back window had a diamond-shaped caution sign attached on the inside: "Baby in Car." Jennifer hadn't been a baby when Helen bought that sign. It just seemed to her that people tended to care more the younger the victim, so if they were the kind who'd be extra cautious for a child they'd be even more so for a baby. The first few times they went out after she'd gotten the sign Jennifer kept asking, "Where's the baby? Where's the baby?"

A long sticker ran along the left side of the rear bumper: "Have you hugged your kid today?" Some prankster had taken a black marking pen and closed off the bottom of the "h," turning it into a "b." People could get to your car, do something like that in broad daylight, in a public parking lot somewhere, and nobody stopped them. If they could do that they could do anything. Sometimes she had to leave Jennifer alone in the car—but always just for a few minutes, when she had to get something *very* quickly. Helen kept intending to get a new sticker to put over the old one, but hadn't found exactly the right one yet. She wanted one with the bright red heart that glowed at night.

She looked around for the raincoat. The strange man from the grocery stared at her from a green pickup parked several rows away. Women in white coats were climbing into their expensive-looking cars, gazing surreptitiously from under their broad hats. Fallow women who might pay any amount of money for a child. Everywhere she looked, strange men carrying no groceries walked up and down the long aisles of automobiles, searching for stray children.

• • •

Dinner preparation was long and confusing that evening. Helen kept forgetting how to prepare dishes she'd fixed countless times before. She'd chop vegetables until there was nothing left. She'd forget where she was in a recipe and add the same thing twice. Too much garlic. The pepper shaker was empty.

She'd been at it so long the roast she'd thawed had already drained quite a bit of blood. Its butcher-paper wrapper, spread like a dried layer of skin over her kitchen counter, had filled with the bright red broth. Helen stood over it, poking at it absently with a large fork. In the meat she saw Jennifer's small red mouth, the plump curve of her behind stripped of its outer layer of flesh.

Helen dropped the fork onto the meat and walked into the living room. Dinner would have to be late. Jennifer would complain, but a sweet before dinner would take care of that. It wasn't good for her, of course, but very little seemed to be good for children these days. Not like when she was a child. Her parents had it easy with her—they always knew what was the right thing to do. Everyone knew. Now it seemed so easy to be wrong. If you weren't unintentionally poisoning your children with some food additive, you were allowing them to be traumatized by something that hadn't even existed when you were a child.

"Are you all right?" she called up the stairs.

"Yes, Mommy," came Jennifer's soft, distant voice. Helen had put her into the bath, watched her a few minutes, then left to prepare dinner. She didn't like doing that. But dinner was late as it was, and she didn't want to keep her daughter up too late. Every now and then she'd called up the stairs just to check on her. But she didn't like leaving her in the bath alone like that.

The front door rattled once, softly.

Helen stopped where she was, stood perfectly still. "Is she still breathing?" her father used to ask while standing over her bed.

"Of course," her mother would always reply, then lower her face over Helen's, checking for herself. They always thought she was asleep but she almost never was. In fact, this survey of her respiration had become a kind of bedtime ritual for her, until she could hardly go to sleep without it.

Now she asked Jennifer every night, "Are you breathing?" She could almost believe that Jennifer would forget to breathe if she didn't ask her. And each time she would wonder if Jennifer was feigning sleep just as she had. "Are you still breathing?" she would ask, clearly, almost angrily, as if daring Jennifer to open her eyes and reply.

The doorknob rattled again, ever so slightly, as if someone were picking the lock. Helen held her breath. She wondered if adults could die from crib death, simply forget to breathe, or hold their breath too long. Or was it a death reserved just for children? Perhaps they got lost in their dreams—children dreamed so intensely, or at least she remembered it so—and forgot to return home. You did not need to breathe in a dream.

The door sighed, softly, as if finally releasing a long-held breath. Helen moved up to the door at an angle. Several thick, frosted panes were set into the door, and the light at the other end of the porch made them translucent.

A dark outline swayed in the panes, its lines distorted, doubled. Helen could smell cigarette smoke coming from under the door. "Tom?" she whispered.

"Are you breathing?" the voice asked from the other side of her door.

Helen backed away. She could still smell his cigarette smoke, could see it rising like mist from under the door, filling the entranceway like tentative strands of web. She thought about fires. *He's going to burn us out,* she thought, instantly picturing her sweet baby slipping out of an upstairs window, forced out of the house by a lack of air.

"Mommy, I'm *hungry,*" Jennifer said somewhere behind her.

"It's cooking, it's cooking," Helen lied, unable to look away from the door. The smell of smoke was still sharp in the room.

"Comb my hair?" Jennifer asked.

"Of course, of course I will," Helen said, backing toward the sound of her daughter's voice, still looking at the door.

The brush was one she herself had had as a child. She could remember her own mother brushing her hair like this, one hundred strokes each night. Now she ran the brush gently through her own daughter's hair.

Are you breathing? she thought.

"Harder, Mommy," Jennifer said, and Helen brushed just a little harder.

What does she think? Helen used to ask Jennifer what she was thinking about, but she was never satisfied with the vague, childish answers. Children weren't like adults. A child might do anything. Think anything. They were like an entirely different species, and, even though you yourself had once been part of that species, you somehow knew that you remembered incorrectly, that your memories had become distorted and false with the passage of time. She often wondered if her own mother had felt this way.

As she brushed Jennifer's hair, Helen could feel her mother brushing her hair. Sometimes she felt her mother clinging to her hair, her mother's dried-up, featherweight corpse floating behind her like some grotesque hair ribbon. Weighing her down.

Just beneath Jennifer's hairline, Helen could see the coded tattoo she had put there immediately following the divorce. The organization had had thousands of such coded tattoos in its registry, ensuring eventual identification of a missing child. Or a missing child's body. But it bothered Helen that perhaps no one else would ever brush her daughter's hair this way, so if her daughter was missing no one might see this tattoo. The tattoo seemed to have faded a bit, become more a part of the skin. Helen thought of Auschwitz, Belsen.

Her dentist had told her of a process in which he could attach a microdot to the back of one of Jennifer's teeth. He showed her his registration book—it was well over a thousand pages.

She was always so nervous when Jennifer played on the stairs. "Careful of the *gap*!" she'd always call. She wouldn't take Jennifer on a train or plane. There was something about putting her daughter in the hands of a pilot or an engineer whom she did not know. Worse, whom she never even saw. It made her feel like a murderess.

Everyone watched mothers. Mothers needed watching.

She had not smelled the cigarette smoke for some time. The door glass was clear, unshadowed. Jennifer had fallen asleep on the couch, the brush in her arms like a doll, a child.

Helen returned to the kitchen to finish making dinner. She cut the meat up with clean, precise strokes, then stood back and gazed at the bloody morsels of herself, spread out on the paper.

. . .

The park was full of strangers that day, but Jennifer didn't mind. That made Helen angry. Jennifer just would not see the danger, had never seen it.

Men with their shirt sleeves rolled up, their fingers dirty. At least they would leave fingerprints behind.

Jennifer had been uncontrollable all day. Running up and down among the rich, fallow women, the Italian men with no groceries, the women in their white canvas butcher's coats, the Arabs, the pornographers, the molesters, the scouts from the private adoption agencies out looking for children to match their clients' requirements. The strangers.

She was too young, too alien, to understand the danger. She did not think the way adults think. She made Helen afraid. She could not stop her.

She saw Jennifer running away. Everyone was looking at her. People watched mothers, strangers watched mothers, because mothers needed watching. Jennifer ran away and Helen chased her for a very long time. Finally Helen had to go back to the empty house alone.

When the police took Helen down to identify the body, she knew exactly what had happened. She knew exactly what to say. She told them about the strangers.

TABLE FOR NONE

William Relling Jr.

William Relling Jr. was born in 1954 in St. Louis, Missouri. He has worked as truck driver, camp counselor, carnival ride operator, janitor, stock boy, warehouseman, librarian, musician, hospital orderly, junior high school teacher, magazine editor, and college professor. His practical experience shows in the admirable matter-of-factness of his writing, a matter-of-factness that makes his jolting moments of horror even more jolting. A full-time writer since 1983, he has published stories in *Cavalier, Dude, Whispers, Night Cry, The Horror Show,* and *The Year's Best Horror Stories.* His first novel, *Brujo,* was published by Tor Books in 1986, and since then he has written *New Moon,* its sequel, *Silent Moon,* and a mainstream thriller, *Azriel.* He now lives in the Fairfax District of Los Angeles, "close to the center of the known universe." He says he likes it a lot.

Mr. Capillari was listening to the *slup slup slup* of his windshield wipers and the tattoo of the rain on the roof and the radio voice fading in and out amid sharp crackles of static. There came a burst of lightning that he could see far ahead of him in the purple-gray gloom, and the radio suddenly spat at him. Mr. Capillari reached for the tuning knob, twisting it gently between his sausage fingertips. The static abruptly grew louder and Mr. Capillari grumbled aloud unhappily: "Ahhh!" His hand moved to switch the radio off.

Too far away, he thought. *Too far out in the middle of nowhere to pick up anything worthwhile even if I wasn't in the middle of a storm . . .*

Mr. Capillari shook his head, frowning to himself. It was a miserable late afternoon, the third miserable day in a row of not one sale. And now the storm on top of everything else, making it all that much *more* miserable. He had traveled nearly eight hundred miles in his automobile during the past seventy-two hours, and his shoulders ached and his skin felt sticky and his eyes were raw from straining to see the slick two-lane blacktop ahead of him through wipers that only smeared the rain. He could feel a dull pain throbbing in his forehead in time with each *slup* of the wipers, and all Mr. Capillari could think of was that he wished he were home.

Why do I put up with it? he wondered. It certainly wasn't for the sake of his customers, because Mr. Capillari never let on to them how he truly felt; if there was one thing he had learned from his mother it was that politeness and circumspection were the keys to success. "Do unto others as you would have them do unto you," Mother had said to him many times. And she was right, of course, because Mother was *always* right. (Though on occasion he had been known to modify Mother's admonition to: "Do unto others *before* they do unto you.") Mr. Capillari knew that the reason why he was the single best sales representative his company had was that he took his mother's advice to heart. Because of Mother, Mr. Capillari could usually charm anyone he wanted into buying just about anything he had to sell.

Mr. Capillari smiled to himself grimly, thinking: *If only they knew . . .*

If only Mr. Capillari's customers and his colleagues at the company knew what he *really* thought of them, how superior he was to all of them, how he merely tolerated their low manners and their simpering ignorance and their slights. (He knew that his co-workers snickered at him behind his back—he was *Mister* Capillari to all of them, because never did he allow any of them to call him by his first name; he was corpulent, haughty Mr. Capillari—who they believed had no real reason to be haughty at all in spite of his exemplary sales record. And wasn't it strange, they asked each other, that Mr. Capillari still lived with his mother? At his age?)

Mr. Capillari's eyes narrowed. Let them say what they wanted to about him, that he could condone. But when any of them said anything at all about his mother . . .

Just then his stomach began to rumble, and a sudden awareness of the emptiness in his belly pulled him from his dark abstraction. Mr. Capillari quickly realized that it was hours since he had last eaten: a late breakfast in his hotel's dining room—a ham and cheese omelet and hash brown potatoes and a double rasher of bacon and a stack of buttermilk pancakes washed down with a pot of coffee. He had eaten it all, cleaning his plate as Mother had always taught him was the proper thing to do. Though the omelet was cold and the potatoes too greasy and the bacon limply undercooked and the pancakes rubbery and the coffee bitter; the only way he was able to assuage his displeasure was by leaving a mere twenty-five-cent tip, conspicuously in a puddle of imitation maple syrup in the middle of the plate that had held his pancakes.

It was always the same, whenever he was on the road. His years as a traveling salesman had demonstrated to him incontrovertibly that nothing he ate could ever compare with his mother's cooking. But whenever he told this to Mother she would chide him for being foolish. Why didn't he simply find another job? she would ask.

He couldn't seem to make her understand that it wasn't the job that he didn't care for; he enjoyed traveling and he enjoyed selling. But then Mother invariably insisted that her son would do well at any job he chose—it was her way of praising him backhandedly, and it always made Mr. Capillari smile to think of it. He and Mother could never argue for very long, because he knew that *she* knew that he made a great deal of money for them, much more than he would be able to make if he had a job that brought him home every night. It wasn't the job at all.

It was the meals.

The feeling of emptiness in Mr. Capillari's stomach had become a cavernous pit deep inside him, and the hunger made his head throb more ferociously. He lifted his left hand from the steering wheel and glanced at his wristwatch. It was only a little before five P.M. and Mr. Capillari let out a low, disconsolate moan. What with the rain, he was still a good five hours from home. At least.

I'll never make it, Mr. Capillari sighed to himself.

It was at that moment that he chanced to look up, and he saw something ahead of him through the rain-smeared windshield, between the sweeping wiper blades. It was a sign perched atop a tall pole, a sign that glowed electric blue against the gray-shrouded sky, its letters distorted by the rain: "DALY'S." And beneath that, in smaller letters made of orange neon was the word "Eat." The place had come upon him unexpectedly, as he couldn't remember ever having seen or heard of a café so far out on this highway, all by itself.

"Oh well," Mr. Capillari sighed aloud. "Any port in a storm." He smiled at his little joke as he flipped on his turn signal and eased a heavy foot on to his brakes. The car slowed and Mr. Capillari spun the steering wheel, guiding the vehicle off the wet highway into the parking lot that lay beneath the sign. The car's tires crunched on gravel as Mr. Capillari straightened the wheel and pulled forward toward the low building that looked depressingly the same as any of a thousand other roadside cafés Mr. Capillari had seen in his life.

His headlights reflected back at him off glass windows as he brought his car to a halt before the café's front doors. There were no other vehicles in the lot, and Mr. Capillari thought for a moment that perhaps the place was deserted—until he saw the "Open" sign hanging inside the front door. Then he could see inside the rain-speckled windows to where a young woman dressed in a pink uniform was standing behind a counter; she had her back to the windows, and she was putting pies into a cabinet mounted into a wall beside a slot that Mr. Capillari guessed opened into the kitchen itself.

He switched off the ignition, unsnapped the seat belt encircling his wide belly and, steeling himself, pushed open the driver's-side door and clambered out into the rain. He trotted across the parking lot, splashing through puddles.

He pulled the door open and heard the tiny jingle of a bell announcing his entrance. The young woman behind the counter turned around to see Mr. Capillari stamping his wet feet on the mat that lay inside the door. She looked at him and smiled.

"Sit anywhere you like, mister," the woman said, and Mr. Capillari forced himself to return the woman's vacuous smile as he let the door close behind him.

He looked around the small café and understood immediately why the waitress seemed so happy to see him. Except for her and the figure he could see through the slot in the wall behind her—who Mr. Capillari assumed was the cook—the place was deserted. And as far as he could tell he was the only customer to have come in all day.

He eased himself into the second booth from the window and was surprised at how comfortable the cushion and back of the booth seemed to feel; more often than not the seats in places like this caused spasms of agony in his lower back. But it actually felt good to sit in the booth, and as Mr. Capillari settled himself, the young woman came up to the table, set a tall glass of ice water before him, handed him a menu laminated in plastic and asked politely if she might not get him a cup of coffee from a pot that she had just made herself, fresh, not ten minutes before. Mr. Capillari accepted.

Then he opened the menu, and the good feeling that had begun to envelop him suddenly evaporated. Mr. Capillari shook his head sadly, and he muttered aloud, barely above a whisper: "My God. Same old sh—"

He caught himself as the woman returned to set a steaming mug of coffee before him. Mr. Capillari smiled at her, handed back the menu, and asked: "So what's good tonight?"

She took a pencil from behind her ear, opened the menu, and tapped a small handwritten note that had been paper-clipped to its upper right-hand corner. The note read: "Nitely Specials. All You Can Eat. $3.75. Dessert and coffee included."

"It's really good," the waitress said, smiling at him a smile that seemed to Mr. Capillari to be meant to convince him of her absolute sincerity. "If you like spaghetti."

Mr. Capillari patted his stomach. "That I do," he said.

She pulled a check pad from her apron pocket. "So that's it?" she asked. "The special?"

Mr. Capillari nodded. "Though I should probably warn you, I can eat a whole lot more than three dollars and seventy-five cents' worth of spaghetti. If it's good."

"It's *very* good," she said as she turned away, still writing his order on her pad. Mr. Capillari watched her as she moved back behind the counter, tore the check off the pad and pressed it under a clamp attached to an aluminum wheel set in the wall slot that opened on to the rear kitchen. "One special," she called to the figure that Mr. Capillari could see behind the slot. He heard a deep, male voice call back to her: "Coming right up!"

Mr. Capillari reached for the mug before him, lifted it to his lips and blew gently at the wisps of steam rising from the dark coffee. He sniffed, taking in the rich, earthy aroma and once again found himself feeling pleasantly surprised. He sipped at the mug, and his eyes widened with delight. The coffee tasted as delicious as it smelled.

As he drank his coffee, Mr. Capillari looked around and actually felt himself growing more and more impressed with the little café. He hadn't noticed when he first came in that the floor and the counter and each of the booths were all spotlessly clean, gleaming in the light from fluorescent lamps hung overhead. The table at which he sat shined, his knife and fork and soup spoon glittering. The glass salt and pepper shakers standing beside the napkin holder next to the wall of the booth were both full. *This is amazing,* he said to himself, feeling astounded that he hadn't known about this place before and wondering why no one else was here . . .

The young woman appeared beside him once more, balancing on one hand a huge plate piled high with spaghetti smothered in red sauce, and a smaller plate of garlic bread on the other hand. Mr. Capillari pulled a napkin from the dispenser and unfolded it in his lap, then leaned back against the booth as the waitress set the plates before him on the table. "Enjoy," she said cheerily, then moved away, walking back behind the counter and out of sight through a swinging door that led into the kitchen.

Mr. Capillari turned from watching the young woman to the massive plate of food in front of him, and for the first time in his life he could actually feel himself starting to tremble in anticipation. *This is impossible,* he whispered to himself in disbelief.

A luscious fragrance tantalized him, and he could already taste the flavors before he had even reached for his fork: the thick tomato sauce, the onions and garlic, the spices—oregano and thyme and *fresh* basil. He twirled his fork gently into the noodles and could tell just by touch that they had been cooked perfectly *al dente.* As Mr. Capillari leaned forward and took his first bite he could feel his heart pounding in anticipation. *It can't be this good,* he told himself as he lifted the first forkful into his mouth. *It can't be . . .*

But it was.

So good, in fact, that Mr. Capillari could not restrain himself from cleaning the plate within minutes. And just as he laid down his fork to reach for a piece of garlic bread to dab at the sauce that remained there, the waitress was once more at the end of the table, smiling at him. "I love to watch a man eat," she said. "Especially one who enjoys it so much. Can I get you some more?"

"Please do," said Mr. Capillari.

She was soon back with new plates of spaghetti and bread. Mr. Capillari nodded to her gratefully, then attacked the spaghetti at once. She was back a few minutes later to remove the empty plate and ask him if he wanted thirds.

"I can't," he protested unconvincingly. "I already feel like such a glutton, and it's like I'm stealing from you—"

"Not at all," the waitress told him. "Just like it says on our menu—all you can eat."

Mr. Capillari mirrored the young woman's smile as he said to her: "If you insist . . ."

But by the time he was three-quarters through with his third plateful, Mr. Capillari laid down his fork, certain that he had stuffed himself to bursting. He could feel his massive belly pushing against his shirt, straining its buttons, and unconsciously he reached down to loosen the buckle of his belt. He leaned back into the booth, steepling his fingers atop his stomach, and he exhaled a deep, satisfied "Ahhhhhhhhhhhhhhhh."

The waitress had reappeared to fill his coffee mug, and she paused to ask him: "Did you like it?"

Mr. Capillari smiled at the young woman, this time genuinely. "My dear, I can say with all candor that this is the first restaurant I've ever eaten in whose food is as good as any home cooking I've had."

The waitress beamed.

"Is it possible for you to call out the cook so that I can thank him personally?" Mr. Capillari asked.

"I'd be happy to," she answered. Then she called over her shoulder toward the kitchen door: "Tim!"

She turned back and nodded toward Mr. Capillari's plate. "Can I get you some more?" she asked.

Mr. Capillari shook his head. "I couldn't swallow another morsel—"

He paused when he noticed that she was suddenly frowning, a dark expression that Mr. Capillari found immediately unsettling. Then her smile returned and she said as she reached for his plate: "Let me get you another plate . . ."

Mr. Capillari raised his hands in protest. "No, no, my dear, please—"

She was frowning again, but before Mr. Capillari could say anything more he looked past her to see a huge, silver-bearded man emerging from the kitchen door behind the counter. The man was dressed in white, wearing a chef's hat and apron, and he came out from around the corner of the counter looking nothing so much like an enormous, lumbering polar bear. The man was as wide as Mr. Capillari himself and looked to be at least twice as tall. Fortunately, the cook was smiling as he came up to Mr. Capillari's booth—until he saw the young woman standing there, her mouth turned down unhappily.

"Something wrong?" the cook asked, eyeing Mr. Capillari with displeased uncertainty.

Mr. Capillari twisted uncomfortably in his seat. "Nothing's wrong," he said quickly, smiling his most charming salesman's smile. "As I was telling your waitress, the meal was excellent. I ate nearly three helpings."

The cook smiled broadly in return, showing sharp, white teeth. "Then you'll be wanting some more—"

"That's what I tried to tell the young lady," said Mr. Capillari. "I'm full. I've had enough—"

But Mr. Capillari's words caught in his throat as he watched the huge man's expression metamorphose into a horrifying scowl, his eyes reddening with fury. Suddenly a massive hand shot out across the table, grabbing Mr. Capillari by the front of his shirt, lifting him off the seat as if he weighed no more than a feather pillow. The cook turned to the young woman beside him and hissed: "Get some *more*!"

Then with his other hand the cook swept clear Mr. Capillari's table, sending plates and silverware, the mug of coffee and glass of water crashing to the floor. Then he hurled Mr. Capillari to the table, pinning him there with a thick forearm. Mr. Capillari squirmed, struggling vainly, crying out: "No . . . NOOOOOOOOOO . . ."

Just as the waitress reappeared carrying a huge metal pot filled with steaming food. She held the pot up for the cook to see, and he tersely nodded his approval. Then he leaned atop Mr. Capillari, pressing him down on the hard table, and he whispered: "Now . . ."

"You don't understand," Mr. Capillari screeched, trying to twist himself free of the man's massive hands. "I just couldn't take another bite—"

"No, *you* don't understand," the cook barked, cutting him off. The man brought his face close, smiling evilly at Mr. Capillari, showing again his sharp teeth.

"You don't understand," he repeated, barely above a whisper. "It's *all* you can eat."

Then he reached down to pry Mr. Capillari's jaws open, as the waitress came forward with a long wooden spoon, laden with sauce-drenched spaghetti. As she brought the food closer, ever closer, Mr. Capillari wanted desperately to cry out in abject terror.

But he couldn't. He just couldn't.

Because Mother had always taught him it wasn't polite to scream with his mouth full.

LITTLE MISS MUFFET

Peter Valentine Timlett

From his home in Canterbury, Kent, Peter Valentine Timlett sent me his own unsurpassable biography: "He was born in 1933, an Aquarian. A bronchial asthmatic, he inhales a particularly fierce pipe and excuses himself on the grounds that every man is entitled to one foolishness. Author of the *Seedbearers* trilogy, he has two young daughters who taught him everything he knows, though not everything that *they* know. He is still learning, and when he is no longer capable of learning he will have died. His politics are centrist, his philosophy Platonistic, his humor Rabelaisian. As a writer of horror he finds he cannot surpass in fiction the horror of a society that needs charities to combat child abuse." His story has a particularly British charm to it: like a Cadbury's chocolate with a soft but poisoned center.

Little Miss Muffet sat on a tuffet,
Eating her curds and whey.
There came a great spider and sat down beside her,
And frightened Miss Muffet away.

The only bus of the day set her down in the middle of the village at precisely twelve noon. She was the only passenger to alight, and none were waiting to board. The driver gave her a friendly wave, and the bus pulled away, the dust spurting from its wheels as it climbed through the gears.

The village really was quite beautiful, she thought. Along the side of the main street, and in between the houses, were dozens of huge old horse-chestnut trees that were now, at the end of June, in full leaf of the most richly glorious green, each tree towering above the surrounding houses like a great green sentinel set to guard and protect those who lived within its shade.

She had been told by her solicitor that the entire village was part of a 20,000-acre estate that had once belonged to a wealthy family whose line had terminated with the decease of the only male heir, killed at the Normandy landing during the war. The estate was now managed by an Estate Office that was responsible to the Board of Trustees in London. They must have been a family of some artistic taste, she thought, for the red-brick houses and stone cottages that apparently housed the estate workers were not set in dreary rows of unimaginative regimentation but were scattered, as it were, higgledy-piggledy amongst the trees, some facing this way and some facing that way, in a quite charming and delightfully random manner.

Some five years ago, the solicitor had said, the estate had faced a period of financial loss and had decided to sell some of its cottages, but only one had actually been sold before the financial climate had changed for the better and the Board had been able, with some relief, to rescind its earlier decision. Thus her brother, George, had been the only private owner in the whole village, a speck of individuality in what was one of the few remaining almost feudal estates in England, and on her brother's death that pinprick of private ownership had passed to her. She remembered the solicitor thoughtfully cleaning his glasses with a spotless handkerchief. "The Trustees of the estate are anxious to re-purchase the property. You could, if you wish, sell it back to them for a tidy sum, a very tidy sum indeed."

Perhaps she would, but first she simply had to take possession of her inheritance and live in it for at least a few months. A lifetime of being imprisoned in one of London's more dreary suburbs had engendered in her a fierce dream that one day she would live in a beautifully rural village such as this. Perhaps later, when the novelty had worn off, she would be able to look at the matter more objectively, from the financial viewpoint, but at the moment she was too excited even to think of selling.

She picked up her suitcase and walked across to what appeared to be the only shop in the village, an all-purpose grocery store cum post office with a single petrol-pump outside. Hopefully two more suitcases would be arriving today by British Rail, and these three suitcases contained her entire worldly goods. Not much after three decades of working as a secretary in a small family firm, but they were her very own and she had no debts to follow her from London. The only advice her father had ever given her was: "Remember, Amelia, be careful whom you marry, and avoid getting into debt. If you can do that you will be free to go anywhere and do anything." Well, her marriage to Henry, though of short duration, had been successful right up to the day he had died, even though they had not been blessed with children, and since then she had indeed managed to keep herself free of debt, a minor triumph in a world that revolved around mortgages, bank loans, overdrafts, and hire purchase. Not that she had been able to go anywhere or do anything, until now, but at least she had always *felt* free, and that feeling of security she quite clearly owed to her father, God bless him and keep him.

There were three men in the shop, one behind the counter and two in front of it, and all three eyed her curiously as she came in. "Good morning," she said, politely but firmly. She had heard that these village communities were rather resentful of strangers and she was not going to tolerate that sort of obstructive opposition. The knowledge of being a property owner gave her a quite alien but quite delicious feeling of authority. "I wonder if you might direct me to Chandira Cottage." An odd name, she had always thought, but then her brother had been a somewhat odd man, with an odd and secretly amused way of doing things. She would like to re-name it by its old name, the one it had before George bought it, a much more pleasant and simple name, but Chandira Cottage was the name on the deeds. She would have a word with her solicitor as soon as possible. Perhaps the deeds could be altered.

"You mean the old Rose Cottage," said the man behind the counter. "It's down that road there, Back Lane," he said, pointing out of the window, "about a hundred yards. But it's all locked up now, and has been for months, ever since George Moffat died."

"That's all right, I have the key," she said, patting her handbag. She hesitated for a moment. She had a horror of divulging too much information about herself to strangers. One had to be so careful. But these people would have to know sooner or later, and it might as well be now. "Mr. Moffat was my brother and he left the cottage to me in his will. I am Miss Amelia Moffat." One of her few acts of female emancipation had been to alter her name legally and officially back to her maiden name when Henry died. She had been married for only three years, not long enough for her new name to have become a habit, and she felt much more comfortable as Miss Amelia Moffat, and it stopped all those tedious questions that most widows had to endure.

"Ah, in that case I have a letter for you," said the man, and rummaged beneath the post office counter. "Here it is. I was going to keep it for a week and then return it to sender."

She took the letter and put it in her handbag. "Thank you. And now if you'll excuse me I'll get along to the cottage. I've had a very tiring journey."

"Of course. My name is Frost, Bill Frost. My wife and I run this place. We keep most things here, and we shut at five," he added.

She nodded pleasantly. "Thank you, Mr. Frost. Perhaps I'll call back this afternoon for a few things when I've unpacked." The other two men had not said a word, but they nodded in a friendly fashion as she left the shop and crossed the road.

They watched her go, a small dumpy woman, neat and precise in dress and speech, about fifty or so as far as they could tell. "Funny old biddy," said one of them.

Bill Frost grinned. "A real Little Miss Muffet."

The others laughed. "You'd better stock up with curds and whey, then!" and they fell about laughing at their own wit.

The cottage was charming, quite delightful, and there were actually roses round the door in the best traditional manner. The garden was small but quite adequate, though woefully overgrown. George had died in the middle of March and since then spring had come and gone, and the riot of growth had occurred unchecked. But to judge by the mass of colours struggling amid the crowded flower-beds the garden was very well stocked indeed. There was nothing wrong that could not be put right with a weeding fork and a lawn mower. Perhaps she could get a man in to help.

In the porchway were her other two suitcases with a folded British Rail delivery note in the letter-box. They would not have dared do that in London. Two unattended suitcases would not have lasted five minutes in London before being snapped up by a passing thief. It was nice to know that some of the old virtues were still alive in rural areas.

She took the keys from her handbag and opened the door and carried the suitcases into the tiny hallway one by one. She tried the electric light but there was no response, and she felt a little burst of anger that the Electricity Board had obviously not carried out her instructions to re-connect. But the water was on and so was the gas supply to the stove, so she wouldn't starve. Having satisfied herself on this point she then took a leisurely tour of the cottage.

All the rooms were adequately curtained and carpeted. There was plenty of furniture, thought the armchairs were those heavy button-backed leather affairs that seem so typically male, but they would serve her well enough until she could get something more to her own taste. By the standards of London bed-sitting-rooms and so-called flatlets, the kitchen seemed delightfully huge, being at least twenty-three or twenty-four feet long, but what delighted her more than anything was that every room, including the kitchen, had heavy oak beams across the ceiling, every city dweller's dream of what a country cottage ought to look like.

There were three small bedrooms upstairs and two rooms downstairs, in addition to the kitchen and tiny bathroom. In the second of the two downstairs rooms, the one she was already beginning to think of as the back parlour, there were a dozen or so glass display cases. The lids of all the cases had been removed and were propped against the wall. Inside each case were several small rocks and some dried-up lengths of twigs with dead leaves upon them, but apart from that they were all empty. She could not think what they had been used for, unless they had been aquaria, but there was no indication that they had ever contained water and certainly no aerator attachments, and anyway she felt sure that George had not been one to keep tropical fish.

She went down to the shop and purchased a few things to keep her going for a few days. There were several other people in there and so Mr. Frost was not disposed to chat, for which she was thankful. On her return she made a cup of tea and sank down into one of the great leather armchairs. It was odd how little she knew of her brother George. There had been fifteen years between them and he had already left home by the time she was old enough to go to school. He had gone to sea as a deck-hand in the Merchant Navy and throughout her entire childhood and teens she had seen him no more than three or four times. Her parents had died within six months of each other, between her twenty-second and twenty-third birthdays, while George was in the Far East. When he returned she was already established in a small bed-sitting-room in

Kensington with an adequate if unexciting secretarial job, and thus did not require his help, though there was little help that he could have offered anyway, situated as he was. She remembered that uncomfortable afternoon she had spent with him at the cemetery. They really had absolutely nothing in common, save the odd quirk of having shared the same parents, and George was quite clearly a withdrawn and taciturn man, though he did have that tiny amused smile in his eyes as though he could always see some joke that was hidden from others. She had been quite relieved when the ordeal was over and George had boarded the train to rejoin his ship. That was thirty years ago and since then she had seen him precisely three times at family gatherings, two funerals and a wedding. It was only after his death that she discovered that he had left the sea twenty years earlier and had spent some years working at Whipsnade Zoo, and had then joined the British Museum where he remained for fifteen years until his retirement a year before his death by a heart attack. She did not even know what his job had been at the Museum. She had intended writing to the curator but for one reason or another she had not found the time as yet.

She sighed and shook her head. It really was quite odd how little she knew of him, and in a vague way she felt rather guilty, though heaven knows it was no fault of hers. She had once offered to make a home for him but he smiled that odd little smile of his and said briefly: "Thank you, but you would not enjoy either my company or my particular hobby, and I am too set in my ways to adjust to others." She had naturally asked him about his hobby but he quite bluntly and even rudely steered her onto other subjects and she never did discover what it was. Perhaps it had been tropical fish after all.

She took the empty cup into the kitchen and rinsed it under the tap, and then dried it meticulously and put it away in the cupboard. She had always been a neat and tidy person. She then went upstairs to unpack, and it was while she was hanging up her dresses in the wardrobe that she caught sight of a large spider that scuttled along the carpet by the skirting board and disappeared under the bed. She dropped the dresses and fled out onto the landing, her heart thumping furiously. Of all the horrors in the world those large revolting house-spiders were the very worst. She would rather face anything else than a spider.

She had heard it said that the best way to cure arachneophobia was to shut the person in a room full of spiders until he or she grew used to it and realised that they were too insignificant and harmless to be feared. Such a stupid and dangerous solution could only have been thought up by someone who had no fear of spiders. If they tried that with her she knew that she would go quite literally insane with terror.

She had two theories about the fear of spiders. It was quite possible that those who suffered from the phobia had been terrified as a baby by having a spider crawl into their cot. The other notion was a very vague and almost esoteric theory concerning the number eight. She had no fear of anything with four, six, or even a hundred legs, like moths or beetles or centipedes or any other insect. It was only spiders, and as far as she was aware the spider was the only insect with eight legs. Why the number eight should be of such particular significance she had no idea, and she was quite prepared to admit that the theory was as irrational as the phobia itself. But no explanation, not even the right one, could dispel the fear which seemed to get worse, not better, as she grew older. And it was not as though she had learnt the fear from her parents. On many occasions she had seen her mother pick up a particularly large and revolting specimen in her hand and carry it into the garden, and her mother had *never* teased her about the fear or had ever tried to make her do the same.

She gathered her courage and peeped round the bedroom door but there was no sign of the horrible thing. Somehow she had got to find it and kill it. There was no way that she could sleep in that bed knowing that a spider was loose somewhere in the room. She went downstairs to fetch a broom, and with the handle end of it she poked at the dresses that still lay on the bedroom floor where she had dropped them. Such was the irrationality of her fear that she *knew* that the spider would not be in the clothing but still she could not pick those dresses up with her hands. She poked the broom-handle under the bundle and gingerly lifted the dresses out onto the landing, and still using the broom-handle she turned them over and over and over again until she was absolutely certain that the spider was not there. Even then it took an effort of will to pick up the dresses and creep into the bedroom to hang them in the wardrobe.

It must be under the bed. It was the only place that it could be hiding. But the coverlet hung down to the floor on all sides and she could not see under. Using the broom-handle again she lifted the coverlet clear and turned it over on top of the bed. Remaining by the door she knelt down and peered under the bed but she could see nothing from this distance. She took off one of her shoes and held it tightly in her right hand, and then cautiously and very, very slowly she crept a little closer until she was right by the bed itself, but still she could see nothing beneath it. Fortunately it was a single bed, and on castors, so she would be able to move it out quite easily. With her right hand grasping the shoe, she took hold of the edge of the bed with her left hand and moved it away from the wall a few inches.

The spider ran out just where she was kneeling and scuttled into the folds of her skirt. With a terrified shriek she leapt to her feet and frantically beat at her clothing again and again with her shoe but the spider clung to her skirt by her knee until finally it fell to the floor and scuttled away towards the wardrobe. It had to be now, before it escaped, for even in her terror she knew that she would not be able to go through all that again, and in a panic of fear she ran after the spider and smashed it with her shoe again and again and again until there was nothing left of it but a few broken bits of legs that twitched obscenely as though they had independent life of their own. She then sat down on the bed, her whole body convulsing with nausea, and burst into tears.

It was a full ten minutes before she recovered sufficiently to change her shoes and go downstairs, but even then she was still trembling and her legs and head still itched as though insects were running across her skin. To take her mind off it she made herself a small omelette and another cup of tea and by the time the meal was finished she was more or less back to normal.

Perhaps it was some subconscious deduction that had not yet filtered through to her conscious mind, but she then decided that she really ought to phone the British Museum to see if she could discover some more information about George. For three months she had not bothered to pursue that possibility but now suddenly it seemed a matter of urgency. It was now a quarter to five on a Friday. If she did not do it now she would have to wait until Monday. There was no phone in the house but she had noticed a call-box at the other end of the village. She grabbed her handbag and hurried out of the cottage.

By the time she had looked up the number and placed the call it was close on five o'clock. "I'm sorry," said the Museum operator, "but all departments are closed now, and the switch-board is just about to close as well. Perhaps you could phone again on Monday."

"But all I want to know is what job my brother had with you—he retired about a year ago—George Moffat."

"I'm sorry but I really can't—George Moffat did you say?"

"Yes, I'm his sister. He died in March this year."

"Oh, I am sorry to hear that. I didn't know him well. He retired just after I came. I went to his leaving party. But I don't know very much about him, and I really have to close the board now. Sorry I can't help."

The girl was obviously eager to catch a train or bus home. "But I only want to know what his job was."

"I really don't know exactly, something to do with insects, spiders I think. He used to look after them or something—and I really must close now. Do phone again on Monday. Goodbye."

"Wait, just a moment—" but the phone had gone dead. She replaced the receiver slowly and walked back through the village. She thought of explaining matters to Mr. Frost to see if he could help, but the shop was closed and locked, and anyway what could he do save laugh at her for being foolish. It couldn't possibly be what she feared, it really couldn't.

She was most reluctant to enter the cottage again. She pushed open the front door and stepped into the hallway and examined every nook and cranny, and then did the same in the kitchen. An hour later she had gone through every room in the cottage and had gingerly examined every crevice and corner and every piece of furniture. She then picked up the remains of the dead spider on a shovel and peered at it as closely as she dared. There wasn't much left but what few bits remained certainly *looked* like a perfectly normal British house-spider. She gave a shudder of disgust and tipped the contents into the dustbin outside, and then went into the downstairs back parlour and examined the empty glass display cases to make sure that they really were empty.

She was being very childish, she told herself, acting like a foolish old maid. She must expect the occasional spider. This was a country cottage, not a London flat, but nevertheless her skin was crawling with the very thought of those hideous insects. She remembered seeing a television programme once where a man had one of those huge South American bird-eating spiders, and to demonstrate how harmless it was he let it crawl up his bare arm. That programme had given her a really dreadful nightmare. She couldn't help it. She simply had a horror of the loathsome things, and no amount of explanation would change that.

Did George ever do that, let one of those things crawl up his arm? The very thought of it made her shudder. No wonder he had said that she wouldn't like his hobby. She looked at the display cases again. Had they contained his collection? If so then who had removed the lids, and where were the inmates now? No, stop it, she told herself firmly, you'll frighten yourself silly. But just in case, just to cover the million-to-one chance that she was right, she would stay upstairs with the light on all night in the room farthest away from the back parlour. After all they couldn't be all through the house, could they? She would stay awake all night. The loss of a night's sleep would do her no harm, and in the morning she would phone the police and explain that although it was a million-to-one chance it was just barely possible that there was a poisonous spider loose in the house. Surely they would understand that she was not being foolish, merely prudent.

Dusk was beginning to draw in and the rooms were already quite shadowy, and she walked over and clicked the light switch. Oh God, she had forgotten that the electricity was disconnected! What to do now? There was no other bus today and the nearest town was ten miles away. She couldn't possibly walk that far, and what would the hotel man think if a lone woman without luggage arrived after midnight, and anyway she only had a little money in the bank, not enough to squander on hotel bills. And she couldn't knock at one of the village houses and ask for a bed for the night. What would they think of her? She would never be able to live that down.

She went out into the hallway and wound a nylon scarf tightly around her head. She then put on her gloves, her biggest and heaviest topcoat, and her strongest and stoutest shoes and went upstairs to the back bedroom and arranged two chairs facing each other. She sat on one and put her feet up on the other. To get at her a spider would have to crawl up one of the thin chair-legs and surely it wouldn't do that.

It was now quite dark and getting darker every minute. Did spiders come out at night? Thank God that it was June, it would be light by five A.M. Surely she could hang on until then. It was her own fault. She should have investigated her brother's circumstances more closely before coming down here. She had always known that he was odd, but how on earth could anyone have guessed that he collected spiders? What a revolting hobby. How could any *normal* person keep those disgusting things as pets!

Her skin was itching furiously in a dozen places and she rubbed her legs quite hard. If there *was* any spider in there the rubbing would kill it, wouldn't it. And anyway it was only an itch, a tickle, but how could she tell the difference? If a spider crawled up her leg how would she know the difference between that and an itch?

George had never liked her very much, that was why he had stayed away from her, and why he had been so rude about sharing a house with her. Though heaven knows why. She had done him no harm, no harm at all. Perhaps he had been odd enough to blame her for their parents' deaths. That would explain it. There was certainly no other reason why he should have an aversion towards her.

Suddenly her leg tickled more strongly than before and she slapped at it in sudden panic, but the tickle was still there and getting higher. Oh God, it was crawling up her leg! She leapt from the chair and beat at her clothing frantically, again and again until finally she leant back against the wall exhausted.

If only the moon would shine. It was so dark she could not see anything at all. Oh God, there could be a dozen spiders on her and she would not be able to see them! It was all so clear to her now. It was revenge. George blamed her for their parents' deaths and this was his revenge. It was all so clear. He must have had one or two earlier heart attacks and this had given him time to plan his revenge, to alter his will to leave her this cottage so that sooner or later she would come down and walk into his trap. And the day he died he must have lived for a few minutes after his final attack, just long enough to remove the lids on the display cases and let the spiders escape throughout the house. A dozen cases, say four or five spiders in each, oh God, there must be fifty of the filthy things crawling all over the place.

She began to cry, weakly and hysterically as she leant against the wall, and then suddenly one of the loathsome things crawled across her face and she tore at her scarf and let out shriek after shriek of demented terror and plunged from the room and fell headlong down the stairs from top to bottom.

It was a warm still summer night and her shrieks had been heard a hundred yards away. It was Bill Frost who phoned the local policeman and the doctor and it was he who met them at the cottage. They forced open the front door and went in. "No lights," said the doctor, flicking the switch. "Disconnected?"

Bill Frost shook his head. "No, they re-connected a couple of days ago. I saw their van. Probably switched off at the mains." He went through into the kitchen and struck a match. "Thought so," he said, and switched on the main power switch and the lights came flooding on.

They found her at the bottom of the stairs, quite dead. While the doctor was examining her the other two went through into the living room. The constable picked up her handbag and rummaged around in it. "Might be something to tell us who to contact." He pulled out the unopened letter and then after some hesitation he tore it open. "It's from her solicitor," he said. "Dear Miss Moffat," he read aloud, "I did not mention it before in case you formed high hopes that could not be fulfilled. Apparently your brother was quite an expert on spiders and kept his own collection. I imagine you have seen the display cases. In his will he instructed me as one of the trustees to arrange to sell the collection to a zoo, and specified Whipsnade in particular. The matter had to be arranged quickly, otherwise the specimens would not have survived. By my instructions and authority the Whipsnade people collected the specimens from your brother's cottage a few days after his death and they have all apparently settled in quite happily at the zoo's insect house. Some of the spiders were quite rare and I enclose a cheque that I feel sure you will find most satisfactory indeed. Incidentally, I imagine that you will by now have guessed why your brother named the house Chandira Cottage. The word 'chandira' is simply an anagram of 'arachnid' which as you know is derived from the Greek word for 'spider.' Perhaps he thought it a more attractive name than Spider Cottage. If you have had any further thoughts about selling the property do please let me know."

The doctor came in to join them. "What's that?"

"Nothing much. Letter from her solicitor. Something about her brother's will. She is dead, I presume?"

"Oh yes, quite dead. Broke her neck in the fall. There'll have to be an inquest, of course, but it's a straightforward case of accidental death."

"Curious though," said the constable. "It's a hot summer's night and yet she's dressed up like it's winter. The sweat must have been running all over her body."

The doctor shrugged. "Yes, a little odd perhaps, but these old biddies get some funny ideas at times."

NIGHT WATCH

C. Dean Andersson

Modern horror fiction has many different faces: from the hauntingly psychological to the splatter-punk school. Dean Andersson's work is upfront and raw, and concerns itself centrally with the nightmares of physical pain, but at the same time he doesn't neglect the reasons why pain is inflicted or accepted. He began his novel-writing career under the pen-name of Asa Drake, and wrote the heroic-fantasy Hel trilogy about a Scandinavian warrior woman called Bloodsong. Asa Drake also wrote a Dracula tale called *Crimson Kisses* and a Lovecraft-style horror fantasy entitled *The Lair of Ancient Dreams.* Dean's first book under his own name was *Torture Tomb,* followed by *Raw Pain Max*—horror novels set in and around the Dallas-Fort Worth metroplex, where he lives. "Night Watch" is his first published short story.

"A squirrel's nothing but a tree-rat," her husband said, grinning at her from a shadowy corner of the bedroom, "a rodent that lives in trees, a filthy killer that will kill your babies if he gets the chance . . ."

Her bedroom window exploded inward, spraying shards of glass as a gigantic dark head pushed its way inside, eyes burning red, fur bristling, razor teeth bared.

She ran screaming toward the crib in the corner. Broken glass sliced her bare feet.

The monster squirrel reached the crib first, clamped its teeth into the flesh of her baby, raised her screaming, bleeding baby into the air, leaped out of the broken window and was gone into the night, leaving her wailing horror-stricken on shard-shredded knees in a pool of warm blood, her blood, and her baby's.

From outside came a crunching sound. Her baby's cries cut off in mid-scream, but hers continued on and on . . .

. . . and she woke up still hearing the screams. The screams in her mind slowly became wounded whimperings.

Comforting moonlight squeezed between the slats of the miniblinds that covered her bedroom window. A mockingbird was singing its nightsong somewhere outside in the trees. The digital clock radio on the bedside table indicated 3:24 A.M. At least she'd gotten some rest this time before the nightmares came back.

She knew she wouldn't be sleepy again until dawn, but she couldn't rest after sunrise either, because when it was light she had to again start watching for the squirrel.

Outside the mockingbird stopped singing. The angle of the moonlight creeping between the blinds changed as Luna made her way serenely across the heavens. A neighbor's dog barked excitedly several times, then fell silent. The mockingbird started back through its long and complex song.

Her baby started to cry. She hurried to the crib in the corner of the bedroom. The crib was filled only with shadows. Her son's crying was only in her mind. For a moment she'd forgotten, had believed everything was still all right. But it would never be all right, not ever again.

The pain of her loss crushed down upon her once more. She went whimpering back to bed.

Two hours and ten minutes later, with the sky outside brightening, she began to feel sleepy and nearly dozed off.

No! she scolded herself. If she slept during the day the squirrel would somehow know and sneak across the roof to kill again. If she slept, the babies would die, and they mustn't die. There had been too much death, too many dead babies. There mustn't be any more.

She got up and went into the living room, tensely listening for the sound of a squirrel's claws clicking on shingles across the roof.

A sliding glass door that opened onto a fenced backyard dominated her small living room. Birds were pecking for food in the back lawn's unmowed grass. There were no squirrels in sight, especially one particular squirrel missing part of his tail, which is why she called him Shorttail, a baby-killing monster.

A few feet to the left of the sliding door, the outer wall of her one-story brick house made a right angle. Hungry cheeping came from the house sparrow nest beneath the overhanging eaves along that wall. As she watched, the mother sparrow emerged from the nest and flew away to get more food for her babies.

It's going to be all right, babies, she told them with her thoughts. *Good babies. Good little babies . . .*

She sat down in a rocking chair placed so she could view the nest and the stretch of roof that led to it. She'd spent the daylight hours of the last three days in that chair, ever since the first sparrow baby had been murdered.

Morning was the most dangerous time. That was when the squirrels usually came, when the first baby bird had been killed.

She had been sitting in the recliner when it happened. She'd been sitting there a very long time, it seemed, waiting for something, and hadn't wanted to get up. But she'd made herself go look when she heard the mother sparrow's screams, screams she could still hear in her mind, cries of helpless panic, utter disbelieving horror, pain, insane terror. Sometimes it seemed that the remembered screams were her own.

When she looked out the glass door she'd seen sparrows everywhere, on the roof and hovering and swooping in the air near the nest, chittering and fussing while the mother sparrow kept shrieking her horror because under the eaves a dark shape was huddled on the ledge near the nest, a squirrel, Shorttail, a dead baby dangling lifelessly from his mouth.

When she saw the squirrel she'd rushed into the backyard screaming and yelling and waving her hands to scare him away, but he had arrogantly ignored her like he was ignoring the maddened sparrows. Then he had climbed leisurely back onto the roof and run away across the shingles, the baby still dangling from his mouth.

The sparrows pursued him.

She was still standing there looking helplessly at the violated nest when the mother sparrow returned and went hesitantly, still frightened, back into the nest, back to the scene of horror to check on her remaining babies.

She'd envied the mother sparrow at that moment more than she'd ever envied anyone or thing. Other babies. The mother sparrow had *other* babies. Her thoughts had skittered then to her own pain, and back in the living room she'd found herself looking at the baby rattle on the floor near the recliner.

The squirrel didn't come that morning or that afternoon either. Darkness returned. She went back to bed. She slept.

The nightmare began with a man's laughter. The roof creaked as something crept across the shingles.

She rushed into the living room. A man, silhouetted in moonlight, was crouching on the roof. He felt her terrified gaze and met it. Cold laughter poured from his grinning mouth as he began to reach under the eaves into the mother sparrow's nest . . .

She jerked awake.

In time, the sun rose again, and again she took her place in the rocker to watch for the squirrel and hope he wouldn't return. She felt certain that in only a few more days the baby sparrows would fly. Shorttail couldn't hurt them then, and she could finally rest. But until then, she had to keep her watch. She had to save the babies.

That night, her nightmare began with an argument. Her husband had been out all night. He'd come home drunk. He was hitting her again. It was worse than usual. He wasn't satisfied this time when her nose and lip began to bleed. He hit her until she fell to the floor, and when she fell to the floor he kicked her until she was numb and stunned and scarcely able to move.

But still he was not satisfied. He brought her son to the bed and drunkenly threatened to beat the baby too, because he knew that would give her the most pain of all. And in his drunkenness he lifted the baby up high. And dropped him.

Her son's screams stopped when he hit the floor.

She woke up.

There was laughter in the house. Her husband's laughter.

It's only in my mind, she told herself. *Only in my mind.*

The laughter went away. The sun rose. She resumed watching for the squirrel.

Shorttail made a second run on the nest shortly before 10:00 A.M.

She was in the backyard this time before he climbed under the eaves. He ignored her again at first, but when she got onto the roof with him his fur bristled, he shook his tail in anger, then turned and ran. The massed sparrow tribe pursued him. The babies had been saved.

She returned to the rocking chair to continue her watch.

When her nightmare began that night, she was still crouched in the corner. Blood was oozing from her son's tiny mouth, staining the bedroom rug. Both she and her husband were silent, momentarily mute with horror. Then she began to crawl on her hands and knees across the floor and her husband began drunkenly trying to awaken their dead baby, all the while mumbling over and over that he was sorry and hadn't meant it and . . .

. . . and she kept screaming with rage into her gag and tearing at her bonds and then her right hand suddenly pulled free. She freed her left hand. She freed her feet. She grabbed the heavy flashlight her husband kept beside the bed and got down from the bed and came up behind him where he was still crouched mumbling over their son's corpse and she hit him with the flashlight again and again and . . .

She woke up. Her husband stood in the doorway across the room, laughing at her. His head showed no signs of the blows she'd given him with the flashlight. Then she remembered that their fight had only been a dream.

No, her dead husband spoke in her mind, *more than a dream.* He laughed again. *I've come back to take custody of our son's soul. You can't stop me. Don't even try.*

You can't take what you can't find, she answered. It was her turn to laugh, and she did.

Tell me where he is. Don't make me have to force you.

She laughed some more, then replied, *You don't frighten me now. You're dead. You can't hurt me or my son with your physical strength ever again.*

A part of her wanted to believe she was still dreaming, but her thoughts were suddenly coming clearer than they'd been in days and she knew it was not a dream.

Again she laughed at the angry but helpless ghost in the doorway. Her laughter drove him away.

Shorttail didn't return that day. Late in the afternoon she saw the babies for the first time when they came out to look around on the ledge beneath the eaves. They had all their feathers. She felt certain they would fly the next morning. *Good babies,* she told them from her rocking chair. *You're going to make it, babies. You're going to live to fly free.*

That night for the first time in many long nights she had no nightmares. Her dead husband's laughter awakened her shortly after 4:00 A.M.

He was at the foot of the bed this time. And he wasn't alone.

Maybe I can't make you tell where you've hidden my son's soul, but He can, he grinned, jerking his thumb toward the one he'd brought with him.

The hulking monstrosity towered nearly to the ceiling. It growled like a beast. Its eyes burned red. It reached out to touch her with demon-hot, soul-rending claws.

It will do you no good, she told the demon-thing. *Torture me all you want. I'll never give you my son. I can't. I remember all of it now. My son's soul is no longer here because I gave him to the Moon.*

The demon drew angrily back, then went away, but it didn't go empty-handed. It took with it her husband's screaming ghost.

In the morning she saw the baby sparrows fly free of the nest. Her watch was done. She looked into the backyard. It was so green, so beautiful, so alive. But she no longer belonged. It was time to go. Time to rest. Time to heal.

She turned to the recliner, looked first at the baby rattle on the floor, and then, for the first time since the mother sparrow's screams had roused her from her numbed stupor, she looked at what sat in the chair, at her corpse and the baby's it held in its arms.

Both bodies were already badly decomposed. So was her husband's in the bedroom on the bloodstained rug near the empty crib.

She supposed it would be the smell that would finally bring their family tragedy to light. A neighbor or someone else would eventually smell death and investigate. Then the police would come and find the empty sleeping-pill bottle she'd left beside the bathroom sink, but they wouldn't find a note because she hadn't written one. And they'd never find out about the Moon, about how the Moon had come into the living room that first night after she'd died in the recliner.

The Moon's light had swirled and spun and become a pale Woman with black wings, and she'd immediately given the Woman her baby's soul. She'd later wondered why she had entrusted her son to the Woman so readily and unquestioningly, but reasoning didn't work with the Moon. It had felt right and she'd done it and been glad. But it hadn't felt right for her to go with the Woman too, and now she knew why. She hadn't fought back soon enough to save her own baby, but she'd saved others and it didn't matter if they were only sparrows. They were alive and that was the most precious thing there was and she'd owed it to the world and herself somehow, so it had been the right thing to do. But it was finally over, and now she could rest.

She eased back into the recliner, back into her decaying corpse, and fell asleep.

And, of course, that night the Moon came back for her soul.

THE LAST GIFT

Peter Tremayne

I didn't realize until he had sent me his contribution to *Scare Care* that Peter Tremayne and I had worked together in another life as junior newspaper reporters in Sussex. Since then Peter has made a notable and characterful name for himself in the British horror/fantasy field, particularly with his Celtic and Cornish-based stories. He has published over twenty horror novels and numerous short stories. Under another name he is an expert on Celtic history and culture and his stories have been translated into all six Celtic languages. In addition he is the only fantasy writer to have been initiated a Bard of the Cornish Gorsedd and to hold honorary bardship of the Welsh and Breton Gorseddau. "The Last Gift" has all the haunting qualities of the best of Peter's Cornish tales.

Children?

I cannot say that I am fond of children; especially solemn-faced boys who stare at you with eyes the colour of grey, lonely seas; children with cadaver-pale faces and hair the colour of bleached corn; children who gaze in silent judgement as if penetrating your innermost secret thoughts. They make me ill-at-ease. Their presence causes me to remember things which I do not wish to recall. They disturb me.

Yet it was not always so.

Many years ago I was on a walking tour of west Cornwall. It was nothing ambitious. I simply set out from Penzance carrying a rucksack and enough money to stay at guest houses en route. My intention was to walk along the coastal paths until I reached St. Ives. It was to be a leisurely trip, a walk without a pre-determined schedule, in which I would stay where my fancy took me and stay as long as I wanted.

I had reached Nanjizal Beach and spent a lazy afternoon on its broad white sands, resting in the warmth of the autumnal sunshine. The scenery was beautiful and I lay breathing it into my being. I had initially intended to make Land's End that evening but I realised, with the sun swiftly sinking to the sea's dim level, that it would be too late to traverse the two miles to my objective. I was not worried; there was no hurry. Instead I climbed the rocky path by the towering granite cliff called Carn Voel towards the village of Trevilley.

Every guest house, with its welcoming "Bed and Breakfast" sign, was filled, in spite of the lateness of the season. I swiftly grew tired of trudging from door to door and with tiredness came irritability. Then at one cottage I found a friendly and helpful youth who, while shaking his head and proclaiming "mum's full up," stretched a hand towards a high, narrow path which ran across the hills towards the sea.

"Do 'ee try at Mrs. Trevossow's place up by Pendenick Point. 'Tis only a half-hour walk from here."

"Mrs. Trevossow?"

"Ay," nodded the youth, "Widow Trevossow, folks call her. Keeps a cottage up on the Point. Gwennol Cottage. You can't miss it. She sometimes lets."

"Zeb!"

The woman's voice was unduly sharp. She appeared, stout arms folded across a faded pinafore, and gazed in disapproval at the youth. The sameness of their features proclaimed their relationship.

The boy gave a defensive shrug. "I thought . . ." he began.

The woman interrupted him with a sniff.

"My boy's mistook, sir," she said to me. "Mrs. Trevossow don't let rooms. Leastways, not now."

This remark was made almost under her breath.

"Sorry we can't oblige 'ee. You'd best take the road to Travescan. 'Tis not far. I'm certain sure they do have rooms to let."

I thanked her and turned up the path.

I do not know what it was that made me hesitate and pause when I came to the rotting wooden sign post whose opposing arms proclaimed "Pendenick Point" one way and "Trevescan" in the other direction. Some strange instinct, as if I were not in charge of my actions, caused my feet to turn in the direction of Pendenick Point. Along the lonely path, across the granite-strewn hills made purple with heather, I cursed myself for all kinds of a fool. Why should I waste my time in this fashion? I had not gone a mile when I realised how silly my inexplicable impulse had been. Yet I pressed on.

Pendenick Point is a formidable surge of granite, a mile from Land's End, at the end of the Cornish peninsula. It is a comfortless and isolated place, shaped by the rise and fall of countless tides and the ceaseless pounding of the Atlantic storms. Few stretches of Cornwall's wild and desolate coastline were so dreaded by sailors in the days of sailing ships than these high ramparts of grey granite, wielded together by clayslate and greenstone, hardened into countless gnarled and twisted shapes.

As I walked along the cliff path towards the solitary cottage which I could now see, I felt the atmosphere of brooding melancholia which haunted the place; I recalled the tales of wraiths and spirits who make bloody sacrifice of unwary travellers; I remembered the tales of malevolent giants and buried treasure hidden in the innumerable granite caves among the hills. Beneath me, at the foot of the cliffs, the angry seas were black, tinged with frothing foam. A warning light scattered the waters from a distant lighthouse high on the battlemented cliffs. The sun was entirely gone from the sky and dusk lay like a thick shroud, mingling with a drifting deep sea fog which crept stealthily inshore. I shivered in the chill of the autumn evening.

The cottage, which defied the sharp Atlantic winds, was a stout grey granite structure with tiny windows and a dark slate roof. The small windows winked with a welcoming, flickering light, light enough for me to make out the painted wooden sign which confirmed it as Gwennol Cottage.

My knock on the stout wooden door was answered after a moment by a young girl. I can see her vision of loveliness even now, after all these years. I estimated her to be scarcely out of her teens; a willowy figure, but well-proportioned. She had bright blue eyes, set wide apart in a fair-skinned face which had just a touch of red along the high cheekbones. There was a hint of freckles across her delicately set nose. The mouth was perfectly shaped, and naturally red. Her hair was a tumble of dark blackness. She stared at me with a curious expression, midway between amusement and inquiry.

"Is Mrs. Trevossow in?" I asked at length, clearing my throat before speaking.

"I'm Mrs. Trevossow," the girl replied, her eyes downcast for a moment.

"Oh, then is it your mother-in-law who lets rooms?"

The girl frowned.

"My mother-in-law has been dead these many years. I let rooms now and again. What makes you ask for my mother-in-law?"

I was embarrassed.

"It was . . . well . . . I was told that Mrs. Trevossow was a widow and . . ."

The girl sighed.

"You were told right. My husband, Sobey Trevossow, was drowned out there."

She jerked her pretty head towards the restless sea.

"He was a fisherman."

"I'm sorry," I replied awkwardly.

"No need," her answer was almost indifferent in tone. "I've got over it. You said you wanted a room?"

I nodded.

"Just bed and breakfast. I'm hiking along the coast."

"Come in, then," she smiled. "The evening has turned chilly."

I followed her into a small and cosy parlour where a hearty log fire roared in an open fireplace. There was a table laid for supper. She saw me glance wistfully at it.

"Have you eaten?"

"Not since lunchtime," I confessed.

"Then you are welcome to join me. My son is staying with a schoolfriend, otherwise he would be here tonight."

My face must have shown my astonishment but she did not appear to notice. Surely she was not old enough to have a son, let alone one of school age?

She showed me to a bedroom leading off from the parlour. It smelt slightly musty from disuse but the bed linen was crisp and fresh and the room was not unduly cold. I had slept in worse places.

"This is fine," I smiled, dumping my coat and rucksack on the bed.

Mrs. Trevossow bit her lip and frowned. She appeared to be trying to make up her mind about something.

"Are you nervous?" she suddenly asked.

I stared at her and she went on.

"I'd best tell you. The night they recovered my Sobey from the sea they laid him out in this room."

I smiled and shook my head.

"I don't believe in ghosties, ghoulies and long-leggedy beasties, if that's what you mean," said I.

Her lip drooped in answering smile.

"How much is the room?"

Mrs. Trevossow named a price with which I had no argument; in fact, it seemed ridiculously cheap.

The business concluded, I followed her back into the living room, and we fell to the supper she had been preparing when I arrived. I cannot remember exactly all that we spoke of over that supper. I recall mentioning my astonishment at how youthful she was to be a mother, a widowed mother at that. She blushed prettily and accused me of flattery. Then we went on to speak of Cornwall. I expressed fascination at the tenacity with which some of the old Celtic traditions, and even the language itself, clung limpet-like to the granite peninsula. Solemnly, so she informed me, in secluded spots such as Trevilley, men and women dreamed the old dreams and remembered the ancient folklore, tales and customs that were ancient before Christianity was brought into the land.

Then we went on to speak of the harsher realities of life; of how it was difficult to wrest a living, an existence, amidst such lonely beauty. We spoke of the task of fulfilling the primeval urge to do battle with land or sea to earn our living. At the mention of the sea, she grew sad and I apologized for my clumsiness in reminding her of her misfortune.

"No, no, it happened a long time ago," she smiled wistfully. "I am fully recovered. The wife of a fisherman has to learn to live with the moodiness of the sea as well as her husband. Sobey Trevossow and I had happiness in our lives. It would be selfish and wrong of me to remember him with unhappiness and sorrow. Besides, did he not leave me a last gift . . . my son?"

I could not fault her simple philosophical outlook.

The clock began to chime and I arose with an apology.

"I'd best get to bed. I have a long trek in the morning."

"I trust you sleep well," she smiled. "Goodnight."

I bade her "Goodnight" and went to my room. I undressed and was asleep as soon as my head touched the pillow.

I awoke with a curious sensation of being wet and cold. The rational part of my brain told me that I was still lying snug and warm in the small bed in the cottage. Yet I began to shiver uncontrollably. Then there came a sudden constriction to my throat. I began to taste brine on my lips. I coughed and began to struggle for breath, threshing about in the bed, desperately trying to search for breath. As abruptly as it came, the constriction was gone but the cold and dampness remained.

There was also something else . . .

Something which I could not understand. There seemed to be an alien presence in my mind. I cannot describe the impression in any better form. Thoughts came into my mind which were not my thoughts; thoughts flowed across my consciousness with a grim arrogance, threatening to absorb my individuality. I held a hand to my forehead, rubbing my temples as if to disperse them, but the thoughts persisted.

I found my body answering the commands of this alien presence, rising slowly from the bed like a somnambulist.

I stood up, peering round the room. Part of my mind registered surprise at how familiar every item was in that little bedroom. Then I was turning for the door, striding into the parlour beyond. It was eerily lit by the dying red embers of the fire and deathly quiet save for the hollow *tick-tock* of a clock on the mantelshelf. That small rational part of me which remained tried to stop and question what I was doing. Yet some power within me turned my footsteps towards the door on the far side of the parlour. My outstretched fingers reached the cold, brass doorknob and turned it gently.

Moonlight dappled the bedroom beyond; it glinted on the old brass bedstead of the Victorian double bed and chased shadows across the white sheets between which lay the sleeping figure of Mrs. Trevossow. I found myself moving to her bedside and gazing down. And as I gazed down at her sleeping form I was seized with a terrible desire, a desire I could not control. Yet was the desire really mine? Those strange, alien thoughts within me urged me forward, urged my body forward, sought to compel it. My breath came in short jerks and I moved even nearer.

The motion must have woken her. Her eyelids fluttered and she turned yawning and peered up at me through the semi-gloom.

Her eyes, those intense blue eyes, met mine and she stared silently for a while. There was a curious light in them. My rational mind wondered why she was not afraid, why she did not make a protest. All she did was utter a long, low sigh.

"So you've come then, Sobey?" she whispered.

There was a shuddering, voluptuous quality to her voice.

"Aye, I've come," I replied in a voice that was not my own.

The rational part of my mind which remained tried to apologise for this intrusion, tried to leave, but the alien thoughts cascaded across them.

Mrs. Trevossow lay back on her pillows, wildly desirable, her hands stretching up to greet me, a groan of anticipatory pleasure sighed from her soft white throat.

That alien force, some animal instinct, took over my thoughts and I plunged into a rapturous love-making which drove all other sensibilities from my mind until I finally fell asleep with exhaustion.

When I awoke the sun was shining through the small cottage window and I found myself lying snug and warm in the small bed in which I had originally gone to sleep. As I came awake and collected my scattered thoughts I began to realise that I had been the victim of a dream, a wild exotic dream, but a dream nonetheless. I lay in bed, feeling the warmth of the bedclothes, the rough homespun blankets, and marvelling at the realism of that dream, remembering the cold dampness, the constriction and the alien thoughts which had pounded in my mind. Had it been real? No, no, of course not!

There was a tap on the door.

I eased myself nervously up on the pillows.

"Come in!"

A small boy entered; he was perhaps ten years of age. He was a solemn-faced child, with eyes the colour of grey, lonely seas; a child with a cadaver-pale face and hair the colour of bleached corn. He stared at me as if penetrating my innermost thoughts, gazing in silent judgement.

I coughed to clear my anxious throat.

"Hello," I said.

The child stared at me long and thoughtfully before saying softly:

"Mum says breakfast is ready."

"I'll be right out," I replied, swinging out of the bed before the implication of what the boy had said registered in my mind. When I turned to question him, he had vanished behind the closing door.

His *mother*?

Was this Mrs. Trevossow's son? But he was all of ten years old and Mrs. Trevossow was scarcely out of her teens, I would swear to it.

Shaking my head in perplexity, I crossed to the wash basin and made a hasty toilet, threw on my clothes and went into the parlour. A table was laid for breakfast with three places. The boy was sitting solemnly at the end of the table, staring at me with those remote, lonely eyes of his. Beyond, from the kitchen, came the reassuring sizzle of cooking bacon, its smell perfuming the air with normality.

I forced a smile at the child.

"Hello," I said.

He made no reply but sat still, his eyes unblinking, opaque yet with a restless quality like the seas which I could hear stirring outside the cottage walls.

"You are not Mrs. Trevossow's boy, surely?" I asked, feeling a little ridiculous.

"Ah, you're up then?"

Mrs. Trevossow stood at the kitchen door holding a plate in her hand.

I raised my head at her voice. My eyes bulged, my jaw drooped foolishly. Was I going mad?

"Are you all right?" asked the woman.

The rapidity of my thoughts made me feel faint. Where was the young girl who had greeted me last night? The young girl with whom I had spent such a pleasant evening? The young girl of whom I had dreamt so erotically during the night, that wild dream of sensual love-making?

The woman who stood framed in the doorway was beautiful still, but she had grey streaks in her hair, dark shadows beneath her eyes. The firm flesh of girlhood was now wrinkling, there were lines of aging around her neck. Yet she was clearly the same person. It was just that she had aged ten years or more during the night!

"Are you all right?" she repeated in a worried voice, moving forward to set my breakfast on the table.

"I . . . that is . . ." I jerked my head up to stare at her hopefully. "Mrs. Trevossow?"

She waited patiently.

"Yes?" she prompted, mistaking my question for a preamble.

I dropped my head in confusion.

"I'm sorry," I managed to say. "I had rather a disturbed night."

She sat down and poured the coffee.

"Sorry I am for that," she said. "I hope my silly remark last night didn't disturb you."

I frowned, trying to dredge forth memories from my pounding sensibilities.

"Silly talk?"

"About Sobey."

"Sobey?"

I must have sounded stupid.

"My late husband."

I tried to recollect what she had said.

"Sorry . . . I don't see the connection."

"Don't you remember?" There was a rebuke in her voice. "I mentioned that Sobey was laid out in the room in which you slept after they recovered his body from the sea."

A coldness gripped my stomach in an excruciating spasm.

The memory did return and with it the vivid recollection of the night—the cold dampness, the constriction of my throat, the taste of brine on my lips . . .

I noticed the boy was watching my face closely.

I made no attempt to pull myself together, my thoughts were illogical, unreasonable.

"I just didn't sleep too well, that's all."

Mrs. Trevossow smiled at the irritability in my voice and sighed. "Some folks can be nervous of a thing like that. You'd be surprised. I'm not afraid of the dead nor the Otherworld. Thank God for it! Otherwise young Sobey there might not have been born."

She nodded to the boy.

I frowned trying to fathom her meaning.

"Last night was the tenth anniversary of my Sobey's death," she went on, pouring more coffee. "Ten years ago, yesterday, Sobey went out to chase the herring shoals, in his little boat—the *Gwennol.* That's the word for swallow in the old tongue. Sobey named his boat after our cottage."

Gwennol Cottage. I nodded in remembrance.

Mrs. Trevossow sighed.

"I remember that day as if it were yesterday indeed. You are not eating," she suddenly observed.

Automatically, I reached for a piece of toast.

"I was preparing for Sobey to be away two or maybe three days. But you can imagine my surprise when I was awakened during the night by him entering the bedroom. I questioned him and he dismissed my questions with that raucous laugh of his. He was born with a gift of laughter. He felt the whole world was made for his pleasure and was simply there to derive merriment from. He was a man in love with life. He loved life desperately."

She paused, her pert features had been moulded now by approaching middle-age into a humorous homeliness.

"More coffee?" she asked.

"No, go on," I whispered.

"Oh yes, of course. Well, Sobey dismissed my questions and came straightway to bed."

She rolled her eyes and chuckled.

"That was a night and no mistake. God! How we loved! I'll always remember that night. Finally, in the early hours, I slept exhausted and when I awoke, my Sobey was gone."

I coloured slightly in my embarrassment at her candid confession of intimacy and glanced nervously at the boy.

He still sat staring at me with those wide grey eyes of his.

"I was up doing my chores when they came to tell me that Sobey's boat had gone down during the night, during a storm off Pendenick Point. All the crew were gone, too."

"What's that?" I demanded. "Are you telling me that your husband left his boat and crew during a storm and came back to . . . to, er, sleep with you while his crew drowned?''

She smiled wistfully and shook her head.

''Oh no, Sobey was drowned with his crew.''

''Then how. . . ?''

''How? That's more than I can say. All I know is that just about the time *Gwennol* foundered, Sobey came to me and made love.''

The woman was clearly irrational!

She raised her bright blue eyes to mine as if reading my thoughts. She shook her head and nodded towards the boy.

''Nine months to the day after that, little Sobey was born.''

I stared open-mouthed from her to the child and back again.

''Yes,'' she went on, ''Sobey loved life. He knew how much I wanted a family. He returned that night to ensure that I had a son to remember him by. It was his last gift to me. His last gift.''

My mouth worked, I tried to say something. But what could one say to someone so clearly demented?

Demented?

My mind filled with strange thoughts; of the memories of the previous night. The cold, the wetness, the feeling of drowning with the taste of the salt sea on my lips. Of the bizarre optical illusion of Mrs. Trevossow ten years younger and of the wild erotic dream of making love to her. I raised my hands to massage my temples, to make the images go away. They did not go.

''You mustn't be afraid,'' smiled Mrs. Trevossow. ''There's nothing to be afraid about. We Cornish are an ancient people, we still live close to nature; we have not lost our psychic reality like you upcountry people. There is no difference between what is real in nature and that which you would call supernatural. They are two aspects of one entity. Death is meaningless. Souls do not die. There is no reason to be afraid of the Otherworld.''

I forced a smile to placate her insanity.

''Of course not,'' I said, a little too heartily. ''But it's getting late and I really must be on my way. Thanks very much for your hospitality.''

I thrust some notes at her and turned for the door, grabbing my rucksack on the way.

"Goodbye," came her soft voice. "Perhaps we will see you again . . . soon perhaps."

I paused outside, reassured by the cold breath of the sea blowing across the cliff tops; reassured by the blue canopy of the sky and the sun, hanging like a bright golden blob high against it; reassured by the curious wail of the gulls wheeling and darting over head.

I turned and hurried up the path to where the track to Trevilley started. A large granite rock sprawled by the path just by the outcrop known as Pendenick Point.

A small figure sat atop it, knees drawn up to chin, arms folded around them, gazing at me with those large sea-faded eyes. God knows how the boy had contrived to reach the spot ahead of me.

My step faltered as I approached.

I forced my troubled gaze to meet his and found myself shivering slightly.

"Dewheles, tasyk!" he whispered softly, his breath like a sigh upon the breeze.

"What's that?" I frowned.

"Dewheles!"

Then the boy was gone, scampering back to the cottage.

I hesitated a moment before hurrying on towards Trevilley. The strange words of the boy burned in my mind. I recognised them as the old Cornish language but that was all. I had no knowledge of it. After a while I paused and noted them down—phonetically—in my pocket diary. Then I pressed on, determined to pick up the threads of my interrupted holiday, determined to drive the unquiet night from my mind. Yet I could not. The memory haunted me, even after I returned home.

It was some months later, while staying with a friend at Cambridge, that I found an opportunity to obtain a translation to the Cornish words which the boy had uttered. My friend had invited a fellow don to dinner who was a lecturer in Celtic studies and had a working knowledge of the language. I passed him my phonetics and he recognised them without difficulty.

"Dewheles!" he muttered. "Well, that is the simple command—'come back!' And as for *tasyk* . . . *tas* means father and *tasyk* would be the more familiar form, 'daddy' for example. 'Come back, Daddy.' That's an odd phrase to pick up."

I found myself shivering with a sudden cold.

The memory of the night returned. Had Sobey Trevossow lived again through my body? Had the child recognised the spirit of his father in me? Such things were impossible! Yet Sobey Trevossow loved life; wanted to live still . . . to live again through me!

I have come to avoid solemn-faced boys who stare at me with eyes the colour of grey, lonely seas; children with cadaver-pale faces and hair the colour of bleached corn; children who gaze in silent judgement as if penetrating my innermost secret thoughts. They make me ill-at-ease. Their presence forces me to recall things I have no wish to. They disturb me.

The years have passed, but with each succeeding year, especially at the time of the anniversary of Sobey Trevossow's death and my visit to Gwennol Cottage, I have this feeling of some alien force entering my mind, drawing me back to Trevilley, to that lonesome cottage high on the granite ramparts. Sobey Trevossow wants to live again. And each year I hear the soft whispering of the boy's voice.

"Dewheles, tasyk! Dewheles!"

"Come back, Father! Come back!"

Only this morning I started from my troubled sleep crying: *"Y-fynnaf dos! Y-fynnaf dos!"*

And I, I—who know no words of the ancient tongue—know that I am promising to return . . . to return . . .

MANNY AGONISTES

James Kisner

I can't think why, but there seem to be more horror writers in Indiana than fleas on a vampire bat's back. Jim Kisner is another Hoosier, a protégé of William E. Wilson, who encouraged him to write his first horror novel, *Nero's Vice,* which won immediate acclaim from *The New York Times Book Review.* Since then, Jim has written *Slice of Life* and *Strands* and short stories for *Grue* and *Dementia* magazines, as well as Jerry Williamson's *Masques* anthology. Jim is an instructor for Writer's Digest School and contributes a regular column on horror to *Mystery Scene* magazine. "Manny Agonistes" is a fine example of the am-I-awake? quality that Jim's stories evoke so vividly.

The woman stared at him with strange, almost hostile, curiosity, as if she had never seen a naked old man before. It was the most interest he had seen in a woman's eyes in many years. He looked away. He could still feel her gaze crawling over his skin, probing at him like a nasty child. He tried to put her out of his mind by shutting his eyes tight and crawling into the void that always seemed to be waiting for him, always there for him to take refuge.

The blackness cleared away instantly as he remembered a sight from his youth, from the summer of 1905, when he had glimpsed a flower in such a perfect moment of beauty that its image had persisted in his memory all these years as if it were a snapshot. Or a particularly well wrought painting.

He had tried to capture its essence on paper, but his limited palette was not equal to the task of committing nature to such a two-dimensional medium. The colors turned harsh and muddy under his brush, as if he were painting the future of the flower—its withered replica several days hence—not the flower as it was now, in this special moment, in this fleeting present. After a while, he ceased trying and instead painted the dull, dark gray building that was only a backdrop to the flower.

He opened his eyes briefly and glanced over at the woman. She was still staring at him. Why him, he wondered, when there were so many others to see? Why him, when there were so many others that needed her soft, caring eyes to assuage their suffering? Why single him out, above the rest?

He returned to the snapshot in his mind: the rose seen from a little distance, its delicate petals wrapping around a different reality, enfolding a simpler way of life, a life only half- remembered now, the details blurred by time's unseemly pace.

A strange odor drifted by. Pain gnawed at the base of his spine. He had been standing too long. What was all the waiting for anyhow? What did it prove? Surely, it would make no difference if things were to move along just a bit more quickly.

Impatient, even now. Impatient for the end.

The rose petals swirled suddenly and the snapshot became animated. The fragile pink laminae of the flower spun and smeared to become a single blotch of color on something alive, not something exhumed from memory.

The children, he thought. *The children know me for what I am. What am I?*

He realized his eyes were open again, fixed on the woman who was staring at him. No, it was more specific than that; he was watching her left breast. It was alive, yet not alive, unpurposeful now, perhaps even unwanted. She was not a young woman, somewhere between forty and fifty, and a bit fat in the middle. She was not really that unpleasant to look at, even in contrast with the younger women, whose trivial natures were always so unappealing, even when he himself had been young.

The intensity of her staring increased, though there was nothing in her eyes that denied him looking at her.

Did she perhaps know him? Should he know her? Was she really staring at him, after all? Some of the details of her face were so indistinct. Her hair was an orange blur, her lips a pink smudge.

Full lips, blood-full, full of blood, ready to burst.

Why had they taken his glasses? With glasses, he might be able to tell who she was.

Should he yell at her? Call out, "I am Emanuel . . . ! Do you know me? Do I know you?"

Something flashed behind his eyes. A fleeting glimpse of—what? No! For an instant it seemed he was behind *her* eyes, inside her head, looking out—at himself. But that was impossible. It had to be a weird sort of temporary insanity.

He shouldn't call out then. Besides, the people who took his glasses wouldn't like it. Yet he yearned to get closer to her. Chat. Say harmless sexual things. Yes, that would be nice after so many years without female companionship. A man needed . . .

Stop it! Emanuel told himself.

Sometimes the mind's perversities were impossible to control, even with prayer. You found yourself contemplating the most vile and disgusting things, even in synagogue, when you were supposed to be in a near holy state, not a perverted one.

Was there forgiveness for that? For the strange mental caprices human beings were apt to experience—for the unbidden dark thoughts that invaded the chaste soul?

But am I chaste?

Now his senses veered off to a different kind of perversity—directed at his own person—by twisting the pain in his back out of proportion, raising it from a dull ache to a sharp edge slicing through his spine; he imagined it was what a scalpel felt like if there were no anesthetic.

The children did know him. So did the others—the old, the women, the dark men watching them all. But who—who was he? What did they know about him that he did not know himself?

Am I chaste?

He knew the slicing pain wasn't real. Couldn't be. It was only because the long waiting was amplifying every sensation, and he had so little patience now he was unable to endure even the most minor discomforts.

Impatient for the end.

God! When would it be over?

Why? Why did they regard him so—when he had done nothing wrong? *Nothing*. Ever.

He tried to block the pain out of his awareness by concentrating on other sensations: the close smell of the others, the warmth of their bodies, the whispered undercurrents of fear and dread that brought a twisted, wan kind of excitement to the moment.

Despite the cold dread urgency of the waiting, he had to admit the press of people was not altogether unpleasant. In fifty-seven years of life, Emanuel had normally shunned people, avoiding physical contact of any kind whenever possible. Now that he was naked and compelled to stand for endless hours with other naked people, he wondered why he had always been so reticent to touch.

There were so many children in the line.

He thought of the children then, not just those around him, but others, millions of them, their small frail faces watching and waiting. It was as if he could see them all in his mind, from a vantage point high above them, as if he were sailing over them like some dark god.

His own childhood suddenly seemed a brief cruel joke, a time in which there was only toil and hatred and—

When another man brushed against him with cool, silently uncommunicative flesh barely contacting his own slack skin, there was a tiny burst of energy between them, like electricity. It lingered a few seconds, even after the involuntary flinching of himself and the other man, who had touched him only by accident—not wanting to, wanting really to keep his distance, despite the impossibility of doing so under the crowded conditions.

Emanuel wished secretly there was more of that—just touching. It was what he missed the most in life, after all. It was the single ingredient that might have made a difference. And now . . .

The pain radiated savagely through his nervous system, knives cutting deep and deeper, severing parts that would never mend. Then the awful racking pain subsided abruptly—so abruptly it seemed to him he might have died.

Might as well, he thought. *Nothing left anyhow*. Except the certainty of more pain, more suffering. More hell. He looked down at his pale, pudgy body with its toneless muscles and miscellaneous scars. No wonder that woman kept staring at him—he was the ugliest of the lot!

Was she still watching?

She was.

So were the children.

The two lines were beginning to converge, forcing the men and women to come together. These people—they who had taken his glasses, and stripped all of them, men and women, and forced them out into this vast concrete field—they had no sense of modesty or decorum, and no concern for the feelings of others.

The woman was only a few feet away now, and he could peer directly into her eyes. What he saw chilled him, as a feeling of evanescent recognition passed between them.

They knew each other completely in that brief exchange of glances; it was as if the intimacy nurtured over a lifetime of closeness were compressed into a few seconds.

But it was not an intimacy of warmth; it was a sharing of complex obscenities and ugly passions, of monstrous deeds and perverted acts—beyond the boundaries of common human lust, beyond anything a tired old man or even the most knowing woman could envision.

There had been a time with whores. There had been a time when flesh was bought and sold, and it was nothing like this, nothing at all.

He and the woman, the woman and he, Emanuel, shared the truth they had both been ignoring.

Now Emanuel knew, and the woman knew.

But more than that, Emanuel remembered.

I did nothing wrong!

The smell of death drifted through the ranks of the naked men, the naked women, and the naked children.

Emanuel remembered he had been the woman.

They were all herded towards the squat gray building; as they approached it, other odors blew over them, stenches that clung to their damp, shivering skins like clammy meat.

Emanuel remembered some of the others too. He had been that frail man a few feet ahead of him. He had been that child clutched by its mother. And he had been a woman lying on a table somewhere as maniac doctors cut her apart alive in the name of a dogmatic, purely insane science that didn't exist.

He also remembered—now in vivid, minute detail—every miserable second of the last fifty-seven years, from the exact instant he was pulled from the womb to the present moment's excruciating awareness, a moment in which he was being jostled ever closer to those gaping doors where an end waited for all of them, except him.

He recalled the painful minutiae of the woman's life too—and the lives of the others—the lives he had lived so far.

Don't they understand? Don't they realize I did nothing wrong? Why can't I make them hear me? Why can't I speak what is in my mind?

That was the terror of it, after all, going through each successive, miserable existence, and never remembering until it was too late, never realizing it was happening again—until he was almost inside the building—at a moment when protests were useless. He could not tell them who he really was now. Nor could he explain how he was trapped inside a pathetic shell that was not really him at all! His voice could not form the words in any case. He could control none of it.

There was no meaningful way to resist; there was no meaning.

They were inside now, crowded within the familiar walls. The men in the uniforms shouted stupid, insignificant words at them—lies about what was going to happen to them which no one believed, especially Emanuel.

And he reflected on his future, as the gas seared his lungs and the men and the women and the children thrashed against him in the throes of death—knowing once more who he was, and knowing this would happen to him a million more times, and then millions more—as some urgent agency in the universe made him pay for each separate, miserable individual life he had caused to be taken.

Then, as his present awareness flickered and faded, the snapshot of the flower suddenly superimposed itself on his vision.

The rose . . .

He closed his eyes and reached for the vision, hoping it could sustain him through the last few seconds of this life, praying it would be enough to displace the awful pain—not of his body dying—but of knowing.

It wasn't the rose, after all, but a botched painting of it like something done by a madman, or worse.

Rough men with coarse voices were talking outside the building. He could barely hear them, but he knew what they were saying.

"Heil, Hitler!" they said.

And he wondered again why he had to endure the final mockery of his own name echoing through the void until the next time, the next last breath, the next—

The children knew why.

FAMILY MAN

Jeff Gelb

Without moonlighters, today's horror fiction would lose much of its richness and creative variety. Jeff Gelb is one of the very best of those writers who plow the furrow of "normal" work during the day, and return home to create horror and fantasy stories in their spare time. Days, Jeff sells advertising space for a leading music industry trade sheet, *Radio & Records;* his nights are spent writing horror tales for men's magazines. His first novel, *Specters,* was published by Bart Books early last year, and he has collaborated on an anthology of erotic horror entitled *Hot Blood.* A new-age music lover and EC comic freak (and who isn't!), Jeff lives in Redondo Beach, California, with his wife and son. His obvious love for his family is one of the strongest qualities of the story you are about to read.

After the funeral, I returned to the home Sarah and I had shared for the last twenty-six years. As soon as I entered the comfortable colonial house, I knew I'd have to move. Sarah's presence was everywhere. She'd decorated the whole thing, and spent hours each week keeping it spotless. Whenever I smelled Comet, or Lysol, or furniture polish, I was immediately reminded of her.

And right then, that was something I didn't want. I mean, don't get me wrong—I loved my wife, always have. She and I went back a long way—to high school, in fact, where she was the homecoming queen and I was the class president. It was pretty stereotypical, but somehow it worked. It worked even though we married two months before I was drafted into the Big War. It worked even though we had to live with my folks for the first three years of our marriage, in the attic of a cramped little dump on the wrong side of town, till I got settled in at Kodak. It worked even though our kid, Jerry, was a mistake who almost miscarried during a particularly rough pregnancy that kept Sarah off her feet most of the time. After that, we'd decided not to chance a second pregnancy, and I got real good with rubbers till Sarah went through menopause.

Yeah, we were pretty damn good together. Jerry, now thirty-four and living out on the West Coast with a wife and kid of his own, would tease us about still being on our honeymoon after forty years. He wasn't quite right, but he wasn't far from it. It really was a pretty solid relationship.

Even when I'd chosen early retirement from Kodak, finally sick to death of the bureaucracy and the politics, with no real idea of what I wanted to do next, she was right there for me. Sarah urged me into my "second career" as an accounting teacher and tutor out at the community college.

Hey, it was no one-way street. Throughout our life together, I was the breadwinner, putting food on the table and putting Jerry through college.

The first time they found cancer, I drove her to chemo every day and then made dinner every night. I always was a better cook than she, anyway, though I never told her that.

The second time they found cancer, I visited her twice a day in the hospital. No matter how hard it got to watch her waste away, losing weight and strength and the will to live, I was there.

But now she was gone, and our beautiful house seemed like it was closing in on me. Funny—in fifty-nine years, I never realized I was claustrophobic. But now I could hardly breathe in there. Although it was late fall and already in the thirties, I had to open all the windows to let in the sweet, fresh air, and to let out the stuffy aromas of cleansers. It kind of felt like I was setting her soul free, to soar wherever souls soar after they leave their fragile human shells.

Wherever Sarah was now, I hoped she was happier than I was. I just had to get out of that house, had to get out of town, in fact. Back at the funeral, Jerry had invited me back to Los Angeles to spend some time with his family, and truth to tell, it was a pretty appealing invitation. Sarah and I had visited Jer once a year every year since his radio career had taken him from Rochester to Southern California some dozen years ago. We'd come to love the area, for its proximity to the ocean and its great climate. In fact, last time Sarah and I were out there, we'd taken a semi-serious look at some houses in Santa Monica, thinking of resettling. But the prices were outrageous, especially for a couple on a limited income.

By the time Jer got back to the house, I'd already packed a bag. We left for California the next day and I knew the moment I stepped off the plane and breathed the salty air that I was going to move out there for good. It was the right thing to do: fresh start, close to Jerry. Sarah would have approved.

Funny thing: I'd just paid the last monthly mortgage bill not more than four months ago, and now that I owned the house free and clear, I was selling it. Damn thing sold in a jiffy, too. Nice houses in nice neighborhoods like ours were being snapped up by the baby boomers.

I made an incredible profit on the house. When I looked at the check, I almost started crying. I mean, back in '59, when we'd moved there, it had taken all of my savings to come up with the down payment on a place that cost 25 G's. Now here was this handsome lawyer plunking down 40 percent of $85,000 without even blinking. I wished Sarah were there to spend the money with me. I felt guilty that we'd never taken the trip to Israel she'd always dreamed of.

I promised Jer and his wife, Hope, that I would only stay with them till I learned my way around and bought a car (I'd sold the one back in Rochester, along with just about all my possessions—it was time for a clean sweep). They were real understanding, but the baby woke me up every morning by 6:30 with his wailing, and I felt like I was just getting in their way in the kitchen or the bathroom. Finally I admitted to myself that their house was too small for three adults, so I kicked myself in the butt, bought a little Toyota Corolla and started looking for a house to call my own.

Jesus, the housing is expensive out here! I had this fantasy that the money I'd made off my house in Rochester would pay for a home out here and maybe even leave me a little nest egg. Boy, was I wrong. It took me about two days to stop looking at homes altogether and switch my thinking to condos. But my heart wasn't in it. After a lifetime of using gardening and lawn-mowing as therapy and exercise, living in a glorified apartment with a Japanese gardener wasn't my style.

I was pretty confused, I have to admit, and more than a little depressed. I was really missing Sarah—I mean Christ, you don't forget forty years in forty days. Jerry understood—I could see it in his eyes. But there's only so much an offspring can do to replace a wife. And he had his own problems, with money and a career he didn't like but felt trapped in. I probably felt as sorry for him as he did for me.

It was a scorcher of a winter's day in January (fortunately, I had retained enough of a sense of humor to appreciate the irony of that thought after a lifetime spent shoveling snow out of my driveway in Rochester). I was headed for UCLA to look into tutoring positions when I got caught in one of those quintessential Southern California freeway traffic jams, where you never see the accident or stalled vehicle that caused the logjam, but you're trapped in it nonetheless for hours on end. I got sick of breathing in exhaust fumes so I took an early exit.

I knew I'd get lost negotiating surface streets but anything was better than that freeway. So I attempted to fake my way up to Westwood. It didn't take but five minutes to find myself in an area of town I'd never traversed before. Kinda nice, too, with older homes that had been well kept. There were even trees, for God's sake, though these trees kept their leaves even in the dead of California winter, you should pardon the expression.

I took to driving up and down these streets I'd never seen before, allowing myself to reminisce about similar-looking streets on which I'd grown up back in Rochester. Finally I looked at my watch and figured I'd better get on to Westwood if I wanted to talk to anyone about getting work. And that's when I saw it.

The house sat by itself, on a big corner lot, sharing the space with a lamppost and a ''Dead End'' sign. Behind it was one of those bizarre oil rigs you see all the time in California. State-owned property, I guessed. The house itself was colonial, kind of like the home I'd recently sold. That's what caught my eye. That, and the hand-painted ''For Sale'' sign that stood in the tall grass of the front lawn. That lawn needed tending, I thought with a smile. My fingers itched for a lawn mower and a pair of shears.

On impulse, I parked in the driveway and strode up to the front door. As I awaited an answer to my knocking, I looked up the street. Quiet neighborhood, all right. Probably full of UCLA professors, undoubtedly way out of my price range.

A young girl, maybe fourteen, answered the door. Pretty as a picture, too, with delicate features and long blond hair. She looked like she could afford to spend a little more time in the sun. Maybe she'd been ill.

''Uh . . . hi,'' I started sheepishly. ''Saw the sign out front,'' I pointed.

''You want to talk to Irv,'' she enthused, opening the screen door and pulling me inside the house.

''Irv's your father?'' I asked as I looked around. It was a beautifully furnished place, with lots of warm colors and little touches that were unmistakenly feminine. Suddenly my heart ached for Sarah.

''You like my new dress?'' she asked, twirling around so I could admire the new outfit, something long and flowing and cottony. ''Irv bought it for me.''

''Very nice,'' I smiled. Cute kid, I thought, but I was a little surprised she'd let a stranger into the house. ''Uh . . . is Irv . . . is your father home?'' I asked.

The girl turned, smiling, and yelled up the carpeted staircase. ''Irv! Company!'' She turned back to me, obviously happy for the attention. ''Do you think the boys would like this dress?''

I gave it the once-over. ''I'm not exactly up on the latest styles, but I think it's quite lovely. And so are you. What's your name?''

She blushed sweetly. ''Becky,'' she giggled, and ran upstairs. Still at that shy age, I figured, just before she realizes how pretty she really is and then starts setting her traps to catch all the cutest, richest kids in town. I smiled and for a moment wished that Sarah and I had tried a second pregnancy. It would have been nice to birth a daughter as sweet as this girl.

I peeked beyond the living room and saw a well-appointed kitchen, complete with dishwasher and microwave (never used one myself, but you're never too old to learn).

I heard footsteps tromping down the stairs and turned to see a boy of not more than ten, robot toy in hand, running to meet me.

''Well, you're sure not Irv,'' I said, and met his outstretched hand.

He gave me a surprisingly hearty handshake. He reminded me a bit of myself at his age, except for the glasses.

"I'm Robert, how do you do. Irv's shaving. You here to see the house?"

"Sure am, Robert. It looks nice from here."

He held out his toy robot. "You want to play?"

I laughed, which felt great. I realized I hadn't laughed in over two months. "Maybe later." His face turned sour. These kids were sure starved for attention, I thought.

He said, "You like libraries?"

"Libraries?" I shrugged. "Haven't been in one in years."

He shook his head, took my hand in his and guided me through the living room to a room full of bookshelves, all of them stuffed with books. A leather armchair faced the stone fireplace that dominated one wall. It was a very masculine, very warm room. I loved it immediately.

In fact, I loved that whole house, I realized as I stood there waiting for the mysterious missing Irv. I felt a tinge of depression as I guessed that the place was surely way beyond my price range.

"Maybe I'd better come back," I offered as I started to back out of the room.

I detected a subtle aroma of lilacs, which instantly made me long for Rochester. And then she entered the room.

"Please don't leave," she said. She was obviously the younger girl's mother, with the same ivory, unlined skin and delicate features. I felt my heart flutter, and felt kind of embarrassed.

"Don't tell me you're Irv," I joked.

She laughed and shook her head, and I noticed the soft light from a window glinting off her long golden hair. She was really stunningly attractive for her age—which was maybe forty.

"I'm Barbara. Irv's coming any minute now. He's . . ."

"Shaving, I know. Listen, I hate to barge in on you people. I was just admiring the house and thought I could take a peek. It's really very nice."

"Hi there!"

I must have jumped visibly, because I heard the little boy laugh. I turned toward the voice.

"Irv?"

"That's me!" He held out his hand and I took it, almost recoiling.

His hand was as cold and slimy as a dead fish, his grasp not nearly as strong as the boy's had been. He wiped perspiration from his forehead. "Here about the house?"

"Well, yes, I am. Though, to be honest, I doubt I could afford it."

"Oh, you'd be surprised. Actually, it's been on the market awhile and no one's bit.

"Let me show you the rest of the house," Irv offered, perhaps a bit too enthusiastically. Nevertheless, I was curious, so I followed him, somewhat reluctant to leave his radiant wife behind. They seemed so full of life, while Irv was . . . well, not exactly Mr. Excitement, let's say.

The house, though, that was something else again. For starters, it was gigantic: three bedrooms, the kids' rooms full of toys and pop star posters, and the master bedroom dominated by a huge water bed (funny, Irv didn't seem the type). Three bathrooms, a full-sized dining room, fully equipped laundry room. Even a basement, which I understood to be a rarity in a California home.

After the tour, Irv brought me back to the living room, where the kids were playing checkers while their mother was absorbed in her knitting. It was the sort of family scene that tugged at my heart. I guess I was lonelier than I realized.

They all looked up at me and smiled as I entered the room with Irv.

"Well," the woman asked, her bright white teeth shining, "do you like it?"

"Are you gonna buy it?" the boy asked excitedly.

"Well, I . . . it's a little big. I'm a widower, you see."

The woman looked as if she were about to cry. "I'm so sorry," she offered. And I knew she really was. I looked at Irv. What the hell did such a classy woman see in this shlub, I wondered.

"It's only two thousand square feet," Irv said, interrupting my thoughts. "Looks bigger than it is."

"Well . . ." I was uncomfortable talking money in front of the man's family, but obviously he wasn't.

"Sixty-nine five."

"I beg your pardon?" I asked.

"Sixty-nine five," Irv repeated. "That's what I'm asking."

I shook my head. I was about to say that was a steal but decided real fast to keep my mouth shut. I did manage, "That's quite reasonable, Irv. What's wrong? Got termites?"

Irv stole a quick glance at Barbara before answering. "God, no! Got the inspection forms right here in the desk," he said as he ran to an antique rolltop in one corner of the room. I smiled at Irv's wife while he retrieved the papers. I examined them and found he was right: the place had been checked out just last month, and there were no termites.

"I have to admit I'm interested," I said. The young boy cheered, and his mother shushed him. "Very interested," I added, thinking about how I could buy the place with cash and still have that nest egg I'd dreamed of. This whole thing was like a dream, I thought as I stood there in Irv's house.

"Would you mind," I asked, "telling me just why you're selling?"

Irv got real quiet for a moment, and I was suddenly scared that he was going to say that he had the Bic C or some other dread disease. I felt like a damned fool for prying.

Finally he said, "I . . . I'm getting a divorce." He looked at his beautiful wife and children. "Guess you could say I'm just not a family man."

I felt terribly embarrassed for Irv and his family. "I'm very sorry I asked," I stammered, suddenly wanting to get out of there very badly, and back into the dying sunlight of the late afternoon.

"I'll have to think about it," I said as I backed toward the door, nearly tripping over a throw rug.

"Sixty-five five," Irv said.

I almost laughed. "Believe me," I said, "it's not the price. I just . . . want to think it over, that's all."

Irv looked like he'd just eaten a raw onion. "I . . . have to be out of here by the end of the month. Going back home, to Idaho."

"I see," I said, not really aware of what I was saying. I was looking into Barbara's eyes, and seeing a lot of pain there. I guess it had really been a rotten marriage. I wondered where she and the kids would move, once they'd gotten their settlement.

"Well," I said finally, "I'll get in touch."

Irv scribbled his name and phone number on a slip of paper, thought for a moment, then scrawled something else and handed it to me. "Call me," he said. "Please."

"Right," I answered, waving at the kids, who waved back, their faces brave fronts indeed. Obviously the whole family was going through hell.

I gazed one more time at the beautiful woman, trying to cement her features in my memory, knowing I'd never see her again. She'd move to Idaho or Nebraska or Bakersfield and marry some country bumpkin farmer who'd show her off to his friends like she was a prize cow. It was all terribly sad.

In my car, I looked at the paper Irv had given me. On the other side of the page with his name and number, he'd written: "Fifty-five five."

Jesus.

. . .

A few days went by and I found I couldn't get the house, or its sad inhabitants, off my mind. I finally figured I'd be doing everyone a favor by buying the place. Old Irv could go back to Idaho and grow roots like a potato, and the rest of his family could get a fresh start someplace else. So I called a realtor and had him look into the place. I wasn't too surprised to find out the reason the house hadn't sold before: a fire in its electrical wiring had burned the place to the ground ten years ago. It had been rebuilt by the tenant who sold it to Irv, who, surprisingly, had only lived there for a few months before putting the place on the market. Maybe there was still something wrong with the wiring, or maybe the plumbing was ready to go.

I had the realtor hire some guys to give the house the once-over, and when they came back with their okays, I revisited Irv with my checkbook. He was surprised but delighted to see me again. The guy seemed really stressed out; he looked like he hadn't slept since my last visit.

Irv hovered over me like a pesky fly while I signed the check and the papers, and I thought he was going to kiss me as I left, he was so jubilant. I'd been hoping to catch his family to wish them well, but Irv explained they'd gone into town to do some shopping.

On my way out, Irv's realtor confided that his client "wasn't well," and he pointed to the side of his head, making circles. No kidding, I thought.

But Irv's mental health wasn't my concern. I looked back at the house—at my house, or what would be my house in a week, after Irv and his family had moved out. Had I made the right move? Sarah had always claimed I worried too much, that I should go more by instinct. I shrugged. Okay, Sarah, I thought—this one's for you.

. . .

Jer wanted to come with me the day I moved in, but I nixed that idea. I guess I wanted to be alone with my thoughts as I started a new life in my new house. So I parked alone in the driveway and sat there for a while, giving the house the once-over. I smiled, thinking that it really was an exceptional buy. Jer had nearly plutzed when I told him how much I'd paid for the place—he'd paid nearly double for his small three-bedroom place almost ten years ago.

I stood on the front porch awhile, getting the feel of the place. I looked around. The front lawn was in desperate need of attention by now, or the neighbors were bound to start bitching. I decided to run out and buy a lawn mower tomorrow.

I turned the key and let myself in. Surprisingly, the place still smelled of lilacs. I liked the delicate aroma and hoped it would last awhile—it would make the big place seem a little less lonely. I looked around the living room. Was I crazy to have purchased a place so big?

I walked through each room of the house like I was discovering it for the first time. And with each step, I felt better about the purchase. It really was too big for me, but what the hell. If I found a tutoring job, I'd hire a housekeeper for one day a week. Jer told me that's what everyone in California does. Kind of made me wonder who cleans the housekeepers' houses.

I took my time walking up the stairs, admiring the finish on the wooden banister. I had to admit, whoever'd rebuilt this place had done a fine job.

I heard a noise from one of the bedrooms. I was about to run like hell to a neighbor's house and call the police when the little boy, Robert, stepped out of his bedroom, holding a comic book. He was beaming.

''Hi!'' he greeted me innocently.

''Hi,'' I stammered. ''What . . . what are you doing here? I mean, where's Irv?''

''Oh, he moved out,'' Becky said as she joined her brother in the hallway. She had one of those Walkmans, and I could hear some sort of rock music coming from its tiny earphones on either side of that pretty head.

''I don't understand,'' I admitted. The two kids looked at one another somewhat nervously.

''Maybe you better call Mom,'' Robert said. Becky nodded, smiled at me and ran down the hall to the master bedroom, where she knocked at the door. A second later it opened and her mother appeared.

''Well, hello,'' I said, admittedly happy to have the chance to see

Barbara again even if I had no idea why she was here. Then I had a terrible thought.

"Irv did tell you," I said slowly, "that I'd bought the place, didn't he?"

She smiled and nodded, but offered no other response.

I laughed nervously. "Well, I hate to be blunt, but how come you and the children are still here?"

Barbara advanced to my side, taking one of my hands in hers. They were freezing cold. "Would you like some tea? Or a beer, perhaps?"

"Not really."

"Well, let's go downstairs where we can all be comfortable."

"But . . ." Before I could protest further, the kids were dragging at me, laughing as they pulled me along and down the stairs. Somehow I couldn't be angry with any of them, but I was certainly confused.

Barbara and her kids sat together, backs to one wall, while I sat on the floor against the opposite wall. No one spoke—it was all very uncomfortable.

She obviously didn't know what to say, and I felt terrible for her. "Do you need more time," I started, "to get packed up? Because that's fine with me. I'll just come back tomorrow . . . or next week. Whatever," I shrugged.

"We don't really have anywhere else to go," she finally said.

I gulped. "Irv didn't skip town with all the money, did he?"

She laughed and shook her head. There was that subtle lilac aroma again. For an instant, I wondered if I was falling in love with this woman, then I banished the thought. After all, she was just divorced days ago.

"We're kind of stuck here," she said softly.

"Well, I'd be happy to help," I offered. "Do you need someone to help you find a new place?"

She shook her pretty head. "We can't resettle," she said. I noticed the kids had stopped playing and were watching us intently.

I was starting to lose my cool. "Well, I'm sympathetic, but you have to understand, you can't live here . . ."

"Well, we don't really live here," Barbara said, the hint of a smile on her face.

Was this whole family batty? My mouth felt as dry as the skin of a lizard lounging on a desert rock in the noonday sun. "I think I will take you up on that offer for a beer," I said.

Robert bounded to his feet and ran through the kitchen door. I mean to say, he ran *through* the damned thing, like one of those haunted house movies . . .

I looked at Barbara, really looked at her, like a blind man suddenly given the gift of sight. I looked at her alabaster skin, remembered her cold touch.

I must have turned as white as a . . . as a sheet, because the next instant, Barbara floated to my side.

"I'm sorry," she said. "Robert's still young. He tends to . . . forget his manners at times."

Robert came bounding back into the room, using the hallway this time, thank God, beer in hand. I took it from him gingerly and then downed the thing in an instant.

"I'm beginning to understand Irv a little better," I muttered.

Barbara smiled and said, "Irv tried, he really did. He bought us nice clothes and gifts. But he'd never been married before and I'm afraid we were, in the end, a bit much for him."

"Like he said," I recalled aloud, "he isn't a family man."

By now the kids had floated to my side, the three of them forming a semicircle around me. Robert bobbed up and down in the air excitedly.

"Are you?" Barbara asked.

"Am I what?"

"A family man."

I sat back, closed my eyes and thought of the fire that had gutted the house. The realtor never told me a mother and her two children had been killed in it. Probably figured I'd think the house was jinxed or something.

"Mister?" I heard Robert's voice as he tugged at my shirt. "Are you a family man?"

I smiled as I considered my situation. It wasn't exactly perfect but it might have been worse.

I opened my eyes and said, "I could be."

A TOWPATH TALE

Giles Gordon

Apart from being one of London's most outspoken literary agents, Giles Gordon is also a mesmerizing writer of nightmarish short stories. He has published six novels, three collections of short stories, and edited numerous anthologies, including *A Book of Contemporary Nightmares.* He was briefly the theater critic of the *London Daily News.* As an agent, his clients include Peter Ackroyd, Fay Weldon, Michael Moorcock, and Barry Unsworth. Married with three children, he lives in Chalk Farm, London. "A Towpath Tale" is one of the darkest and most sophisticated stories in this collection, and should not be read by anyone whose marriage hasn't been going too well lately . . .

This was his dream.

He was walking along the towpath of the canal with his wife. Their dog, Mary, named after his mother, mooched on ahead of them. She was a bitch, the dog. A white boxer. The wife was another matter. They did not speak, to each other or to the bitch; less because they were wrapped in their own thoughts, contemplating mortality or immortality, than that they had nothing to say to one another. They had exhausted conversation, subject matter, their totality of knowledge, both information and opinion. Neither sparked excitement off the other, stimulated in any way. Which is not to suggest that had either been exposed to another—a third party, a new person; new to him or to her—knowledge, information *and* opinion might not have returned with a vengeance. With the emphasis, maybe, on vengeance. It wasn't that they had been married for ever, just that it seemed that way. Neither, in truth, could properly remember life—or death—without the other; and when they went to weddings these days, and they'd been to two in the last three months (for years before they'd been to none, either not invited or no one getting married, no one they knew or who wanted to invite them; not that they were more blighted than most couples, at least many), the brides wore white, above and below, and the grooms white shirts, dazzlingly so. Albeit both couples were embarking upon second marriages, that was the surprise, the *energy;* that, more than the commitment. Otherwise there were ferocious, pinched, sardonic funerals—almost always almost late for the distant crematorium, just making it—and subfusc memorial services in churches in the suburbs where the vicar tended to know, at least recall, more about the deceased than most members of the congregation did.

They were together, he and his wife, because they always had been, together.

That was how it seemed.

That was how it was.

This, as I said, was his dream. *His,* not hers. Hers she did not divulge. To him, at any rate.

They were walking along the canal towpath, between Camden lock—the hideous, tacky, bejeaned and bearded market, fuzz lacking Fuzz, stallholders with vacuous pasts, the future next weekend—and Little Venice. Everybody and everything reeked of the sickening, acrid aroma of fast food fat used for days, weeks too long; unfrozen hamburgers, walking disease traps.

Others on the towpath, coming towards them, were merrily dressed as if for a carnival. Some of them, anyway. Those in groups. Those on their own looked melancholy, muttered to themselves. At least their lips moved about, mumbled; not that any words were heard, made out. The gaily garbed people laughed and talked loudly, moved their limbs loosely, floppily. Their mouths were open as if to show off their perfect teeth, their gleaming, incisive quality. It was not that the sound of their laughter disturbed the nipped, concentrated air; it was the mouths open that was horrific, the faces smiling as if to hold reality, everyday existence, at a distance.

They came towards them, these laughing people brightly caparisoned, with children in tow, animals too. The animals were dogs, all dogs; but a different breed for every animal. There were lions to the left, and zebras and gazelle. To the right, a baby elephant, walking between two keepers. The elephant was round like the letter O, its body covered in down. A fluffy elephant. Exotic birds preened themselves, cavorted or looked bored, in Lord Snowdon's executive toy aviary. Humans—humanoids, anyway—moved listlessly about the zoo, a species less exotic than those in captivity.

They walked, in his dream, along the towpath. From point A to point B.

It could have been anywhere yet had this identification, of the zoo, the canal.

People came towards them, mostly in groups. Laughing. No sound, no sound in the dream, but laughing.

One person, a thin man in jeans, black tee-shirt, passed them from behind, didn't look at them, or to left or to right. He was in a hurry, an obsessive rush. Maybe he had somewhere to go, someone or something to see. Maybe he hadn't.

Charon plied the water, for a price, between Camden lock and Little Venice. For a fatuous fee he provided water-rides for the inquisitive or bored. The pleasure boats, long and thin and covered with glass, moved silently through the slick water, the idiot damned peering out through the glass, trapped for a time in their watery bell-jar, transported to their fate. They stared out, across the water, to the towpath, to the zoo; their mouths often open, gasping for air, somehow to grasp life, find a function. They spoke no words, either to those they were with—friends, relatives: what else is there?—or to the world outside; from which, by water and by glass, they were excluded.

The boat throbbed, trembled, stuttered soundlessly, absurdly on, gilding the dank water it glided through.

How she fell in he didn't know. He hadn't *thought* about it, contemplated it happening, made plans. He was, in a manner of speaking, content. What had happened had happened. It wasn't his *fault*. There was no morality about it, no right or wrong; not even a grey area, an ambiguity. On the other hand, on the other hand. No, none of that, no intellectual speculation, no judgement. One moment she was beside him, shrouded elegantly in her long black winter coat, thick black woollen tights, sullen blond hair; the next, in his dream, *I say in his dream,* she was in the water, the canal near Camden Town. A known locality, to him, to her. Near their home. The dream getting the detail right, topographically.

The oily water was not ruffled, not disturbed, distracted by her fall from grace; or if it was, it was by the boat, by passing Charon's load, the boatman and his pleasure cruise. But the boat had gone, and there was nobody else on the towpath, in either direction. And in the zoo only the silent, cut-out animals, pretending to eat. Everybody promenading on that October Sunday afternoon (was the dream *that* specific, on time and date and season?) had vanished, disappeared; as if they'd never been there. If they were photographed by a hidden lens it was in black and white, or sepia; certainly not colour.

She was in the water and somehow he did not realize it. He had not witnessed—let alone assisted, countenanced—her fall, seen or heard the monochrome, monotone splash, the breaking of the waters, disappearance into the womb. And therefore had not cried out, to the Sunday crowd, had not requested kind assistance, caused passers-by to run up dramatically, exercise their ludicrous confusing social concern. Throw her a rope, or a life-belt. Pull her out. By her weeping feet or her sucked waist, not her straggly, streaming hair. Lay her on her back. Don't crowd around. Let her breathe. Is there a medic in the stratosphere, or a vet in the zoo?

He was, then, on his own; with the dog, the bitch, Mary. Walking alone, by the canal. The Regent's Park houses framing the scene, and the railway above, an Inter City train sometimes but not often. In the churchyard the gardener burnt leaves. The scent of burning leaves. In the dream.

He stopped, on the towpath. Ahead of him, sitting on a bench, at right angles to the flow of the canal, were two men, faces bestubbled, besmeared, less by dirt than the living dead, dark bottles by their feet, one derelict with a not quite empty bottle in his fist not offering it to his fellow. Not that they were unconcerned by the woman in the canal, the man observing the water, the dog thinking it a game. The world was excluded from their sombre, forgotten vision.

He peered at the water, more disinterested than uninterested. Her handbag (he'd hardly realised she was holding one, had it with her on the walk) bobbed up, a touch of leather above the cold black water; then sank.

Did he speak in the dream?

"Throw me your handbag," he commanded, in a matter-of-fact voice, not raising it above talking level; not shouting, certainly not; not wanting to cause an exhibition, an incident. Propriety was all, or most.

Then, like the hand and arm triumphantly clutching, presenting Excalibur, she—from, presumably, the mud and grime and muck and filth of the bottom of the canal—hurled the handbag out at him. It landed, soggily, on the towpath; bleeding water. He bent down, excitedly, reached for it; his hands out and thrusting. His fingers touched, made contact. He opened the clasp. There was money in it, not much, not by what you need to survive today, but money. A fiver, a note, and two coins, pounds. Nothing else of any significance. Oh keys, a credit card, library ticket, a bill or two. A handkerchief. But no secret life. Nor birth certificate, nor death certificate. The marriage lines were elsewhere. I *tell* you, *this was a dream.*

The water was still, not even ruffled by wind; hardly a ripple.

Then there were people again, coming towards him.

The animals moved, in the zoo, and dogs. Mary the bitch barked, her tail, stump though it was, wagged. The bark was almost heard, a sound in sleep.

Two young canoeists, dipped in life jackets, paddled past, at dignified Sunday speed. "Lost something?" one called out to him as he stared at the water, as the boxer barked.

The other laughed. They both laughed. He didn't reply, didn't seem to hear.

Then the dog really did bark.

He woke up, from his dream. The dog barked in his dream, was barking as he awoke. The dog barked at the newspaper shoved through the letterbox, thrust there, insistently. News of mayhem and murder and political ineptitude.

He remembered his dream. Told it, later, to the woman beside him, his wife.

"You *would* be interested in the money," she said, laughing mildly, a dull hate in the voice. She thought him mean but he always thought himself generous.

"But there was only a fiver there. And two pounds, coins," he protested, self-righteously.

"That wouldn't worry you."

And she forgot. She didn't remember his dream. He'd told her, early in the morning a few days later, and she fed him into her undernourished nether quarters, an unnourishing snack. The bitch barked at the end of their bed, entered.

Some months later, a Sunday afternoon, autumn, the leaves russet coloured, the water glassy blue, tree branches fingers in the sky, scribbling for identity, they walked by the canal, on the towpath, somewhere between Camden lock and Little Venice, not that they ever went as far as the latter, as to do so meant leaving the towpath, treading the pavement for a while before going below again.

This was for real, this walk; no dream. Mary accompanied them. Mary was the excuse for the walk. She needed exercise. Mary the white boxer bitch was, really, the walk.

She, his wife, wore the coat she'd worn in the dream but he didn't think of that, it wasn't a connection he made. He wasn't, I insist, thinking of the dream. It wasn't at that time in his mind. He hadn't recalled it often, just once or twice. Well, twice. Two or three times.

The coat she'd been wearing in the dream. He couldn't call it, think of it as a nightmare because, in the morning, he hadn't woken up screaming, sweating, hadn't experienced a terrible time exorcising the visions of sleep. The content of the dream had seemed—if not a "good" idea at least a pragmatic one, a way of making sense of his existence, this mortal coil. A means, perhaps, to an end.

They walked on, without speaking; the dog ahead, snivelling and rooting.

He searched to left, to right. In front, behind. Up at the windows. There was, there seemed to be, no one around; in sight. He thrust himself towards her, with his shoulder gave her a tremendous push, butted like a goat at the top of her arm, her shoulder. He used, from a hitherto unexploited, untried angle, the full weight of his body as he did when with an axe he chopped recalcitrant logs, great thicknesses of trees. She was not, naturally, expecting the blow and easily toppled into the liquid, legs following head, her body stunned as it hit the water.

She didn't immediately go under, as he thought she would. Not that he'd thought, not *thought*. Then she began to come to, a bit of movement, a flutter, limbs disturbing the lurching, slopping water.

The dog stopped and watched, surprisingly didn't bark, didn't yelp; not then.

He no longer worried as to whether he was being watched, whether anyone was coming, had seen. He had gone so far. He leant down, stretched his hands into the water, pulled her feet towards him, dragged her in a little, a fraction, then with his full weight, a different fulcrum, held her down, thrust her down. He held her down and pushed her down and her heavy black coat contributed as ballast. She was dead, this was a drowning, an ending of life. And it had, to his bewilderment, been easy. And this was no dream, no dream.

He stared at the water, wanting her back. His wife. He knew he shouldn't have done it, whatever he *wanted*. And he hadn't particularly, especially wanted that.

Then he saw. The bag, her handbag, was coming up out of the dark. It was in her hand, clutched tight by her drowned, drowning fingers. Then the rest of her hand followed, and her arm, and he thought she would rise up to confront, accuse him, and that he wouldn't be able to face.

He was standing at the edge of the canal, on the towpath. He would topple in unless he took a grip, at once. The bag was projected towards him, quite definitely thrust at him. She wanted him to take it.

Didn't she?

But why?

He steadied himself, bent down, ever so nearly toppling in. He snatched it from her. There he was, holding her handbag, and she was in the water. There was, now, no sign of her hand, arm. Certainly no sign of the body, and the water there wasn't deep, not that deep.

Oddest of all, the bag wasn't wet. It was as if he'd torn it from her before pouring her into the canal, or that they'd fought and she'd failed to hold on to the bag. But that hadn't been how it happened, neither in real death nor in the dream.

Mary, the bitch, began to bark. She pawed at the ground, concrete edge of canal and towpath, earth footpath behind. She snarled and cried herself hoarse, baying at the place where the body went in. She made no attempt to plunge (and she was an energetic, ardent swimmer), rescue her, drag her out.

He knew that she'd seen, and he understood.

As to the handbag, he'd take it home. Of course he would. He'd open it there, remove the fiver and the two pound coins he knew he'd find.

Charon came round the corner, from the pleasure boat's berth in Camden lock. He'd unloaded one lot of passengers, commandeered another. There are different forms of death, more alternatives than ways of killing a man, or a woman.

The husband, widower, stood watching, and the boat came near enough to the bank to drag over her body and pull it along underneath, to a deeper part of the canal. The boat stuttered for a second as if it had snagged on a branch, or a tyre, then continued on its wasteful, meaningless cruise.

The body would be found the next day, or the day after.

That night, the bitch came to him. She breathed heavily, as if the experience had been anticipated for a long time. She opened herself to him, dripping, nuzzled and licked, whimpering the while, and he grew and grew, a man, a man again. He was joined with her, no snack but her essence, her essence become his. He came in the bitch and her tongue screamed in his mouth.

"Do not think these things," she barked. "Do not imagine them."

In the morning, he woke up alone. She was not beside him, breathing her normal deep sleep, a world away. Had she gone for an early swim, as sometimes she did but usually only in the summer?

He stretched over, to find his watch. It was time to shave and bathe.

Naked, he walked to the bathroom. Not a sound in the house.

She, his wife, was lying there, in a very full bath, almost overflowing, lying in the water, on her back, submerged. Drowned.

The worst thing was that her face was at peace, undisturbed.

He opened his mouth to scream, then heard the dog, the bitch, somewhere. Barking. In triumph.

MARS WILL HAVE BLOOD

Marc Laidlaw

I have always suspected that Marc Laidlaw has a secret yearning to write every horror, fantasy and science-fiction magazine single-handed. He has been writing, he tells me, for ever; his fiction has appeared in *Omni, Twilight Zone, Night Cry,* Bruce Sterling's *Mirrorshades: the Cyberpunk Anthology,* Dennis Etchison's *Cutting Edge,* and Terry Carr's *Best SF of the Year.* Marc once wrote comic-strip scripts for *Creepy* and *Vampirella* and seems to be embarrassed about this, although I can't think why. His first novel was *Dad's Nuke,* published in 1986; and he has just published *Neon Lotus,* a Tibetan science fantasy about . . . uh . . . a neon lotus. Marc lives in San Francisco with his wife Geraldine, and apart from writing everything else, he is a medical word processor. And photographer. And musician. And film buff. And—

"Too much ichor," said red-faced Jack Magnusson, scowling into a playbook. "The whole tragedy is sopping in it. Blood, blood, blood. No, it won't do for a student production. We're not educating little vampires here."

"That remains to be seen," said Nora Sherman, the English office head. She stared into Magnusson's round obsidian paperweight, which he had pushed to the center of the table. Little Mr. Dean's hand kept darting toward it and receding.

Magnusson, the chairman of Blackstone Intermediate School's Ethics Advisory Committee, threw the playbook at Steve Dean, who was sometimes mistaken for a student. Dean flinched but caught it.

"Well, Jack . . ."

"Speak up, Dean."

"Er, it is *Macbeth,* Jack, and it's on the reading list this year."

Magnusson drew himself up, spreading his halfback shoulders, running a hand through his thinning steel-wool hair. "That curriculum's always been trouble," he said, "but there's no use asking for more. What with the swear-word in *Catcher in the Rye* and the dead horse in *Red Sky at Morning* and the A.V. Department showing *Corpse Grinders* on Back-to-School Night, we're going to start losing constituents to other districts that don't have these problems."

Dean looked ready to cry into the pages of *Macbeth.* Nora Sherman grabbed the book from him and held it dangling by the spine.

She said, "Tirades aside, Jack, you'd better let the kids do Shakespeare this year or there'll be a rebellion. Birnham Wood will move at recess, with Neal Bay heading the insurrection. There's a lot of talent going to waste around here and the kids damn well know it."

Dean stared at her, dazed. "Well said, Nora."

"You stay out of this," she said.

"What do you want from me?" Magnusson asked her. "I can't approve this."

"Perhaps not as it is, but what if it were toned down?"

Magnusson reared back. "Cut out the blood? There'd be nothing left."

"No editing," she said. "We won't use the Shakespeare. We'll write our own version. Improvise. I've seen grade school kids do it with *The Wind in the Willows.* Once we get rid of the poetry, we're not stuck to the plot, and that gives the students considerable freedom. We can change the setting and period."

Magnusson got the book back. "Take it out of Scotland, you mean?"

"I've seen it done. *Romeo and Juliet* transplanted into the Stone Age, or onto Monster Beach. *A Midsummer Night's Dream* is the usual organ donor. Can you imagine it set in German-occupied France? Or in Boston during the Revolutionary War? One was set in Transylvania, but it wasn't exactly bloodless . . ." She trailed off, one metallic blue fingernail tracing the green line of an artery on the back of her hand.

"You could set it in Siberia or the outback," said Mr. Dean. He sat up and reached for the book, but Magnusson ignored him and held the captive copy spread masklike before his face. Dean dropped back into his seat and gazed into the paperweight.

"Or the Old West," he said, crossing his arms.

"Too messy, Dean," said Mrs. Sherman. "What I suggest is we give our actor-warriors weapons that won't be as sloppy as bullets and swords. Give them, say, ray-guns and send them off to . . . I don't know, Mars. Sure. Tie it in with the study groups reading *The Martian Chronicles*."

"Mars," said Magnusson, as if the planet were a jawbreaker that refused to dissolve on his tongue.

"With real Martian music," said Mr. Dean.

Mrs. Sherman caught and held his eyes. "I didn't say anything about that."

"No, I did," said Mr. Dean.

"We have to use the band this year," said Magnusson.

"Why?" she asked.

"Because he promised," said Mr. Dean. "We haven't had a musical in the last three years. *The Crucible, Man in the Moon Marigolds, Snake House* . . . The things these kids choose, I swear. They have the sense of humor of morticians. This year we're doing something lighter, a musical 'revue.' I think our own Sheri DuBose could come up with something appropriate in the way of music and songs for *Macbeth*."

"Oh my God," said Nora, sinking.

Magnusson hardly looked at her, though he was smiling with one side of his mouth. "That should keep the kids tame, yes."

"For that you'd need wild-animal tamers," said Mr. Dean. "At least it will keep them happy."

Mrs. Sherman seemed to come out of a coma. "Forget I ever mentioned *Macbeth*. Don't do it to that play. Not that silly girl's music . . ."

''Nora,'' said Mr. Magnusson, shaking his head at her and smiling as if he knew something she didn't. ''So pale. Are you well?''

''Seen Banquo's ghost?'' said Dean, with a chuckle.

''You're not being a very good sport,'' said Magnusson. ''We've all got what we wanted.''

She tightened her metallic-blue mouth, looked at both of them, then put out a hand and touched the copy of *Macbeth* as if to swear upon it. When she was perfectly still, she whispered, ''If you get Sheri DuBose, I get Ricardo Rivera.''

Mr. Dean jumped as if he had been grabbed; but before he could form a word or stop her, her hand shot out and touched the black paperweight in the center of the table.

''Ha!'' she said. ''Motion passed.''

Dean slumped back in his chair.

''All right,'' said Magnusson. ''Let's move on to athletics.''

. . .

Lunch bag in hand, Ricardo Rivera hurried across the quadrangle toward the crowd of twelve- and thirteen-year-old students that had gathered at the back of the auditorium by the stage door.

He was a small boy, green-eyed, with dark curly hair, fine-cut features, and a grin that some might call elfin. The grin was partly imaginary because at that moment he thought he was to be the next Macbeth.

At the edge of the group he asked Sheri DuBose if the cast list for *Macbeth's Martian Revue* had been posted, though it obviously hadn't.

''Not yet, Ricardo,'' she said. ''Mr. Dean wants me to write the songs, though.'' She smiled. ''I have it on good authority.''

'''Good authority,''' mimicked Bruce Vicks, pigging his nose at her with a finger. ''Sheri DuPug,'' he said.

Sheri snorted and turned away, forgetting about Ricardo.

'''If it were done when 'tis done,''' Ricardo said, ''then 'tis best it were done when it's best it were . . . now wait a minute.'' His audition piece was already sliding from memory.

''Here come de prez,'' somebody said.

Ricardo jumped to look over the heads of the others and saw a tall boy with longish sun-bleached hair, a sure and smiling freckled face, and the lopsided walk of a skateboarder.

Ricardo waved at him, "Hey, Neal, over here!"

Neal Bay joined the crowd, smiling at everyone.

"Good job, Neal," said Randy Keane, shaking Neal's hand. "You better remember your campaign promise for lots of movies."

"Won't forget," said Neal. "I've already got *The Red Balloon* on order."

Keane groaned and laughed. "That stinker?"

Ricardo pushed his way to Neal's side. "The list's not up yet."

"Duh," said Neal. "My brilliant campaign manager. I can see the list isn't up yet, dipstick. I don't know how I won with you on my side."

Ricardo ignored the insult and lowered his voice to a whisper. "I hear Cory gave you trouble yesterday."

"Trouble? Who told you that?"

"At student council."

"No trouble, except maybe for you. I just asked Cory about a few of the things you told me."

Ricardo stepped back. "I told you? Like what?"

"Oh, like how you said that Lisa Freuhoff told you Cory was fixing the elections."

"That's what Lisa said," said Ricardo, backing away but pointing at Neal. "I didn't say it was true."

"Yeah? And how she swore I'd be sorry if I won. She'd get even, you said. I never asked where you heard that one."

"Lisa said it," Ricardo said.

Neal crossed his arms, rolled his eyes, and smirked. "Yeah? Well, Cory and I are a team now."

"But she was your-your enemy!"

"We were never enemies. We always knew one of us would win, and the other would be vice-president. You just *wanted* us to be enemies."

Ricardo fell silent, trying to imagine what Neal meant.

"We've been good friends, Neal," he said. "You shouldn't just treat me like this now that you've won. You'll still see me around. Maybe you'll even get the part of Banquo. You did a great audition."

"Banquo?" Neal laughed. "I'm going to be Mister Macbeth, Junior."

"No way," said Ricardo. The idea was laughable, and he laughed.

Then he turned his tongue back to the more important issue. "Cory was always nasty to you. Remember that time in the cafeteria?"

"You shut up," Neal said, taking a step to hook his forefinger into the soft flesh and glands under Ricardo's jaw. The bigger boy grinned, and it was not the kind of smile that makes one comfortable.

Ricardo moaned until Neal let him slip free. There were tears in his eyes, and his voice didn't carry.

"Bet you don't even get Malcolm's part," he said. "Bet you don't even get to be a Murderer."

Neal started forward.

"It's a fight!"

A cry from the direction of the door interrupted them. Mr. Dean stepped outside, wincing at the sunlight and the students. He waved a sheet of ditto paper as if it were a pennant. Everyone cheered. He tacked it to the door and slipped back in before he could be trapped by the kids.

As Ricardo struggled forward, he dropped his lunch bag. He bent down, but before he could grab it a Hush Puppy squashed the sack, spilling the guts of a peanut butter and banana sandwich onto the asphalt. Rising, suddenly hungry, he heard someone say, "Awright! Macbeth for President!"

"No," Ricardo said in disbelief. "Oh, no."

President Bay appeared above him, looking down his long, straight nose. "Sorry, buddy, you're Banquo. Sorry for both of us, I mean. I'd just as soon not see you on that stage."

Ricardo felt his face scrunch up with anger. "Banquo," he said. "Banquo gets killed halfway through, then he's just a-a-a ghost. I wanted—"

"Don't be a wussy," Neal said.

"A wussy?" Ricardo said. His anger passed and he felt weak. "Neal, see if I was second choice."

"You dummy, you're not even my understudy. Be glad you got anything."

"But you can't do it, Neal, you don't have the time. You're already president, isn't that enough?"

"President no thanks to you, when all you did was tell me lies about Cory Fordyce, which is pretty screwed considering how you've got the hots for her."

Around them, kids were staring and starting to laugh. Some even looked frightened in a tentative, eager way.

"The hots," someone repeated.

Ricardo tripped on an ankle out of nowhere, and falling backward grabbed the nearest object: Neal's chest. He heard a rip as he continued to fall, and when he landed he had a handful of torn, threadbare cotton with *Primo Beer* written across it.

He looked slowly up at a bare-chested, raging Neal, and something happened to freeze them in time. Something kept his words in his mouth and Neal's fists in the air. Everything stopped and Ricardo sat suspended outside of the world.

Until Cory Fordyce looked in.

Long blond hair, Miss Clairol curls, rosy cheeks and lips, pale blue eyes. All he could see of her was her face; the crowd hid the rest. She was peering around Neal, while Neal turned slowly to look at her.

"Hello, Cory," Neal said, smiling as his fingers uncurled.

She scowled past him and looked down at Ricardo. "What did you tell him about me, Ricardo?"

"I didn't say a thing!" Ricardo shouted. "Lisa said! Ask Lisa!"

Neal stepped forward with a shout, swinging his arm as if he were bowling. Ricardo's face went numb with pain; he wasn't sure why. He lay back on the asphalt, smelling a cloud of tarry, rusty, bloody smoke rising around him. Neal's fist floated above in slow motion, a white planet spattered in blood. Ricardo's awareness roamed into the dark.

. . .

"Ricardo?" A woman's voice. "This is Mrs. Ensign, the nurse. We've called your mother. I'm afraid she'll have to take you to the hospital. Your nose is quite broken. Breathe through your mouth and you won't have so much trouble."

His face felt like a pane of safety glass, shattered but clinging together. She wiped his eyes with a wet cloth as the sounds of typewriters and telephones filled his ears.

Jars rattled and a fluorescent light appeared. Mrs. Ensign stood above, shaking a thermometer. Then she shook her head.

"If I did that you wouldn't be able to breathe," she said. "Poor boy."

"Bisses Edsid, could I see a cast list for *Bacbeth's Bartiad Revue?*"

"A catalyst for who?"

"Cast list, cast list. I cad't talk right."

"Can you read right? Stay put, I'll get you the list."

When she returned, she had a ditto so fresh it fumed. She held it before his face so that he could read:

MACBETH'S MARTIAN REVUE

Macbeth. . . . . Neal Bay
Banquo . . . . Ricardo Rivera
Lady Macbeth . . . . Cory Fordyce

"That's all," he said.

She left him alone with his pain.

Why me? he thought. Why me?

That was an old thought, worn thin over the years of his childhood. It hardly captured his present frustration, which felt like the undertow at high tide.

Why Neal? he thought. Better.

Why Neal, the sun-tanned surfer, instead of me, the brainy twerp? I'm not such a bad bodysurfer.

And why Neal, with the perfect dumb joke that makes all the girls laugh (except Cory usually, but probably now she'll laugh), instead of me, s-s-stuttering R-R-Ricardo?

Yeah? Why does Neal get to be President Bloody Macbeth of the Blackstone Intermediate Bloody Spaceways and the Planet of Bloody Blood; when I get to be Good Ol' Banquo the Friendly Ghost?

Why does Neal get Cory while I get . . . I get . . .

Cory. Thinking of her was like swallowing a Superball. He had never gotten over the bruises she'd given him the previous year, when he had let himself have a crush on her even while knowing that she hated him, even while knowing for certain that his affection would make her crueler.

In moments of pain, her image always brightened to torment him. He had never known as much pain as he felt now, and her face had never been so bright.

. . .

That night he cried out in his sleep. His mother found him sitting half-awake in his bed, describing in a senseless rush the events of some nightmare on another world: a planet of blood where starships of rusted metal crashed into the ruins of red cities; where a bloody sun and moon chased each other round and round while the stars howled in a hungry chorus, and seas of blood drenched everything in red. He fell back asleep without truly waking, leaving her clinging to his seemingly empty body, leaving her afraid.

On the table by his bedside, she saw his English assignment: Ray Bradbury's *The Martian Chronicles.*

"I'll call the office in the morning," she promised her son. "That place is giving you nightmares."

• • •

Mrs. Sherman sighed when she saw Ricardo in home room 408 the next morning. His bandaged nose was the subject of several disputes between first and second bells. As the students punched their new day's schedules into computer cards and copied each other's math homework, she watched him gazing into space. Near the end of the period, she checked his schedule and saw that he had no class after home room.

"Would you please come see me at fourth bell?" she asked.

"Yes, Mrs. Sherman," said Ricardo, and he shuffled away without having met her eyes.

He wandered into the department office at third bell and was waiting for her when she got free of Mr. Ezra and Miss Bachary, who each claimed to have the room for the next period. The scheduling computer was down again.

"Everyone defended Neal," he said, when she was sitting at her desk. He looked about eighty years old when he said it. She wanted to tell him to look up, to smile.

"They said you started it?" she asked.

He nodded. "I let them give my part away. Newt got it. David Deacon, I mean. He's even shorter than me. I don't know why Mr. Dean thinks Banquo's a shrimp."

"Have you taken your story to Mr. Magnusson?" she asked.

"He and Mr. Bay go golfing together," he said. "I don't want to be in the stupid play anyway."

"Maybe it's for the better, Ricardo," she said. "I thought of you when we chose *Macbeth*. Mr. Dean will need a student playwright, someone who can write, to polish what the actors come up with and read it back to them better than before."

Ricardo looked up, astonished. "You mean me?"

She smiled. "That could be, but it depends on you."

"I'd do it! I have an idea about-about Macbeth's mother!"

"Fine, Ricardo. I've talked to David Deacon since he was chosen, by the way. He's in my science fiction class and he loves Mars. He said he'd be glad to help you learn what you need to know to write a story on Mars."

"Write a story on Mars," Ricardo said to himself. "Wow."

"—gladly share his fine ideas about the angry red planet, that grisly world of war and blood."

She looked past him, through the filing cabinets, up at the clock.

"And *Macbeth,*" she intoned, "all black and red, dark night and dark blood. A haunted planet, a cursed play. Did you know there was a curse put on the play? It's bad luck for an actor to hear the Scotsman's name, unless they're in the play. If you listen long enough, you'll hear stories about the strange things that happen when people perform *Macbeth.*"

Ricardo's gaze followed the path her eyes traced upward, ever upward.

"Use your gift, Ricardo."

"Okay, Mrs. Sherman, I'll give it a try."

"A-plus, Ricardo," she said. "You're A-plus material."

• • •

The new Banquo, David "Newt" Deacon, was a nerd. He even had a bowl-head haircut. When Ricardo found him in the audiovisual room, he had toilet plungers strapped to both legs and was filming himself with an upside-down video camera while extolling the virtues of "Human Housefly Sucker-Cups." He looked a bit like a housefly himself, wearing bug-eyed glasses with quarter-inch-thick lenses.

Newt shed his plungers and turned off the video recorder.

"Ricky River?" he asked.

"Ricardo Rivera."

Newt shook his head, as if clearing it. "Thought that couldn't be right."

"Mrs. Sherman sent me."

"Oh, I know. Excuse me a second." He went poking through shelves cluttered with tape reels and charred copper wire, speaking over his shoulder. "She's neat, huh? She said I'd tell you everything you ever wanted to know about Mars, right?"

"I guess I know as much as anybody. I read *The Martian Chronicles.*"

"Oh," Newt said. "That's just the beginning."

When he came out of the cupboard, holding a burned-out electromagnet, his cheeks were sucked in between his molars. He stared at Ricardo's bandages.

"Neal was my best friend once," he said. "Back in fifth grade, we did everything together. He got ideas for all these neat things—squirt-gun burglar traps and stuff—and I built 'em. But he kept taking and breaking them. Now it figures he's president. And going with Cary Fordyce, too."

"Cory," said Ricardo.

Newt unwound some of the scorched copper wire from the motor and began winding it around the fingers of his left hand as he talked.

"Here's what I thought would work for Mars on the stage: all red lights; we'd make big castles out of red foam rubber—sandstone-looking stuff. I wanted to do a sandstorm—they're really bad on Mars—but Mr. Dean said no, too messy. We get an avalanche at least. The space suits are gonna be kind of a cross between space suits and kilts."

"How about canals?" Ricardo asked.

"There aren't any canals," Newt said emphatically. "Didn't you ever see *Robinson Crusoe on Mars?*"

"No, but-but I think I know how Mars looks." He looked up and saw a clock with its hands skipping backward. The office reset speeding clocks several times a day. "It has two moons, a red sky, towers, and Martians who nobody ever sees . . . I bet I could write it so everyone acted like they would if they were really up there."

"Make it good and bloody," said Newt, fidgeting with the prongs of an electric plug. The other end of the wire was hooked to the motor, now strapped to his left hand.

"Yeah," Ricardo sighed, "except they won't let us have any blood in it."

"Aw, there's this great word from horror stories that no one would ever mind."

Ricardo leaned closer. "Tell me."

Newt's hand exploded. He yanked the plug out of the wall socket while Ricardo, in shock, peered at the smouldering hand.

"You did that to yourself?"

Grinning, Newt unwrapped his hand and held it out. The fingers and palm were powdered with carbon but unharmed.

"Mr. Dean's letting me do the special effects," he said. "Now, you were asking about a good word for blood?"

. . .

A small flame licked up and seared Ricardo's heart each time Cory and Neal shared the stage. Two weeks after the primaries, their political sessions were notorious; according to Lisa Freuhoff, they would as soon ogle each other as filibuster. Sunk deep into a folding chair, Ricardo daily watched them declare their sappy Martian version of love while a piano student rapped out accompaniment. When the ruddy stage lighting lingered in their eyes even off the stage, he saw it as the glow of lust and hated it. Cory tried none of the tricks she had played on Ricardo last year. She and Neal were at each other's mercy.

One afternoon, between scenes, Neal jumped from the stage and sauntered over to Ricardo.

"What a quay-zar," Neal said.

Ricardo drew up his knees and sank down into the safety of his own lap. "What are you trying to prove, Bay?"

"Nothing you haven't proved already. That you're a lying little wimp. If your mouth and fingers are both really connected to your brain, then everything you're writing is probably a lie, too."

Ricardo sat up and set the script book down. He was getting hot now.

"Neal, would you just fuck off?"

Of course, of course his voice had to break when he said the worst word he knew.

"Ooooh! What nasty words! They're just what I'd expect from a nasty little boy like you. Nasty little fag."

Neal spun away and leapt back onto the stage without using his hands. Ricardo lapsed into a fever of pent rage; he almost smote his breast in public.

"Just because I don't have a bitch for a girlfriend!"

Sheri DuBose, who was passing behind him, gasped.

He blushed, felt his ears burning. When she was gone, he looked at Cory Fordyce, alone at the center of the stage. He covered her with a hand, imagining the bitch-queen of them all in her place. Lady Macbeth, with long black hair and vampire teeth and bloody lips and hungry eyes. In his mind, the Lady consumed Cory, another bitch, and he began to smile.

"I don't care if I'm not Macbeth or Banquo or any of you," he whispered, giggling.

He held his pen up before his eyes, concentrating on it until he went slightly cross-eyed. His thinking also did something like doubling; he suddenly thought of himself as every one of them. He could be Duncan, murdered in his sand castle, and any or all of the three witches who danced across the viewscreen of the starship *Silex;* he could be the comical porter of the air-lock. The whole time the players thought they were creating the play, he had actually been writing new lines and getting the actors to learn them.

Over Christmas break, he was left to polish the script and prepare a final version. He lost interest in the mundane holiday and often had to be coerced to take part in family affairs such as ornamenting the tree and visiting relatives.

For two solid weeks he breathed the sands of Mars and haunted the winding stairs of a crumbling Martian castle. Instead of carols, he heard phantom birds cawing from the high thin air as murder sneaked through the two-mooned night. His dreams were premonitions of laser-fire, in which no blood was allowed. The holes in Duncan's chest smouldered, cauterized. And always, just before he woke, the sand dunes of the Birnham Waste came humping forward, crawling, alive . . .

He wrote and rewrote. Sometimes he stared at the wall and the soccer trophies and the Certificates of Merit and the pencils in the papier-mâché holder he'd made in third grade. He stared at these objects but all the while saw blood, only blood, blood swirling into sand, spraying in the wind, blood that the school would never allow, everywhere the substance that the Committee had forbidden.

The days passed in a red dream.

("Merry Christmas, darl— Ricardo, did you even sleep?")

On New Year's Day, inspired by the changing year, he took a silver pin and pricked his fingertips; squeezed out bright beads and droplets that splashed the fresh-typed manuscript; chanted, "By the pricking of my thumbs, Neal Bay is overcome!"

He smeared a little blood on each page. For a while he watched it dry, then he licked his fingers clean of blood and ink.

"Excellent job, Mr. Rivera," said Mr. Dean the next day. "Sheri turned in the final draft of her songs; I hope you two got together over the holidays? Then I guess that should do it. Listen, if you're not too busy this trimester, why don't you lend a hand building sets?"

Ricardo could have cackled and rubbed his hands together, but he had more control than that. He nodded and went looking for a hammer.

That afternoon he worked on the stage, doing quiet tasks with glue and thumbtacks in the dark wings while the actors looked over their new script.

Cory Fordyce said, ''But I don't remember . . . Morris, this isn't our play.''

''What else would it be?'' said Mr. Dean. His word outweighed that of Morris Fluornoy, the student director. ''I'll expect you to have it memorized by Friday. Don't forget, opening night's only two months away.''

''But this is scary,'' said Lady Macbeth.

''It's supposed to be,'' said Newt, who had already complimented Ricardo on his script. ''It's Mars. Didn't you ever see *Planet of the Vampire Women*?''

Ricardo resumed hammering. In his hands, the first of the Martian towers began to rise. The flunkies in set construction were used to taking orders; it was easy to shape their understanding of Martian architecture. He explained how low gravity and rarefied air required all structures to be warped until they could withstand ion storms and colloidal temperature gradients.

So, under his direction, they built something like a huge Cubist monster with a low, foam-rubber belly, giraffe-long legs, and a vast fanged mouth missing the lower jaw. They painted it red-orange, stapled a slit sheet of clear plastic between the front legs, and finally gave it wheels. Ricardo discovered a talent for painting, and covered it with writhing figures, deliberately crude glyphs of torment.

Portcullis-cum-air-lock. Hell-gate. Beast. It stood like a watchdog, always somewhere on the stage, its upper regions hidden from the audience by hanging backdrops and the proscenium arch.

Another of Ricardo's talents also came in handy. He proved an excellent mimic, and so created a variety of unusual sound effects once he'd made friends with the sound technician. The obscure bird of night called, when it called, in a high voice familiar to Neal; and each time it called, the sandy-haired athlete grew slightly pale inside his skier's tan. The bird's cry, Neal once said to Cory within Ricardo's hearing, sounded almost like a voice. He didn't know that the words, Ricardo's taunts, had been accelerated and run together until no sense could be made of them.

Neal became an ever more haggard Macbeth, in his plastic kilt and rakish cellophane visor. He started crossing the stage to avoid the young playwright and set-builder.

But Lady Macbeth—that is, Cory Fordyce—seemed to grow ever bolder.

Ricardo noticed her watching him as he went about his business in the shadows. One day he climbed a ladder all the way up to the catwalk, where spotlights and unused backdrops hung. He stood directly over her as she read a hologram from her husband who was fighting rebels in space. Ricardo concentrated on the top of her head, and within seconds she looked straight up at him, though he had climbed aloft in perfect silence, unobserved until now. He pretended to adjust a red gel on a spotlight while she continued her speech.

When he descended she walked proudly toward him, seeming to drink up the red light as she came, seeming to swell and tower as it filled her. Her hair caught scarlet highlights, her mouth wettened with blood, her eyes swam in red tears.

"Ricardo," she said, "what are you up to?"

He backed away and she moved closer, forcing him into a corner.

"What are you doing to us?" she repeated.

Ricardo could summon no strength to meet the red glare in her eyes. Her intonation was that of Lady Macbeth in speeches he had written. She had such power over him. He felt his own power ebbing, leaking swiftly onto the ground, unstoppable.

She followed him along the row of ropes that dangled up into darkness.

"Don't you run," she said, "I want to talk to you. Sometimes you make me so mad—"

He saw a door and rushed through it, and turned with a cry as he realized his mistake. He had fled into the light cage. He turned to see her, triumphant and angry as she grabbed the wirework door and slammed it shut upon him.

The last of his strength left him. He slumped backward, catching his elbows on light levers, and so drew the theater into darkness with him as he fell.

When they found the source of trouble, they sent him out to sit in the auditorium until he felt better.

Cory came onstage. For a moment the lights were all wrong, pale white instead of red. She looked like a porcelain doll, eyes wide but blank. When she saw Ricardo, she looked over his head. Though he was the only one in the empty auditorium, she looked everywhere but at him.

"We'll try Lady Macbeth's song now," said Morris.

"It's Neal I want," Ricardo whispered. "Stay out of my way."

He felt murderous and guilty, but the alternative was worse. If he didn't hate, then there would be nothing left for him at all. He did not want to be numb. If no one loved him, then he would see that they hated him; for though love was but a dream one forgot upon waking, hate worked in full daylight. Hate brought bright red visions of double lunacy, of a crimson planet spinning through a velvet-black void.

The piano played a few notes and Cory sang:

"Should I? Could I?
Would I do this deed?
How will—I kill
Duncan and mislead
The Martian warriors who'll
Find him in his bed?
The noble fighters
Who'll see he's really dead?
With Duncan's last breath,
He'll see a Macbeth,
But will it be my Lord or me?
Should it be my Lord or me?"

Ricardo groaned at Sheri's song. It was so bad it might ruin the rest of the show.

Neal entered and they began a duet.

"Will we? Shall we?
How can we protect our fate?
Still we . . . will be
Taking risks so very great."

The monster of hell-gate loomed suddenly flimsy and ridiculous above the awkward singers.

"Dare we? Care we?"

Ricardo answered, "No!"

He rushed down the row of folding chairs, kicking a few out of his way. The piano stopped and the singers fell quiet. The actors and crew came out on the stage to see him.

"That stuff stinks!" he said.

"Mr. Rivera," said Mr. Dean, aiming a quivering finger at the door, "you are out of bounds. Now leave and don't bother returning."

"I won't have to come back," he said. "I'll hear everybody booing on opening night, even way out where I live."

Cory's eyes flashed red and he stayed a moment to look at her. Hate mauled his heart. He slammed his way outside to face a cloudy sky of blue with no trace of red in it.

. . .

Even then, he did not abandon the play. Whenever possible, he entered the auditorium before crew and cast arrived, and stayed hidden up in the dark catwalks until all had gone. Cory never saw him, for her eyes were always on Neal. Ricardo's eyes, in the meantime, opened to the full scheme of performance, the total effect of actors and words, lighting and music—such as it was—working in dramatic fusion.

With silver pins he pricked his thumbs and dribbled his blood over everything, investing the play with his own power. He bled on the net full of foam boulders intended for the avalanche scene. He daubed the witches' robes down in the costume rooms; these were worn by three members of Neal and Cory's cabinet. Let them wear his blood, and though they were enemies their gestures might carry some of his power.

There were rumors, whispers, stories that he overheard from his high place. A girl in the costume room had seen the witches' robes moving all by themselves. A boy working late on the set had seen a woman in red-black tatters standing in the light cage. Shreds of music drifted over the stage when the tape player was disconnected. Others saw severed heads that vanished. Then the hell-beast rolled swiftly across the stage with no hands pushing it.

Only Ricardo saw Newt at his tricks.

He thought of nothing but *Macbeth's Martian Revue*. He never again wondered, "Why him instead of me?" His power carried him beyond all that. In daydreams he communed with Shakespeare and saw at first hand the awful history that had provoked the play: Macbeth's veiled mother (where could she have come from, except his dreams?) pointing the finger of guilt at Duncan. He dipped a hand into eternity and sipped from the splashing spring of the witches' queen Hecate: a fount of blood in a dark forest. Not even the Ethics Advisory Committee could spoil that sanguine vision or censor its red power, no more than they could stop his Mars from coming into being as he imagined it.

Vampire dreams. Huddled like a bat in the loft, he watched the actors. He hid by the speaker where the night-bird cried, and sometimes joined its voice with his own. Even Newt looked worried then, and he had wished aloud for ghostly visitations.

Cory also came into her own, and nothing strange or out of place could touch her. She led Neal around by the hand; leaned against him during critique sessions; and one afternoon, while Ricardo watched, she kissed him backstage. The kiss lasted too long and Ricardo gasped for air. Neal's hands on her hips, clutching and tense, pulled her forward; while her hands rested smooth and relaxed upon his shoulders, and drew gentle curves, and never needed to tug because he fell toward her of his own will. Ricardo, too, almost fell. Later he lay on his back, panting, dreaming of the plunge he had nearly taken.

Opening night came as if without warning, but Ricardo had been ready for a long time.

"Banquo!" he called through the stage door. "Banquo, psst!"

Newt spied him and came over, looking wary at first, then startled. He wore pointed ears, Mr. Spock style.

"You!" he said. "You're not supposed to—"

"Come outside a minute," Ricardo said.

They stood in the lunch quadrangle. It was dark except for a moth-battered floodlight above the stage door.

"Are you going to see the show?" Newt asked. "It shaped up pretty well, except for those dumb songs."

"I want a favor," Ricardo said. "No one but you will know, all right?"

"What kind of favor?"

Ricardo held up a paper sack. "I've got a space suit in here, kilt and visor with Banquo's emblem on 'em. I want to play your ghost tonight."

"What? You can't—"

Ricardo lunged and caught Newt by the throat. He held him against the wall.

"I don't want to hurt you, Deacon, but I will. Just let me play Banquo's ghost. We'll switch places, it's a short scene. No one'll know it's me except for you."

"Why?" Newt asked. "It's crazy."

"That's right. And if Neal asks, it was you playing the ghost, not me."

Newt took a deep breath. "Let go."

"Not till you agree."

Newt shrugged. "I don't care if you're the ghost. Be my guest. It's still pretty weird."

"Yeah. Go on, get ready. I'll be hiding backstage."

Newt went back inside. Ricardo went to a rest room and changed into the space suit. He fit a cap over his curls and pulled down the visor, thus resembling a dozen others in the cast. A tube of Vampire Blood, left over from Halloween, went into a tunic pocket.

When he returned to the auditorium, the play began with an orchestral flourish that seemed to catch up and echo the coughs of the audience. The Blackstone Intermediate School Band forged on to the end of the overture, then continued a few bars past that and sputtered into silence.

He peered through the backstage curtains and saw the set of Macbeth's spaceship, the *Silex,* much resembling the deck of the *Enterprise* from *Star Trek.* On the viewscreen—a framework with blue gauze stretched across it—three hags from Cory's campaign appeared cackling prophecies.

Neal Macbeth set his jaw and told the hags to get out of the way, he needed to see to make a landing. He was taking his shipful of space pirates to fight for the planet Mars.

"Aye, the red planet," said one witch. "That swollen, infected orb of death and decay. Beware you do not stab the crawling sands, for your own ichor may flow below the surface."

"Ichor in crawling sands?" said Macbeth. "What is this?"

Newt Banquo, Macbeth's second in command, leapt at the screen brandishing his ray-gun. The witches vanished amid shrieks and groans from the sound system.

The irrepressible space pirates broke into song:

''Oh we're on our way to Mars,
We've come from far-off stars,
Though the place we're really
Fondest of is Earth.
Oh it's been an endless trip
But the captain of our ship
Knows pretty much just what
A light-year's worth.
So Hip-Hip Hooray, Macbeth!
Hip-Hip Hooray, Macbeth!''

The audience started laughing, tentatively at first. Ricardo shivered, feeling their hilarity grow.

As if on cue, the spaceship's flimsy viewscreen trembled and would have toppled except for Newt, who caught and held it till the stagehands had anchored it from behind.

Coolly, Newt turned to his pale captain and said, ''They don't make these screens like they used to.''

The audience never had a chance to breathe.

Ricardo backed into the sets, unable to watch. The laughter went on, but he only half heard it. How could something with so much of himself in it appear so absurd? What had become of his life's blood, his offering of labor?

''Please,'' he prayed to the catwalks. ''Please don't let them laugh.''

Not all of the original spirit was lost. The laughter died out gradually, though never completely, and the lengthening silences seemed full of increasing horror. Much of the action, unseen to him, must have struck the crowd as gruesome. Murder and betrayal, the beast of hell-gate, the cry of the obscene bird: all cast a spell of red darkness that was nearly but never quite broken each time a DuBose song came up. Relief and dismay were blended in the laughter.

Ricardo smiled. There was still hope. He affixed Vulcan points to his ears and painted his nose with gooey Vampire Blood. When Newt came looking for him, he stepped out from behind a set-piece.

"You enter over there," Newt whispered, taking his hiding place. "You look really gross."

"Thanks."

"Break a leg."

Ricardo pulled down his visor and peeked through a curtain at the scene. Macbeth and Lady Macbeth were entertaining officers around an octagonal table. As he waited for his cue, he looked into the audience and immediately spied Mrs. Sherman in the front row, beyond the band, her jewelry glittering in the footlights. He hoped she wouldn't recognize him.

"Let's drink this toast in Venusian slug-ichor!" said Macbeth.

The officers raised their goblets.

Someone strode down the front row, a huge man with silvery hair and a dark red furious face. It was Mr. Magnusson, come to summon Mrs. Sherman from her seat. All around them, parents watched, while politely pretending to see nothing.

Ricardo heard his cue. He took a deep breath and strode onstage, aware of the two adults leaving together. Mr. Dean looked after them in horror, his conductor's wand drooping. The music swooned.

Neal spotted Ricardo in his costume, and his eyes widened with melodrama. "By the cosmos!" he cried.

"What is it, my Lord?" said Lady Macbeth, her eyes passing through Ricardo as he shambled forward. He heard the expectant breathing of the audience at his side, now invisible in the red glare of footlights. The whole set, everything around him, appeared to be drenched in blood. His insane hieroglyphs crawled over the walls, red-on-red, luminous.

"But-but-but," said Neal. "You-you-you . . ."

Ricardo walked offstage, turned on his heel, and waited to re-enter. His visor was steamed with the sweat of stage fright. He tried to find his breath.

"My lord?" said Cory Fordyce. "What is it? Have you seen some nightmare with your eyes wide open?"

"Didn't you see him?" Neal asked.

"See who?"

"Nothing, it must be nothing. I am tired, my dear. However, I'll let nothing stop our celebrations. I propose a toast to—"

Backstage, Ricardo heard a growing commotion. Mr. Magnusson, pulling Mrs. Sherman after him, came through a stage door.

"No, Jack," Mrs. Sherman whispered. "You can't just stop the show. If you were going to come late, you shouldn't have come at all. You're drunk, Jack."

"Ichor," said Mr. Magnusson, almost spitting. "Ichor! That's practically blood! It was the first word I heard. I'll pull down the curtain myself if I have to."

Morris Fluornoy bumped into Ricardo. He was running from the adults.

"What's going on?" Ricardo asked.

"We're in trouble!" Morris said, and blinked in puzzlement. He stooped to look under the visor. "Hey . . . Ricardo?"

"My cue," Ricardo said.

He slipped back onto the stage and stood at Neal's side. His pointed ears and Banquo's emblems were enough to tell the audience who he was, but now it was time to show Neal alone. He stepped before his former friend and slipped the visor up an inch or so, until Neal could see his grin while the audience saw only the back of his head. Another inch of raised visor exposed the tip of his bloodied nose. Finally Ricardo stared full into Neal's face. He rolled up his eyes until the whites were showing, and with his hand smeared Vampire Blood all over his face.

Neal turned ghastly green.

"Hello, my friend," Ricardo whispered.

Cory looked over and yelled, "You!"

The visor dropped. Ricardo turned and ran till he was tangled in the wings. Where was the backstage door? He saw Lady Macbeth scowling after him and Neal still gaping. He ripped off the ears and wiped the red goo on his sleeve.

"Newt?" he whispered. "Trade off."

"All right," said a deep voice that echoed through the back stage. Mr. Magnusson came storming around the backdrop, intent on the light cage.

"Jack," said Mrs. Sherman, just behind him, still trying to whisper. "Jack, they'll murder you."

"If not them, their parents," he said.

Actors rushed from the stage and the next scene began in chaos.

Neal and Cory charged Ricardo.

Mr. Magnusson opened the door to the light cage.

Ricardo turned toward the backstage door but Neal veered to cut him off. The next thing he saw was the ladder.

He was climbing.

Cory cried, "I'll get him!"

The ladder shuddered as if it were trying to throw him. Looking down past his feet, he saw Lady Macbeth climbing up. Below her, Mr. Magnusson swore at the array of light switches, asked "Which is which?" of the terrified operator, then snarled and stalked out of the cage.

Ricardo reached the top and looked out over the stage. The catwalk was the narrowest of tracks across the deepest of pits. At the bottom, three witches chanted around their cauldron while their red and black queen Hecate—played by Sheri DuBose—rose with her arms outspread to take in all the stage. She met his eyes and screamed.

The band faltered, stopped. Mr. Dean climbed onto the stage and met Mr. Magnusson and Mrs. Sherman at the witches' cauldron; there they stood looking out at the audience. The proper witches backed away. Sheri still stood looking up at Ricardo. He realized he had better move. A door opened onto the roof at the other side of the catwalk.

Mr. Magnusson began, "We apologize—"

Cory's feet banged on the ladder. Ricardo scuttled over the abyss. Below, Hecate screamed again, pointing now.

"Don't do it!" she cried.

Murmurs from the audience, yells from the darkened regions of the stage. The Committee looked up at him.

Halfway out, he heard Cory speak after him:

"Ricardo, don't be stupid. You can't get out that way. Come on back and face the music."

Her voice was soft.

He took a tentative step.

"Please," she said. The word was like nothing he had ever heard.

He turned to face her, and crouched with both hands holding the plank. She stood at the end of the catwalk, her red robes flowing into space. She was barefoot tonight, raven-haired, seeming much older and crueler than ever, despite her gentle word.

"Don't come out," he said.

She took a step.

Glancing down, he saw all of them, Neal and Newt and the faculty, all of them looking up at him with rubies for eyes.

"What is it you want, Ricardo?" she asked. He looked up. "Attention?"

Her face seemed to crack into pieces, everything he recognized in it crumbling away. She was smiling, reaching out to him, yet she was sad. He knew that look: pity. It drove him back.

She took a step. The catwalk shuddered like a diving board.

"Don't," he said, and turned to run.

One foot missed the plank.

He fell, bleating.

Cory screamed. Newt was already running through the darkness below, pushing the hell-beast like a cradle to catch him. Ricardo's clawing hands triggered the net full of foam boulders and he plunged amid a shower of soft Martian rocks.

As he fell, he dreamed with regret of all the scenes that would not be seen tonight because the show was spoiled. There would be no Lady Macbeth sleepwalking, sniffing the ozone left on her fingers by the firing of ray-guns. There would be no attack by Birnham Waste, where soldiers disguised as sand dunes advanced on Macbeth. Macbeth's disconcerted cry of "Ichor!" would not be heard, for he would never casually thrust a spear-point in that same sand. Ricardo saw all the things that should have been and would have been, if not for his fall.

Falling took longer than it should have.

Above him he saw no catwalk receding, no backdrops rushing past, no dwindling floodlights. There was instead a sky of crimson so dark, so deep that it was almost black; wherein, high up, like the smiling white eyes of a slick red beast, were two tiny horned moons. It was his dream, Mars as he had come to see it, and now it had him.

With much ripping of foam and splintering of wood and creaking of chicken wire, he landed. The belly of the hell-beast split wide, dropping him on the floor. A few boulders tumbled through after him.

A little figure scurried to him, a small boy swathed in red, with wide shiny eyes beneath a strange cowl.

"I'm here," said Newt. "Ricardo, can you answer?"

The mound of foam on which he lay collapsed, spilling him out from under the hell-beast. Ricardo's eyes blurred over for a moment, then his vision began to brighten.

"Newt!" he said.

"I'm here."

"I can see Mars. I really see it. I—I'm going . . ."

"Wow, Ricardo! Great! How is it?"

"Just like I im—"

He shrieked, his eyes fixed on the Martian firmament that no one else could see. He wailed as the moontips burst the membrane of sky and the red heavens poured down around him. Up he rose through the dark flood, like a bubble in a bottle of burgundy, and it seemed he would never reach the surface, never breathe again. For the air of Mars was thin, thin and cold, cold as death.

MY NAME IS DOLLY

William F. Nolan

If you create an idea that achieves the international recognition of *Logan's Run,* it's hard sometimes to be remembered for anything else. But quite apart from *Logan's Run,* which became an MGM movie and a CBS television series, Bill Nolan has written a truly handsome body of horror and science fiction work which stands among the finest in its field. Twice winner of the Edgar Allan Poe Special Award Scroll from Mystery Writers of America, he has written forty-six books (including the horror-story collections *Things Beyond Midnight* and *Nightshapes*) and sold over one hundred short stories, and he can boast credits on countless TV and movie productions, including more than fifteen "Movies of the Week." This story has a terrible aptness for *Scare Care,* and displays Bill's skill for black conciseness at its best.

MONDAY—Today I met the witch—which is a good place to start this diary. (I had to look up how to spell it. First I spelled it dairy but that's a place you get milk and from this you're going to get blood—I hope—so it is plenty different.)

Let me tell you about Meg. She's maybe a thousand years old I guess. (A witch can live forever, right?) She's all gnarly like the bark of an oak tree, her skin I mean, and she has real big eyes. Like looking into deep dark caves and you don't know what's down there. Her nose is hooked and she has sharp teeth like a cat's are. When she smiles some of them are missing. Her hair is all wild and clumpy and she smells bad. Guess she hasn't had a shower for a real long time. Wears a long black dress with holes bit in it. By rats most likely. She lives in this old deserted cobwebby boathouse they don't use anymore on the lake—and it's full of fat gray rats. Meg doesn't seem to mind.

My name is Dolly. Short for Dorothy like in the Oz books. Only nobody ever calls me Dorothy. I'm still a kid and not very tall and I've got red hair and freckles. (I really *hate* freckles! When I was real little I tried to rub them off but you can't. They stick just like tattoos do.)

Reason I went out to the lake to see old Meg is because of how much I hate my father. Well, he's not really my father, since I'm adopted and I don't know my real father. Maybe he's a nice man and not like Mr. Brubaker who adopted me. Mrs. Brubaker died of the flu last winter which is when Mr. Brubaker began to molest me. (I looked up the word molest and it's the right one for what he keeps trying to do with me.) When I won't let him he gets really mad and slaps me and I run out of the house until he's all calmed down again. Then he'll get special nice and offer me cookies with chocolate chunks in them which are my very favorite kind. He wants me to like him so he can molest me later.

Last week I heard about the witch who lives by the lake. A friend at school told me. Some of the kids used to go down there to throw rocks at her until she put a spell on Lucy Akins and Lucy ran away and no one's seen her since. Probably she's dead. The kids leave old Meg alone now.

I thought maybe Meg could put a spell on Mr. Brubaker for five dollars. (I saved up that much.) Which is why I went to see her. She said she couldn't because she can't put spells on people unless she can see them up close and look in their eyes like she did to Lucy Atkins.

The lake was black and smelly with big gas bubbles breaking in it and the boathouse was cold and damp and the rats scared me but old Meg was the only way I knew to get even with Mr. Brubaker. She kept my five dollars and told me she was going into town soon and would look around for something to use against Mr. Brubaker. I promised to come see her on Friday after school.

We'll have his blood, she said.

FRIDAY NIGHT—I went to see old Meg again and she gave me the doll to take home. A real big one, as tall as I am, with freckles and red hair just like mine. And in a pretty pink dress with little black slippers with red bows on them. The doll's eyes open and close and she has a big metal key in her back where you wind her up. When you do she opens her big dark eyes and says hello, my name is Dolly. Same as mine. I asked Meg where she found Dolly and she said at Mr. Carter's toy store. But I've been in there lots of times and I've never seen a doll like this for five dollars. Take her home, Meg told me, and she'll be your friend. I was real excited and ran off pulling Dolly behind me. She has a box with wheels on it you put her inside and pull along the sidewalk.

She's too big to carry.

MONDAY—Mr. Brubaker doesn't like Dolly. He says she's damn strange. That's his words, damn strange. But she's my new friend so I don't care what he says about her. He wouldn't let me take her to school.

SATURDAY—I took some of Mr. Brubaker's hair to old Meg today. She asked me to cut some off while he was asleep at night and it was really hard to do without waking him up but I got some and gave it to her. She wanted me to bring Dolly and I did and Meg said that Dolly was going to be her agent. That's the word. Agent. (I try to get all the words right.)

Dolly had opened her deep dark eyes and seen Mr. Brubaker and old Meg said that was all she needed. She wrapped two of Mr. Brubaker's hairs around the big metal key in Dolly's back and told me not to wind her up again until Sunday afternoon when Mr. Brubaker was home watching his sports. He always does that on Sunday.

So I said okay.

SUNDAY NIGHT—This afternoon, like always, Mr. Brubaker was watching a sports game on the television when I set Dolly right in front of him and did just what old Meg told me to do. I wound her up with the big key and then took the key out of her back and put it in her right hand. It was long and sharp and Dolly opened her eyes and said hello, my name is Dolly, and stuck the metal key in Mr. Brubaker's chest. There was a lot of blood. (I told you there would be.)

Mr. Brubaker picked Dolly up and threw the front of her into the fire. I mean, that's how she landed, just the front of her at the edge of the fire. (It's winter now, and real cold in the house without a fire.) After he did that he fell down and didn't get up. He was dead so I called Dr. Thompson.

The police came with him and rescued Dolly out of the fire when I told them what happened. Her nice red hair was mostly burnt away and the whole left side of her face was burnt real bad and the paint had all peeled back and blistered. And one of her arms had burnt clear off and her pink dress was all char-colored and with big fire holes in it. The policeman who rescued her said that a toy doll couldn't kill anybody and that I must have stuck the key into Mr. Brubaker's chest and blamed it on Dolly. They took me away to a home for bad children.

I didn't tell anybody about old Meg.

TUESDAY—It is a long time later and my hair is real pretty now and my face is almost healed. The lady who runs this house says there will always be big scars on the left side of my face but I was lucky not to lose my eye on that side. It is hard to eat and play with the other kids with just one arm but that's okay because I can still hear Mr. Brubaker screaming and see all the blood coming out of his chest and that's nice.

I wish I could tell old Meg thank you. I forgot to—and you should always thank people for doing nice things for you.

THE NIGHT GIL RHYS FIRST MET HIS LOVE

Alan Rodgers

Originally from Florida, but now living and working in New York, the quiet-spoken Alan Rodgers is one of the most demanding and respected young editors working in horror/fantasy, and apart from that he writes a mean story himself. He has edited *Night Cry* magazine, and from 1983 to 1987 worked on the editorial staff of *Twilight Zone*. His contribution to Jerry Williamson's *Masques II* anthology was a memorably chilling tale called "The Boy Who Came Back From the Dead," and I can never forget the way that the boy's mother screamed but didn't drop the porcelain casserole dish she was carrying. Alan's first novel, *The Children,* was recently published by Bantam. You've met Alan . . . now (shudder) meet Gil . . .

At the age of twenty-three, convulsing with the need for heroin on the sidewalk of a wide, dirty street, Gilman Rhys was a virgin. The fact bothered and distracted him.

It was three in the morning and he wasn't ready for the fit at all—he thought he'd been through the last of that weeks ago—and the neighborhood was hard and nasty. It wasn't the worst place (that was over in the projects where everyone had been hungry for a long time); thirty years ago this had been a shopping district, and while there were homes on the side streets, no one lived here—most of the houses were deserted or condemned. After seven P.M. most of the nasties went home and left the street to the bums and winos. But even if he had been squirming his way through a fit in the middle of the projects, he wouldn't have been scared. Gil had torn a *mean* monkey off his back, and he'd been desperate enough for long enough that being scared wasn't possible. It would be a while before anything ordinary would scare him.

Besides, if worse came to worst he had his pig-sticker—a beautiful switchblade stiletto he'd scrounged off the body of a Latino after a gang war—in his back pocket. He'd had to use it before. No one sensible ever robs street people—they don't have much and what they do have smells bad—but more than once he'd had to cope with kids from the high school when they came cruising around looking for fun. Fearless or not, though, Gil didn't want any trouble. He'd got himself in a deep pit with junk, and he'd spent a lot of time and heart crawling out of it. He'd done lots of things that he was lots less than proud of, but what he'd done was done with, now, and all he wanted out of life was the chance to make something out of it he could live with.

The woman passed him on her way from the parking lot to the all-night diner. She was dressed like she had money—not an awful lot of money, not like she'd got it all from her folks, but more like the kind of money you have to make yourself. "Are you all right?" she asked. Her voice was neutral, not frightened or concerned.

He lied to her automatically: "I'll be okay. I fell. I'll get up in a minute," he said. He looked up to see her, wary of her, and he saw that her eyes were turquoise, alive with light and color. A long sensuous chill crawled up his backbone, raising hairs and goose-down on his forearms and the sides of his face. Some queer denizen of his id, set loose by the chaos in his forebrain, recognized her. It told him so.

That's her, it said. *She's the one.*

Gil shook his head, not understanding the voice or its genesis at all, and his ears began to ring.

You'll know her if you'll think of it for just a moment. She's yours.

"What?" he asked, thinking she had spoken. But she had already gone.

After a few moments, he got up, brushed himself off (which didn't do much good), and followed her into the diner.

When he got there he saw her sitting in a booth by one of the diner's big plate-glass windows, so he sat at the counter not far from her. The thing in his id was still shouting at him, but it had given up on words. It was stomping around on his heart and his gut like a child making a racket, trying to get its mother's attention by pounding on the walls with blocks. It made him afraid (the nasty, jittery kind of fear that turns mean and violent at any provocation), it exhilarated him, made him desire, made him lonely. None of it made any sense. Gil shifted in his seat uncomfortably.

The waitress looked at him from where she stood, further down the counter, and raised an eyebrow at him. "Coffee?" she asked.

He nodded.

She walked to the urn, poured a cup, and brought it to him. When she was done (just from seeing him she knew him well enough not to offer him a menu) he turned back toward the woman with the blue-blue eyes. He wanted to speak to her, to ask her what she'd said to him out there. But he was shy of her. Women frightened him in a way that thugs and nasties and even high school ruffians didn't. He thought that was funny, sometimes: him, a mean, nasty, grimy junkie, afraid of women. But thinking it was funny didn't change it any.

She saw him looking at her, and her face jumped like suddenly she'd recognized him. But she didn't say anything. She looked away from him very pointedly, and she lit a cigarette. The index finger of her left hand—the one nearest him—drummed on the scratched Formica tabletop.

Then the man in the kitchen set her ham and eggs and potatoes and toast on the stainless-steel shelf in the window between the kitchen and the counter, and the waitress went to get it, and for a moment the whole agenda of the diner changed. Gil was thinking he was hungry, and he had money, because he'd been to work at Manpower every day for at least a couple of weeks now, but he was way out of the habit of spending money on food, and it was hard to do. Gil couldn't see into the kitchen because of the angle from where he was sitting, but he could smell things cooking, and he was tempted. Then the waitress was setting the plate in front of that strange woman, and Gil saw her staring at him, not straight on, but at his reflection in the plate-glass window. That spooked him, because her eyes were even bluer and ghostlier in *her* reflection than they were that first time he saw them, out on the street. And Gil forgot all about food.

The waitress started wiping the counter, down at the far end. After a few strokes she didn't look too happy about it at all, and she turned to Gil, not looking like business, the way waitresses usually do, but looking like she just wanted to talk to somebody. Gil wasn't in the mood for that, not at all. He was still trying to screw up his courage to talk to the girl. There was something important there, and it needed attending to.

''More coffee?'' the waitress asked.

Gil's right hand was fiddling around with the spoon, trying to stir up the sugar even though it was already dissolved. He turned away from the girl's reflection to answer the waitress, swiveled his seat so he could sit in a more ordinary position.

''Pardon?''

''I asked if you wanted more coffee.''

''Oh, no''—he gestured with the cup—''thanks. Still almost full.''

But the waitress wouldn't go away. And what could Gil do? So, after a while, just to be polite, he said, ''Nice weather, huh?''

The waitress nodded. (The weather had been horrible, actually—too humid, too hot, too many clouds.)

He sipped from his coffee cup. His seat felt uncomfortable.

''It's been slow tonight,'' the waitress told him.

He nodded.

She began to tell him about the night's trade. She was the sort of woman, Gil thought, who'd take hold of his ear and never relinquish it. After just a little while he found himself wondering if she could go on forever, and then he began to think that she could. He didn't want to listen; everything inside him shouted and shoved at him, trying to get him to *do* something, to get him *away* from the woman. But something about her pinned him where he sat, left him unable to do anything but nod and smile in response. He turned to look at the woman with the strange eyes . . .

. . . and she was sipping the last of her coffee, dabbing the corners of her mouth with a napkin, fussing with her purse, and getting up to pay her check. She stood at the register for a long while, waiting for the waitress to finish with Gil and take her money. Gil watched her, awed by her for reasons he didn't understand. She looked back at him as though she knew him very well.

Then the waitress finally made her way to the register, and the strange woman paid, and she left.

Gil wanted to leave right then, he wanted to follow her to wherever she was going, and . . . he didn't know what. But he didn't dare. He knew that. He had to be careful; a junkie couldn't just go following strange women out of restaurants. It wasn't wise.

So he set his teeth and resigned himself to sit on the stool and wait out five or ten minutes of listening to the waitress, or staring into the distance, or *whatever* happened next. Maybe then, he thought, he'd try to find the woman. He had to talk to her. He had to . . . something. He didn't know what. He really didn't know. But whatever it was, he couldn't just run after her, screaming and shaking and acting like a lunatic.

At least that's what Gil was telling himself when the waitress got back from the register and put her hand on top of his, all warm and moist, and looked deep and soulfully into his eyes. She smiled at him dirty-like and the hackles went up on the back of his neck and he wanted to scream.

"There's nobody here," she said, "but you and me and the cook. And he's half deaf, or deafer. We could lock the place up, and—"

Gil didn't hear any more than that. He couldn't stand to listen. He got off his stool and bolted. He had to run, to get the hell *away* from that woman. He was at the door when he realized that he hadn't paid, so he took a dollar bill out of his shirt pocket (he liked to keep a little folding money where it was real handy so no one could see his wallet) and threw it at the register.

He only ran a few yards after he'd got out of the place. The waitress wasn't going to follow him; he knew that as soon as he calmed down for a minute.

Before he even realized what he was doing, he found himself looking for the woman with the turquoise eyes, but she was nowhere in sight, in either direction. Gil even walked up the block to see if she had taken the side street, then walked back past the diner to check the major cross street at the block's other end. He didn't see her, though. He didn't see anyone at all.

. . .

He spent the whole night looking for her. Not looking in the sort of places where you'd expect a well-dressed white woman to go; Gil didn't even know those well enough to look in them. But he went to all the places *he* knew—the ones that he could picture her in, anyway. Gas stations, all-night newspaper stands, the twenty-four-hour grocery down at Kennedy and Rome. Places like that.

It didn't surprise him that she wasn't in any of them. Not *really*. But he'd hoped, he'd really hoped . . .

When he was too tired to look anymore, when he was too tired to even *think* about looking anymore, it was quarter till five in the morning, and his boardinghouse had closed up tight as a clam at nine-thirty. He went down to the park by the river, planning to stake out a bench and try to get at least a couple of hours' worth of sleep before the morning-shift cops came to shoo him away.

Maybe it was just pure chance that she was there, in the park, almost looking like she was waiting for him. But he never thought so. Not then or even later.

She was sitting on just the bench where he'd planned to sleep, which was way out of the way, in this really narrow little finger of the park (with the river on one side and the base wall of the expressway on the other) that was shielded from the rest of it by a bushy-thick clump of pine trees.

''Hello,'' he said. He sat down on the bench beside her, but not close. Not close at all. She turned to look at him, and the words he was going to say, whatever they were, got confused and stumbled all over each other. After a while he said, ''You're beautiful.'' But she didn't say anything, not for a long time.

She looked frightened, uneasy, and somehow at the same time not afraid of him at all. ''Why do you say that?'' she asked, finally. Her smile was gracious and flattered and a little coy. ''Even if it is true, it's not the sort of thing strangers often come up to me and say.''

''I . . .'' He didn't have an answer for her. His face had fixed itself into an awkward, uncomfortable position. Everything was jumbled up, and he suspected she'd had a mindful hand in the jumbling. He found himself being more honest than he meant to be, more honest than was sensible. ''I'm alone, I guess. Because I'm lonely.''

She was quiet for a long while after he said that, and he really thought he'd said quite enough, thank you. "It's horrible to feel lonely, isn't it? I suppose that that is what I was feeling, too. Would you like to talk? Isn't the river beautiful this time of day?"

"That's deep and meaningful," he sneered—then brought himself up short: *What do I have to be hostile about . . . ?* And even more, *Why would I want to alienate her . . . ?* He didn't understand any of it, least of all himself. "I'm sorry. I shouldn't say things like that." He teased the roots of the grass with the toe of his work boot. "You're right. The river is beautiful."

"It's all right," she said. "Don't worry about it." She was staring at the dawn-lit corner of the sky. The sun had begun to edge its way onto the horizon. "You were in the diner. And on the street before that."

He blushed.

"You were staring at me."

"*No . . . !*" His throat choked on itself; he couldn't say anything else. But he wanted to deny it, loud and long, even if it meant she'd know he was lying. That thing in the back of his head was screaming again, *You too, you were staring too.* But Gil knew that wasn't the thing to say. Oh no.

"Let's walk," she said. Her voice sounded somehow compassionate, almost as though she thought she was offering him a mercy.

What could he do? His ears were ringing with a tone so high he could barely hear it, and he could feel his blood pounding in the back of his skull like it was all about to break open. He got up and followed her, trying to look as cool and nonchalant as he possibly could.

"I feel as though I've always known you," she said after they'd taken a few steps. *Dumb,* was the first thing he thought. Then, a moment later, *Ludicrous . . . !* He could feel the jumpy id-thing in the back of his head stretching to find the word; it'd been a long time since any part of him had to use words like that.

But what she said settled in after a minute or two, and eventually he realized that she was right, that recognition was exactly what he was feeling.

"Yes," he said, agreeing with her. It was hard to say; he was still uneasy, his throat and his vocal cords still constricted and tense. "Maybe that's what it is."

She let that ride for a while, and they walked without talking until they were over by the pine trees.

"Do you come here often?" she asked.

He shrugged. "No, not often. Just when I need to."

"It's a good spot for sunrises," she said, and she pointed. Prosaically enough, the sun was rising over the river in all its gold and crimson glory. Gil had never really looked at it from here before; that really wasn't his sort of thing. If he was here and it was dawn it was pretty certain he'd be sleeping, or trying to.

But he still looked when she pointed, and he saw the sun's disk three-quarters risen over the horizon, and he even reveled in the glory and the overstatement of it. He saw a pattern in the wondrously golden-backlit clouds.

"Can you see that?" he asked. "Over there, to the left of the sun?"

She shook her head. "It looks like a cloud to me."

Gil felt silly, but he didn't let that stop him. "Can't you see the big golden dragon? And that ray of sunlight is the dragon breathing fire. That's the head, there's the tail, and those over there are the arms and legs. The big cloud over there is a wing; the other one's behind it."

She smiled again. "Do you always notice that sort of thing?"

"I don't know," he said. He kneeled down, looking at something in the grass. "I guess not." He wanted to tell her a lie, to tell her that he always did, but he couldn't think fast enough, and he told her the truth by accident, before he'd even had the chance to tell his voice not to. Part of him was trembling, anxious, scared, but the part of him that was talking and moving and doing, that was cool and calm as he ever was, just like nothing at all was happening. Being calm like that scared Gil probably more than anything else.

He stood up, and he was holding a flower: a tiny yellow buttercup.

She looked at it. "For me?" she asked.

"Yes." He reached over and held it under her chin. "What is it they say you are if it shows yellow underneath you?"

"I don't know."

He threaded the flower into her hair.

"Well?" she asked, and when he didn't answer she asked again. "What did you see?"

"I couldn't tell," he said. "I can't see from here."

As he moved his hand away she caught it. She kissed him, softly and gently, on the lips. She *touched* him. "Love me," she said.

And—

Again . . .

—just like the other times, he felt it reaching up from deep inside him, twisting him, making him . . .

Again . . . !

. . . want to *do* things, cruel, violent things, and suddenly like a daydream the world was made of blood, red, red, red, and he knew he had—

Again!

—to run or else he'd be doing something he could never undo, and he tried to break away from her but she had her arms around him *tight* and he couldn't get loose, and she was loving him, and *God* it was fine, and he had to get away but he couldn't even make himself try anymore, and—

—and—

—and suddenly he had the pig-sticker, the beautiful switchblade, in his hand, and when he pushed its button he almost came, and it was all much, much too late. He drove the knife into her back and into her neck, and her belly, and her sides, and in his mind's eye the world was made of redness. And even though his eyes were closed because he couldn't bear to see what he was doing he was coming, and again, and again.

And then he was drowsy and weak in the knees with the satiation of a lifetime's unfulfilled lust. He fell to the ground, and his eyes opened, and he almost shrieked from fear of seeing what he'd done . . .

. . . but he didn't, he gasped instead, because she was smiling at him, and there was nothing wrong with her at all.

Where he'd cut her there was mist wisping out of gloriously gaping holes, and when reflex curiosity made him reach out and touch her he realized that she wasn't made of flesh and blood at all, but ghost; her arm was cool and powdery in his fingers for a moment, and then it was not there to touch at all. He saw it pass through his hand just the way one dim reflection supersedes another on a window.

But when she reached out to take the knife from him her touch was as real and cold as anything he'd ever felt and her smile was as lazy-lusty as any he'd ever imagined, and when she spoke to him her voice was as real as it had ever been.

"Your turn." She said it just like when the girl is going to give the guy a back rub in the movies. Her voice was just exactly the lover's coo he'd always dreamed.

MODELS

John Maclay

John Maclay's "Models" is one of the most original and moving portrayals of childhood grief that I can remember reading. John has two sons himself, now aged twenty-one and nineteen, and the elder of the two was his model for "Models." Since 1981, John has been the small-press publisher of thirty-six books of fiction and local history—and, separately, since 1984, the published author of more than two dozen short stories and a co-written novel. A former advertising executive, he lives with his wife and two sons in Baltimore, Maryland.

"Dad, tonight can we build models?"

The man hesitates, thinking of a nap he was going to take, a television program he was going to watch. But he looks at the six-year-old boy, and answers, "Yes, I guess so."

The boy is excited as they climb to the third floor. They sit down at a table, tear the cellophane from a brightly colored box, spill out the plastic parts, and start to assemble an airplane.

The man tries to be interested in the job.

"After we're done with this one," he says, "we'll have only two more to go, then you'll have models of all the different kinds of airliners." The boy smiles in reply.

The man does more of the work than he should, since he's impatient to finish. He narrates the steps, the boy breaking in to say, "I can do that," or "Let me put on the wing." But when the boy falters, the man takes over.

Their work finally absorbs them, and they lose track of time. When his mother comes upstairs, says that the boy simply must go to bed, they are almost done. The next day they put on the decals, and set the model on the shelf with the others.

As they study the airplane, the boy remembers his father's hesitation the night before. "Why doesn't Dad always want to do things with me?" he thinks. But then he smiles. After all, he did have a good time. The man in turn remembers his own childhood. "I must be more of a father," he decides. "Not just . . . a model."

Two weeks later, the man has to go on a business trip. His wife and son drive him to the airport, the boy anxious to see the real airplanes, after the models. He is excited by the wide, polished floors of the terminal, the hurrying people, the smell of jet fuel, and the great machines rushing skyward. His father bends over to kiss him, and he feels secure. He watches the man go down the long tunnel to the plane, then turn and wave.

The boy and his mother stand at a window. "That's Daddy's plane," she says, "the one with the red stripe. He'll be home on Tuesday, and he'll bring you a present."

But it isn't Daddy's plane at all. He *mustn't* have control of it, thinks the boy, as it roars down the runway, lifts for a moment, then plunges into the woods and explodes in a ball of flame and a column of black smoke, like something on television. No one has control, not the trucks and men rushing toward the woods, or the screaming people around him. He looks at his mother's twisted face, and can't recognize it. But he doesn't cry. Daddy can't be in the ball of flame. He'll be home on Tuesday.

But Daddy doesn't come home anymore. The boy wanders around the quiet house, climbing to the third floor, where the row of model airplanes and two untouched boxes are. He opens one, tries to fit the parts together as his father taught him. But he can't, so he cries now, with a rage against all mechanical things. He throws the pieces on the floor, tramples them into sharp shards of plastic. He goes to the shelf, takes down a finished airplane, ready to destroy it too. Maybe, he thinks, that will bring back his father. But suddenly he sees its red stripe, and stops. He peers into one of the tiny windows. And miraculously, there is Daddy in the model, staring straight ahead, with a toy dog on his lap, a present for him. It's Tuesday now, and the boy feels a little better. He dries his tears and goes down to his mother.

Until he goes to college and the model airplanes are given away, the boy sometimes takes down the one with the red stripe, and looks into the window again. He usually does this when something bad has happened to him, or when he feels insecure. His father seems ever closer to him then. Soon the boy becomes a man, takes a job as a salesman, and travels the country in airplanes. He enjoys his trips, especially the conversations with the older men in the seats next to his. It is then that he remembers, not the little man he saw in the plastic plane, but his real father's voice and warmth beside him as they sat building models.

CRUSTACEAN REVENGE

Guy N. Smith

Guy N. Smith is one of those people whose sheer industriousness makes you feel exhausted just to hear about it. He and his wife Jean live on Black Hill, on the border of South Shropshire and Wales, an ancient Bronze Age backwater of Britain, still breathtakingly beautiful. There they run a 7½-acre smallholding which is run entirely organically, and also a mail-order business in horror/fantasy/SF first editions, Black Hill Books. A one-time banker, fifty-year-old Guy wrote *Werewolf by Moonlight* in 1975, and since then has published what seems like a new horror book every week. For me, though, his most memorable creation will always be *The Crabs,* and here is a new crustacean adventure for those who have a taste for devilish shellfish.

Klin was sweating profusely as he pulled the boat up on the rocky beach of the small island. He shaded his eyes against the glare of the afternoon sun, and stared back out to sea. Even a fisherman of his experience and calibre could not hold back the tiny shivers which ran up his spine and neck as he saw the cruel coral reefs, half-submerged beneath the water. Five hundred yards of them, a maze that protected this tiny island from casual visitors, claimed the lives of the unwary. There were few men who would have made it, would have had the courage to risk it. And Klin was one of those.

Tall and rangy, he topped six feet, his bronze muscular body clad only in a tattered pair of khaki shorts, a pair of scuffed sandals his only other attire. An unkempt mane of jet-black beard tumbled down to his broad chest, hiding features that were handsome in a wild sort of way. It was impossible to judge his age to within fifteen years but if you looked closely you saw flecks of grey in the dark hair, a wrinkle in the mahogany skin. But it was his eyes you noticed most of all, dark like the rest of him, penetrating, reading more of you than you read of him. And you felt uncomfortable in his presence for no reason that you could logically define. You dropped your gaze and admitted to yourself that in some inexplicable way you were afraid of this man. You didn't like him but you respected him.

Klin turned back, surveyed the island, the almost impenetrable mangrove swamp that had grown back since the last time he had set foot on this uncharted scrap of wasteland ten years ago. He recalled the fire that had ravaged it, started by his own hand, the wall of flames that swept terrifyingly inland, finally destroying those . . .

He grimaced at the memory of the giant crustaceans, the huge killer crabs which had ravaged the Great Barrier Reef, armoured invincible monsters that had virtually destroyed the millionaire paradise of Hayman Island in their insatiable hatred of Mankind and their relentless craving for human flesh and blood. A long time ago but Klin would never forget; sometimes they came back to him in his nightmares, the castanet-like clicking of their pincers, sheer malevolence burning out of their tiny eyes. Many was the time that he had awoken screaming, his flesh lathered in sweat, staring into the darkness of his beach hut and telling himself that it was only another dream. They weren't there, they couldn't be because the fire had destroyed them all. And even when he had harnessed logic and dispersed the terrible fantasies of the nocturnal hours he still had his doubts. And during the last few weeks those doubts had crept back and now he knew that the killer crabs were alive again, that some of them had survived and bred. And once again they were hungry for human flesh and blood; they *remembered* and wanted a terrible revenge for what Man had done to them. Which was why Klin had come back to this island.

They had got that girl off the beach on Hayman on the last full moon, a young millionairess who got her kicks out of nude bathing. She had gone down to the water just after midnight; Klin had observed her from the doorway of his hut and it had done exciting things to him, reminded him of another beautiful rich girl who had once figured in his life. Caroline du Brunner had been a crab victim, too. Now this other girl was asking for trouble. No, not from the crabs because they were all dead years ago but from inshore killer sharks and there were plenty of them about this summer.

Klin watched her swim right out, almost yielded to temptation and went down to the water to join her. She would have liked that, pretended at first that she wasn't going to let a common fisherman . . . But she'd change her mind, women always did where Klin was concerned. Maybe if he had gone then, she wouldn't be dead now. Or else they would both be dead. He grinned wryly to himself.

She had swum back to the beach, come up out of the tide, lithe and sensuous, shaking herself like a dog. *And next second they had got her!*

There were just two of them, as big as cows, moving with deceptive speed. Maybe if she had run she might have escaped their lumbering charge but instead she froze to the spot. The crustaceans got her by the legs first, snapped one and amputated the other, the blood from the ragged stump spouting thick and dark in the wan moonlight. She fell forward and they stood back and let her thresh and crawl a yard or so; Klin sensed their unholy gloating, their delight at her agony. Then they were on her again, pincers moving in obscenely and opening her thighs wide, making her do the splits, wrenching her limbs out of their sockets. A tender shapely breast was snapped off neatly, the soft flesh conveyed to a waiting mouth. In the stillness between the screams Klin heard the slurping, the munching, heaved at the revolting gluttony of creatures that had no right to live on this planet.

Those claws were gigantic scalpels in the hands of a butcherous surgeon carrying out an abdominal operation, slitting her open from crotch to throat, blood spraying the crabs as they delved into the incision and pulled out yards of intestine, sucking it up like tripe out of a barrel. Their appetite was whetted, the foregames were over.

Her screams grew fainter until they finally died away. Now she was just a dismembered heap of bloody flesh, unrecognisable for what she had once been, the power of her riches futile against these behemoths from out of the ocean. The crabs fed, crunched the bones and masticated noisily. Klin looked back towards the Royal Hayman Hotel; lights shone from every window and the faint strains of an orchestra tuning up reached his ears from the open ballroom window. Nobody had heard the girl's screams, and if they had they couldn't have given a shit, Klin reflected, because it wasn't them that were getting mangled up, and even if there were killer crabs in the sea then what the hell. Maybe most of them had never even read what had happened here once and, in any case, they would be gone by the end of the week. The crabs were somebody else's problem.

Klin reflected why he had not done anything. Not that the girl could have been saved once the crabs got her. Maybe he should have raised the alarm. But he didn't, and only now, standing here on the beach of the most dangerous island in Australia's Great Barrier Reef, did he understand why he hadn't. Because he had a personal score to settle with the monsters; *he hated them as much as they hated Mankind!* Maybe there were only a few of the bastards, the beginnings of a new strain of mutants, and if that was the case then that was swell. Whatever, he had to get them himself, the way he and Professor Davenport and Shannon of the Shark Patrol, the biggest bullshitter on Hayman, had once done. This time it had to be Klin's own show. He had a score to settle; they had snatched Caroline du Brunner from him, left him the way he had always been, a womaniser without a woman. And, Jesus Christ, they'd pay for that!

I'm gettin' crazier in my old age, he told himself as he beached the boat, lifted out the double-barrelled .500 Express that had once belonged to Harvey Logan, a big-game hunter who had called in at Hayman and thought he was going to bag himself a crab trophy. The rifle had proved inadequate, a toy would have served as well, but somehow it gave Klin a feeling of reassurance. It bucked and you heard the slug whine, heard it strike and ricochet. You didn't feel so vulnerable. I'm crazy, he decided as he walked up the sloping beach and remembered that suitcase full of money that was still buried amongst the pines behind the hotel. It had been Frank Burke's ill-gotten loot, which in turn had been stolen by the girl who called herself Caroline du Brunner. She was a con-girl but it didn't matter because by the time she got her hands on that money she was as wealthy as the image she had created. Thanks to the crabs, that dough had come Klin's way. After it was all over he could have sailed right out of Barbecue Bay to a life of ease. Wealth would only have taken the challenge out of life, he had told himself, but that was not the real reason he had stayed on. These crabs had become an obsession, he would never get them out of his system until he had killed the last one with his own hands. Moonlight nights he got thinking about them most, a kind of masochistic worship that kept you on Barbecue Bay. Just waiting.

Until now.

This island hadn't changed any, Klin noted. He remembered seeing it from the Patrol's chopper that time, roughly circular, its shores bounded by treacherous coral reefs. The swamp was spread over most of it, patches of water visible here and there, most of the land hidden by an impenetrable tangle of mangroves. A mangrove swamp can grow up in a few years, the seedlings sometimes drifting for hundreds of miles with the current, capable of remaining alive for a year, even longer, sprouting additional roots and top growth whilst still afloat. Then they get washed up somewhere, take root and spread. Like they had done on this island that didn't even have a name and where nobody came because of the reefs.

Beneath the top foliage was dead dry wood that would blaze and start a forest fire once you got it going. That was what had happened here. It had been Davenport's idea once they found out that the crabs were spawning here. Let 'em all come up out of the ocean, big ones carrying their young on their backs the way crustaceans do; let 'em get right into the heart of the swamp and then set the whole island on fire from different points. A gigantic ring of flames that even the crabs could not get through. Jesus, Klin still heard their cries of rage and pain as the fire got to them, roasted them alive. But they hadn't got the Big One, the one they called Queen Crab. She had been blinded but she had not died. Maybe there had been a male lurking somewhere in the ocean depths and they had got together, made out and started the whole thing off once more. Klin lit a cheroot, rattled his box of matches; the sound was as reassuring as the weight of Harvey Logan's gun under his arm because the big fisherman knew exactly what he had to do. An old motto of his, "What you've done once you can do again.'' And, by Christ, if he didn't do just that he was going to finish up as crab-bait for sure.

The mangroves had drifted in again after the fire and re-populated the island just like the crabs had done. The scenery was as familiar as if it was only yesterday when Shannon had put the chopper down and Davenport had said, ''This is the place, all right.'' And now it was the place again.

The narrow waterway was still there, the water no deeper than a few inches, the bed thick mud and coral, the mangrove branches overhead shutting out the sunlight and creating its own atmosphere of gloomy eeriness, restricting visibility to a few yards. In places the water was a dark red colour caused by the tannic acid from the mangroves.

Klin's progress was slow, stopping to listen at frequent intervals, but there was no sound other than the distant muffled waves on the coral. He did not expect to hear anything else for it was only mid-afternoon and the crabs would not move until the moon rose. But he needed time; time to build his fires, a task that several men had completed the last time and one that he must now carry out single-handed. Not so thorough, more chancy, because he must rely on the flames spreading from one starting point for he would not have time to circle the island lighting individual crustacean funeral pyres. He must rely on the wind and there was precious little of that.

Klin built his first fire a quarter of a mile into the mangrove forest. The crabs would doubtless follow this watercourse and he would have to try and cut off their retreat whilst the flames got a hold. He had just finished when his ears picked up a faint noise, one that had his heartbeat speeding up, every whipcord muscle in his body tensing. A clicking, a long way away . . . Relief as he recognised the sound, just the clicking of the shells of bivalves. The rustling of small, ordinary crabs scuttling away through the undergrowth at his approach. God, he was edgy.

The foul stench of decay was stifling, the heat intense and overpowering, his body awash with sweat. It had him thinking about that hidden money again . . . there was still time to cut and run, to leave this place and forget that it had ever existed. But he knew he would stay, that forces beyond his ken had called him here just as they had called the crabs. He was a puppet in the hand of Fate.

At length he reached the big clearing. It was maybe a hundred yards in circumference, a sheet of stagnant reddish-brown water where for some reason the mangroves had not rooted, a foul stinking lake. And it was to this place that he knew the crabs would come clicking their way in the silvery moonlight, the place where he must trap them and burn them. His pulses pounded at the thought and his dark eyes took on an expression that was maniacal as his obsession neared its peak. He savoured his own hate, the malignant driving force that burned up logic and clear thinking. He stood there for maybe half an hour, a clairvoyant viewing future happenings and lusting in what he saw. He smelled the smoke, felt the intense heat from the crackling flames as they leaped from one tree to another, a circle of fire consuming everything in its path. He heard the shrill cries of the trapped crabs, their squeals of pain and fear, heard their flesh sizzling. There was a pain in his chest but he ignored it; his vision was blurred because of the smoke which smarted his eyes and his dizziness was due to the suffocating atmosphere.

Then his fantasy was gone and he knew there was work to be done, piles of deadwood to be built, and when the time came he must sprint as the torch-bearer from Olympia had once done, pushing his brand into each tinder-dry heap; then back down the watercourse, lighting that final fire, running and hoping that he would make it back to his boat in time. Pausing on the beach to fire round after round back into the swamp from Harvey Logan's .500 Express, a final defiant gesture of victory. Shouting "It was Klin that did this, you bastards! D'you hear me, it was *Klin!*"

Then he was busy, oblivious of the heat and the stench, gathering dead branches and piling them up, relishing his task and only finishing it when darkness dropped its curtain over the island. Then he took up his position some fifty yards from where that sluggish stream oozed its way out of the forest, and waited. In one sweaty hand he held the gun, in the other his matches.

Just waiting and listening. And hoping that his intuition had not let him down and that the crabs would come as they had come ten years ago, a shambling army that would be defeated in a fiery hell.

. . .

The moon was almost at its zenith when Klin heard them coming, the muffled clicking growing louder by the second, a scraping of many pincers on coral. He tensed, peered into the shadows, mentally urged the monsters to come this way.

Then he saw them, silhouettes in the ethereal light, creatures that seemed far bigger than when he had last seen them, ungainly as they bore their offspring aloft, all making for . . .

Oh, merciful God, they weren't heading into that foul swamp lake, they were fanning out into the forest itself, finding a dozen tiny tributaries, going into those godawful everglades! Realisation numbed Klin, had him cursing incoherently, trying to will his enemy back into the clearing, but nothing would deter the crabs from their destination.

Click-click-clickety-click.

He could have pressed himself back against the bole of any one of a dozen different mangrove trees around him, climbed up into their boughs and been safe, but Klin dispelled any thought of skulking the night hours away. His fury was already beginning to erupt into a terrible rage, the hunter thwarted when his plans had seemed foolproof, crustacean cunning outwitting the guile of Man. For they *knew,* Jesus Christ they knew, had sensed this trap through an instinct evolved from their ancestors who had perished here; they saw the dangers of the lake, headed away from it where they could not be trapped by fire.

And, above all, they smelled an enemy in their midst, scented Man in their domain!

The Big One was there leading them, Klin recognised the Queen Crab by her very size, a giant amongst giants, a leader upon which the rest fawned. Pincers aloft, antennae waving, searching the shadows for Klin just as he had been scanning them for her. A pincer circled, pointed into the dense mangroves, and he knew that his hiding place had been discovered!

Perhaps he could have run, stumbled away from them in the darkness, made it back to the boat. The thought did not enter his enraged brain for never would he flee in the face of a foe. The matchbox fell from his fingers, rattled once in its futility as it struck the ground. And then the rifle came up to his shoulder, Klin's blurred vision seeking and finding a sight in the uncertain light. The big female, her gargoyle-like face lit up by the red glow from her eyes, triumph and hatred merging in her contorted expression. *There he is, the one who burned us before. Take him and feast on his flesh and blood.*

The report of the .500 was blanketed by the thick mangrove forest, a dull clap of thunder rolling through the trees trying to find a way out, the flash of sheet lightning that lit up the entire scene, magnified it a hundredfold. Impact—the heavy slug finding its mark on the flesh beneath the shell, a dull thud, the crab seeming to check but only momentarily. A crustacean scream of rage and hate, crabs coming from all sides, answering the cry of the one who controlled their every movement.

Klin fired again, reloaded, discharged both barrels, the recoil throwing him back against a twisted tree trunk. The smell of burned cordite was sharp in his lungs, the pain in his shoulder seeming to spread across into his chest, a crippling agony that robbed him of his strength to lift his weapon but somehow he still managed to reload. This time he fired from the hip, the gun bucking, the hammers gouging his hand viciously so that blood rushed from a severed vein.

The iron stench of human blood, how those crabs scented it, came at him in a shambling invincible wave. Still firing, the force of the bullets chipping their protective shells but not stopping them.

And then the final impact took Klin in the chest, a bone-shattering blow that threw him back into the mud so that he lay there looking up at the mangrove canopy above him, tracing patterns with his failing eyesight where the moonbeams made a criss-cross over his head; breathless, writhing, wondering what in hell they had fired back at him. A missile of some kind, somehow they had learned how to propel it accurately and with such force that it was capable of shattering a human breastbone. Oh God, the pain was excruciating . . .

The moonlight was fading, blackness tinged with red creeping in, numbing him so that he scarcely felt it when his outstretched legs were seized. Just mental agony, seeing again that girl being ripped apart on the beach back on Hayman Island, mutilated beyond recognition, then every last shred of her eaten so that the searchers found nothing and blamed it on the sharks.

Cursing. Then laughing hysterically at the irony of it all when everything began to fade and he felt himself starting to fall into that yawning bottomless chasm beneath him. Klin, the hunter of Barbecue Bay, had fallen into his own trap but nobody would ever know. The islanders wouldn't be able to bloody well laugh at him because . . . oh, shit, you should have told the Shark Patrol and had this place blasted to hell. No, it *is* hell and I wouldn't have had it any other way.

He mustered up one last laugh and hoped they heard and understood, knew that he had not gone down screaming at the last.

SARAH'S SONG

Roderick Hudgins

It took me a long time to decide to include "Sarah's Song" in *Scare Care,* for reasons which will be obvious when you read it. But Roderick's writing is fine and his heart is well attuned to the feelings of children, and in the end the sheer quality of the story won the day. Born in Suffolk, Virginia, Roderick graduated from Woodbridge High School with the hope of being a professional baseball player. Instead he became a sergeant in the U.S. Air Force. Twenty-seven years old, he now lives in Caribou, Maine, with his wife Jacki and his daughter Megan, where he has been working on his first novel. "Sarah's Song" will haunt you for a very long time to come.

Charlie Dore was singing ''Pilot of the Airwaves.'' The voice came slow and melodic on the tiny radio. The tiny radio which sat on the old dresser in the bedroom of the secluded white house on the lonely country road. The bedroom with the old furniture and the old curtains that swayed in the breeze. Outside was a warm June midmorning; a blazing yellow sun, highlighted by a deep blue sky. Freshly washed clothes fluttered on a clothesline. Off in the distance a dog barked; closer, a sparrow chirped.

Back inside, in the sitting room, *The Price Is Right* played on the oversized Montgomery Ward television set. In the kitchen, water ran over dirty breakfast dishes and the back screen door banged softly against its jamb. And upstairs, in the room with the tiny radio and the old furniture and the swaying curtains, came the crisply audible, steady sound of: THUMP . . . THUMP . . . THUMP . . .

It started early that morning with Wilbur, her oldest brother. Sarah had found him in the barn cleaning out the animal stalls. She crept up to the hayloft, careful not to make any noise, and there she found what she needed to do the job. And what an excellent job it did!

The pitchfork went through the back of Wilbur's neck and down his back cleanly; almost silently. The sound it made was like that of a spade entering moist earth. At first, Wilbur only stood stock-still; eyes wide, mouth agape. Then his mouth began to move, but no sounds came out. Blood ran from one nostril, then flowed from one corner of his mouth. Wilbur fell face-first to the barn floor. Blood slowly started to seep up through the holes made by the pitchfork.

Next, there was Sarah's year-older sister, Celia. Celia was standing at the kitchen sink preparing water for the breakfast dishes. Her long auburn hair was drawn into a ponytail behind her head and she wore only a skimpy pink nightie. The same nightie their momma had told Celia time and time again not to wear, because it was "too barin'" for a house with two growing boys. But Celia wore it anyway; she'd always been proud of what it revealed. That was why Sarah had never cared for Celia.

Sarah knew what it was Celia did with the red-haired boy with the big teeth in the clearing out in Old Man Curtis' woods. She had followed Celia out there once without Celia's knowing it. From her hiding place behind the big oak stump covered by white honeysuckle, she'd watched as the red-haired boy had his way with Celia. The boy touched Celia's breasts, slid his dusty, freckled hand up her dress and even touched her secret place. Sarah didn't know what they were doing, but she knew it was bad. Because Celia had quipped teasingly that it wasn't for goodie-goodie, dumb-witted girls like her. Celia always teased her; not openly and outright, but sneakily, coyly, so neither Momma nor Daddy would notice. Celia teased until Sarah thought her own curiosity would kill her. But then Sarah had learned what the bad thing was, and she didn't want to do it. Celia would be damned to hell for doing it.

While Celia stood at the kitchen sink about to do the dishes, Sarah stealthily sneaked to the pantry and removed the huge butcher's knife from the top shelf. The knife Momma called "Daddy's hog-killin' knife."

The large knife was as beautiful as it was menacing. Its handle was hickory, with a solid brass ring protruding from its end. The blade was bluish steel, polished to a high gloss and sharpened to split hairs. But hairs weren't what Sarah intended to split.

From the doorway of the pantry she watched Celia. Sarah loved her sister dearly, but Celia was too cruel. Too, too cruel.

Sarah took great pains to be silent; she didn't want to alert Romy, in the next room. When she struck, it was with catlike abandon; quick and quiet, but fierce and to the point. She'd sprung up behind Celia, covered Celia's mouth with her hand, pulled her sister's head back and glided the razor-sharp edge of the knife across Celia's throat. Sarah then pushed Celia's head back down until it touched her chin to her chest, muffling the gurgling noises made by the spewing blood. Sarah had seen this on the Tuesday night movie a couple of nights before, the one about Viet Nam. It worked, just like in the movie.

With Celia out of the way, it was time now for little Romy. He'd begun to stir in the sitting room, rising to change the channel from *Romper Room* to *The Flintstones*. Besides her mother, Romy would be hardest. Sarah loved her little brother very much and hated the idea of having to destroy him. Poor little Romy. His brown eyes wide and curious, with all the wonders around him. The stubby five-year-old fingers pushing his sandy blond hair out of his face. Romy was a brat at times, but he was still Sarah's favorite.

But the voice had said Romy, too. The voice had said *all* of them, kill them all.

The voice told her they were mean and hateful without exception. And deep down Sarah knew it was true. Celia and Wilbur, always teasing, calling her "retard." Once Celia'd used a word Sarah had never heard: "You iddy-itt!" Celia had screamed at her when she dropped a dish trying to help with the dinner dishes. Sarah'd had no idea what the word meant, but she knew it was mean; mean just like Celia. Momma and Daddy had scolded Celia and Wilbur many times, saying she *wasn't* a retard, only "slow." Her momma helped her feel good but she oftened wondered about Daddy. Daddy liked to hug and touch her, but his hugs and touches were peculiar ones. One time he'd even touched her secret place and made her touch his. She had struggled and tried to pull away, but he was too strong. "Relax," her daddy had said. "Sarah, you're nineteen now. You're a woman. Time for you to learn about this." Her momma came in and her daddy had lied and said they were just "funnin'."

Sarah felt strange toward her father; she loved him, but she also feared him. When she did away with her father, it would be like removing an aggravating burden. If little Romy was the hardest to kill, Daddy was going to be easiest. But she'd worry about her father later, when he came home from work.

Right now, it was little Romy's turn.

Romy was sitting again on the dirty, legless sofa, holding a tennis ball in both hands and watching Fred Flintstone harangue his wife, Wilma, for some unknown reason. Sarah crept up behind the sofa, an ice pick gripped tightly in her right hand. Romy shifted, working himself now to the edge of the couch. Sarah watched him; a stream of saliva tracked from the corner of her mouth. *Run, Romy. Run.* The words formed in her head, but nothing left her mouth. The thought was severed completely when she grabbed Romy by his hair with her free hand and rammed the ice pick into the base of his skull with the other.

Romy tensed; his tennis ball flew from his hands and bounced across the floor. His hands jerked out spasmodically, seeming to reach for the ball, and then all life left him. Blood poured from his nostrils, over his chin and down onto his white Dallas Cowboys football shirt. A dark stain began to spread about the crotch of his tan Garanimals jeans.

Sarah stared at the slumped body, held up now only by the ice pick in the back of his head. She stared unbelievingly at what she had done. A car raced by on the road outside, snapping Sarah from the temporary trance. A gust of wind blew some papers off a table, making Sarah jump and notice that she still held fast to the wooden handle of the ice pick. Quickly, she yanked her hand away.

Outside, Sarah's mother sang to herself while she hung the clothes to dry. Romy's body fell forward, the head thumping the floor. Sarah jumped again and, this time, emitted a startled shriek.

Easy, Sarah. Calm down. The voice from the tiny radio wafted down, casting its spell once more. *It's all right. You've done well. Now, all you have to do is one more—then wait for Daddy to get home.*

Her composure regained, Sarah turned and started for the back door. As she walked through the kitchen, taking a giant step over Celia's body, she caught a glimpse of her mother through the window over the sink. She had hoped to find an easy, painless way for Momma, but none came to mind. She went out the back door and crossed the yard to the woodshed where the hatchets were kept.

The woodshed was old; it smelled of damp mildew. It had been hastily built years ago and its walls now peeled dingy gray paint. Inside the shed was cool darkness; a welcome relief from the humid June morning.

Sarah stepped inside (glancing back one last time to make sure no one had seen her), closed the door behind her and paused to allow her eyes to adjust to the dark. From the rear wall of the shed, dim streaks of sunlight managed to filter through a tiny, very dusty window, only minutely illuminating the interior of the shack.

Sarah took a deep breath, separating the sweet smell of sawdust from that of mildew. The scent brought back pleasant memories from a time long since past.

When Sarah was a little girl, she had spent long hours playing in the shed. Of course, it was in much better repair then, not nearly as neglected and dilapidated as it now appeared.

It was Sarah's own special place, when she was younger; a place where no one bothered her. No furtive whispering or half-pitying stares from townsfolk. None of the cruel teasing from other children. Almost all her memories about the old—the better—woodshed were good ones. The single bad recollection was the time Momma found her playing with her special baby doll.

Sarah's mother had come out to call her to dinner and found her sitting on a wooden toolbox cradling her baby doll which was wrapped in an old pink tablecloth. Sarah had glanced up at her momma and smiled a lopsided smile.

Her mother was always kind, always knew what to say to make her feel better. She'd never noticed the unfocused right eye, the ugly harelip, or the lack of intelligence caused by an unexplained birth defect. But upon seeing what Sarah had wrapped in the tablecloth, her mother's kindness and seemingly perpetual patience evaporated.

"Whatcha got, darlin'?"

"My baby doll. My *special* baby doll," Sarah'd said happily, struggling with her deformed lip.

"The one Daddy gave you for Christmas?" Momma squatted down beside her.

"No, ma'am. I found it."

"Found it where?"

"In the field 'cross the road," Sarah'd said.

"Can Mommy see her?"

"Well . . . I reckon. Just be careful, she's only a little baby." She had gently placed the tiny bundle in her mother's arms, all the while blushing proudly.

But a putrid odor wafted up from it.

"Oh, *Christ* . . ." was all Sarah's mother managed before flinging the bundle across the shed. It struck a far wall and fell to the dirt floor. The tablecloth came open and the carcass of the dead rat rolled out.

"Sarah Elliott! What is the matter with you?" Each word was harshly accentuated. "That is not a play toy!"

Sarah said nothing. This was a side she'd never seen from her mother. Tears slowly slid down each cheek.

Mrs. Elliott checked her temper and ordered Sarah to go into the house and take a bath before dinner.

Now as Sarah stood in the shed recalling the incident, the malformed smile faded from her lips. She knew that that one bad time hadn't made her mother a mean or terrible person, yet the voice said her mother was evil and had to be destroyed. But who—or what—*was* this voice that could only be reached on *her* radio?

For the past three weeks Sarah had spent hours in her room, listening to the battered little radio on her dresser emitting a soft, enticing voice. It soothed her, comforted her; it encouraged her to right all the wrongs in her life. But the voice always said the wrongs were those people she loved most: her family. And wasn't that strange? But it also made sense. Because townsfolk and teasing children she could stay away from, but the family was always there.

But who *was* this voice? While it made her feel wonderful—like a real person—how did she know she could trust it? Momma'd told her never to trust strangers, and Sarah didn't recognize the voice; therefore it must be a stranger. Yet it was so kind, and entrancing. She hadn't been able to help falling under its spell.

Her mother's humming from the clothesline snapped Sarah's reflections in two. She reached up, grabbed the middle of three hatchets that hung on the rear wall. It was fairly new; the handle was sanded to a smooth finish, and the head had recently been sharpened. Sarah stared at the edge, amazed at how *right* the hatchet felt in her hand. She grinned, turned on her heel and started toward the door.

Christine Elliott ran the back of her hand across her sweat-dampened forehead. Then she removed the comb from the bun of her hair, letting it fall to her shoulders for the soft breeze to cool her hot, moist scalp. She saw Sarah leave the woodshed and begin walking in her direction. Christine smiled warmly, then waved to her daughter.

But the smile left Christine's lips and turned to puzzlement when Sarah got closer.

The girl's hands were behind her back, as if playing a game, but the look in her eyes was unsettling even to a mother. Sarah's eyes gazed straight ahead, and appeared to be glazed over. A lump had formed in Christine Elliott's throat by the time Sarah stood before her.

"Hey, darlin'," Christine murmured, her voice cracking.

Sarah blinked, seemed to awaken at the sound of her mother's familiar drawl. "Hi, Momma."

"You okay?" Christine's tired, gray eyes studied her daughter's face.

"Yes, Momma, I'm fine." She watched her mother nervously raise a wet bedsheet and turn back to the clothesline. "But I have something I want to tell you."

"What is it, sweetie?" Christine swiveled, met Sarah's eyes. "You know you can tell Momma anything." She had to squint slightly in the blazing midday sun.

Sarah's eyes grew soft. "I love you, Momma."

Christine felt tears form in her eyes one moment before the hatchet came down with deft ferocity and force, embedded in her forehead, between the maternal eyes and partly through the nose. She never knew what had happened, and stumbled backward, slightly, then fell on top of her freshly washed linen.

Sarah turned and stared toward her own bedroom window. The thin white curtains blew inward from the mild breeze, and the little, battered radio on the old dresser again emitted the soft, melodic voice. She followed the lulling sound up to her room, pausing along the way to retrieve the huge butcher's knife. She squatted down next to the dresser, the knife held out in front of her between both hands, and listened to the soothing tones from the radio. While she listened, she thought of her father, pictured him dearly. Her lips curled into a completely covert sneer and, rhythmically, she began to poke the floor with the knife. The strokes made huge, permanent gashes.

Sarah listened to the radio, and waited for her father.

THUMP . . .

THUMP . . .

THUMP . . .

THE AVENGER OF DEATH

Harlan Ellison

Harlan Ellison suggested that maybe it was "sententious" for him to remark that "money is lovely, but serving the commonweal makes the air draw fresher in the nostrils." Sententious, nothing. The warmth and immediacy with which all of the horror writers in this collection responded to my appeal (Harlan included) showed that their desire to help children has nothing whatsoever to do with self-regard. What can I say about Harlan Ellison, except that he's a brilliant and celebrated one-man dynamo of science fiction and fantasy, with more Hugos and Nebulas to his name than anybody else? A denizen of Sherman Oaks, California, he has written *Star Trek* and *Outer Limits* episodes, motion picture scripts, more than thirty books and that *Canadian Review* called him the best living short story writer.

The first one Pen Robinson killed came to his attention partially through the good offices of the Manhattan branch of the Federal Bureau of Investigation. He had been holding a dusty copy of *Burke's Peerage* when they took him into custody.

They came for him—two frosty agents who had bought their suits at the same Big & Tall Men's Shop—just after two-thirty on Saturday.

The bookstore was busier than usual, "just off Broadway, rare books and technical texts in Good Condition," because of the two Puerto Rican boys who had approached him the previous Monday as he was unlocking the shop. They had braced him, suggesting a way in which he—Meester Robinson of Robinson's Good Used Books—could attract new business, "guaranteed *absolutamente*." For a small fee, they would undertake to slip under the windshield wipers of every automobile parked between Eighth Avenue and Park, between 42nd and 59th Streets, a flier advertising whatever Meester Robinson wanted to push that week.

Pen had gone to the Kinko instant print shop on Lexington, and had ordered three thousand fliers extolling the arcane virtues of books scented with shelf dust and written by men and women who had vanished into the lonely posterity of the Dewey Decimal System.

The boys had been as good as their word, and mailboxes, doorways, lunch counters—and windshields—had worn his fliers throughout the week. Pen had paid them gladly; and Saturday was busier than usual when the FBI chilled the doorknob of the shop, entering to take him into custody.

One moment he had been standing there, dusting *Burke's Peerage*, and the next he was crossing the sidewalk on 51st Street, being sternly guided by a cold hand, slipping as effortlessly as an exhalation, into the velour darkness of the black limo double-parked in front of the shop. Fifteen minutes later he was somewhere in the towering abyss of the Pan Am Building, seated in a moderately comfortable knockoff of an Eames design, being punctiliously but courteously questioned by a man half his age. Pen Robinson, at age fifty-five, looked no older than forty; and his judgment of the inquisitor's youth may have been faulty. He was under no misapprehension about the quality of the man's eyes, however.

He thought, *I'm glad I never have to look out of those eyes.* He knew he would not like the world seen from that side.

"You called a bicycle shop in Queens yesterday," said the wearer of the bad eyes.

"Uh, yes . . ." Pen was wary.

"Why did you call that number, Mr. Robinson?"

"It was a wrong number."

"Whom," he said precisely, "were you looking for at that number?"

Pen furrowed his brow. He had no idea where this was going.

"They said they were from the FBI. The men who brought me here. I never asked to see their identification. I suppose it's against the law to say you're from the FBI if you're not. Are you really the FBI?"

The young man neither nodded nor blinked. "Whom were you seeking at that number, sir?"

"Maybe I ought to ask to see your credentials. I don't even know your name . . . there's nothing on the door out there. How do I know you're—"

The young man leaned forward, resting his pale, freckled hands on his desk blotter. The desk was empty of all but the leather-framed blotter, and a pair of pale, freckled hands. "You don't want to get yourself in any deeper, do you, Mr. Robinson? You're only here for a visit; you understand that the liaison we share, at the moment, does not involve the possibility of arrest, imprisonment, detainment, any of that. You understand that, don't you?"

Pen was frightened. People vanished, it happened all the time; and not just in Latin American dictatorships. Right here in the United States, it could happen: Judge Crater, hundreds of children every year, Jimmy Hoffa. And those who vanished into *apparats* controlled by people who spent their time spying on one another. There had to be hidden places where the vanished were taken. And from there to other locations . . . from which one never returned . . . or if you did, the years would have been stolen, and your loved ones would never recognize you . . . to come back as an old, old man they did not know. There were no loved ones: Pen was alone in the world. But that only made it worse. If they decided he would never return, who but the New York State tax assessor would try to find him.

"Look, I don't know what this is all about," he said, trying to get back to whatever safe place he had unknowingly abandoned. "But this is all crazy; it's a mistake of some kind. Why don't I just tell you what that call was about?"

"Why don't you tell me that, Mr. Robinson?" No resonance: flat silver panes of reflective glass.

So he told him how inconsequential it had been.

"I bought a library at an estate sale. From an agent in Detroit. It was one of the last elements of the dissolved estate of a man who had worked for GM for many years. I was told there were hundreds of technical journals and books of design." He paused a beat to clarify. "My store specializes in technical texts."

The eyes blinked. Pen took that as encouragement.

"I was opening the crates . . . so I could catalogue what had come. I was slapping them."

Another blink. Pen was beginning to get the drill: he clarified.

"Slapping them. Flat banging two books together to get the dust off them. Then I turn each one upside-down and riffle the pages; for good measure. A check fell out of one of them. I picked it up, and it was a check that had been written by a man named Henry Chatley. The address was in Queens. It was a perfectly good check drawn to cash, in the amount of something like one hundred and fifty dollars. It was only two weeks since it had been written, it was a check someone could cash. I called the number on the face of it. A man answered and said it was some bicycle repair shop. I thought I'd misdialed, and called back, and got the same man. I dialed very carefully the second time. So I didn't know what to do."

The mouth beneath the eyes moved. "How did it get there?"

"How did *what* get there? The shop, the man, what?"

"The check, Mr. Robinson. How did the check get into that book?"

"How am I supposed to know?"

"You say you bought these books from the library of a man who lived in Detroit."

"Yes. He died, and they liquidated his assets to pay outstanding taxes."

"This was an old book?"

Pen shrugged. "I didn't check the copyright, but I'd say it had been in his library for years, yes, I think I can say that."

"What was the title of this book, that you say the check fell from?"

"I'm not *saying* it fell, it *did* fall. I didn't make this up!" He felt anger rising despite his caution. "And what if I *am* making it up, what's the problem here? I did a decent thing, I made a good samaritan phone call; I got a number that had been changed. Obviously, that's the answer. What is it you *think* this is all about?"

"I don't think it's about anything, sir. I'm asking a few questions."

There wasn't anything to say to that, so Pen sat and waited. It had to stop sometime; perhaps now.

"So you don't know Henry Chatley."

Pen said, very seriously, sitting forward and placing his hands opposite the pale, freckled pair: "I wouldn't know Henry Chatley if he walked through that door. I have never *met* a Henry Chatley; I have never *heard* of a Henry Chatley; and I wish to god I'd never seen his damned check! Now does that satisfy you? Have I been here long enough for you to run me through your computers or whatever you do, long enough for you to understand I'm a used-book seller and not Ashenden the Secret Agent?''

The young man with the bad eyes said nothing. He looked at all the parts of Pen's face, as if certain duplicity would reveal itself in dark lines if he applied enough visual pressure. Finally, he said, ''Thank you, Mr. Robinson.''

Pen was astonished. It was over, as abruptly as that. His inquisitor obviously meant for him to go.

''That's it?'' he said. Now he was annoyed. It seemed he should have ended with a bit more fanfare . . . *something*!

''That's it, sir.''

''Not even going to tell me what this has been about, are you? Not even a word, right? Just let me march out and find my way back to my place of business, from which you dragged me for this waste of time!''

''Goodbye, Mr. Robinson.'' The door opened behind him, and he felt a chill. The cold hand touched him again, and he knew it was time to get up, now, right now, and go with the agent.

Three minutes later, he was on the street.

He was hailing a cab when it hit him. How *did* that two-week-old check, written on a New York bank, by a man whose phone number had been changed with such impossible swiftness that it had already been reassigned to a bicycle repair shop in Queens, get into a book that had sat on an old man's bookshelf in Detroit for possibly decades? And who the hell was Henry Chatley?

• • •

In the cab going back uptown, he felt as if he stood poised before a membrane. Where he stood, on this side, it was the real world, the mimetic universe, a place of order, even if this thing with the FBI made no sense, was something out of *Alice*. On the other side, through that translucent curtain, lay a great many small items, only imperfectly seen, but probably very important. Where the check had come from, how it had gotten into the book, who Henry Chatley was . . . or had been. He had an overwhelming sense of certainty that Henry Chatley, whoever, wherever, was dead.

But how to get through the membrane?

He needed a trope, a metaphor, a puff of smoke, a rabbit for the hat. Twenty minutes later, back in the shop, near to closing time, the rabbit manifested itself.

While he had been at the Pan Am Building, his clerks had tended to the benefits proffered by the two Puerto Rican boys. The shop was empty.

He decided to lock up early, cleared the cash register, gave out the paychecks, and watched as the clerks wandered up the street, seeking weekend euphoria. He stared out the front window for a time, then locked the doors and stared out the window for a longer time. In all, it had been only twenty minutes, yet in that time he had resisted the impulse to find the book again: not once, but a hundred times.

Finally, he went back into the storeroom, to the stack of books he had removed from the crate the day before. He had not lied to the inquisitor. He really *didn't* know which book it had been. When the check had floated to the floor, he had laid the book on the stack beside the crate, and had taken no further notice of it. If all was as it had been, the book should still be there.

It was. One of the clerks had placed a folded newspaper atop the stack, but otherwise, everything was as it had been. He picked up the book. *Elements of Structural Design,* with a copyright notice of 1926. Pen held the book in both hands, and stared at it; then, as he flipped the pages, he discovered two more pieces of paper.

The first was part of a press release for a book titled *Tian Wen: A Chinese Book of Origins*. It had been torn off, possibly having been used as a bookmark. It bore an excerpt from the twenty-three-hundred-year-old Taoist catalogue of mythology, philosophy and pre-Imperial legend. It read as follows:

1

Of the beginning of old,
Who spoke the tale?

2

When above and below were not yet formed,
Who was there to question?

3

When dark and bright were obscured,
Who could distinguish?

He had no idea what it meant. He *never* understood such riddles, though apparently entire nations found the words urgently meaningful. The only one of such epigraphs that had ever made sense to him was: *The oxen are slow, but the Earth is patient.* That seemed peculiarly appropriate now, even if the three excerpts from *Tian Wen* were not.

So he continued flipping the pages of the book, and came, at last, to the stiff file card wedged into the spine fold. Printed on the card were the words ***Chatley*** and ***Where the Woodbine Twineth.*** Under these words, written in a fine hand, with an ink pen, was the direction ***Take by truck, corner 82nd and Amsterdam, Friday, 7:17 P.M.***

He took the IRT uptown to 79th and Broadway, and walked quickly to 82nd and Amsterdam. He expected to find a shop, or an apartment, or something that related. He found nothing but the dead faces of apartment buildings as night fell.

But he knew he had been intended to find *something*. However the three seemingly disconnected pieces of paper had found their way into that book, he understood in his meat and bones that it was he, Pen Robinson, who had been meant to discover the puzzle, and to solve it. He had never been a mystic, lived life surely in the pragmatic universe of shelf dust and self-prepared meals after work, and knew there was a logical explanation waiting for him here on the corner of 82nd Street and Amsterdam Avenue.

He loitered. He leaned against a wall and studied the street. Nothing, for the longest time. He looked to the rooftops, and then to the filthy New York sky. Nothing, for a longer time. He felt his eyes closing. He knew he shouldn't be weary, nothing really exhausting had happened to him that day. Perplexing, emotionally taxing, but not truly something to make the flesh sag. But the waiting was beginning to take its measure of him.

And the rabbit came again.

Across the street, directly opposite his station, a pale blue light pulsed softly from the stairwell leading down to a basement apartment. He studied it for a while, and then slowly walked across 82nd to the apartment building. He looked over the wrought iron railing, leaning between heavy black plastic bags of garbage waiting for the truck some distant morning. In the stairwell, lying on his back, was a man with a hole in his chest. From the hole pulsed a distressingly blue light, and as Pen watched, the hole expanded slightly, and the glowing light colored the man's anguished face. He was in terrible pain.

Pen walked to the gate in the railing, slipped the latch, and walked down the stone steps to the filthy bottom. He knelt beside the man, and looked into his face. "Henry Chatley," he said. He knew who this had to be.

The man looked up at him, and nodded with the tiniest movement. "You found the termination order," he said, the words sighing from between lips that barely moved.

The glow pulsed steadily, as Chatley's chest was being eaten away; and Pen could see inside him. It was like looking into a cauldron of soup being roiled by an invisible ladle. "What's happening to you?" Pen said urgently. He felt he should be doing something for Chatley, but this new strangeness was more frightening than anything that had yet happened. "Is there something I can do?"

The man made an attempt to smile. It was a thin rictus, the corners of his mouth twitching for just an instant. The sound coming from the glowing hole in his chest was faint, but if Pen leaned closer he could make out the unmistakable keening of mountain winds. Whatever was happening to Chatley, it had been intended that he would suffer. Pen asked again if there was some help he could offer: a hospital, moving the man's limbs to a more comfortable position, some kind of cover that would block the hole?

Chatley shook his head without much actual movement. "I took George S. Patton and Bert Lahr."

Pen said, "What? Say again, please: I couldn't make that out."

"Patton and Bert Lahr. And Huey Long and Groucho Marx. I took them."

"Took them? Took them where? Were you a cabdriver? What?"

"I took them where the woodbine twineth. And Ansel Adams. I took him."

"Who are you, Mr. Chatley? What are you saying to me?"

Chatley looked up, and for a moment there were ages in his eyes. And enormous measures of pure pain. And the sense of things rushing away from the lens of his sight, while mountain winds howled. "I worked for the Dust Man. I collected for him. Got notices and did the actual work."

Pen had no idea what he meant.

That was not quite true.

He had an idea, but it lay so far beyond the membrane, on the shadowy side of other realities, that he could not countenance it.

Chatley said, "The Dust Man. The reaper. He laughs when he calls himself Boneyard Bill."

"He did this to you?"

"I did this to myself. He gave me a termination order for you. I didn't do it. So he had George fulfill the order on me."

Pen remembered the file card in the book. "Take by truck."

Chatley was speaking so softly now, Pen had to lean in almost to his mouth. The blue glow had spread, the hole was gigantic, nearly from armpit to armpit. "George isn't as adept as he should be. The truck threw me over the railing. I've been waiting for you. I'm glad you came." These words were spoken so haltingly, so filled with dying air, that it took him several minutes to release them.

"Why didn't you take me?" Pen asked.

Chatley would have shrugged, had he been able. As it was, he twitched terribly, saying, "If it hadn't been you, it would have been my next order. Should have been the woman before you. The order was an epileptic seizure, death all alone, in the evening, dressed to go out to dinner with her daughter." He closed his eyes against the pain, and said, "Her name was Emily Austin. In California. It should have been her, but I was still afraid. I'm still afraid; it hurts very much; Bill likes to hurt. But he may not be done with me. There was a taker once, a while ago, Ottmar, he got word back to some of us . . . the same way I got the papers into the book for you to find . . . he said it didn't stop after Bill had his way. Not for orders like you or Emily Austin, you're on the books. But for us, the takers. Bill likes to hurt. He doesn't get as much of a chance as he'd like."

"Can I help you in *any* way?"

Chatley opened his eyes. There was distance behind the color. He was on his way. The blue glow had eaten its way down through his stomach. "You know."

"I can't do that," Pen said, wishing he hadn't.

"Then why ask?"

"What would I have to do? I don't think I can do it, but what would that be . . . to help . . . ?"

Chatley told him. It was simple, but it was unpleasant. Then he said, "You can always tell one of us by the eyes." And he described the bad eyes Pen had seen watching him across a desk earlier that day. He lay silently for a long time, as the blue glow ate away the flesh and the bones and Pen could see the maelstrom swirling inside him. Then he said, "If you're going to do it, please now. It's very bad now. It's very bad."

And so Henry Chatley became the first for Pen Robinson.

But when Chatley was gone, perhaps having been saved from the Dust Man's special attentions on that other plain beyond the membrane, Pen realized he had not asked what the Chinese epigraphs meant, nor why he had written a check for cash in the amount of one hundred and fifty dollars, nor how he—using Ottmar's method—had been able to get the papers into that old book, nor what had turned him against the Dust Man, nor what had finally broadened his courage to defy Bill, nor what the takers posing as FBI men had sought to find out from Pen (but perhaps it had only been a matter of needing to be convinced Pen was an unsuspecting bystander), nor the answers to the other questions that now would never go into the solving of the puzzle, the passage through the membrane.

And one morning very soon, the truck would pick up a black plastic bag filled with remaining parts.

• • •

Pen gave over the running of the shop to the clerks.

He wandered the city, looking into people's faces.

He found the taker who had fulfilled the orders on P. T. Barnum and Babe Ruth and Adlai Stevenson, among others. Those were the names she remembered best, the ones she would tell him about. He found her eating dinner alone at the Russian Tea Room, and he followed her home, and did what he would never have thought himself capable of doing. He forced his way into her building, then into her apartment. He tied her to a chair and asked her more than a hundred questions. Chatley had died before he could answer those questions, more than a hundred Pen had been too distracted to ask. She possessed the bad eyes Henry Chatley had described, so Pen was able to do what he had to do. But she only knew a few things, despite her age. She did as she was told. Had been doing it for a very long time; and Pen learned that it was because of the gift of *a very long time* that many takers hired on.

It seemed to Pen a poor reason for working at such an unpleasant job. And when she told him, with resignation, that now he would have to put her out of Bill's reach, because of finding her and talking to her and interfering with her anonymity and making her suspect in

Bill's eyeless sockets, he said he couldn't do that, and she began to cry, which Pen thought was shameless of her, and she told him some of what it would be like, but he already knew that because he had crouched beside Chatley, and she said if he had even a spark of human kindness, a vestige of human decency, he would do what had to be done, and he thought that was even crueler of her to say, because where did human kindness and human decency enter into *her* job description? Had she said anything to Babe Ruth when she took him? Had Adlai Stevenson given her unassailable reasons for demonstrating human decency and kindness?

"You mustn't leave me for Bill!"

"It would serve you right."

"*Please*! Show some compassion!"

"My god, this is an obscenity!"

But in the end, he did it. Because thinking about all the reasons why he *couldn't* do it, which were all the reasons she had ignored and *did* do it, made him so desolately angry that he couldn't stop himself. And so with the second one he became the avenger of Death.

• • •

He found the taker who had gotten Ernie Pyle, and he killed him. He found the taker who had arranged for John Lennon and Fiorello La Guardia and Brendan Behan, and he killed him. He found the taker who had gotten Mackenzie King and Marilyn Monroe and Frank Herbert, and he killed her. He found the taker who had gotten Sergei Rachmaninoff and Eleanor Roosevelt and Helen Keller, and he killed him. He sat behind the one who had taken Emiliano Zapata and Leon Trotsky and Amelia Earhardt and Aleister Crowley, as she stolidly watched an Arnold Schwarzenegger movie. She was a very old, blue-haired woman, and she studied the film as if preparing for a final exam. And Pen waited for a car crash, reached into her lap, pulled out a knitting needle; and he killed her. He saw the taker who had been his inquisitor, and he followed him into a restaurant, and when he went to the men's toilet followed him again, and didn't even ask whom he had gotten, because he knew the list would be long and filled with people whose names he would not know, and which the taker would not remember, and he simply killed him. But not once did he ask the question that transcended in simplicity and importance, all the hundreds of questions he *did* get answered.

Not once did he ask a taker why the Dust Man was not making any effort to stop him from decimating the ranks of his chosen agents, why he was allowing Pen Robinson to course through the city being the avenger of Death.

. . .

On the first day of winter, in Central Park, near the statue of Alice, he saw a taker about to put his hands on a child climbing a rock. Pen moved in, feeling his years in his aching bones, and he was about to use the ice pick on the man whose hand stretched toward the little girl, when he felt a chill that was not part of the season, and a hand dropped onto his shoulder. The voice behind him said, "No, I think not, Pen. That will be enough. It's certainly enough for me."

In the moment before the cold hand turned him away, Pen saw the taker reach to the child, and touch her on the ankle, and the child fell. It lay on the crackling icy grass, and the taker moved off, casting only a momentary glance at Pen and his companion. The taker was frightened.

Then Pen was turned, without seeming effort, and he looked at the face of the Dust Man. He had not seen that face in forty-one years.

Tears came to his eyes, and he reached out to touch the chest of the reaper, the reiver, the slayer of nations; and he said, "You went away and I never got to say goodbye."

Pen Robinson's father, who had died in a mill accident when Pen was fourteen, smiled down at his boy and said, "I'm sorry, Pen. But I've spent a long time getting back to you, and I've missed you."

Now Pen could see clearly through the membrane; and he understood why Henry Chatley had been permitted to contact him; and why he had found it so effortless after a quiet, empty, essentially lonely life of shelf dust and cold meals prepared after work, to do the things he had done.

And he walked with the Dust Man, whose name was Bill, as had been his father's name, through the membrane and straight into a long lifetime position in the family business.

CABLE

Frank Coffey

Will this man Coffey ever be serious? Probably never; and that's what gives his horror fiction such a combination of terror and charm. Frank is a New York-based novelist and screenwriter, and he and I first touched base when he produced an anthology (recently reprinted) called *Modern Masters of Horror*. He tells me that his hobby is donning a Packer Backer knit hat and defrauding old biddies with bogus fortune telling. Harrumph, Frank.

It started on Saturday, March 14. Right before *The Pee Wee Herman Show* was supposed to come on. We'd just gotten cable, and I was looking forward to seeing Pee Wee clear and sharp for the first time.

I was about to be disappointed.

Instead of Pee Wee a rerun of an ancient *Lassie* episode came on. Pure black-and-white American banality.

I called my wife.

"Didn't I tell you that installation guy was a low-grade moron?"

"What's the matter, Jerry?" My wife has a way of getting to the heart of things. A logical thinker, her mother always says.

"Lassie's on instead of Pee Wee." (I know this sounds stupid—you can imagine how it felt to say it. On the other hand, it was true.) "The cable's on the fritz."

Naturally, she checked to see if I was, in her words, "overreacting." Again, *Lassie*'s hegemony remained intact.

"That's weird."

"Tell me something I don't know." I was not in good humor.

Some guys play golf on Saturday mornings. Or jog. Tennis is popular. I watch kid's TV. And Pee Wee's my favorite geek. Faced with a Pee Wee-less weekend, naturally I was an unhappy camper. Who wouldn't be?

"It looks so *phony,*" my wife remarked.

"Poor production values to start with. Plus a lot of the old nitrate film partially decomposed before the studios realized what was going on." I do a fair amount of entertainment work. I take lots of meetings.

"You know," Joan said, "Lassie looks a little like Phoebe."

This was perceptive. "They're collies, Joan. Of course they look alike." Patience is not one of my strengths. And Phoebe not one of my favorite conversational topics, being a nasty little beast with a history of accidents involving Persian rugs and mailmen. Currently she was AWOL . . . a mercifully common occurrence.

"I'm using my imagination. Try it sometime."

I grunted. Politely. The dig is part of Joan's latest campaign. "You act like an alter kocker" is the gist of it, meaning I'm increasingly humorless, inflexible and formal. For my part I answer that I'm supposed to be humorless, inflexible and formal. I'm a forty-year-old lawyer.

I looked back at the screen. Joan was right, Lassie looked a lot like Phoebe. An awful lot. I watched Timmy put his arms around Lassie. Even as a kid I'd always loathed the little brownnoser.

I called the cable company and gave them hell. They said they'd send somebody, I said I wouldn't hold my breath . . . and the conversation deteriorated from there though I got some satisfaction from slamming the phone down in the middle of a painfully insincere apology.

When I got back to the tube, Lassie was racing across a street after Timmy. Timmy made it, Lassie was whacked by a Good Humor truck and splashed all over the road.

. . .

After a lunch of three Beck's and Cheese Whiz on toast I called George McBride, my scintillating, endlessly fascinating next-door neighbor. I knew Lassie's intestines did not belong spread all over the road. Something was wrong.

"Your cable on the fritz?" I wanted to start slowly.

"Jerry boy, when you gonna hit those hedges? This baby's on the market as of too-day."

After I assured George that I was every bit as concerned as he about the effect on property values of untrimmed shrubbery, he announced that *Lassie* had been on his cable system too. The kids had a fit missing Pee Wee. Damned-us thing he'd ever seen, but, good buddy, everything was A-okay now. He went on to say that he'd sat his fat ass down in a Laz-E-Boy and watched the whole show and damned if it didn't bring back some pretty freakin' fine memories. He didn't mention Lassie's insides.

I thanked him for allowing me to share his boyhood reminiscences, reported that even as we spoke my clippers were being honed to bush-lethal edge, and hung up.

In one of life's little miracles the cable guy showed up at six-fifteen, complained only briefly about the hour and blamed "system-wide amplifier problems." In a small hydraulically operated box he rose to the top of a telephone pole in front of our house, performed a brief, inscrutable repair and left our cable-powered, remote-controlled television set operating at peak technological efficiency.

Sunday I flew to California, performed a brief, inscrutable legal repair to an actress's thirty-four-page contract with Paramount (a two-line part in a breathtakingly original all-new slasher film), collected a well-deserved bonus in her hot tub and flew back east Wednesday in time for *St. Elsewhere*.

"Phoebe's dead."

Joan wasn't upset, she was just reporting the facts. I'm the emotional one.

"What happened?"

"She was run over by a truck. It happened Saturday morning. They didn't call us till yesterday."

"What kind of a truck?" I spat this out a little too quickly and Joan shot me a quizzical look.

"A Good Humor truck. What difference does that make?"

I suppressed a gasp. Things were getting a little strange.

"Don't you have anything to say?"

"It's sorta scary." (This was honest, and therefore a slip-up; I told you I was emotional.)

A pedantic look spread gleefully across Joan's face. "Grow up, Jerry. Cancer's scary. AIDS is scary. Pets die every day and besides Phebes was eleven and . . ."

"I know that's old for a collie. But geez . . ."

"Don't make me out the cold bitch again, Jerry. I'm not gonna listen to that bull. I was the one who scraped her off the road, I was the one who buried her with the kids and I was the one who had to take two Tranxenes to get to sleep Tuesday night."

I thought of Hollis, my actress, and realized that at no time in California had I had any trouble falling to sleep.

"Sorry," I said, then poured myself another stiff scotch and plopped on to the couch just as *St. Elsewhere* was to begin.

Timing is everything in life and mine was spectacularly bad. *The Dick Van Dyke Show* was on *St. Elsewhere*'s channel.

"Christ almighty." I slammed my hard rock glass down and it cleaved neatly in two. Scotch rivers meandered across a three-hundred-year-old oak table, then dripped on to the rug. Modern American telecommunications had turned on me.

I walked slowly into the kitchen, fate tagging behind.

"How long has this been going on?"

"What been going on?" she said quickly, with an odd little catch in her voice.

"The cable." I was trying not to be impatient. "It's gone wacko again."

"There hasn't been anything wrong with it."

"There is now."

We marched with military precision into the family room.

Joan took one look at the young Mary Tyler Moore and sat down. "Look at that figure. God, that woman was a knock-out."

"Still is."

Joan let out a brittle laugh. "At her age? Who you trying to kid?"

I sat down beside her and we watched the show. It wasn't half bad. Richard Deacon, the actor who played the next-door neighbor, was blustering about in his febrile, overobnoxious way. A guy we love to hate.

"Do you know something," I remarked, "he looks a little like George."

"George who?"

"McBride."

"How much have you had to drink?"

I'd had three. I decided to drop it.

Deacon had just scored yet another psychological victory over a guileless Van Dyke when the phone rang. Joan got up to get it. That's when Richard Deacon grabbed his chest, let out a groan and crashed through a low, Scandinavian-style coffee table on to Mary's Electrolux-clean rug. This was a new episode for me and its raw effectiveness caused a quiver of self-reproach: who was I to scorn the old sitcoms? This was good stuff.

That's when I heard Joan crying.

It was my night for the Tranxene. Didn't work. George McBride was a classic bore. Pedestrian is a word that could have been invented to describe his mind. That doesn't mean he deserved to keel over with a massive heart attack at age thirty-six. Clichés have a right to life like the rest of us.

. . .

Obviously Richard Deacon didn't die on the set of *The Dick Van Dyke Show*. I know, I checked a TV encyclopedia. On the other hand I know what I saw. So I called the cable company again. They were polite. Apparently I have one crackerjack cable franchise in my town. And sure enough, a Cinemax rerun of a *Dick Van Dyke* episode had inadvertently run on Wednesday last when *St. Elsewhere* should have been on. They said it was a mystery to them.

But I knew that already. The pressing question was the nature of the mystery. And how could I raise said question?

Well, I couldn't. Except to my wife.

"Are you all right?"

"Jesus, Joan, I know it sounds crazy."

"It *is* crazy."

"Listen . . .

"You got that look in your eyes again. It's like . . ."

"Wait a . . ."

"Sparks flying. You're scaring me."

I shut up. It was hopeless. I even closed my eyes. Didn't want the sparks to detonate any marital explosions.

When I opened my eyes Joan was gone. So were little Pete and Sophie. The only thing that wasn't gone was what I saw on *The Dick Van Dyke Show*.

We talked the next day. She was at her mother's. Yes, of course I'd go talk to Dr. Shirvier. Probably I should never have stopped. And yes, I understood that given the circumstances it would be best if, for a while, I stayed in a hotel. And no, I wouldn't hold it against her; it was a very difficult time what with the biological clock ticking away and me seeing the bimbo in California.

What? Wait a minute.

George let it slip. It was one night when he'd had too much to drink.

What else did he let slip?

It wasn't like that.

But, of course, it was exactly like that, and on some level I'd known it all along.

. . .

After I moved out, my California bimbo's contract developed a flaw . . . or rather a flaw emerged. Somehow I had overlooked both video-rights profit participation and character-based toy licensing.

Immediately thereafter Messrs. Bain & Palmer overlooked their promise of partnership. Bain, Palmer & Rhodes was not to be.

It was an equitable, thoroughly gentlemanly parting.

I remarried. A Sony 26″ black matrix Trinitron.

When, finally, my new home (rented) was wired for cable I felt a dark little bubble of joy burst open in me. The first show I watched was a re-run of *The Fugitive*. You know, the show in which a doctor is arrested for the murder of his wife. Unjustly, I might add.

. . .

When Joan's body was found in our old house the police hippity-hopped across town to see me. They didn't believe my story about the one-armed man. I asked them to call the cable company, but they wouldn't. My lawyer finally did . . . they couldn't really help me. Nobody thought Joan looked anything like Richard Kimble's wife and as one particularly brutish cop observed, "So what if she did?"

Ironically, Josh, my lawyer, is on retainer with the cable company now, plus he gets free HBO. Josh is my brother.

. . .

According to my cellmate, Raphael, a scumbucket first-class, there's a rumor going through the block that we're going to be cable-wired soon; way up here in the Adirondacks they've had cable for over twenty years—hell, you can't see a thing without it, I mean one fuzzy channel out of Schenectady—but, for obvious political reasons, the wire never got over the wall into the Big House. I hear Showtime is running *The Prisoner,* one of my favorites and, let's face it, what could be more appropriate? Raphael has never seen *The Prisoner,* he's too busy being one . . . and, unfortunately, he's very good at all its myriad facets.

The more I think about it—and I've got lots of time to think—the more I realize that Raphael is the spitting image of Patrick McGoohan. I've always liked McGoohan, but Raphael's getting on my nerves. When the cable comes something'll have to give.

. . .

Of course, there'll be other shows to enjoy in the years to come. It's not like my life's over. Josh told me that. He also said you gotta think positively, you gotta look for the good.

So I decided to look for a good part for him. Maybe on *The Untouchables.* Or *Naked City.* If the cable comes in, and it will eventually, I'll find something to suit him. He can bet on it.

SPICES OF THE WORLD

Felice Picano

I particularly enjoyed Felice Picano's story because it is set in a London seen through the eyes of a native New Yorker: rancid, decaying, and strange. Your own city always becomes alarming when you perceive it through other people's eyes. Felice was born in 1944 and graduated with honors from New York University. He used to be a hippie in the sixties. The beard, the beads, you know the kind of thing. These days, he is the much-respected author of such novels as *Smart As the Devil, Eyes,* and *Lure.* For me, "Spices of the World" shows Felice at his most elegant and threatening. I can understand why many critics regard him as one of the finest stylists writing in horror fiction today.

The little square he had been directed to lay unfashionably northeast of St. Paul's Cathdedral and Ludgate Hill, a forlorn, small plaza with an unclipped, irregular common and a few dilapidated wrought-iron benches deeply set in weeds. Row houses loomed on each side, four stories high and built in the era of the Reform Act, displaying—at least—in their exterior detail that the area had once been populous, more than likely genteel: generous oystershells of water troughs for awaiting carriage horses, grotesqueries of concrete balustrades cracked here and there and so poorly mended their iron framework showed through, other details of external trim—pilasters and false Doricisms—in pretentious abundance. All had fallen into an inexorable slow disrepair. Only one of the four surrounding rows looked recently painted, and that a bilious brown. The other three slabs of buildings peeled coats of *fin de siècle* canary yellow to reveal previous coats of Prussian blue, questionable lavender, even the original dusky brickwork.

The minute they arrived at the address David had given, the cabdriver called out that he would wait—doubtless he sensed as strongly as David that this was hardly the type of neighborhood a well-dressed passenger would wish to remain stranded in. As soon as David stepped out of the Austin Princess and looked about, he couldn't be certain whether or not he'd imagined quickly hidden stares from behind grimy windows through curtains unironed for a decade. When he turned to the driver for confirmation of what he thought he'd seen, he was met by the indifferent headlines of a lurid daily newspaper.

V. R. Bardash, Spices of the World, was only one of several shops dug into below-street-level openings on the southern—and gloomiest—row of the square, and the only one still open for business. Signs in English, Arabic, and what he took to be Urdu and Pali script declared the place and its wares. ''Peppers, Salts, Cumins, Corianders, Gingers, Turmerics, Nutmegs, Cloves, Chilis of All Varieties, Sizes, and Powers'' read its enigmatic advertisement, causing David to wonder exactly how many different sorts of ginger and clove actually existed.

He pushed open one of the filthy, narrow, mullioned doors into a tiny, narrow shop. The single room seemed lighted by two high windows which opened to God only knew where—certainly not onto the streetside which had been without any apparent venting. In the strong, sharply defined late afternoon sunlight, the air seemed so filled with particles of dust he immediately began to cough before realizing it wasn't dust but instead the powdery emanations of hundreds of spices that he was breathing in, a cacophony of odors so overwhelming as to stop him briefly, his hand still on the door handle, exhaling forcefully to retain a clear head.

Tall, mostly bare, sagging wooden shelves on either wall dominated the shop. About halfway down their great height and centrally placed as though to spotlight them, three or four small cellophane-wrapped packages huddled together, their garishly printed boxfronts and indecipherable writing declaring them undeniably of Eastern provenance although in no way explicating their contents. Two long sagging deal counters fronted the shelves, extending virtually from front to back of the shop. These were less sparsely laden, with small sacks, hempen edges rolled back to reveal brown lengths of vanilla beans, knobs of mahogany-colored cloves, balls of nutmeg and allspice, twisted tiny tan mannequins of ginger root and long yellow strips of dried papaya and other fruits unrecognizable to David in this form. The extremely limited floorspace was reduced to a single, nearly impassable aisle leading to a discolored paisley curtain, which no doubt opened upon a back room or office or living quarters. Knee-high rucksacks of other spices—among them giant balls of green peppers but most of them unknown to David and more than a little otherworldy in shape and hue—crowded about his legs, more or less tripping him into immobility by threatening to spill over with each step he took attempting to brush past.

In the fortnight since the letter from Lahore had arrived with its urgent request from the Mazudrah family, David had been all over London and several of its more squalid suburbs attempting to locate his old friend, and failing most emphatically. Something indefinable besides the actual contents of the fractured English of the communication had suggested that Rajinder was in serious trouble, political trouble perhaps, something to do with Sikhs and sects and bombs and assassinations half a world away. How this could be, David wasn't certain. Although he hadn't seen Raji in almost four years, surely the clever, overintelligent philosopher who could minutely dissect Kant and Wittgenstein, who derided nationalism as "the folly of the senses in our century," couldn't have changed so utterly: could he?

So far, David's quest had not answered that question satisfactorily. On the debit side, there had been that slender, red-nosed, whining barrister, Monica something or other, who gushed close to an hour about Raji's work with the Ealing factory workers, only to admit she hadn't seen or heard from him in months. Not to mention that arthritically deformed, garrulous, retired railway man in East Grinstead, with whom Raji had boarded as recently as six months ago, and who'd insisted to David that there was "no wog born good as the lad," despite his intimations that Raji's bed-sitter had been a meeting place once a week for several unsavory types. "They told me they were studying the niceties of the *Mahabharata,* whatever that is," the old railway pensioner had said. "But some of them toffs didn't look like they read more than the pony listings, if you know what I mean."

On the plus side, David would have to place Mrs. Arrowhead, an aging, pincushion-shaped secretary of the United Baptist Mission to the Heathen, where Raji had worked almost two years. She'd been unstinting in her praise of young Mazudrah—"Such a good example to the neighboring young West Indians, he was. Liked his tea strong, always a sign of a God-fearing man. After he came to us, we had no more break-ins or vandalism." Mrs. Arrowhead said she'd been delighted when Raji took the post in the bursar's office at Brighton College, even though it had meant the Mission losing him. Ian McQuith, head bursar at the seaside institution, had nothing but praise for the young man, insisting that without Raji's help they would have never reorganized their past decade of files. Yet, even McQuith had wondered aloud over some of the more "sinister types—actors and suchlike" at the college in whose company Raji was sometimes to be found. And Mrs. Arrowhead had insinuated that she hadn't ever discovered the methods which Mazudrah had used to intimidate local toughs from harassing the Mission.

A checkered recent past, David had to admit, quite different from what he'd expected of his brilliant pal. And now all leads to Rajinder's whereabouts seemed to have ended. As though he'd evaporated into the sky, as the prophet Isaiah was said to have been taken up in a chariot of fire. David had thought to hire a private investigator. But if for some reason—good or otherwise—Raji were in hiding, a stranger's inquiries would send him even deeper in. Whereas word of David looking for him ought to be far less threatening. Even so, the search had been long enough and sufficiently fruitless that he'd fallen back to this address, the first one Raji ever had in England. Should this fail, David would have to concede defeat and write back to Lahore with the bad news.

Although he'd jangled the shop bell as he entered, no one had responded. David cautiously stepped back and once more roughly rang the bell, peering into the dusty corners to see if any object reacted.

He'd decided the shop was abandoned when the paisley curtain furled back an inch from one lower edge and a large pair of frightened dark eyes looked out at him so briefly that he'd scarcely gotten over his surprise when the face was gone again.

"Hello? Anyone here?" he called out. "Mr. Bardash!"

The curtains ballooned out a bit before a small stout figure stepped out and made a sketch of a salaam: the owner of the dark eyes—or rather, a remarkable pair of pistachio-colored eyes, large eyes, childlike eyes.

"Good afternoon, sahib," the man's voice fluted in a ridiculously high register for an adult. "Can I be of assistance to you in your purchase of many spices?"

"I was looking for Mr. Bardash. Mr. V. R. Bardash," David said, watching the turbanned, rotund little man easily pick his way toward him through the seemingly impossible paths of overflowing sacks.

"Deceased!" the man chirped, joyful as a robin at daybreak.

Before David could react, the man moved deftly behind a nearby counter, and smilingly sung out, "I am Mr. V. R. Bardash's nephew. R. J. Bardash. Perhaps you will not be too unforgiving if I offer to assist you in the selection of your spice purchases, taking the place of my distinguished uncle. I cannot pretend to his vast knowledge of each and every variety, alas," he twittered merrily, "for I have not personally journeyed to all of the many spice islands in the several hemispheres whence they derive." He all but sparkled, as he added, "Yet I will attempt my greatest endeavors."

"Actually, I'm not looking for any spices."

"Not looking for any spices?" Bardash tittered, as though David were clearly making a joke.

"Fascinating as they seem to be," David conceded. "I'm actually looking for a person.

"Fascinating indeed are spices," Bardash twinkled. "This, for example. I wonder, can you tell me what it is?" He held a longish well-dried-out gourd, slightly bent in the middle and speckled brown against a more general ecru color.

"Why, no. I'm afraid not."

''Neither can I,'' he giggled. ''It has been in this shop for years. Since I was a boy. Mr. V. R. Bardash knew what it was. But he would not tell. Even as he lay breathing his last, I pleaded, 'Uncle, esteemed uncle, I beg you, tell me what the object is, in what it consists, what it contains.' He would not tell. I thought perhaps *inside*.'' Bardash shook the gourd and something did seem to rattle within. ''Ought I chop it open, do you recommend?'' he sang out in countertenor, making a machete-like motion with his tiny fist. ''Or is it better to leave it as it arrived, unchopped?''

He seemed to hesitate, as though David could answer him. In fact, David was about to say yes, by all means, chop it open to see what's within, when the shop owner interrupted.

''Yet . . . if I chop it open, I may not be able to sell it. And who knows if what is within will then go quickly to rot. But perhaps one day some distinguished person like yourself will step into this shop, see the object, and cry out, 'Aha! There! That'—whatever it's name will prove to be—'that is *exactly* what I've been searching for!''' Bardash's eyes glittered in merriment and potential profit. ''And then I will know what it is, and I will still be able to sell it. Don't you think?''

Unable to follow the little man well enough to know what to think, never mind how to answer, David merely said, ''Perhaps you have a point there. I was asking about Mr. Mazudrah. An old friend of mine. I believe he used to lodge with your uncle. At least this was the name and address he gave. Mr. Rajinder Mazudrah.''

''Then again,'' Bardash giggled, ''what if no one does eventually come into the shop to identify the object? What then, eh? It is possible, you will admit. Even likely, given the fact that as yet no one *has* come in to identify its properties or better still, to purchase it.''

David felt as though some test were being proposed to him, a code whose secret he did not know. Once more he was about to say yes, that by all means Bardash should chop open the blasted thing, when the little round spice merchant wagged a beringed index finger at him.

''What then? I'll tell you. Then I will still have the ambiguous pleasure of possessing a mystery. There is much pleasure in possessing a mystery, don't you think?''

''Yes, of course there is,'' David said, relieved he'd not fallen into the trap. "Very wise of you indeed. Now, about Mr. Mazudrah? You know him?"

"The name is not entirely unfamiliar."

"Rajinder Mazudrah is his full name. At least all that he gave us." David suddenly felt on uncertain ground. Had Raji another name? A middle one? Or more than one? Had it been a kindness, a courtesy on his part to merely give out the usual Occidental two names, instead of a string of them as he might have in his own country? And what if there were some honorary title he'd also possessed, all unknowing to David?

Only slightly daunted by these new questions, David decided to go on. "He used to work as a tailor for my father before he went to university in Manchester. Mr. Wechsler. Of Wechsler's Fine Haberdashery on Regent Street? Say, four years ago."

"An estimable business, haberdashery," was Bardash's cryptic response.

"We were friends, Raji and I," David tried. It was possible this fellow thought David was a constable or government man in plainclothes, and that Raji was in some sort of official trouble. "He used to board with your uncle, he told us. Or at least nearby here. He gave my father this address."

"Alas, I did not reside here with Mr. V. R. Bardash four years ago, but upon a neighboring square with my cousin, Mr. L. S. Bardash."

"I must find Mr. Mazudrah. It's a matter of some importance."

"I think not," Bardash chirruped happily.

"You think not what? That he's here?"

"Oh, you are an *amusing* gentleman. Who could be here but myself? And my daughter?"

"Naturally, I didn't mean to imply that you were hiding him."

"*Most* amusing gentleman," Bardash tittered into his tiny fat fist.

"You do know of whom I'm speaking, don't you?"

"Yes, surely, I do. Mr. Rajinder Mazudrah, who used to live with my uncle some four years ago or so, or nearby, and who used to work for your father, Mr. Wechsler of Wechsler's Fine Haberdashery on Regent Street."

"Good," David said, somewhat relieved, until he realized that the spice merchant hadn't told him anything about Mazudrah that he,

David, hadn't already a minute past just told Bardash. ''Perhaps I ought to describe him.''

The large pistachio eyes twinkled in merry agreement.

''Well, first of all,'' David began, ''he was, well, somewhere between yourself and myself.''

''This cannot be?'' Bardash sputtered, ''for then we could see him.''

''I meant in height. He was neither short like yourself, nor tall like myself.'' Equally inane: such a description could signify any of a million men. ''Lightly complected, he was,'' David added unsteadily, ''like yourself. Or rather not as olive-complected as yourself, yet not quite as highly complected as I am.''

''Yes, yes?'' Bardash went on, all ears.

''Well, I don't know what else.'' What else, indeed. That in age, Mazudrah was somewhere between the two of them, as he was in race, and . . . ''You're certain you know him?''

''With such a description, how could I not?''

''Well, then perhaps you might tell me where Mr. Mazudrah might be. It's rather urgent that I see him.''

''I think not,'' the little man sang out.

''You don't know? Is that what you're saying?''

''I wonder, can you perhaps tell me what this object is?'' Bardash held up a small brown knob of a thing.

''You say you *don't* know where he is, or that you do know and won't tell me?''

''Neither, sahib. I clearly said neither of the two.''

''But you clearly said 'I think not.'''

''Indeed, sahib. And did you take that to mean I know of Mazudrah's whereabouts and will not tell you?''

As David no longer knew what he'd meant, he merely gaped at the spice merchant, who once more picked up the small brown object.

''It is somewhat like this object,'' Bardash said, his voice restored to its chirruping manner. ''I wonder, can you tell me what it is?''

Indifferently: ''I haven't a clue.''

''An artichoke!'' He tittered. ''So many things we don't know because they have changed in some manner. And how should you know a dried artichoke when you see one? No, believe me, sahib, it is better to possess a mystery. Even an ambiguous mystery. Far more valuable,'' he trilled.

"Is there *anyone* who might be able to tell me where Mr. Mazudrah is now?" David tried, and as the little man merely smiled and rolled the obscenely dried artichoke from one hand to another, he asked, "Are you trying to tell me that Mazudrah is transformed in some drastic and unrecognizable manner?"

"You are a *truly* amusing gentleman. I was merely speaking of artichokes. I wonder, can you tell me what this other object is?"

"You needn't be afraid for his sake. We were great friends, you know."

"Were you indeed, sahib?"

"Well, I mean to say, we were great friends at one time."

"Four years ago, you said, sahib?"

"Yes, but we didn't have a falling out or anything of that sort, you understand. He merely left."

"Left, sahib?"

"Yes, just up and left. Although I assure you we were *great* friends."

"Yes, I understand."

"One remains friendly after four years, you know. Even after one has just up and left, you see. It does happen. He wouldn't be purposely hiding from me. There's no reason for it. He hasn't an idea I'm looking for him, you understand. There would be nothing in the world to even suggest that after four years, upon some whim or other, I'd suddenly come looking for him, would there? Would there? *Would there?* I ask you."

David's head throbbed with possibilities he'd never before entertained, thoughts which had come spewing into his mind simultaneous with his absurd bout of self-defense. What if Raji were actively hiding from him? What if he didn't wish to be found? What if all this were some sort of blind? A smokescreen? A . . . ? And he, David, a complete ass to have come this far, to have tracked him down to this ridiculous shop, this absurd spice merchant?

"Of course not, sahib. Not if you say not," Bardash sweetly answered. In his hand he now held a small greenish object, a cross between a dried-out lizard and a hairy plant. "I wonder, sahib, if you can tell me what this object is?"

David stared. Three objects, three tests, as in some mad Oriental tale. David had already failed the first two. Looking at the object before him he knew that once again he would not be able to say what it was—some rare medicinal root? A large, specially preserved caterpillar? And failing to answer that question too, he would be ridiculed, humiliated, and who only knew, perhaps asked to identify another and another more outlandish even than these. Before he could reach across the counter and throttle the little beggar, he spun around and was outside the doors, leaping up the steps onto the street.

Inexplicably—how long had he been in the shop?—the cab was gone. The square abandoned.

He could have sworn the driver had said he would wait for him, had put up a newspaper and begun reading the telly listings. And now he was gone! David was certain he saw a bright sari behind one of the curtained windows flash suddenly into and out of view on the floor directly above V. R. Bardash, Spices of the World.

An apalling thought crossed his mind. That last object . . . was it? . . . could it possibly be . . . a . . . scalp? Raji's scalp?

He turned to face the shop doors' grime-stained windows. They didn't seem in any way different, yet, as a result of his going in them and meeting Bardash and asking and being asked and . . . they were quite ghastly different. As though some dark deed carefully withheld until these past few minutes and his arrival here must no longer wait but be accomplished with all haste, and with utter ruthlessness.

He rushed down the steps to the shop door and shook the handle. It was locked, damn it! And though he rang and rang and rattled the door and could hear the shop bell echo shrilly within, no one answered.

When he finally ascended onto the street, many curtained windows in the row above the shop were filled with veiled faces openly—mockingly—staring down at him.

Suddenly, and with an unshakeable certainty, David knew he would never see his friend again. He thought he would scream something at them, that he was going to find a bobby, a dozen bobbies and half of Scotland Yard, until he found Raji. But as he watched, all the curtains closed, shades were drawn. Filled with horror and despair, he turned and began to walk away, feeling the curtains open behind him, the shades lift, the eyes once more watching, laughing. He hastened now, damning his legs for moving so slowly, barely able to restrain himself from breaking into a full run, certain that if he turned, looked, there would be footsteps behind him, men in poorly wrapped turbans, filthy *dhotis*. His breath was coming tighter, a stitch beginning in his side. And now he did begin to run, to run until he was approaching the end of the row and around the building, out of the hellish square.

He dashed across a narrow lane and dared himself to stop, to stop and look back. Damn it! He wouldn't be made a fool of by some damned Pakis.

He steeled himself, stopped, and turned. A figure he hadn't noticed collided with him.

"So sorry," David said, politeness mechanically rising to the occasion.

The man who pulled back was short and turbanned, with flowing bright *dhoti*.

David suddenly felt dizzy. His vision blurred, he began to stagger.

"I wonder," the voice said in a remarkable basso voice, "can you tell me . . . ?"

David didn't remain for the question, didn't even look at the questioner. He was running, running, running now for sanity, for his very life down the lane into the next street, running directly into the blaring horn and brightly red bonnet of an oncoming omnibus.

. . .

At the brief inquest, Rajinder Mazudrah identified his friend's corpse. Yes, he testified, he'd witnessed the accident. Yes, he'd wondered why his friend hadn't recognized him, indeed had run from him with such haste, as though in terror. Mazudrah had been returning to the spice shop he'd been attempting to inventory and sell off as a favor to a cousin in Lahore. He had been at the family solicitor's barely a half hour. He couldn't remain away long, he explained to sympathetic officials, as another, more distant relative, Mr. R. J. Bardash, was temporarily living behind the shop, despite its lack of space or amenities.

This cousin insisted upon believing he was a merchant in an active business, Mazudrah told them, indeed he insisted upon believing many even more fanciful things. There had been a previous somewhat unfortunate incident when a stranger wandered into the shop thinking it open for business. But surely that needn't be gone into. It couldn't possibly cast light upon this tragedy. All they needed to know, Rajinder assured them, was that his cousin Bardash had only been out of the sanitorium a few days and although he'd been placed in a sort of halfway house he'd refused to go.

It made little difference really, Mazudrah said. His cousin might be mentally unstable, even untrustworthy: he could hardly be considered dangerous.

DOWN TO THE CORE

David B. Silva

Dave says that the more he learns about writing, the less he knows. But he owns the most beautiful word processor that I ever came across. He has served since 1982 as editor for *The Horror Show,* a quarterly magazine dedicated to horror fiction, and has published the work of Dean Koontz, Robert Bloch, and Rick McCammon. As a writer, he's had stories published in numerous small press publications, as well as *Masques, Masques II,* and *The Year's Best Horror Stories.* His second novel, *Thirteen,* was published in 1988, and he has recently finished a third. "Down to the Core" exhibits a strange coldness which doesn't accord with Dave's personality, but which should chill you to the core . . .

It was the first time Braden Chapman had seen the dancer.

She was living in apartment 713, one block over, where an elderly Jewish man had recently died. The Jew had kept full-blown photographs of the Holocaust on those same apartment walls. Like monuments. And Braden had often wondered if the old man had ever stopped being a prisoner to his forty-year-old memories. A poem called ''The Past Is Tomorrow'' came almost effortlessly out of that man and his photographs, as did a dozen other poems. Then a month ago, after Braden watched the man's dull, ancient eyes sink even deeper into the cavity of his skull, the Jew had finally died. *Forty years of nightmare specters,* Braden had written in his notebook, *of rictus masks, of degradation still breathing on the other side of time, now he sleeps, side by side with the nightmares, because without the one there cannot be the other.*

But now . . . now those same sad walls held paintings by Quinn and soft airbrushed photos of dancers in leotards, and they were brighter walls, because now it was *her* apartment, number 713.

Braden peered again through the Linitron telescope that was set on a tripod in his living room, twenty floors above the San Francisco streets. It was nearing seven o'clock on a Wednesday night. Nightfall was beginning to darken the sky, to wash away the dirty gray walls of the City, bringing up the streetlights, the brightly colored neons atop the skyline that reminded Braden of the plastic side of life. Sometimes when he looked out over the City it seemed as if nothing were real out there, as if everything were one illusion draped brightly over another. No substance at all, just glitter.

She stretched, the new tenant in 713, and the soft, airbrushed dancer in the photo on the wall behind her seemed to shadow her slow movements, reaching ceilingward, arching her back, then slowly lowering her arms again. She was wearing white, skintight leotards that absorbed the contours of her slim body as she moved. Her legs were long, graceful limbs, like wings, the way she moved them.

Braden looked up from the telescope, thinking how different she was from the old man who had lived there before her, what a contrast of character the two of them made. One old, one young. One rigid, one flexible. One living for the past, one living for the future.

He took a notebook from the bookshelf next to the window, folded back a page of penciled doodles and disjointed notes. On a fresh page he wrote: *statue dancer, liberty chancer,* thinking for a moment, then circling the words *dancer* and *liberty,* and tapping the tip of the pencil against those two words because there was something there he thought he might be able to use.

When he looked up again, the dancer was gone. And when she didn't return after a few minutes, he wrote at the top of the notebook: *Golden Gate Apartments, 713, 6:45 P.M.*

You do something long enough, often enough, it becomes almost a compulsion, whether you enjoy it or not. Like sitting through *The Love Boat* on Saturday nights, hating every second of it, but not being strong enough to turn the damn tv off and face yourself straight on. You do it because it's something you've come to know well. Braden had come to know *The Love Boat* too well; and he thought he had come to know his business well enough not to be surprised. But that wasn't the case. He *was* surprised when he looked through the telescope at the Aladdin Apartment Building across the street, because there it was . . .

. . . another telescope

. . . looking back at him.

"Caught looking where you shouldn't be looking," his mother would have said.

Like when he was seven and his mother happened upon him and Alicia Manson in the bathroom, stark naked; her trying to figure out why she was missing some parts, him wondering why on earth God had gone through all the trouble of making boys and girls different.

Caught looking where you shouldn't be looking.

Braden felt a cold shiver ride up his spine on a rush of adrenaline. It felt surprisingly good. Like a cold shower on a hot summer day. In the back of his mind he realized it was the first time in longer than he could remember when he had felt anything at all. He wondered how he had let that happen and decided distantly that it had come about much the same way watching *The Love Boat* had come about. Being detached was more comfortable than being involved.

He had been holding the telescope with both hands, now he let go and sat up straight in the chair. The Aladdin was all nightshades of shadow and light against the background of the City. Oddly out of focus and dream-like without the telescope. But no less nightmarish now that he knew someone was watching him from that building over there on the other side of the street, watching *him* the way he usually watched *them*. Something was wrong about that. Not just unsettling, but *wrong*.

The notebook slipped off his lap. Braden took a stab at catching it, missed it, and it hit the floor just as the phone rang. For a moment, he thought his heart was going to explode right out of his throat, out into the stale apartment air. Like a bad fear he couldn't keep down.

He made a grab for the phone before it could ring again, and came away with the receiver in his hand, wondering, *what if it's . . .*

(who?)

(the watcher from the Aladdin?)

"Braden?"

"Diane?"

"Don't you say hello when you answer the phone these days?"

"Oh Christ, it's you, sis." He sank back into the chair.

"Who were you expecting?"

"I don't know . . . the guy across the street maybe . . . someone . . . just not you, I guess."

"Braden, you okay?"

"Someone's watching me, sis." Across the street, the Aladdin was staring back at him through a hundred window-eyes. Dark, shadowy pupils. Fluorescent sclerae. Each window-eye looking so much like the next that for a moment he forgot which one had nearly scared the shakes out of him. "Across the street, in the Aladdin, someone's watching me through a telescope."

"You know what I want to say, don't you?" He thought she was going to break out laughing. Her voice was free, light as a song, and sometimes when it hurt the most, she would break out laughing at you without even realizing what she was doing. It was something she seemed to have a knack for . . . laughing at the wrong time. "Sooner or later," she added, "someone was bound to catch on to your little voyeur fetish, Braden. Feels a bit different when you're on the other end of the telescope, doesn't it?"

She was right, he *did* feel different. The word he wanted to use was . . . *exposed*. That's as close as he could come to describing it. He started counting, six floors up from street level, then across the face of the building, right to left, past the marquee, sixteen windows altogether. Until he found the window he was looking for. It was difficult to see beyond shadow and light. The apartment number was 666.

Aladdin Apartments, number 666.

"You still there, Braden?"

"He's just sitting there, watching me—"

"Close your drapes if it bothers you that much."

"—as if he were waiting for something to happen."

"He'll get bored, Braden. We all get bored."

"Why would he be watching *me*?"

"Maybe he doesn't have a tv," Diane said. She sounded far away. "Look, I just called to remind you about the special on Channel 9, the documentary on graffiti in the cities. Thought you might be able to cannibalize a few ideas." There was a short silence before she added, "Is any of this finding its way to your nerve center, Braden?"

"Why would *anyone* be watching me?" he asked again.

Then his sister sighed, and hung up on him.

Absently, he replaced the receiver. The call had seemed more like a dream than reality. But now he was awake again and he was wrapping both hands around the Linitron, leaning forward to see if he was still being watched.

Which he was.

What the hell is going on?

Another shudder ran through him. He tried to keep it from breaking loose, tensing the muscles in his feet and hands, but it was a losing cause. Then he got up and closed the living room drapes. He would open them again, peek out to see if the watcher was still watching, find that he was, and close them again, on and off again, all through the PBS Special on graffiti, through *Dynasty* and *Hotel*, all through the long night.

. . .

They got together again in the morning.

Briefly.

The watcher and Braden.

Him looking out, the watcher looking in.

Even in daylight, with the sun nearly overhead, the watcher was a faceless, almost formless dark shadow. Not a person anymore—didn't he ever eat or sleep? didn't he ever go to the bathroom? empty his bladder? his bowels?—but now a *thing*. Like the guards in the old Holocaust photographs on the walls of Golden Gate Apartment 713. Not human at all. Just a mindless *thing*.

Braden took in a deep breath, then drew the drapes again. He sat in front of the television, in the easy rocker, his notebook open in his lap. *Love American Style* was on, mostly for the background noise. *Takes away the loneliness,* he was in the habit of telling Diane when she pestered him about his television being on all day. She knew it was just a line. They both knew it was just a line. The television *had* to be on. He was its audience.

In his notebook, Braden wrote:

They're watching.
A thousand midnight eyes.
Looking out,
To see who's looking in.
Past magnifying lens.
Past iris, green and blue, brown and hazel.
Past dilated pupil.
Inside.
Because they want to know who's in here.
Where darkness is mute, silence is black.
Where the secrets are kept.
But it's not the thousand midnight eyes I fear.
It's only two.
Only your eyes, I fear.
Because you know.

He stopped, pen in hand, then scratched absently at a rash which had broken out on his forearm sometime during the night. He thought there would be something more of the poem coming—maybe something about how frightening the unknown could be—but it never seemed to gel and after a while it didn't seem to matter anymore.

All that really mattered were the two eyes he knew he'd find looking back at him if he peeked out the window at Aladdin 666. Like a nightmare. Eyes that were watching him whenever he was watching them. And when he closed the curtains again . . . well, then those nightmare eyes might be watching, and they might not be. You never could be sure. That's the way it was with a nightmare.

• • •

It was 6:40 P.M.

Daylight was slipping into dusk.

The lights were off, the apartment darkened except for the dim glow emitting from the television screen. Braden was sitting in his chair, behind the Linitron, the notebook in his lap. The curtains were drawn around the telescope the way you cup your hands around your eyes to keep the bright sun from whitewashing a view you don't want to miss. The view: Golden Gate Apartments, 713. And the sun . . . the sun was those godawful *eyes* that he knew were still watching him.

It had become almost a game now.

The watcher and the watched.

Like a child's game of nerves.

Green Light . . . pull the curtains open just a little wider, enough to look out, to let yourself breathe a little bit freer, to feel like you've won something even if you haven't.

Red Light . . . wait, don't let him see the curtains moving, don't let him see you looking out while he's looking in, he'll catch you then, you'll lose then, and the stakes are higher than you imagine.

"Christ," Braden muttered. He scratched at the rash on his arm—it had spread up past his elbow and he thought it might be an allergic reaction to something he had eaten. The heart of the rash was a bright red, like a sunburn. Around the edges, the skin was turning gray, around the gray . . . white. Absently, he rubbed the side of his pen across his arm. A heavy tiredness had settled over him during the day. He thought it was the emotional strain beginning to take its toll, and wondered, *What if the watcher* never *stops watching? What if this goes on for a week? a month? a year? Or even worse*—because there was a quirky kind of expectation growing inside him now—*what if the next time I pull back the curtain, there's no one at all watching? What then?*

That was how unnerved he had become.

A man walking the edge.

His initial pleasure in feeling something . . . *anything* . . . after being so comfortable for so long in his detachment had suddenly started sliding down a mountainside of uneasiness. Waiting at the bottom, there was a gully of dry hot fear.

All along the block, the streetlights flickered, then buzzed on. It was closing in on 6:45. Night shadows were beginning to fall impressionistically across the faces of the buildings.

Braden leaned forward, put his eye to the telescope again. He was hoping to find the dancer in 713 back again. And she was. She had one leg propped up on a chair, her arms reaching high overhead then slowly descending until her fingers were almost touching her toes, her face almost touching her knee. She was still beautiful—her movement still innocence—but she was different tonight.

Before, when she had stretched, her body seemed as if it could do anything she willed it to do. But tonight, she seemed . . .

. . . older.

. . . somehow less magnificent, not quite as free.

Next to the word *liberty* which Braden had written the night before, he penciled in the word *free,* and under that, *old.* In a way that he couldn't yet define, she was becoming like the old man with the photos of the Holocaust on his walls. Succumbing to something within herself.

Braden wrote: *the apartment, what if there's something twisted and evil about the apartment?* Funny how you sometimes hide yourself from the obvious. Now that he was thinking about it, there had been a handful of times when he had sat back in his chair and wondered if he was playing witness to that old man's greatest fear come true. The man had survived the *camps,* for crissakes! Once you've stood eye-to-eye with the glowering eyes of death, maybe you can't ever be free of that death gaze again? Maybe the holocaust had followed him around until he couldn't resist its glances another single moment, and then . . . maybe then, after it had taken the old man into its valley of darkness, it had made its cold home in that apartment one block over, and that's where it was right now. In 713. Breathing out its cold breath into the same rooms where the beautiful young dancer was breathing in. Each breath a little more constricting, a little less . . .

Braden wrote:

Who's the guest
and who's the host
When no one's been invited, but everyone is there?
Not the cold walls, sucking up your last warm breath.
They aren't supposed to be there with you,
those cold walls that belong to someone else's past, but
are now,
are now,
suddenly . . . your *future.*

His dream that night was a nightmare, and he couldn't quite remember it by the time he got out of bed the next morning. Those were the worst nightmares, when he couldn't remember them clearly. Those were the ones that were trying to tell him something he didn't want to hear. And they were the ones that always kept coming back.

This one came back alive.

It took him a while to wake up. He went through the routine of getting dressed, brushing his teeth, taking note of how much farther the rash on his arm had spread. Something was wrong with him, he could see that. The discoloration covered all of his left arm now, and half of his upper body. There were bits of flesh around the edges that looked as if they had been charred . . . black and flaky and dead. But there was no pain, and that was one reason keeping him away from a visit to the doctor. The other reason was the *watcher*.

It had come to him sometime during the night—maybe during the nightmare—this idea that what was really going on in Golden Gate 713 was an unveiling of the soul. There had been death at the soul of that old man. Forty years ago, during the Holocaust, he had weaved himself a protective cocoon and in Golden Gate 713 he had emerged again only to come face-to-face with the same death he had tried to escape. Because it had become part of his soul by then. Part of who he was. The same way the fear of aging was part of the soul of the young dancer who had taken his place.

An unveiling of the soul.

That's what was going on down the street from him.

Not because there was something magical about Golden Gate 713, but because anytime you watch something close enough, long enough, a natural unveiling takes place. Like the lifting of morning fog.

The nightmare was starting to come back to Braden now. It had been one of those sightless dreams. He had to struggle to get his eyes opened wide enough to see past his blindness. Everything was dark shadow. He was staring—squinting, really—into the bathroom mirror. In his right hand he was holding a Schick disposable razor. There was a fog of hot, thick steam rising around him. For some reason he couldn't quite understand, he felt he had to hurry. To get back to his watching, perhaps. *Don't want to miss the young dancer, because she's going to start aging tonight. She's going to stretch out to touch her toes and the skin's going to loosen, then wrinkle, then start drip-*

ping right off her arms like hot wax. Someone in the dream had Krazy-glued his eyelids shut. He was looking out through a sliver of light, trying to make some sort of sense out of his steamy reflection (it didn't look like him, it looked like the old man in 713, the lather like chapped flesh; for a moment, he thought he could actually see the flesh drying out and cracking, but it wasn't flesh, it was lather). The razor blade suddenly felt like a scythe in his hand, big enough to shave grain off the face of the earth. He placed it against his cheek, took a slow cautious swipe and . . . a long, sweeping sheath of flesh came away . . . and underneath there was . . .

nothing

a black hole

no muscle

no cartilage

no bone

nothing

and he had started to scream . . .

He pulled back the living room curtains now and stood in front of the window, looking out. It felt as if it were a long, long time since he had last seen the sunlight. Across the street, 666 was in morning shadow. The sky and the shadows, even the City itself, had a cool purple feeling that reminded him of late fall mornings when he was a boy walking the beach. Just the purple morning and him. As if he were the only person left on the good earth. Sometimes lately that sense of aloneness had come back to him, spent a day or a week, sometimes even a month with him.

Through the lens, the Aladdin began as a grayish-white blur, like an indistinguishable thundercloud against an already-gray sky. He focused. The gray-white tint darkened, and he could see the dull aluminum frame around the window. A reflection of light from somewhere on the street below glinted off the glass as if it were a mirror.

Braden felt his stomach tighten.

He cupped his hands around the telescope. On the other side of the window, on the other side of the street, he could see the dark outline of a man taking a deep breath. Like a deep breath of his own. *Because the breaths . . . they're one and the same, aren't they?* Then the man's face came into focus for the first time and Braden was looking into the lens of a telescope at himself, looking into the lens of a telescope at himself . . .

face-to-face
one part of him here, another part of him there
both the same, and both different
like twins
except the Braden Chapman on *that* end of the telescope had no eyes. He was looking over the top of the telescope, through two huge holes, black as a starless night and just as endless, and the side of his face was covered with a plethoric redness, peeling gray around the edges, pasty white around the gray, like the dry sugary crust of a cherry tart.

. . .

It was after nightfall when he finally got hold of Diane. Sometime during the day—he couldn't remember when—he had stripped off his clothes and was naked now, pacing back and forth in front of the living room window. There were little bits of dry skin flaking and falling off him like fluttering white butterflies. The notebook was sitting in his chair. Across the yellow paper he had scribbled the hard-to-read words: *an empty soul*.

"You believe in the yin and the yang?" Braden asked his sister over the phone.

"What goes around comes around?"

"Close enough."

"I never gave it much thought."

"And the soul, Diane? Do you believe you have a soul? That we *all* have some part of us on the inside, buried beneath the flesh and the bone, that's the real essence of our being? Something that carries on after we die?"

There was a pause on the other end of the phone. Then, "Are you okay, Braden?"

"Just answer the question, goddammit!"

"You want me to come over?"

"No!" He glanced out the window, across the street in the direction of Aladdin 666. It was all city lights and neons out there. *No substance at all, just glitter*. And when he couldn't look past it any longer, he forced himself to face his reflection in the living room window. The realization had already run cold through him, but it didn't change the shock he felt. He was shedding. Like a snake. Shedding his skin, one dry flaky layer at a time, until whatever was underneath would be uncovered in all its rawness. And he was beginning to understand what that rawness was going to be . . .

"Braden?"

"No," he said again, softer this time. "No need to come over, sis, I'll be all right."

"You sure?"

He thought for a moment, not much about her question—he wasn't sure of anything anymore—but about what was happening to him. Then he asked, "You ever think that what I do is wrong, sis?"

"How do you mean?"

"Looking at the world through my telescope. Being a spectator instead of a participant. If you really think about it, what I do is feed off other people. Sometimes I wonder if that's because deep down inside me there's nothing for me to draw on. It's empty inside me. So I feed off other people, and they suffer for it."

"Where do you get this garbage, Braden?"

It wasn't garbage. Not at all. He understood that much. But when he ran it through his mind again—*so I feed off people, and they suffer for it*—it sounded like something without much sense. Like trying to take blame for someone else's cancer. You can't give someone cancer just by coughing on them, no need holding on to your guilt if all you did was cough. And you can't feed off people just by watching them through your Linitron . . .

"Does come across a little smelly, doesn't it?" he said.

"Like a walk through the sewers."

"Sorry."

"You sure you're okay?"

"I'm fine, honest."

"I can still come over."

"No need," he told her again, then he asked her about how her day had gone, about what she had done over the weekend, about her newest boyfriend, and a mouthful of other safe, uninvolved questions. He said goodbye after that, and she said goodbye, and when he hung up, he found himself standing all alone again in the living room. The window looking out over the world.

The chair behind the telescope was cold when he sat down. Across the street and down the block, in Golden Gate 713, the dancer would be going through her stretching exercises about this time. A little older tonight than last night. *Because anytime you watch something close enough, long enough, a natural unveiling takes place.*

The flaking had spread over his entire body now. He brushed a hand across his thigh, watched a storm of white, dead skin kick up, and noticed a small spot where it appeared as if the last layer of flesh had finally peeled away. Much longer and there wouldn't be anything left of him—like there hadn't been anything left of the old man after he caught the gaze of death during the Holocaust.

Around the edges of the raw spot there was a fillet of dying skin. Braden took a pinch of it, pulled gently, started to peel back the final layer of himself.

. . . *anytime you watch something close enough* . . .

There wasn't a doubt about what he was going to find.

It was going to be dark under there.

A black abyss.

Endless.

Because that's what emptiness was like.

And for Braden Chapman, there was nothing left in the world to see.

JUNK

Stephen Laws

Stephen Laws was born in Newcastle-upon-Tyne, England, in 1952. His native Northeast has featured in three novels of supernatural terror: *Ghost Train,* in which a resurrected demon takes possession of a train on the King's Cross, London to Edinburgh route (and the advertisement for which was banned by British Rail), *Spectre,* where an unknown terror stalks the inner-city streets of Newcastle, and *The Wyrm,* where something that isn't spelled correctly stalks the Border Country. Stephen is an opponent of the "gross-out" school of horror writing and his story "Junk" reflects that opposition. He tells me, "I want to take people where their worst fears live, and bring them back in one piece."

The nightmare began on a warm, sultry August afternoon. McLaren had been standing outside his ramshackle ''office,'' leaning against the rusting hulk of a Ford Cortina, his belly full of beer after a boozing session at the pub around the corner. For half an hour he had stood there, smoking one of the cheap cigars his brother-in-law brought him back from Spain regularly. The cheap aroma seemed to radiate from him continuously: in his clothes, his hair, his breath.

From his vantage point, he had a clear view of the entire junkyard from which he made his living. He watched as Tony Bastable manoeuvred the jib of the crane, bringing the huge mechanical claw down heavily onto a battered Austin Allegro, crushing the roof like tissue paper. It gave McLaren a curious sense of satisfaction to see the car crushed like that. Only the week before, some fat cat had been sitting behind the wheel of that car, probably on his way to some big business meeting. Looking forward to champagne and caviar; not realising that the articulated truck just ahead of him was about to jack-knife on a patch of oil on the motorway and that his nice new Allegro was going to slam, bang right into the back of it, leaving lots of little pieces of fat cat all over the road.

The Allegro was hoisted into the air and swung across the yard to The Crusher. In a few minutes, all that would remain would be a solid cube of metal.

McLaren took the cigar from between his teeth and crumpled it in his hand in much the same way that the mechanical claw had just crushed the Allegro.

"You are, no doubt, the proprietor of this establishment?"

The voice which sounded from behind McLaren made him jump forward a couple of feet, shoulders hunched up into his bull neck as if expecting an attack. But it was not a loud voice. Silky soft and with a thick accent.

"What the hell do you want to creep up on me like that for?" boomed McLaren, taking in the tall, angular figure which appeared to have materialised from nowhere. The stranger was tall, impeccably dressed and wore a homburg hat.

"My apologies. I assume that you were engrossed in your thoughts," said The Stranger. His pale face had an expression of vulpine amusement. When he smiled, McLaren could see two rows of perfectly even teeth that would have put the Osmond brothers to shame. Striking eyes sparkled with amusement beneath dark, heavy brows.

"Never mind. What do you want?" McLaren thought: *Only Jews wear homburgs. But he doesn't look Jewish. That accent sounds . . . I dunno . . . Hungarian or something*. The Stranger had his hands clasped at chest level, as if he were about to pray. Big white pulpy fingers writhed like a handful of worms.

"I am looking for certain . . . bits and pieces."

"Well, bits and pieces are what you see scattered all over the yard, mister. What you looking for in particular?"

"May I browse for a while?"

"This isn't a bloody library, mister. Now, what do you want?"

"Ah, a businessman," said The Stranger, in a way that McLaren didn't like one bit. Like he was being humoured or something. "You have it in mind to make an immediate transaction. Very well. I require a transmission from a 1963 Ford Cortina."

McLaren opened his fingers and let the crumpled cigar fall to the ground before dusting off his hands. "Pretty specific. But we don't have one in working order."

The Stranger smiled again as if to humour him. The afternoon sun seemed to be playing tricks with his eyes and teeth, which seemed to capture and reflect the light. McLaren noted in particular the curious effect the sun played on his eyes. It was like the photograph that he'd taken at his nephew's wedding last spring. The flash cube had turned everyone's irises a deep reflective red. And now The Stranger stood before him, like some forgotten and uninvited intruder at that wedding, grinning into the camera.

"The transmission need not be in working order."

From the other side of the yard, McLaren heard The Crusher begin to growl, followed by the squealing shriek of metal as the Allegro began its first crushing compression.

"Indeed, the condition of the transmission is not, within limits, of outstanding importance."

Again, the silky voice. The eyes with their stolen embers of sun. The scream of tortured metal.

"However, I do require that the equipment in question be taken from a 1963 Ford Cortina . . . *any* 1963 Ford Cortina . . . But the automobile must have ended its days as the result of a crash. And at least one passenger in the car must have been killed instantaneously."

"Get out of my junkyard, mister. Before I set my dog on you. I've got a business to run. I suggest that you save however much you were going to pay me and use it on a shrink. Now, get out." McLaren turned away from The Stranger to lean on the wreck behind him. "Atlas!" he shouted. On the other side of the yard was a shed which Jackie Shannon, the night watchman, laughingly called the "office." The shed was surrounded by a mesh fence, and McLaren's Alsatian dog prowled restlessly back and forth like a caged wild animal . . . which, in effect, it was. On hearing its name called, the dog leapt up against the mesh with a sharp, ringing clatter. McLaren smiled and turned back to The Stranger to see if he had taken the point.

The Stranger now stood less than three feet away from him. Silently, he appeared to have glided uncomfortably close to McLaren while his back was turned. The Stranger's grin was wider but there was no trace of humour on the face. The eyes burned with amber fire now, which came not from the sun, but from within. McLaren involuntarily pressed himself back against the wreck.

The Stranger's thumbs began to intertwine back and forth, back and forth in the white nest of his fingers. The squealing of metal against metal seemed to be reaching a new crescendo as The Stranger spoke again, his soft, satin voice still silken clear over the cacophony.

"At least one fatality, Mr. McLaren."

How does he know my name? thought McLaren with something like panic beginning to take hold. *Because your name's on the sign over the gate, that's why, you idiot!* But the answer failed to stem the fear which crept over him. His uneasiness in The Stranger's company had now turned to an unreasoning terror. Sweat trickled between his shoulderblades and moulded his shirt to his back. It ran down his face and dripped from the tip of his bulbous nose.

"Age or sex is immaterial. But I expect you to provide me with my requirements by tomorrow evening at the same time. Do I make myself clear?"

McLaren could not find his voice. It lay shrivelled and fearful in the pit of his stomach.

"Do I make myself clear?" said the vulpine face again as it began to move terribly and hypnotically closer.

"Yes!" McLaren's fear had found the mislaid response. The face halted inches from his own and McLaren could see now without any question that the flames of hell burned hungrily in The Stranger's eyes. A white hand like the dried, shrivelled husk of a dead spider moved to McLaren's chest and he felt something being pushed into his top jerkin pocket.

"Tomorrow, Mr. McLaren."

McLaren wanted to look away from that horrible face but was afraid that if he did, those frighteningly sharp teeth would dart quickly forward for his throat.

And then The Stranger was gone, turning sharply on his heels and striding purposefully towards the junkyard gates. The screeching sound had dwindled to a dull churning and crunching. Atlas gave vent to a long, low, pitiful howl. McLaren turned to see the dog slinking back from the mesh fence towards the shed. When he looked back to watch the departing figure, there was no one in sight. But that was crazy! It was a good three-minute walk to the gates.

But The Stranger was gone.

Tomorrow.

McLaren wiped the sweat from his face. His hand was trembling violently. Now able to move at last, he pushed himself away from the wreck and began to pick his way nervously amidst the junk towards the shed, casting anxious glances back over his shoulder.

Tony was still concentrating on The Crusher. "Hi, Frank!" he called as McLaren stumbled quickly to the mesh gate and let himself in without once looking his way. "Up yours then, you bastard!" he growled under his breath as a four-foot metal cube of Austin Allegro trundled past on a conveyor belt.

McLaren moved quickly to the shed. Atlas rounded the corner, glanced sheepishly at his master and then, as if sensing the fear which still lingered around McLaren like an invisible cloud of his rancid cigar smoke, slunk away out of sight again. McLaren clattered across the shed to a small safe, twisted the dials to the right combination and pulled out a bottle of MacInlays and a glass. Sitting at a cluttered table in the centre of the room, McLaren poured a glassful and downed it in one, staring out through the grease-stained window which overlooked the spot where he had encountered The Stranger. He drank another and then remembered the something that The Stranger had stuffed into his top pocket. Fingers still trembling, he pulled out twenty ten-pound notes.

Two hundred quid! For a lousy transmission that doesn't have to work.

A 1963 Ford Cortina which has been involved in an accident, a voice seemed to echo somewhere. *And at least one person must have been killed instantaneously in the wreck.*

McLaren drank again and watched as Tony climbed into the crane, swung the jib over The Crusher, plucked up the metal cube from the conveyor belt and swung it across the yard, late afternoon sun glinting on the wrinkled metal.

• • •

McLaren spent four of the crisp brand-new ten-pound notes on booze in the Crane and Lever that night. And as the alcohol seeped into his corpulent bulk, the unreasoning fear which had overcome him in the presence of The Stranger began gradually to dissolve. By closing time in the pub, he had rationalised the situation completely. The man was an eccentric, a queer, a pervert. He got his kicks from weird mementoes. Hadn't he once read somewhere that pieces from the car wreck which had killed James Dean in the fifties were treasured souvenirs? So what if this fella was sick? He had paid two hundred smackers, cash in advance, and the stuff he wanted didn't even have to be in working order. And, anyway, he knew for a fact that there was a battered Cortina just behind the compound with its transmission intact. It was useless, of course; strictly junk value. Two kids on a bender had been cut out of the car on the Coast Road. One of them had been dead on arrival at the County Hospital. McLaren had always been interested in how his cars came to the junkyard. Now it looked as if his interest was going to pay off.

On the following day, when the effects of the alcohol had worn off, McLaren's reasoning did not seem as watertight as it had previously. He suffered from butterflies in the stomach from the moment he climbed out of bed and they stayed with him as he supervised the extraction of the transmission from the Cortina. His nervousness also angered him so that when Tony asked him why the hell he was bothering with this piece of junk, McLaren had told him to get the hell on with it and earn his living.

As the afternoon crept on towards the appointed time, McLaren's apprehension and temper grew. By 4:00 P.M. the bottle of whisky in his safe was empty. Atlas had sensed his master's discomfort and was keeping well out of the way under the table in the "office." At 4:31 P.M. the dog looked up, sniffed the air, snarled and then slunk quickly out of the office.

McLaren knew before looking out of the window that The Stranger would be standing in the same place as yesterday, hands held clasped in front of him, staring at the office.

McLaren made his way over to the silent figure, trying to avoid looking at the face with the ivory glint of teeth and the twin orbs of copper-fire. There was a twelve-foot gap between them when McLaren stopped. The transmission rested against the twisted hulk of machinery which McLaren now leant against, waiting for The Stranger to break the silence.

"This is the transmission I requested?"

"Yeah . . ."

"Capital, capital. I think that this will suit my purpose admirably."

Bloody creep.

"I trust that you can store this equipment for me in a secure place here in your yard?" The silky smooth voice purred like a contented cat gloating over a recently slaughtered mouse.

"Well . . ."

"For a suitable fee, of course." The Stranger's thumbs were intertwining again as he surveyed the battered transmission.

"How long do you want me to keep it for you?" ventured McLaren, wiping the sweat from his brow and averting his gaze from The Stranger to scan the junkyard behind him unnecessarily.

"Not for long. I have numerous other requirements which I trust you will be able to provide."

Look, mister. Why don't you take your junk and just clear off? Leave me alone. Take your eyes and your teeth to someone else.

"Like what?"

"A rear axle from a 1971 Morris Marina. Undamaged. And the driver must have suffered leg injuries in the crash. Fatal or otherwise, but the leg injuries are the important factor."

Jesus!

Thirty seconds and thirty pounds later, McLaren was walking back to the office, feeling his hands shaking again and not wanting to turn around in case he really did see The Stranger suddenly vanish in a puff of smoke. Tomorrow. Same time, same place. That evening, there were two new whisky bottles in the safe and another on the office table.

And so the days began to blur into each other.

McLaren fought his fear with the whisky bottle and decided, at the height of his drunkenness, on various means of dealing with The Stranger: How about the threat of physical violence? Setting the dog on him and telling him never to come back? (If, that is, Atlas could be persuaded to stop crawling on his belly.) Hiring a couple of heavies from the Crane and Lever to lean on him? Calling the police to complain about the nuisance?

But every evening at the allotted time, McLaren found himself standing trembling beside the twisted hulk with The Stranger as he showed him the latest acquisition. McLaren was becoming a very rich man. But for the first time in his life, the money meant nothing to him. He hoped fervently that each latest piece of junk would be the last. But it never was.

> The rear seat from an Anglia: the back-seat passenger must have been killed, preferably decapitated.
>
> The front wheels from a Volkswagen: condition irrelevant. But two bystanders must have been injured in the crash. At least one fatality required. Leg injuries essential.
>
> An unruptured petrol tank from a Datsun Cherry: one child fatality required.

And for reasons McLaren could not explain, he found himself obeying The Stranger's strictly specific requirements to the letter even though they were becoming more and more bizarre, more and more difficult to find. Panic often threatened to overtake him on his quest, which now took him to other junkyard owners: men who had once called him friend but now only took his money, noted his whisky-tainted breath and, shaking their heads sadly, directed him to the required junk. Somehow, McLaren succeeded in meeting The Stranger's requirements every time.

Until, that is, The Stranger made his request for the *unmarked windscreen from a hit-and-run car. No particular model of car necessary. But the victim must have suffered damage to the eyes.*

McLaren knew immediately that, this time, he would never be able to meet The Stranger's requirements. It was impossible. How the hell could he provide something like that?

On The Stranger's next visit, he said so.

And then wished that he hadn't as The Stranger turned his doll-like visage on him and the ember-filled eyes sparkled displeasure. When

The Stranger smiled, it was with the face of something that had been dead for a long time. McLaren burbled that he would have the windscreen ready for him at the same time tomorrow night.

When The Stranger had gone, McLaren stood looking miserably at the pile of junk which lay cluttered in the middle of his junkyard. The recently acquired two hundred and fifty pounds fluttered loosely in one dangling hand. The pile made no sense at all. He could make no reason of this ill-assorted heap of scrap metal. It was useless. Rubbish. Junk. When McLaren moved towards the office at last, he failed to notice that two of The Stranger's ten-pound notes had fallen from his loose grasp and now lay fluttering on the muddy ground.

The following day passed agonisingly slowly for McLaren in a whisky-sodden haze. He had tried everywhere for the windscreen knowing that the request was impossible. How the hell would anyone know if any of his own cars or any of the wrecks in the other junkyards he visited were hit-and-run? Only the police were apt to have that kind of information. And in one of the junkyards he visited that day, the owner had threatened to give him a good working over after he had made his sick request.

At three o'clock that afternoon, McLaren sat in his office trying to drown the fear in his guts once more with alcohol. After a while, it seemed to be working. But McLaren knew that he must keep himself sufficiently "topped-up" to carry out the plan which he had finally prepared. He was faced with no other alternative. And if his fear of The Stranger was allowed to surface, he would never be able to do it.

First of all, he made a none-too-steady tour of the junkyard and found an intact windscreen from a Citroën. Then he called Tony over and instructed him to take it out carefully . . . *very carefully* . . . ignoring the look of disgust on his employee's face. What the hell? He was drunk and he knew it, and only by staying drunk was he going to solve his problem.

By the time that Tony had propped the windscreen up against the pile of junk which had been accumulated by The Stranger, the sun was beginning to sink in the late afternoon sky.

"Mind if I ask a question?" said Tony, lighting a cigarette as he cast a glance over the peculiar debris.

McLaren grunted. It could have meant yes or no.

"What the hell's all this stuff for?"

"You get paid to do a job, Tony. And that's all. Just do it and don't stick your nose in." McLaren finished his statement with a rattling belch.

"You always were a pig, McLaren." Tony blew a stream of smoke in his direction. "And until now, I've just put up with it because I needed the work. Now I don't. So you can stuff your job as of now."

McLaren stepped forward.

"Try it and I'll lay you out," said Tony easily. McLaren stopped, swaying slightly. "But before I do go I think I should give you a piece of advice. See a shrink. You're acting pretty weird, McLaren. I think that whisky bottle has addled your brains."

Casting a last, derisory glance at The Stranger's junk, Tony walked past McLaren towards the gates.

Oh, yeah? thought McLaren. *Big man! If you'd been through what I've been through, you wouldn't be so loudmouthed. If you'd had to look into those bloody eyes, just what state would* your *nerves be in?* He wanted to say all of those things to Tony. But only one word would come out.

"Bastard!"

Tony ignored him. Funnily enough, McLaren's parting remark was entirely factual.

Back in the office, McLaren replenished himself, cooing gratefully to the bottle, caressing its neck like some strange glass pet. Underneath the table, Atlas began to make low, grumbling sounds in his throat. It was time.

The Stranger stood in the usual spot, his own angular shadow joining with the sharp, ragged shadows of the surrounding junk as the sun finally began to creep past the horizon. McLaren's hands were no longer trembling as he stood up purposefully, the chair clattering backward to the floor. The dog whined and began to crawl across the floor on its stomach until it had reached the far corner.

Walking stiff-legged, eyes staring, McLaren moved to the bench, found what he was looking for and tucked it tightly into his belt behind him, feeling its hard coolness in the small of his back. The walk across the junkyard to The Stranger seemed to take place in a dream-like slow motion. He seemed to be walking on a moving treadmill and never actually getting any closer.

The Stranger was smiling or grimacing . . . McLaren couldn't decide which . . . but he hoped above everything else that he could not read his mind and see his intention. The Stranger's mouth opened, lips writhing back from glistening teeth, as McLaren arrived.

"You have obtained the necessary?"

"Yes . . . it's over there behind you." *All this whisky and I'm still so goddamned frightened. Can he hear it? Can he hear how frightened I am?*

"Good. Let me see it."

McLaren gestured for him to move forward and The Stranger turned to look at his pile of junk. The windscreen was propped against the transmission. It dimly reflected The Stranger's angular shape as he leaned down to touch it. McLaren had moved up behind him as The Stranger crouched down and stroked the glass.

And then McLaren heard the sharp intake of breath that sounded more like the warning of a rattlesnake about to strike. The Stranger was turning from his crouched position, mouth twisting in a cruel grimace. One eye was swivelling back to look at him like some hideous chameleon.

"This is *not* . . ." began The Stranger as McLaren stepped swiftly forward, fumbling at the small of his back. In the next instant, the spanner had cracked open The Stranger's skull like a ripe melon. The mouth grinned, eyes rolled up to white and The Stranger jerked over backward with the spanner still embedded in his brain, arms and legs writhing in a dance of death. Then he was still.

McLaren stood frozen in position, one arm held out before him in the act of the fatal blow. Stunned, he stared at The Stranger. It had been so easy. So damned easy. One blow. And he was dead.

Lurching away, McLaren vomited a stream of pure alcohol onto the ground, his stomach heaving and straining until there was nothing left to come.

The Stranger lay twisted and angular like some hideous praying mantis, the whites of his dead eyes still reflecting the dying light as McLaren finally moved towards him again. He purposefully avoided those eyes as he leaned behind the twisted car wreck against which The Stranger's junk was propped, trembling fingers finding the oil-smeared tarpaulin he had placed there earlier. McLaren felt so terribly cold, so bloodless, as he threw the tarpaulin on the ground beside the corpse. Wiping one trembling hand across his mouth, he kicked the body over onto the tarpaulin, unable to bring himself to touch The Stranger with his hands. The body rustled easily over onto the sheet. The spanner squelched from its resting place.

Controlling his stomach, McLaren drew the canvas up around the body and rolled it over; once, twice, three times . . . until The Stranger's corpse was firmly wrapped in a cocoon of tarpaulin. McLaren threw an anxious glance back at the office. Jackie Shannon, the night watchman, would be arriving at any time. There wasn't much time. McLaren grabbed the tarpaulin around The Stranger's feet and began to drag his package across the junkyard. The sun had finally slipped past the horizon as McLaren reached the rusted hulk of the Ford Cortina, the jagged piled silhouettes of rusted cars and twisted metal painted with the blue-black of night. It was like some bizarre elephant's graveyard.

Hinges screeched as he pulled open the driver's door and McLaren heard Atlas give vent to a long, solitary howl from the office. Now McLaren would have to use his hands and felt disgust as he roughly bundled the corpse across the driver's seat, still glancing fearfully behind him for any sign of Shannon. Finally, the bundle was stuffed into the car and McLaren slammed the door shut with unnecessary force, feeling the cold sweat on his face, the dull ache in his gut.

Within seconds, he was in the driving cab of the crane. As he had so rightly guessed, Tony had left the keys in the dash. The engine roared into life and the grab swung across the yard to hover like some mythical roc's claw above the wreck and its grisly occupant. The engine gasped and the claw suddenly descended under its own weight, crumpling the roof of the car. The claw tightened, punching in the windows, splintering and cracking the bodywork. In silhouette, it seemed as if some stalking *Tyrannosaurus rex* had caught its prey and was in the process of taking the corpse to its lair.

The black, rectangular maw of The Crusher yawned wide to receive the car as the crane gently lowered the wreck. For five agonisingly long seconds the prey refused to be parted from the hunter, before finally crashing down into the machine. Five minutes later, McLaren stood at The Crusher's control, still furtively looking over his shoulder, eyes darting, fingers twitching, beads of sweat marbling his face.

He set The Crusher in motion.

The squealing and rending of metal was almost too much for him. He turned his back on The Crusher, hands clasped to his ears to deafen the insane cacophony of tortured metal. McLaren tried to shut out the recurring mental image of what must be happening to the tarpaulin-wrapped body in the car. It would all be over soon. But now, as the car began to reach the first stage of its compression before the hydraulic ram could start on the inexorable forward movement which would finally reduce the car to a solid cube of metal, the squealing had taken on a new and decidedly more horrific tone.

It seemed to sound like someone screaming.

No, that can't be! thought McLaren, squeezing his hands tightly over his ears. *He was dead. I know he was dead. I crushed his skull . . .*

The squealing and crunching abruptly subsided to a lower, rumbling noise under the unstoppable grumbling of The Crusher. The conveyor belt began to move.

McLaren moved away from The Crusher controls and around to one side, straining nervously forward to catch sight of the car's remains.

A cube of compressed metal, four feet square, trundled out of The Crusher's maw.

McLaren walked around it. There was no blood. No telltale shoe poking out of the side. No hideous, clutching hands. He turned back to the crane and climbed into the cabin.

The claw descended. The cube was hoisted across the junkyard. McLaren swung the cube up high over the inpenetrable tangle of steel and iron in the middle of his yard, until it dangled over the most inaccessible depths of his junk pile. The claw opened.

The cube plunged into the junk pile with a screeching crash and the pile seemed to shift uncomfortably, adjusting its bulk to take account of this unwelcome intruder. It groaned, murmured, protested. And then, with a final squeal of protest, the cube began to slip. Slowly at first, and then faster and faster the cube slid into the widening, yawning fissure of a junk earthquake.

Perfect! thought McLaren, licking dry lips. *Bloody perfect!*

The cube vanished from sight under an avalanche of metal, a twisted wreath of wiring and steel frame crashing down and effectively burying it from sight for good. The junk heap rumbled once and was still.

Perfect!

"Working late, Mr. McLaren?"

The voice just outside the cab door sent a bolt of electric blue lightning racing through McLaren's heart, bottlenecking in his throat with a convulsive heave. Shannon had climbed up to the cab and watched as McLaren had manoeuvred the cube into the junk heap.

"Just . . . it was . . ." McLaren heard himself say. "Bloody stuff was no good! Just in the way all the time." And then, hastily and defensively: "Wouldn't have had to do it myself if it hadn't been for Bastable. I had to sack the bastard this afternoon!"

"Tony? Really?" Shannon began to climb back down as McLaren switched off and began to follow him, legs like jelly. "Ah, well. I could see it coming. His heart was never in it."

Back at the office, McLaren could hear that Atlas was barking fit to burst again. But this time, it seemed to him that his dog's barking seemed healthier, less fearful. McLaren began to feel a great pressure lifting from him.

"Fancy a glass of whisky?" he asked Shannon.

Shannon's jaw dropped. This kind of offer from McLaren was unknown. "Don't mind if I do," he replied after he had regained his composure, adding mentally: *Sacking people must agree with you. I'd better watch my step.*

McLaren smiled heartily and clapped Shannon's back so heavily that the old man's dentures nearly popped out.

"Celebrating, Mr. McLaren?"

"Just let's say I've got a pressing problem off my mind."

• • •

The nightmare began again a week later.

McLaren had found himself unable to go anywhere near the pile of junk which he had accumulated for The Stranger. Every time he passed it, he promised himself that he would have it gathered up and slung out later. Later. Always later. And then, a week to the day that he had rid himself of that *thing,* he noticed that the junk was gone.

His first reaction was one of relief. He had given no order to any of his men to get rid of the stuff and normally he would have flown into a vindictive rage because of that fact. But not this time. He asked his workmen in as casual and appreciative a manner as possible, who had done it . . . George, Ray and Barney Hill. Even Jackie Shannon. And something like unease began to creep over McLaren as each worker in turn denied having touched any of the stuff. He fought it down. *Somebody* must have moved the bloody stuff. But whatever that person's reason for keeping quiet about it, McLaren decided to be thankful for this not-so-small mercy and ask no more questions. The junk was gone. That was the important thing.

On Thursday morning, McLaren let himself in through the main compound gate for another working day and as he approached the office could see immediately that something was wrong. Shannon was standing in the doorway hopping from foot to foot, obviously waiting anxiously for him. Atlas was pacing back and forward behind the mesh.

"What's up, Jackie?"

"Prowlers, Mr. McLaren. Early this morning; about three o'clock."

"Catch anybody?" asked McLaren, pushing past him into the office and making straight for the freshly boiled kettle.

"Never saw a soul. Heard them, though. I reckon Atlas put the wind up them."

"Where?"

"Over on the other side of the compound. They couldn't have been professionals, Mr. McLaren. They made one hell of a racket. Crashing and banging, pulling the bloody junk about. I let Atlas go and then followed him. I reckon when they heard him barking, they scarpered. They must have been fast, though . . . I didn't see a soul. Not even with those arc lights blazing away."

"Probably kids," said McLaren. *Then why the hell do I feel scared all of a sudden? What the hell's the matter with me?*

"Did you check the fence?"

"No breaks. They must have come over the top. Must have been keen if they wanted to risk losing a bollock on that barbed wire. Shall I report it?"

"Naw," said McLaren, gulping hot, strong tea. "Not worth it. Just keep your eyes open tonight." *Tomorrow night. In the junkyard. In the dark. And I'll be home, drinking whisky. Far away from this place. Far away and safe.*

Why did the junkyard at night suddenly seem such an unpleasant prospect?

McLaren gulped his tea and started a long, unsuccessful day of trying to rid himself of a bloody awful creepy feeling that he thought had vanished with the passing of The Stranger.

. . .

It had been a long, arduous day. McLaren, still feeling clammy, had spent two hours in the Crane and Lever that evening until the whisky had numbed him to it. Returning home, he had finished off a six-pack from the fridge and fallen asleep in front of the television. His dreams were vague and troubled. The images were confused and disturbing. The junkyard at night. The crane. The Crusher. A tall, angular shadow standing up against the compound fence, fingers hooked through the mesh, face obscured apart from two hideously shining red eyes looking straight at him with hungry intent. The sound of The Crusher. The squealing and shrieking of rending metal. The shrieking of steel turning to the shrieking of a human voice. Closer and louder. Closer . . . louder . . . *Close . . . closer . . . here . . . Now!*

McLaren woke with a scream clenched tightly in his teeth; his heart was hammering, and he half expected to find himself standing alone in the junkyard listening to the sounds of shambling footsteps behind him. The familiarity of his living room made him slump backward with a deep sigh. The television buzzed angrily at him, the speckled snowstorm on the screen the sole light in the room.

But why could he still hear the shrieking?

He panicked again. But no, it wasn't The Crusher, or the car, or The Stranger. It was the telephone.

Groaning again, McLaren struggled to his feet, accidentally kicking over an empty beer can with a reverberating clank. He wiped his face, yawned and then answered the telephone.

It was Shannon.

"I'm sorry to bother you so late, Mr. McLaren. But I think you'd better come down here straightaway."

McLaren looked at his watch. It was one-thirty. "What the hell's wrong?"

"It's Atlas. He's been hurt pretty bad."

"How? No . . . wait! I'll be right down!"

As always, the junkyard was brilliantly floodlit, but the harsh black shadows that filled the ragged gaps and crevices of the junk pile brought the crawling taste of fear back to McLaren. The booze had worn off. He felt dry and hollow; and the hollowness was filling up rapidly with that creepy sick feeling again. The gates were open . . . Shannon had obviously seen to that . . . and McLaren's car roared through, kicking up dust. The car screeched to a halt and McLaren flung himself out past the night watchman and into the office, unaware of Shannon's agitated burblings, and realising for the first time (*truly* for the first time) how much he loved that dog and didn't want to lose it. He knew that it was going to be bad.

But not as bad as this.

Atlas lay on a blanket beside the table, making low, hopeless gurgling sounds in the back of his throat. It whimpered when it saw him. McLaren moved forward and saw the blood. The dog's body was covered in deep lacerations, its foreleg almost severed at the knee. Shannon had tied a makeshift tourniquet above the knee with masking tape.

". . . Oh God, Atlas . . ." was all that McLaren could say as he knelt beside his dying dog, knowing that it had lost too much blood to be saved. It licked his hand. McLaren choked back tears.

"What the hell happened here?"

"That's what I've been trying to tell you, Mr. McLaren. There's something weird going on. I don't think I want to work here no more . . ."

"What have you done to my dog?"

"We've been hearing noises all night, Mr. McLaren." Shannon's voice struggled to retain control. "Somebody's out there in the junk, moving stuff around. And every time we got near to where we thought the noise was coming from, it stopped and then started again somewhere else. Atlas was sniffing around at the foot of that big pile of junk in the middle of the yard . . . just like he'd found something in there. Then he started squealing. When I got to him I saw that he'd got his leg caught in some wiring. I couldn't get him loose, Mr. McLaren! He just kept getting more tangled in the junk. He bit me while I was trying to help him. Look!"

Shannon showed him the crescent-shaped mark on his forearm but McLaren was looking beyond him, through the open door and into the junkyard. "Show me, Jackie. Show me where it happened." McLaren's voice was quavering. Instinctively, he knew where it had happened. But he still had to see. "Show me."

"The dog . . . ?"

"He's as good as dead. Show me."

McLaren followed Shannon outside.

"I'm sorry, Mr. McLaren. Really I am. But we just couldn't find whatever was making the noise. It stopped after Atlas was hurt . . ."

"Show me."

They walked through the starkly lit, deeply shadowed automobile graveyard, passing ruined metal carcasses heaped one upon the other. The crane stood its silent dinosaur vigil, dagger-toothed head stooped and waiting. As McLaren had guessed, Shannon headed straight for the centre pile where The Stranger's remains lay buried in a four-foot-cube coffin. McLaren became aware of a buzzing in his head and tried to shake it off, finally realising at last that the sound was coming from one of the arc lights overhead. The first of their multiple shadows reached the pile before them. Shannon pointed at the foot of the pile.

"There. That's where it happened." A pool of Atlas' blood glistened darkly like machine oil.

What am I going to do? thought McLaren desperately.

"Maybe we should get the police . . ." began Shannon.

"No!" snapped McLaren. "No police!" *God knows what they might find if they start snooping around.*

And then the lights started to go out.

During their walk the buzzing sound had grown steadily louder before ending abruptly. At that moment, one of the arc lights beside the office had suddenly gone out. Both men turned to look as another light went out on the far side of the compound. They turned again. Another light went out. And then another. Section by section, the junkyard was being plunged into utter darkness.

"What the . . . ?"

Only one arc light now remained in operation: the light which towered above the centre pile at which they were standing. McLaren and Shannon stood vulnerably in the droning spotlight.

"Power failure?" said Shannon in hopeless dismay.

The last light went out.

McLaren almost allowed his first instinctive reaction to take hold. He had plunged headfirst into his own most recent nightmare and he wanted to run screaming from the junkyard. Fighting to control himself, knowing that he was not going to wake up this time in the safety of his own armchair, McLaren fumbled through the dark to touch Shannon's arm. Shannon jerked in shock at the touch.

"Use the flashlight."

Shannon unfastened the torch from his belt and switched it on, the beam sweeping over the twisted wreckage of the junk pile.

"We'll walk back to the office slowly. No point in breaking our necks on a piece of junk."

Something shifted in the junk pile behind them.

Shannon swung around and the torch beam danced over the pile again.

"Keep walking!" said McLaren, pulling Shannon's arm.

"There's something in there," said Shannon tightly. "I can see . . . sparks . . . or something."

"Come on!"

"No, wait, look there." Shannon switched off the torch. The darkness swamped them again. McLaren could feel his heart racing. Despite himself, he turned to look.

Deep inside the junk pile, obscured by tangled machinery and wiring, McLaren could see a brief spluttering of light. Sparks danced and hissed somewhere in the very heart of the junk pile as if someone was at work in there with an oxyacetylene torch.

"We've got to get out, Jackie!"

The junk shifted again. The sparks crackled and jumped.

"No . . . wait a minute, Mr. McLaren . . . I can see something . . . I can see . . ." Shannon had moved forward, pulling away from McLaren's grip.

"Jackie, I'm going for the police. Come on. It's kids or something." McLaren kept backing away as Shannon put one hand on the pile of junk and strained forward to peer inside. He raised the torch and pointed it through a ragged gap.

"Come on, Jackie!"

"No . . . wait a minute, Mr. McLaren . . . I can see something . . . I can see . . ." Shannon switched on the torch, pushing forward headfirst into a gap in the junk pile.

At first, McLaren thought that he was back on that terrible day again and that he had just switched on The Crusher. The horrifying screech of metal had turned into the screaming of a human voice. The screaming had started again—loud, desperate and horrifying. A screeching and crunching noise that froze McLaren in his tracks. But of course, it was not The Crusher. It was Shannon.

And McLaren could only stand and watch in horror as something unseen began to drag Shannon into the junk pile by his head. The torch clattered down into the pile, providing an angled cross-lit framework of the tangled junk as Shannon thrashed, screamed and kicked. The junk shifted. Shannon slipped further inside, his shrieking now hoarse and mortally desperate. His legs kicked spasmodically, the junk shifted again and Shannon disappeared quivering and silent into the pile. The hissing and spluttering sparks danced again.

At last, McLaren screamed. He turned and ran blindly into the dark, away from the junk pile. Too late, he became aware of something directly before him. Something slammed into his forehead, sparks danced in his brain and he was aware now that he was lying on his back. He groaned, wiped his hand across his head and felt blood. He looked up. A length of girder was protruding from the open window of a ruined Ford Estate car. McLaren had run straight into it. And he knew that the girder had not been there before.

Frantically, he clambered to his feet and began moaning in terror as the pile began to slither and crash behind him like a living thing. McLaren blundered away again, trying to orientate himself and find the direction which would lead him to the office.

But as he ran, he felt like a stranger in someone else's junkyard. The terrain was unknown to him. The landscapes of piled junk, the jagged peaks and valleys of wrecked cars and ruined machinery were completely alien.

It's as if something's been moving the junk around so that I would get lost! McLaren heard himself thinking, blind terror now taking hold. He continued to run, screaming and scrabbling through the junk like an animal as the centre pile crashed and heaved in the darkness. *Something's breaking out! That's what it is . . . he's breaking out!* Jagged steel edges lacerated his hands and shredded his sleeves as he plunged blindly ahead. Something screeched rustily in the darkness behind him.

Please, God, let me get out! I'll be a good boy . . . I promise . . . Just let me out!

McLaren's foot tangled in a broken radio set and he crashed heavily to the ground again, knocking the breath out of his lungs. Sobbing painfully, he scrabbled into the shadows of a rusted car hulk, squeezing himself partially beneath it.

The noises from the centre pile ceased.

McLaren struggled to control his wheezing, now the only sound in the darkness. The centre pile was obscured by other mazed mounds of twisted junk. There was no sound; no movement of any kind. McLaren tried to assess his exact whereabouts in the junkyard, scanning the darkness and the black silhouettes of metal carcasses. None of the junk was familiar. He closed his eyes, hands clasped to heaving chest, and concentrated. He thought quickly back to his first approach towards the centre pile with Shannon, gauged how far his desperate flight had taken him, and then looked around again. If he headed *over there* . . .

And then McLaren heard the first sound off to his right. A hollow, shivering clank from somewhere in the darkness. It didn't come from the centre pile, of that much he was certain. Perhaps, he thought, with rising hope, it was Ray, or George, or . . .

Something moved across the open patch of ground on McLaren's right. Something that was long, twisted and indistinct. It seemed to hop, skip and then turn end over end as it moved quickly across the ragged ground, rattling and clanking. McLaren refused to believe that it was a car exhaust, moving of its own volition and headed in the direction of the centre pile. He also refused to believe it when a car battery began to roll end over end across the yard from the other direction, again on its way to the centre pile. Junk did not move by itself. Tyres did not suddenly squeeze themselves out of the junk and roll sedately away into the darkness. Headlights, axles and car seats did not emerge from the night, scuttling and bouncing on their unknown destination. Even when a rearview mirror whistled past his face, clipping his ear and drawing blood, McLaren did not believe. Things like that only happened in nightmares. And if this was a nightmare, he would be waking up soon. A wild, living tangle of valves and wiring whispered past his arm, like some insane man-made tumbleweed.

The screeching, hammering and grinding from the centre pile began again. McLaren squeezed further under the car wreck, face smeared with blood and rust. This had to be a dream.

For two hours, McLaren lay in that position, listening to the crashing and rending of metal, the hiss and sputtering of something that made sparks. And for two hours, he firmly believed that he would awake at any second in his armchair at home. When he did, he would make straight for the fridge and break open another six-pack. After a while, the procession of ambulatory junk had stopped. Now there was only the noise.

When the noise stopped, McLaren screwed his eyes shut, willing himself to wake up. *It's time to wake up now! This is it! The nightmare's finished. Come on . . .*

Something large and decidedly ferocious coughed once in the darkness and then began to roar throatily. The sound was filled with threat and rage. It was hungry. It wanted somebody. It wanted him.

It began to move in his direction.

McLaren scrabbled out from under the car, sobbing desperately. The roaring sound filled the night air, reverberating and echoing from the mounds of junk. He raced in the direction he had identified earlier.

I want to get out!

McLaren rounded a corner, tottering on one foot, trying to find the office. It was useless. Everything looked so bloody different. Behind him, something large and monstrous ploughed through a mound of junk with explosive force.

He ran. And ran. And ran.

The junkyard was a maze. McLaren was lost. And behind him, getting ever closer as it followed his scent, came a bellowing, fearful Minotaur. McLaren leapt over an old tractor engine with an agility born out of mortal terror and slipped into another unfamiliar alley. The bellowing behind him changed tone to a gasping, hydraulic hiss. It was as if some great animal was angrily drawing in breath and scanning the junk for any sign of its quarry. McLaren pressed tightly and silently into the darkness, holding his breath. The gasping noise began to move away. McLaren listened until the noise had receded into the distance and when it had vanished, he exhaled desperately, heaving air into his lungs. When he had recovered sufficiently, he began to creep forward through the junk, scanning the twisted wreckage for movement, searching desperately for the office. On his left, the dim outline of an arc light reared up against the night sky. Using it as a guide, he searched for the others. One, two, three . . . and *there* was the light with the broken girder.

That means the office is over there!

Quietly, fearfully, McLaren picked his way through the junk to the arc light, slipping between rusted car wrecks, squeezing through gaps and crevices. The night swamped everything. Fighting down claustrophobia, McLaren pushed through yet another tangle of metal. As he pushed at a ruined lawn mower, the junk shifted with a grinding clatter. McLaren froze, expecting the bellowing, hissing unseen thing in the dark to round a corner and roar down upon him. But there was no noise.

McLaren eased through the junk, hope and relief flooding his soul as he saw the dim outline of his office and the compound fence. His car was parked and waiting. Beyond it, the gates were wide open. In one minute flat, he would be roaring away from the nightmare forever.

He ran quickly forward, crouching low and darting anxious glances in the darkness as he made for his car. Something metallic snared his shin in the pitch-blackness. He cursed under his breath at the pain. Finally, he reached the dim outline of his car, knowing that the keys were still in the dash. The doors were not locked. He would be gone in seconds.

Quicker than thought, he wrenched open the door and dived into the driving seat. He slammed the door and reached for the keys. They were gone. He fumbled in the darkness for them. They had not fallen on the floor, as far as he could see. Muttering a short prayer, McLaren reached up for the light switch above the windscreen, which did not seem to be where it should be. His fingers found an unfamiliar switch. He pressed it and a blue light came on overhead.

Now he knew that he was not in his car.

McLaren was sitting in a nightmare tangle of wiring and twisted metal; a bizarre creation of freshly welded junk. Rusted piping throbbed with hideous life. A twisted radiator grille, soldered to the exhaust which McLaren remembered procuring for The Stranger, hissed angry steam. With mounting terror, McLaren recognised the other items of The Stranger's junk, all hideously welded into some nightmarish, contorted and utterly alien design.

He was sitting inside some monstrous machine that only barely resembled a car. He knew now what had chased him in the junkyard.

Something pulsed in the darkness beneath the dashboard. McLaren didn't want to look, but did.

Shannon's severed head gazed up at McLaren, the eye sockets pierced by living wires. But it wasn't the head that made McLaren scream. It was the object on which Shannon's head rested and into which the wiring from his eye sockets had been soldered.

It was the hideous cube of metal which McLaren had buried in the junk pile. The cube which contained the mangled remains of The Stranger.

The eye socket wiring sputtered, Shannon's jaw twitched and McLaren saw the machine's headlights flare on beyond the rusted frame of the shattered windscreen. Now it could see. McLaren scrabbled at the door but could not find a handle.

"Let me out! For God's sake let me . . . !"

A band of corrugated steel flashed from the darkness around his waist, pinning McLaren to the seat like some insane seatbelt. Frantically clawing at the unyielding metal, McLaren failed to see the dashboard slowly open before him. Steam hissed angrily. The interior blue light flickered as the monstrous engine coughed into rumbling life.

"No no no No! No! No! . . ."

A rusted pipe, slick with oil, stabbed outward from the dashboard. McLaren watched it plunge into his chest in a crimson implosion with a look of mild surprise on his face. The pipe tore into his heart, sucking greedily. Beneath McLaren's spasming legs, the tangled cube of metal began to vibrate.

Now refueled, the Doomsday Machine roared out of the yard, scattering junk.

The noise of its coughing, roaring engine was soon swallowed by the beckoning night.

THE WOMAN IN THE WALL

John Daniel

A reporter for the *Chicago Tribune* for over twenty years, John Daniel retired to his home town of Archbold, Ohio, to take care of his wife Ellie and to fulfill a lifelong ambition to write fantasy and ghost stories. He is one of the shyest of all the authors who contributed to *Scare Care,* and almost always publishes his classically crafted short stories under an assortment of *noms-de-plume,* including those of his friends, his local grocery-store manager, and (once) his pet retriever. John's hobbies include Italian cooking and making his own wine. He sounds mild enough, but discover what's waiting for you in John's faintly disguised home town . . .

It was raining in cold dreary sheets that day I moved into 31 Caper Street; scurrying between the uplifted tailgate of my station wagon and the wedged-open front door, with a sodden copy of the *Archman Times* draped over my head.

And when at last it was all over, and I was sitting in my own brown dilapidated chair with rain-streaked boxes stacked around me, I closed my eyes against the raw glare of the single electric bulb and breathed relief.

But what sadness, too. Because Vicky was gone, and Jimmy Junior was gone, and here I was, alone in Archman, Ohio, on a rainy night, with wet shoes, and nothing to show for four years of marriage but old magazines and dog-eared Christmas cards and records I never wanted to listen to, never again.

I rummaged my way through four cardboard boxes until I found a half-empty bottle of Wild Turkey. There was nothing to drink it out of but a lime-encrusted flower vase. I sat under the single bulb and drank myself a toast. To love, to life, to what-the-hell.

You threaten to walk out so many times. You rage and argue and all the time you never believe that one day you're going to do it. And then one day you do. And once you're standing on the wrong side of that door, that's it. Something irrevocable has happened, and you can never, ever go back.

My advice to all discontented husbands: don't argue, don't drink, don't walk through that door.

Now Vicky was working as a secretary in Toledo and Jimmy Junior was classified as the child of a single-parent family and I was preparing to start work as a geography and athletics teacher at Archman Junior High. Your whole life can turn itself upside down that quickly—just because you walked out of that door.

I finished my drink, and lay back for a while, and then I decided I needed a walk, and maybe some supper, too. I left the apartment by the narrow front stairs and walked along Caper Street as far as Main.

It had stopped raining, but the streets were still wet. An occasional car swooshed past, its brake lights bleeding into the glistening blacktop. I thrust my hands into my pockets and looked up at the rapidly clearing sky, and felt that I was two thousand miles away from anybody I knew and loved.

On the corner of Willow and Main, there was a drugstore with steamy windows called Irv's Best. I pushed my way inside and it smelled of meat loaf and grape-flavored gum and *Elf Quest* comics. There was a run-down-looking guy behind the counter with a face like potatoes and a folded paper hat. ''How about a Reuben sandwich and a light beer?'' I asked him.

He poured me the beer. ''You want gas?'' he said. ''This'll give you gas. This, and a Reuben sandwich. You want a guaranteed recipe for gas?''

"I just want a sandwich and a beer, is that all right with you?"

He sniffed. "You headed east?" he asked me.

"I'm not headed anywhere."

He frowned. He obviously didn't understand.

"I'm moving in. I've come to live here."

"You've come to live in Archman? You out of your tree?"

"I'm teaching geography and athletics at the Junior High."

"You *are* out of your tree."

"I don't think so," I told him, and by this time he was making me feel irritated. "I wanted to find someplace quiet, and Archman looks like it."

"Well, you're right there. Archman is someplace quiet all right. Archman is so goddamned quiet they keep sending the sheriff across from Wauseon to see if we're still breathing."

He sniffed more violently, and spent some time wiping the stainless-steel counter with a smeary rag. "There's a church, and a store, and a brickworks, and a library full of books that everybody's read, and that's it."

He was silent and thoughtful for a while, and then he reached out his hand and said, "My name's Carl, by the way. Good to know you. Welcome to Archman."

"What happened to Irv?"

"Irv who?"

"This place is called Irv's Best, isn't it?"

"Oh, that Irv. He died."

. . .

I finished my sandwich and walked back to Caper Street. Carl was right. Archman was the quietest place I've ever been in, *ever*. You could stand in the middle of Main Street at midnight and you couldn't hear anything at all. It was just as if the whole town had been covered by a thick felt blanket. Claustrophobic memories of childhood, underneath a bedspread that was too heavy.

I climbed wearily up the stairs to my first-floor apartment, and closed the door behind me. I undressed, dropping my clothes on the floor. Then I took a shower. The plumbing shuddered so loud I imagined they could probably hear me all the way across town. I soaped myself and whistled a little. *The night they drove Old Dixie down . . . and all the people were singing . . .*

But then, so soft and indistinct that I thought I might have imagined it, I heard a noise in the apartment somewhere.

I listened, feeling that odd tingly feeling you get when your intellect is telling you to be reasonable but your instinct is more than just a little bit alarmed. I never particularly like taking a shower in an empty apartment anyway, it makes me feel *vulnerable*.

The next thing you know, Anthony Perkins is going to come slashing his way through the shower curtain with a twelve-inch carving knife.

I heard the noise again, and this time I shut off the faucet. I listened and listened, but all I could hear now was the soft gurgling of water going down the drain. I stepped out of the shower and picked up my towel. I opened the bathroom door.

There it was again. A soft, insistent, scratching noise. A rat, maybe; or a bird in the eaves. It seemed to be coming from the bedroom. I hesitated outside the door for a while, and then stepped in.

The bedroom was empty. There was a solid red-brick wall at one end, and the three other walls were painted white. I had set up the new divan with the brass headboard which I had bought three days ago at Sear's, but there was nothing else in the room at all. No cupboards for rats or cats to conceal themselves in. No nooks and crannies. Just a plain rectangular room, with a bed. A double bed, which one casualty from a recently broken marriage was hoping from time to time to share with somebody else. God let there be some single women in Archman. Correction, God. Single women under the age of sixty.

I listened a moment longer, but all I could hear was the muffled rattling of a distant freight train. I finished drying myself, and then I climbed into bed and switched out the light. The ceiling was crisscrossed with squares of light from the street outside, on which the shadows of raindrops trembled. I lay with my eyes open feeling more sad and lonely than I had ever been in my whole life. I thought of Vicky. I thought of Jimmy Junior. I let out one tight sob that was more of a cough and then I didn't allow myself any more.

Sleep took me by stealth. I snored once, and jolted, but then I was sleeping again. Two hours of the night passed me by, and then I heard that noise again. A soft, repetitive scritching, like claws against brick. I lay staring at the wall, tensed up, not breathing, and then it came again.

I reached down and switched on the lamp, half-expecting to send a rat scurrying away into the shadows. But the bedroom was bare. I listened and listened and there it was. *Scritch, scritch, scritch.*

There was no doubt about it this time. It was coming from the other side of the wall. Perhaps somebody in the next building had a dog that was locked up for the night. Perhaps they were doing some late-night decorating, scraping off some old wallpaper. Whatever it was, it didn't have anything to do with me—except that if it kept on, I'd have to go next door and complain about it.

I turned off the light, dragged the comforter up around my ears, and made a determined effort to go to sleep. I had almost sunk back into the darkness when the scratching started up again. Angry now, and deeply fatigued, I picked up a heavy bronze ashtray and banged on the wall with it.

"Can you hear me? There's somebody living here now! I'm trying to get some sleep!"

Almost immediately, I received three sharp knocks on the wall in reply.

"Listen!" I yelled. "All I want you to do is to shut up! Do you hear me? No more knocking! Just let me get some sleep!"

There was silence. I stayed where I was, kneeling up in bed, half-expecting to hear another knock, but none came. After a while, I allowed myself to wriggle back under the covers and re-arrange my nest.

An hour passed. I dozed and dreamed. I heard whispering and laughter. Sometimes I was asleep and sometimes I was awake. I thought I could see someone sitting hunched in a hood in the opposite corner of the room, and it turned out to be nothing more than a shadow. Then, later, I woke up sweating and although the room was silent I knew that somebody had been speaking to me. I lay bunched up in my covers, listening, holding my breath, my brain feeling as cold as an empty linoleum corridor.

Somebody said, *"Help me."*

I lifted my head a fraction.

"Help me," the voice repeated. A woman's voice, but very faint.

I sat up in bed, listening so intently that my eardrums sang.

"Please help me, call somebody, please."

I pressed my ear against the brick walls.

"Help me," she repeated, and this time there was no doubt that she was next door, whispering to me through the wall.

"What's wrong?" I called back. "Can you hear me? What's wrong?"

"—lp me," she said.

"Listen!" I shouted. "Are you locked in? What's wrong? Has somebody locked you in? What's happening in there?"

"—me, for God's sake, hel—"

I sat up straight. I didn't know what the hell to do. A strange woman on the opposite side of my bedroom wall was begging me for help, but she wouldn't tell me what was wrong. Either that, or she couldn't hear me. But if she was whispering, and I could hear *her,* then she must be able to hear me yelling.

I climbed out of bed. I went through to the living room, found the phone and picked it up, intent on calling the police. But then I thought I'd better make one last check. I'd called the police once before, when Vicky and I had been arguing, and that experience had been sufficient to make me feel highly prudent about summoning the law. I went back to the bedroom and knocked on the bricks with my ashtray.

"Are you okay?" I called. "Are you hurt, or anything like that? Do you need an ambulance?"

"He's coming," she whispered. *"Please hurry, he's coming!"* Then she screamed, and her scream was so piercing that I shouted out, too, and dragged my pants off the back of the chair, and hop-stumbled into them, and grabbed at my shirt, and wrenched open my door and ran down the stairs to the street not even stopping to think that I was scared.

Outside it was cold and windy, with a fine flying drizzle in the air. I banged at the door of the house next door, Number 29. "Let me in!" I shouted. "Let me in! You touch that woman and I'll call the cops!"

I banged and yelled and yelled and banged, and two or three lights went on, in bedrooms across the street. I tried to wrestle the front door open with my shoulder, but even though it was old and rotten and the gray-green paint was flaking, it wouldn't budge.

I stepped panting into the street and peered up at the second-story windows. They were dark and blank. They looked almost as if they had been boarded up from the inside. I wondered if I ought to shout out again, or find an ax and try to smash the door down, but neighbors were watching me now, hostile and inquisitive, and I decided against it. If anything serious was going on next door at Number 29, I'd better call the police, and leave it to them to break in.

I ran back upstairs, and hammered at the bedroom wall. "It's all right! Hold on! I'm calling the police!"

There was no reply. My God, I thought, he's killed her. He's killed her and I couldn't stop him. I picked up the telephone with shaking hands and dialed the local police station. It was almost a minute before they answered.

. . .

The patrol car parked on the curb outside with its red and blue lights flashing and now the whole neighborhood was awake. A thin gray-haired police officer with a Boy Scout hat was standing on the sidewalk waiting for me when I opened the door. "You the fellow who made the complaint about twenty-nine?"

"That's right. I heard a woman calling for help. Then a scream. She said something about a man coming to get her. I tried to break into the house but I couldn't."

The police officer tirelessly chewed gum and stared at me with interest. "You tried to break in but you couldn't?"

I nodded. "The door was locked, I couldn't budge it."

"The door was locked," he repeated. I was beginning to feel as if one of us was some kind of mental retard.

I inclined my head toward Number 29. "Don't you think you'd better try to get in there, to see what's happened? There's a woman in there and she could have been hurt."

The police officer fastidiously adjusted his hat. "Well, you come along with me, sir, and we'll see just exactly what's been going on."

I closed the front door behind me, and followed him along the sidewalk. Several neighbors had come out into the street and were standing staring at me, their arms folded in suspicion, their faces conspicuously unfriendly.

"You lived here long?" the police officer asked me, without turning around.

"I moved in this afternoon."

''Thought I hadn't seen your face before. I know most faces. Excepting those that want to hide them deliberate.''

To my surprise, he walked straight past the front door of Number 29 without even glancing at it. ''The screaming was coming from here,'' I told him, trying to catch up. ''It was coming from right next door.''

The police officer carried on walking to the corner of Number 29. He turned into the alleyway beside it, and then turned and beckoned me.

''What?'' I said, uncertainly.

''Come on here,'' he said. ''Take a look for yourself.''

I stepped after him into the alleyway, convinced that I was going to witness something terrible. Yet he seemed so calm.

''Look,'' he said, and pointed, and I took one last step forward and saw that behind the brick facade of Number 29 with its tightly locked door and its blanked-out windows there was nothing but a vacant lot, overgrown with grass and dead nettles and strewn with tires and broken bedsteads and other debris.

I raised my eyes slowly up the scabby outside wall of Number 31, and saw the patchy brickwork of my own bedroom wall, twenty feet above the ground. Nobody could have scratched or whispered or screamed at that wall, not unless they had a twenty-foot ladder. An extraordinary unbalancing shudder went through me, and I turned back and stared at the police officer in total perplexity.

He chewed his gum and smiled. ''I'd say you had a nightmare, wouldn't you?'' he asked me.

I stared back at the wall. It was beginning to drizzle more heavily now, and the drizzle made a soft prickling noise among the weeds.

''I don't know,'' I replied. ''It surely didn't *seem* like a nightmare. Not at the time.''

''Best get back to sleep,'' the police officer told me, and without another word he walked back to his patrol car, slammed the door, and drove off.

. . .

The next morning, at Irv's, Carl leaned across the counter and said, ''Heard about your little frack-ass last night.''

''News travels fast,'' I told him, with a mouthful of cheese Danish.

"Ain't much escapes my attention," said Carl. "Jim Kelly said you heard some woman screaming, something like that, in Number Twenty-nine."

"Who's Jim Kelly?"

"Plumber, lives opposite you."

I swallowed Danish and stirred my coffee. "Yes, well, I must have made some kind of mistake. The police officer who showed up said I was probably having a nightmare."

"That's what he always says."

"What do you mean, 'That's what he *always* says'? You mean it's happened before?"

Carl nodded. "All over town. Here, there, and everywhere. John Peebles heard it over on Sycamore; Mrs. Dunning heard it on East Main. In the end, the Chamber of Commerce asked some professor from the University of Chicago to come down and see what the hell was going on. Collective hysterics, that's what he called it, something like that. Community guilt."

"Guilt about what?" I asked him.

"Not what, *who*. Nesta Philips, the local grade-school teacher. She was leaving school one winter afternoon four years ago and that was the last time that anybody saw her. They never found hide nor hair of her, excepting one of the combs she wore in her hair, and that was all clogged up with dried blood. They never found Nesta, and they never found who killed her, and that's why the population of Archman is supposed to hear whispering and screaming just the way you did last night. Kind of makes your hair stand up on end, don't you think? I'm surprised that Dennis didn't tell you."

"Who's Dennis?"

"Dennis is the local deputy. The fellow who said you were probably having a nightmare. You know what they say about Dennis? You can always rely on Dennis to be just. Just plain stupid." Carl snickered at his own joke, and shook his head. "He's as even-handed as the day is long, and twice as dumb."

I swallowed coffee. "It's hard to believe that what I heard last night was just an hallucination. I mean—*I* couldn't be feeling guilty about Nesta Philips, could I? I never even heard of her, till now."

"There's stranger things under the sun than you or I ever dreamed about, fair Horatio," Carl misquoted.

"But she sounded so real. She sounded just like she was right next door."

Carl made a face. "You saw for yourself. There *is* no next door."

"She could almost have been—*inside* the wall."

"You mean, bricked up?" Carl asked me. "You mean she's climbed up a whole story, right inside a cavity wall, just to keep you awake at night? Even if it was possible, it still wouldn't make any sense."

"I don't know," I told him. "*None* of it makes sense, whichever way you look at it."

. . .

It was well past midnight before I heard it again. It had taken me nearly two hours to get myself to sleep, and just when I was beginning to slide into unconsciousness, I heard a *scritch, scritch* and I sat up in bed, startled, wide awake, clutching the covers as tightly as a child.

"Is that you?" I asked, in a choked-up voice.

There was a long silence. Two or three cars swished past on the wet streets outside. "Is that you?" I repeated.

Again, there was a soft scratching, claws on brick.

I hesitated for a while, and then I said, "Are you in any kind of danger?"

No reply.

"Are you trapped? Is that it? Are you trapped inside the wall?"

No reply.

"Listen," I said, more boldly now, "if I'm going to help you, I have to know where you are."

There was a very long silence. I was beginning to think that she wouldn't answer me, but then I heard that fearful, electrifying whisper. *"Help me. Please, help me."*

I leaned against the wall. "But where are you?" I begged her. "I can't do anything until you tell me where you are!"

"Help me, he's coming. Please help me. Please! You don't know what he's going to do to me! Please!"

"Listen to me!" I yelled at her. "I can't do anything! I don't know where you are!"

It was then that she started to sob and scream and beg me to help her, *beg* me. There was nothing else that I could do. I galloped downstairs to my station wagon, dragged out my toolbox, and took out a hammer and a maul and a tire iron. I made such a clanking noise with the tools that a light went on, across the street, and a voice cried out, "For the love of mike!"

Back upstairs in the bedroom, I dragged the bed clear of the wall, and immediately started hammering at the bare brick. As I did so, the woman's voice screamed and screamed, and babbled hysterically for help. I was almost hysterical myself. I kept hammering away, dislodging the mortar with the maul, and then levering the bricks out with the sharp end of the tire iron.

After the third brick had banged on to the floor, there was a loud knocking at my apartment door. "Hey! What the hell's going on! What the hell are you doing in there? Don't you know it's one o'clock in the morning!"

I ignored the shouting, and kept on knocking bricks out of the wall. The voice said, "I'm calling the landlord! I'm going to have you thrown out of here, you inconsiderate bum!"

I dislodged half a dozen more bricks, and they went tumbling across the floor. Now I could see right inside the cavity of the wall. I lifted my bedside lamp and held it up, so that it shone down into the wall where it sounded as if the woman's voice had been coming from.

"Can you see this light?" I shouted. "Can you see this light?"

Silence.

"Can you hear me? Can you see this light?"

Again, silence. I began to have the dreadful feeling that she might have climbed right up inside the wall cavity, all the way to the level of my bedroom—and that my first few blows with the hammer had dislodged her, and sent her dropping twenty feet down to ground level again. She could be wedged inside the wall somewhere, unconscious, or seriously hurt.

Yet the wall cavity was no more than five or six inches wide. Nobody could have crawled up inside it, even if they had been deranged enough to want to. It was too narrow and too dark, and they would have been lacerated by the rough mortar and the razor-sharp edges of the bricks.

I stood staring at the huge hole in my bedroom wall, and dropped my hammer on to the floor. As I did so, I heard the front door of my apartment open. My landlord, Mr. Katz, came in, wrapped in a green padded bathrobe, looking white-faced and furious.

He stared at the wall and spread his hands wide. "What's this? You stupid *momzer!* What have you done to my wall?"

I sat down on the bed. "I thought I heard something inside it."

He looked at me with his mouth wide open. "You thought you heard something *inside* it? Like what?"

"I don't know. It sounded as if somebody was trapped. Maybe it was all my imagination."

"An imagination like yours my brother-in-law should have! He runs a demolition company!"

"I'm sorry, Mr. Katz," I said. I suddenly felt weary and stupid and very alone. "I'm really sorry."

"I should throw you out, you know that?" said Mr. Katz, stepping forward in his mules and peering down into the drafty cavity. "I should throw you out right now, with all these—cardboard boxes after you."

But he turned back again, and said. "You're going to be teaching at the school, right? I know Mrs. Henry, the principal, she and I are good friends. So for her sake, I'll give you a last chance. You repair this damage, you make this wall good, and don't ever again break anything else in this apartment, not so much as a light switch, and we'll forget it ever happened."

He picked up one of the bricks from the floor. "Get new bricks, these are all broke. And get this rug cleaned, too. Then we'll forget it."

He stared at me for a long time without saying anything. Then he laid his hand on my shoulder and said, "You got divorced, maybe that's it. Sometimes a sadness stays in your head, and then comes out some other way, like breaking down walls maybe."

"Maybe," I said, without looking up.

• • •

On Saturday morning I went to the Archman Brickworks down by the river to pick up a dozen matching bricks to repair Mr. Katz's wall. It was a damp, foggy morning. The brick-kilns smoked steadily into the fog. Everywhere around there were huge stacks of recently fired bricks, flettons and marls and engineering bricks. I walked up to a young man who was sitting in a forklift truck reading a copy of *Guns & Ammo* and listening to tinny rock music on a Sony Walkman.

"Office?" I shouted, and he jerked his thumb toward a small shack with a corrugated-iron roof at the side of the main tunnel-kiln building.

In the office, a kerosene heater had raised the temperature until it was almost asphyxiating. A fat red-faced man was shouting at somebody on the telephone. Abruptly, he clamped the telephone down and turned to face me. "Well?" he demanded, "what can I do for *you*?"

"I'm looking for some bricks," I said, lamely.

He dragged out a handkerchief and noisily blew his nose. "I guess you came to the right place. How many do you want?"

"Eleven," I told him. I rested my brown-paper shopping sack on the table, and lifted out one of the bricks from my bedroom wall. "Eleven like this."

The red-faced man took the brick and hefted it in his hand. "This is a handmade job. First-quality facing brick. We don't make these any more."

He handed the brick back. "We may have some left in stock. Come around to the back."

Thankfully, I followed him out of the overheated office into the chill outside. He waddled ahead of me over the gritty, brick-red ground. We passed stack after stack of different-colored bricks, until at last we reached a row of stacks that were protected from the weather by a lean-to roof.

"Here we are," said the red-faced man. "No more'n five dozen left. We used to have a guy who made them special, all by hand, but after he was gone, there wasn't no point in training anybody else to make them. It's all mechanized now. Two tunnel kilns and a Hoffman kiln. You can drive your car down here and pick what you want."

He waddled off again, leaving me to select my eleven bricks. I lifted them up, one by one, making sure that none of them were chipped, and that they matched the pale rosy hue of the sample brick from my bedroom wall. I had almost finished when I thought I heard somebody whisper.

I said, "What?" involuntarily, and looked around. But the brickyard was deserted and foggy. Even the boy in the forklift had gone.

Then I heard it again, and it was unmistakable. *"Help me."*

It was her. It was the woman in the wall. The skin on the back of my hands prickled as if I had been electrocuted.

"Help me. Please, help me."

I stared down at the eleventh brick, resting in the palm of my hand. *"Help me, please, help me,"* she pleaded, and then I knew for sure. I lifted the brick up and held it close to my chest.

The bricks, damn it! She was in the bricks! Her body or her soul or some part of her last agonies alive were mixed into the bricks! That was why they had heard her whispering and pleading in different parts of town! Wherever a wall had been built or patched with any of these bricks, she was there—begging, crying to be saved.

I walked back to the brickyard office, shaken but determined. "How much for the whole stack?" I asked the red-faced man.

"Thought you only wanted eleven," he retorted.

"Well, I did. But they're such beautiful bricks."

"One hundred fifty dollars even. You'll have to carry 'em away yourself, though. My delivery truck's broke."

I counted out $150, and laid it on his desk. "Tell me," I said, as casually as I could manage. "The man who made these bricks . . . is he still alive?"

The red-faced man took out his handkerchief again. "Sure he's still alive. He didn't retire old or nothing. He was just sick of making bricks, that's what he said. His name's Jesse Franks, lives over on Sycamore, right down by the Exxon gas station. He runs his own body shop these days."

"Thanks," I told him. "I'll just drive down and load up the bricks."

"Get Martin to lend you a hand. About time that boy did some hard work."

. . .

I sat in my station wagon for most of Saturday afternoon, catercorner from Jesse Franks's house on Sycamore Street, waiting to catch a glimpse of Jesse Franks himself. I suppose I could have gone straight up and knocked on his front door and introduced myself. After all, he wouldn't have known me from Adam. But for what I had in mind, I preferred to remain unseen and incognito, just in case it all went wrong and I was making a horse's ass out of myself.

I was frightened, too, to tell the truth, because if I *wasn't* making a horse's ass out of myself, then Jesse Franks was not the kind of man I wanted to upset.

It rained, and then the rain cleared. At four o'clock, when the clouds were scurrying like windblown newspapers and it was just beginning to get dark, the front door of his gray weatherboarded house opened, and he stepped out on to the porch. He was wearing a navy reefer coat and a brown woollen hat. He must have been forty-five years old, solidly built. He looked up and down the street for a moment, and then he came down the steps and out of his gate and started to walk southward on Sycamore past the gas station.

He reached the bar on the corner and disappeared inside. I gave him five minutes, while the light steadily failed, and then I opened the door of my station wagon and climbed out. The suspension groaned. I still had the five dozen bricks stacked in the back: I had chosen to come here first, before unloading them and carrying them all the way up the stairs to my apartment.

I crossed the street keeping my head lowered and my coat collar lifted. I went straight into Jesse Franks's front yard, and down the steps that led to his basement. There was a smell of cat's wee and weeds down there. I rattled the door handle but the door was locked. I hesitated for a moment. I could give it all up now, and forget it. Nobody would know the difference. Only Nesta Philips, whose soul was somehow imprisoned in those bricks, and who could never be free.

But she had whispered, *"Help me,"* with such desperation, and I knew that I was the only person who could.

There was a broken triangle of concrete in the yard. I picked it up and, without hesitation, smashed one of the panes of glass in the basement door. I reached inside, and thank God there was the key. The door juddered as I opened it. Inside the basement it was gloomy and dusty and smelled of camphor.

I hurried upstairs, breathless and sweating. I kept imagining Jesse Franks finishing his beer and leaving the bar and walking back along the street. His house was bare and poorly furnished. A sagging sofa with a brown stretch-nylon cover, two secondhand wheel-back chairs. A television set, and a bureau with cracked veneer. No flowers, no ornaments, and only two pictures on the wall, both of wagon trains. In the kitchen, a faucet with a blue rubber anti-splash attachment dripped into a large stained sink. I listened, and the silence was almost more alarming than the sound of somebody coming.

Up in the front bedroom, under the double bed with the sawed-oak frame, I found what I was looking for.

My mouth was as dry as emery paper, and my pulse was skipping as I dragged out a cheap brown-fiber suitcase, locked. I forced open the locks with my screwdriver. Inside, a selection of knives—well-worn knives, with insulating tape around the handles—as well as a cheerfully colored profusion of porno magazines, and a large pungent red rubber apron. Underneath the apron, a woman's dress, beige, neatly folded; a woman's pantyhose, underslip, and bra. All of these items of clothing were jigsawed with dark rusty marks.

I had been to the offices of the *Archman Times* just after lunch, and read everything I could find about Nesta Philips. On the day that she had gone missing, she was wearing a "beige or light brown dress."

I closed the suitcase, and picked it up. I stood for a moment, listening; and then I hurried quickly and quietly downstairs. I tiptoed along the hall to the front door. The best thing to do was walk calmly and normally out of the house, and across the street to my car. But as I reached up toward the door handle, the key sharply turned in the lock on the other side.

Panicking, I tried to retreat down the hallway, but the edge of the suitcase caught on the small hall table, and knives and magazines and clothes went sprawling everywhere. The front door opened and there was Jesse Franks, staring at me in complete amazement.

"Who the—?" he began to ask, but then he saw the stained dress and the red rubber apron and the knives.

"What the hell do you think you're *doing*?" he demanded. His face was bunched-up muscle, with two glassy little pale blue eyes.

I didn't wait to get into conversation. I shouldered him sharply in the chest, twisted away from his grabbing hands, and jumped down the front steps of the house three at a time. I ran across the road and wrenched open the door of my station wagon.

Jesse Franks, however, was right behind him. He caught my arm and swung me away from the wagon. Then he punched me hard in the ribs; and then again, and I staggered back and stumbled over a low wall just behind me.

"You interfering bastard, I'll kill you!" he panted, and he came forward to hit me again.

If it hadn't been for dumb Dennis, I think he might have. But

Dennis had been called out to Sycamore Street by a curtain-twitching old lady across the street, who had seen me breaking in. Just at that moment he came around the corner with his lights flashing and his siren warbling, and Jesse Franks spun awkwardly around as if somebody had body-tackled him.

"You bastard!" he shouted at me, hoarsely. "You called the cops!"

I was too winded to do anything but ineffectually raise one hand.

Jesse clambered heavily into my station wagon, and started the engine.

"That's my wagon!" I protested. But all he did was to give me the finger, and snarl, "If I ever get caught, bastard, I'm going to finish you off for good!"

He swerved away from the side of the road. As he did so, however, a huge gasoline truck emerged from the Exxon station and completely blocked the street. Jesse slewed my station wagon around, and came speeding back toward me.

Dennis saw what he was doing, and turned his patrol car sideways-on to block Jesse's escape.

I can remember what happened next as vividly as if it were a video recording, which I can run and re-run and never forget. Jesse drove my station wagon on to the sidewalk, but it bounced and skidded out of control, and collided head-on with a hydrant.

I started running toward it, but then I stopped. I couldn't believe what I was seeing. Under normal circumstances, Jesse Franks would have easily survived a collision like that. But the crash sent a furious blizzard of bricks hurtling the length of the wagon, smashing and buffeting his head and spraying blood all the way up the windows. I saw him flailing his arms, trying to protect himself, but then a single brick struck the back of his neck and his head jerked sideways at a sickening angle. Some of the bricks burst right through the windshield and tumbled on to the sidewalk in a slush of glass.

Dennis came hurrying over, and tugged open the wagon door. Jesse lay slumped over the steering wheel, with dark blood dripping on to the leg of his pants.

"He's dead," said Dennis, and he was shocked.

"Yes," I said. My stomach knotted itself up, and I had to take a deep breath and look the other way. "He was trying to get away."

"Well, get away from *what*?" asked Dennis. "I was called out because somebody was supposed to be breaking into his house."

"That was me. I was looking for something. Proof that Jesse Franks might have killed Nesta Philips. Go take a look in his hallway. All the evidence is there. Knives, clothes. I guess he was keeping them as some sort of souvenir."

"Jesse Franks killed Nesta Philips?"

I nodded. "That's right, and dismembered her, and baked her in his brick-kiln, I shouldn't be surprised, and powdered up her ashes, and fired them into bricks. That way, nobody would ever find any trace of her."

Dennis stepped away from the wagon and sniffed. "How come *you* did?"

I bent forward and picked up one of the bricks. "They say that the human spirit is immortal, don't they? They say that you never really die."

. . .

They wouldn't grant me permission for a grave at Archman Cemetery, so one day I drove the bricks out to the woods around Hamson Lake, and buried them there, neatly, under four feet of soil. I stood over the grave for a while in the chilly late-afternoon sunshine, and said the Lord's Prayer, and thought about ashes to ashes and dust to dust.

I thought I might have heard a voice, whispering to me; but it was probably nothing more than the wind, blowing through the trees.

The next time Vicky brought Jimmy Junior around, she noticed a framed black-and-white photograph of a young woman on top of my bureau. She contained her inquisitiveness for as long as she could, but then she said, "Is it rude of me to ask who that is?"

"Oh, that's Nesta," I told her.

"Nesta? You never mentioned any Nesta."

"No, she's gone now," I replied. I picked up the photograph and smiled at it regretfully. "We were neighbors, that's all. Just very close neighbors. She lived—" and I pointed toward the wall.

LOOPY

Ruth Rendell

Ruth Rendell is justifiably one of the most-acclaimed mystery writers in the world. Her first novel *From Doon With Death* was published in 1964, and since then she has won one award after another: an Edgar from Mystery Writers of America for her short story "The Fallen Curtain"; Current Crime's silver cup for the best British crime novel of 1975 with *Shake Hands For Ever;* the Crime Writer's Association Gold Dagger for 1976's best crime novel *A Demon in My View;* and the Arts Council National Book Award in 1960 for *Lake of Darkness.* Ruth's stories have been filmed and televised and her books are published in fourteen languages. She has homes in London, and in the picturesque Suffolk village of Polstead.

At the end of the last performance, after the curtain calls, Red Riding Hood put me on a lead and with the rest of the company we went across to the pub. No one had taken make-up off or changed, there was no time for that before. The George closed. I remember prancing across the road and growling at someone on a bicycle. They loved me in the pub—well, some of them loved me. Quite a lot were embarrassed. The funny thing was that I should have been embarrassed myself if I had been one of them. I should have ignored *me* and drunk up my drink and left. Except that it is unlikely I would have been in a pub at all. Normally, I never went near such places. But inside the wolf skin it was very different, everything was different there.

I prowled about for a while, sometimes on all fours, though this is not easy for us who are accustomed to the upright stance, sometimes loping, with my forepaws held close up to my chest. I went up to tables where people were sitting and snuffled my snout at their packets of crisps. If they were smoking I growled and waved my paws in air-cleaning gestures. Lots of them were forthcoming, stroking me and making jokes or pretending terror at my red jaws and wicked little eyes. There was even one lady who took hold of my head and laid it in her lap.

Bounding up to the bar to collect my small dry sherry, I heard Bill Harkness (the First Woodcutter) say to Susan Hayes (Red Riding Hood's Mother):

"Old Colin's really come out of his shell tonight."

And Susan, bless her, said, "He's a real actor, isn't he?"

I was one of the few members of our company who was. I expect this is always true in amateur dramatics. There are one or two real actors, people who could have made their livings on the stage if it was not so overcrowded a profession, and the rest who just come for the fun of it and the social side. Did I ever consider the stage seriously? My father had been a civil servant, both my grandfathers in the ICS. As far back as I can remember it was taken for granted I should get my degree and go into the civil service. I never questioned it. If you have a mother like mine, one in a million, more a friend than a parent, you never feel the need to rebel. Besides, Mother gave me all the support I could have wished for in my acting. Acting as a hobby, that is. For instance, though the company made provision for hiring all the more complicated costumes for that year's Christmas pantomime, Mother made the wolf suit for me herself. It was ten times better than anything we could have hired. The head we had to buy but the body and the limbs she made from a long-haired grey fur fabric such as is manufactured for ladies' coats.

Moira used to say I enjoyed acting so much because it enabled me to lose myself and become, for a while, someone else. She said I disliked what I was and looked for ways to escape. A strange way to talk to the man you intend to marry! But before I approach the subject of Moira or, indeed, continue with this account, I should explain what its purpose is. The psychiatrist attached to this place or who visits it (I am not entirely clear which), one Dr. Vernon-Peak, has asked me to write down some of my feelings and impressions. That, I said, would only be possible in the context of a narrative. Very well, he said, he had no objection. What will become of it when finished I hardly know. Will it constitute a statement to be used in court? Or will it enter Dr. Vernon-Peak's files as another ''case history''? It is all the same to me. I can only tell the truth.

After The George closed, then, we took off our make-up and changed and went our several ways home. Mother was waiting up for me. This was not invariably her habit. If I told her I should be late and to go to bed at her usual time she always did so. But I, quite naturally, was not averse to a welcome when I got home, particularly after a triumph like that one. Besides, I had been looking forward to telling her what an amusing time I had had in the pub.

Our house is late Victorian, double-fronted, of grey limestone, by no means beautiful, but a comfortable well-built place. My grandfather bought it when he retired and came home from India in 1920. Mother was ten at the time, so she has spent most of her life in that house.

Grandfather was quite a famous shot and used to go big-game hunting before that kind of thing became, and rightly so, very much frowned upon. The result was that the place was full of ''trophies of the chase.'' While Grandfather was alive, and he lived to a great age, we had no choice but to put up with the antlers and tusks that sprouted everywhere out of the walls, the elephant's foot umbrella stand, and the snarling maws of *tigris* and *ursa*. We had to grin and bear it, as Mother, who has a fine turn of wit, used to put it. But when Grandfather was at last gathered to his ancestors, reverently and without the least disrespect to him, we took down all those heads and horns and packed them away in trunks. The fur rugs, however, we did not disturb. These days they are worth a fortune and I always felt that the tiger skins scattered across the hall parquet, the snow leopard draped across the back of the sofa and the bear into whose fur one could bury one's toes before the fire, gave to the place a luxurious look. I took off my shoes, I remember, and snuggled my toes in it that night.

Mother, of course, had been to see the show. She had come on the first night and seen me make my onslaught on Red Riding Hood, an attack so sudden and unexpected that the whole audience had jumped to its feet and gasped. (In our version we did not have the wolf actually devour Red Riding Hood. Unanimously, we agreed this would hardly have been the thing at Christmas.) Mother, however, wanted to see me wearing her creation once more, so I put it on and did some prancing and growling for her benefit. Again I noticed how curiously uninhibited I became once inside the wolf skin. For instance, I bounded up to the snow leopard and began snarling at it. I boxed at its great grey-white face and made playful bites at its ears. Down on all fours I went and pounced on the bear, fighting it, actually forcing its neck within the space of my jaws.

How Mother laughed! She said it was as good as anything in the panto and a good deal better than anything they put on television.

"Animal crackers in my soup," she said, wiping her eyes. "There used to be a song that went like that in my youth. How did it go on? Something about lions and tigers loop the loop."

"Well, *lupus* means a wolf in Latin," I said.

"And you're certainly loopy! When you put that suit on I shall have to say you're going all loopy again!"

When I put that suit on again. Did I intend to put it on again? I had not really thought about it. Yes, perhaps if I ever went to a fancy-dress party, a remote enough contingency. Yet what a shame it seemed to waste it, to pack it away like Grandfather's tusks and antlers, after all the labour Mother had put into it. That night I hung it up in my wardrobe and I remember how strange I felt when I took it off that second time, more naked than I usually felt without my clothes, almost as if I had taken off my skin.

Life kept to the "even tenor" of its way. I felt a little flat with no rehearsals to attend and no lines to learn. Christmas came. Traditionally, Mother and I were alone on the Day itself, we would not have had it any other way, but on Boxing Day Moira arrived and Mother invited a couple of neighbours of ours as well. At some stage, I seem to recall, Susan Hayes dropped in with her husband to wish us the "compliments of the season."

Moira and I had been engaged for three years. We would have got married some time before, there was no question of our not being able to afford to marry, but a difficulty had arisen over where we should live. I think I may say in all fairness that the difficulty was entirely of Moira's making. No mother could have been more welcoming to a future daughter-in-law than mine. She actually wanted us to live with her at Simla House, she said we must think of it as our home and of her simply as our housekeeper. But Moira wanted us to buy a place of our own, so we had reached a deadlock, an impasse.

It was unfortunate that on that Boxing Day, after the others had gone, Moira brought the subject up again. Her brother (an estate agent) had told her of a bungalow for sale halfway between Simla House and her parents' home and it was what he called "a real snip." Fortunately, *I* thought, Mother managed to turn the conversation by telling us about the bungalow she and her parents had lived in in India, with its great colonnaded veranda, its English flower garden and its peepul tree. But Moira interrupted her.

"This is *our* future we're talking about, not your past. I thought Colin and I were getting married."

Mother was quite alarmed. "Aren't you? Surely Colin hasn't broken things off?"

"I suppose you don't consider the possibility *I* might break things off?"

Poor Mother could not help smiling at that. She smiled to cover her hurt. Moira could upset her very easily. For some reason this made Moira angry.

"I'm too old and unattractive to have any choice in the matter, is that what you mean?"

"Moira," I said.

She took no notice. "You may not realize it," she said, "but marrying me will be the making of Colin. It's what he needs to make a man of him."

It must have slipped out before Mother quite knew what she was saying. She patted Moira's knee. "I can quite see it may be a tough assignment, dear."

There was no quarrel. Mother would never have allowed herself to be drawn into that. But Moira became very huffy and said she wanted to go home, so I had to get the car out and take her. All the way to her parents' house I had to listen to a catalogue of her wrongs at my hands and my mother's. By the time we parted I felt dispirited and nervous. I even wondered if I was doing the right thing, contemplating matrimony in the ''sere and yellow leaf'' of forty-two.

Mother had cleared the things away and gone to bed. I went into my bedroom and began undressing. Opening the wardrobe to hang up my tweed trousers, I caught sight of the wolf suit and on some impulse I put it on.

Once inside the wolf I felt calmer and, yes, happier. I sat down in an armchair but after a while I found it more comfortable to crouch, then lie stretched out, on the floor. Lying there, basking in the warmth from the gas fire on my belly and paws, I found myself remembering tales of man's affinity with wolves, Romulus and Remus suckled by a she-wolf, the ancient myth of the werewolf, abandoned children reared by wolves even in these modern times. All this seemed to deflect my mind from the discord between Moira and my mother and I was able to go to bed reasonably happily and to sleep well.

Perhaps, then, it will not seem so very strange and wonderful that the next time I felt depressed I put the suit on again. Mother was out, so I was able to have the freedom of the whole house, not just of my room. It was dusk at four but instead of putting the lights on, I prowled about the house in the twilight, sometimes catching sight of my lean grey form in the many large mirrors Mother is so fond of. Because there was so little light and our house is crammed with bulky furniture and knick-knacks, the reflection I saw looked not like a man disguised but like a real wolf that has somehow escaped and strayed into a cluttered Victorian room. Or a werewolf, that animal part of man's personality that detaches itself and wanders free while leaving behind the depleted human shape.

I crept up upon the teakwood carving of the antelope and devoured the little creature before it knew what had attacked it. I resumed my battle with the bear and we struggled in front of the fireplace, locked in a desperate hairy embrace. It was then that I heard Mother let herself in at the back door. Time had passed more quickly than I had thought. I had escaped and whisked my hind paws and tail round the bend in the stairs just before she came into the hall.

Dr. Vernon-Peak seems to want to know why I began this at the age of forty-two, or rather, why I had not done it before. I wish I knew. Of course there is the simple solution that I did not have a wolf skin before, but that is not the whole answer. Was it perhaps that until then I did not know what my needs were, though partially I had satisfied them by playing the parts I was given in dramatic productions? There is one other thing. I have told him that I recall, as a very young child, having a close relationship with some large animal, a dog perhaps or a pony, though a search conducted into family history by this same assiduous Vernon-Peak has yielded no evidence that we ever kept a pet. But more of this anon.

Be that as it may, once I had lived inside the wolf, I felt the need to do so more and more. Erect on my hind legs, drawn up to my full height, I do not think I flatter myself unduly when I say I made a fine handsome animal. And having written that, I realize that I have not yet described the wolf suit, taking for granted, I suppose, that those who see this document will also see it. Yet this may not be the case. They have refused to let *me* see it, which makes me wonder if it has been cleaned and made presentable again or if it is still—but, no, there is no point in going into unsavoury details.

I have said that the body and limbs of the suit were made of long-haired grey fur fabric. The stuff of it was coarse, hardly an attractive material for a coat, I should have thought, but very closely similar to a wolf's pelt. Mother made the paws after the fashion of fur gloves but with the padded and stiffened fingers of a pair of leather gloves for the claws. The head we bought from a jokes and games shop. It had tall prick ears, small yellow eyes and a wonderful, half-open mouth, red, voracious-looking and with a double row of white fangs. The opening for me to breathe through was just beneath the lower jaw where the head joined the powerful grey hairy throat.

As the spring came I would sometimes drive out into the countryside, park the car and slip into the skin. It was far from my ambition to be seen by anyone, though. I sought solitude. Whether I should have cared for a ''beastly'' companion, that is something else again. At that time I wanted merely to wander in the woods and copses or along a hedgerow in my wolf's persona. And this I did, choosing unfrequented places, avoiding anywhere that I might come in contact with the human race. I am trying, in writing this, to explain how I felt. Principally, I felt *not human*. And to be not human is to be without human responsibilities and human cares. Inside the wolf, I laid aside with my humanity my apprehensiveness about getting married, my apprehensiveness about *not* getting married, my fear of leaving Mother on her own, my justifiable resentment at not getting the leading part in our new production. All this got left behind with the depleted sleeping man I left behind to become a happy mindless wild creature.

Our wedding had once again been postponed. The purchase of the house Moira and I had finally agreed upon fell through at the last moment. I cannot say I was altogether sorry. It was near enough to my home, in the same street in fact as Simla House, but I had begun to wonder how I would feel passing our dear old house every day yet knowing it was not under that familiar roof I should lay my head.

Moira was very upset.

Yet, "I won't live in the same house as your mother even for three months," she said in answer to my suggestion. "That's a certain recipe for disaster."

"Mother and Daddy lived with Mother's parents for twenty years," I said.

"Yes, and look at the result." It was then that she made that remark about my enjoying playing parts because I disliked my real self.

There was nothing more to be said except that we must keep on house-hunting.

"We can still go to Malta, I suppose," Moira said. "We don't have to cancel that."

Perhaps, but it would be no honeymoon. Anticipating the delights of matrimony was something I had not done up till then and had no intention of doing. And I was on my guard when Moira—Mother was out at her bridge evening—insisted on going up to my bedroom with me, ostensibly to check on the shade of the suit I had bought to get married in. She said she wanted to buy me a tie. Once there, she reclined on my bed, cajoling me to come and sit beside her.

I suppose it was because I was feeling depressed that I put on the wolf skin. I took off my jacket, but nothing more of course in front of Moira, stepped into the wolf skin, fastened it up and adjusted the head. She watched me. She had seen me in it before when she came to the pantomime.

"Why have you put that on?"

I said nothing. What could I have said? The usual contentment filled me, though, and I found myself obeying her command, loping across to the bed where she was. It seemed to come naturally to fawn on her, to rub my great prick-eared head against her breast, to enclose her hands with my paws. All kinds of fantasies filled my wolfish mind and they were of an intense piercing sweetness. If we had been on our holiday then, I do not think moral resolutions would have held me back.

But unlike the lady in The George, Moira did not take hold of my head and lay it in her lap. She jumped up and shouted at me to stop this nonsense, stop it at once, she hated it. So I did as I was told, of course I did, and got sadly out of the skin and hung it back in the cupboard. I took Moira home. On our way we called in at her brother's and looked at fresh lists of houses.

It was on one of these that we eventually settled after another month or so of picking and choosing and stalling, and we fixed our wedding for the middle of December. During the summer the company had done *Blithe Spirit* (in which I had the meagre part of Dr. Bradman, Bill Harkness being Charles Condomine) and the pantomime this year was Cinderella with Susan Hayes in the name part and me as the Elder of the Ugly Sisters. I had calculated I should be back from my honeymoon just in time.

No doubt I would have been. No doubt I would have married and gone away on my honeymoon and come back to play my comic part had I not agreed to go shopping with Moira on her birthday. What happened that day changed everything.

It was a Thursday evening. The stores in the West End stay open late on Thursday. We left our offices at five, met by arrangement and together walked up Bond Street. The last thing I had in view was that we should begin bickering again, though we had seemed to do little else lately. It started with my mentioning our honeymoon. We were outside Asprey's, walking along arm in arm. Since our house would not be ready for us to move into till the middle of January, I suggested we should go back for just two weeks to Simla House. We should be going there for Christmas in any case.

"I thought we'd decided to go to an hotel," Moira said.

"Don't you think that's rather a waste of money?"

"I think," she said in a grim sort of tone, "I think it's money we daren't not spend," and she drew her arm away from mine.

I asked her what on earth she meant.

"Once get you back there with Mummy and you'll never move."

I treated that with the contempt it deserved and said nothing. We walked along in silence. Then Moira began talking in a low monotone, using expressions from paperback psychology which I am glad to say I have never heard from Dr. Vernon-Peak. We crossed the street and entered Selfridge's. Moira was still going on about Oedipus complexes and that nonsense about making a man of me.

"Keep your voice down," I said. "Everyone can hear you."

She shouted at me to shut up, she would say what she pleased. Well, she had repeatedly told me to be a man and to assert myself, so I did just that. I went up to one of the counters, wrote her a cheque for, I must admit, a good deal more than I had originally meant to give her, put it into her hands and walked off, leaving her there.

For a while I felt not displeased with myself but on the way home in the train depression set in. I should have liked to tell Mother about it but Mother would be out, playing bridge. So I had recourse to my other source of comfort, my wolf skin. The phone rang several times while I was gambolling about the rooms but I did not answer it. I knew it was Moira. I was on the floor with Grandfather's stuffed eagle in my paws and my teeth in its neck when Mother walked in.

Bridge had ended early. One of the ladies had been taken ill and rushed to hospital. I had been too intent on my task to see the light come on or hear the door. She stood there in her old fur coat, looking at me. I let the eagle fall, I bowed my head, I wanted to die I was so ashamed and embarrassed. How little I really knew my mother! My dear faithful companion, my only friend! Might I not say, my other self?

She smiled. I could hardly believe it but she was smiling. It was that wonderful, conspiratorial, rather naughty smile of hers. "Hallo," she said. "Are you going all loopy?"

In a moment she was down on her knees beside me, the fur coat enveloping her, and together we worried at the eagle, engaged in battle with the bear, attacked the antelope. Together we bounded into the hall to pounce upon the sleeping tigers. Mother kept laughing (and growling too) saying, what a relief, what a relief! I think we embraced. Next day when I got home she was waiting for me, transformed and ready. She had made herself an animal suit, she must have worked on it all day, out of the snow leopard skin and a length of white fur fabric. I could see her eyes dancing through the gap in its throat.

"You don't know how I've longed to be an animal again," she said. "I used to be animals when you were a baby, I was a dog for a long time and then I was a bear, but your father found out and he didn't like it. I had to stop."

So that was what I dimly remembered. I said she looked like the Queen of the Beasts.

"Do I, Loopy?" she said.

We had a wonderful weekend, Mother and I. Wolf and leopard, we breakfasted together that morning. Then we played. We played all over the house, sometimes fighting, sometimes dancing, hunting of course, carrying off our prey to the lairs we made for ourselves among the furniture. We went out in the car, drove into the country and there in a wood got into our skins and for many happy hours roamed wild among the trees.

There seemed no reason, during those two days, to become human again at all, but on the Tuesday I had a rehearsal, on the Monday morning I had to go off to work. It was coming down to earth, back to what we call reality, with a nasty bang. Still, it had its amusing side too. A lady in the train trod on my toe and I had growled at her before I remembered and turned it into a cough.

All through that weekend neither of us had bothered to answer the phone. In the office I had no choice and it was there that Moira caught me. Marriage had come to seem remote, something grotesque, something that others did, not me. Animals do not marry. But that was not the sort of thing I could say to Moira. I promised to ring her, I said we must meet before the week was out.

I suppose she did tell me she would come over on the Thursday evening and show me what she had bought with the money I had given her. She knew Mother was always out on Thursdays. I suppose Moira did tell me and I failed to take it in. Nothing was important to me but being animals with Mother, Loopy and the Queen of the Beasts.

Each night as soon as I got home we made ourselves ready for our evening's games. How harmless it all was! How innocent! Like the gentle creatures in the dawn of the world before man came. Like the Garden of Eden after Adam and Eve had been sent away.

The lady who had been taken ill at the bridge evening had since died, so this week it was cancelled. But would Mother have gone anyway? Probably not. Our animal capers meant as much to her as they did to me, almost more perhaps, for she had denied herself so long. We were sitting at the dining table, eating our evening meal. Mother had cooked, I recall, a rack of lamb so that we might later gnaw the bones. We never ate it, of course, and I have since wondered what became of it. But we did begin on our soup. The bread was at my end of the table, with the bread board and the long sharp knife.

Moira, when she called and I was alone, was in the habit of letting herself in by the back door. We did not hear her, neither of us heard her, though I do remember Mother's noble head lifted a fraction before Moira came in, her fangs bared and her ears pricked. Moira opened the dining-room door and walked in. I can see her now, the complacent smile on her lips fading and the scream starting to come. She was wearing what must have been my present, a full-length white sheepskin coat.

And then? This is what Dr. Vernon-Peak will particularly wish to know but what I cannot clearly remember. I remember that as the door opened I was holding the bread knife in my paws. I think I remember letting out a low growl and poising myself to spring. But what came after?

The last things I can recall before they brought me here are the blood on my fur and the two wild predatory creatures crouched on the floor over the body of the lamb.

TIME HEALS

Gary A. Braunbeck

Gary A. Braunbeck lives in Newark, Ohio, and smokes far too much for his own good. His stories have been published in *Eldritch Tales, The Horror Show, Twisted,* and *Night Cry*. His movie column "The Eldritch Eye" has been running in *Eldritch Tales* for more than five years. Gary's friends tell him that he ought to get out more. If he stays indoors and continues to write stories like "Time Heals" then I really don't think he ought to listen to them.

VLADIMIR: Was I sleeping, while the others suffered? Am I sleeping now?

Samuel Beckett
Waiting for Godot

They'd just returned home from the hospital when Corbin's wife noticed the ugly bruise on his neck.

"Where in hell did you get that?" she said. "I didn't notice it earlier." Corbin crossed to the bedroom mirror and loosened his shirt collar, staring.

Long and wide, blues into reds into a sickening yellow-tan; it didn't look like a fresh bruise, more like one that was in its last discoloring stages before healing.

"I don't know . . . where—" It looked as if someone had slammed into the side of his neck with an iron or—

—or wait a minute—

—six years old, he was six years old the day Mom had gotten drunk before the Little League baseball game, that's right, and she forgot to iron his uniform, his only uniform, the uniform he was so proud of even though he was just the bat boy, even though he never got to play he was Getting Involved, and Daddy had said that he needed to Get Involved in things, and Corbin did, but Daddy left, anyway, and now Mom was drunk so he stood in the kitchen crying, holding his prized uniform, asking her why she didn't iron it, didn't she want him to look nice, wasn't she proud of him, he was sorry he didn't play but he did help the team, he was a good bat boy, but then she threw her glass and yelled and yanked the iron from the kitchen cabinet, then—

"It's the world's biggest hickey," he said, noticing the slight trembling of his hands. "You'd best learn to tone down those passionate bursts of yours at night, Anita."

"Don't joke," she said. "That thing looks horrible."

You should have seen it twenty-three years ago, he almost said, but didn't. She stood behind him, her face reflected in the mirror, and put her arms around his waist.

"You've hardly said ten words since we left."

He stared at the bruise.

"The doctor said he doesn't expect her to live out the night," said Corbin. Anita made a sympathetic *tsk*-ing sound and pressed her cheek into his back.

"I'm so sorry, hon, I really am. She's such a sweet lady."

". . . yeah . . ." He closed his eyes and allowed himself to become lost in the warmth from his wife's body, her softness, her scents, her—

—the baby kicked.

Anita giggled, then sighed.

''Isn't that the most wonderful feeling?'' she said. Corbin turned toward his wife, placing both his hands on the roundness that was their unborn child.

''First time I felt it,'' he said. Anita's eyes filled with mild surprise.

''You're kidding?''

''That would accomplish all sorts of things, wouldn't it?'' He leaned in to kiss her, but the pain from the bruise caused his neck to cramp. He reached up and massaged the area with his left hand. He noticed the deep cuts—healing cuts—on the base of his palm.

They hadn't been there this morning.

He didn't say anything to his wife about it.

Mom hadn't meant to shove his hand through the window, he knew that.

''Penny for your thoughts,'' said Anita.

''That's about all they're worth at the moment,'' he said. ''I'm tired.''

He crossed over and sat on the bed, feeling his body relax. After a moment he stood, removed his shoes, then took off his pants—

—the gash on his right kneecap?—

—take the damn garbage out right now, Corbin . . I don't care if you can't find your shoes, I will not have that shit smelling up the house and, what? Can't you open the door by yourself, do I have to do everything for you, want me to give you a hand going down the steps?—

—a week. It'd taken that one a week before it stopped seeping.

He looked at Anita; she was staring at the gash, her face pulled tight, worried. Worry looked so ugly on her. Displaced. Disfiguring.

''Please don't ask,'' he said.

''If you like.''

''I like. Just come here and . . . sit with me, will you?'' Anita came and joined him on the bed, her arms enfolding him, warm, loving, I'll always be here for you . . .

He wondered why he couldn't summon up any memory of his mother's arms.

''Anita?''

". . . yes . . ."

"Listen to me . . . just listen, all right? Don't say anything, don't ask anything." He looked at her, she nodded her agreement.

"When she's born—"

"—*he's* born," she corrected.

"I love the way you follow instructions."

"It was never my strong point," she said, kissing his bruised neck.

"Whatever. When that kid is born, I want to tell you right now—and I hope this doesn't sound corny—that I will never, *never* raise a hand against it. I swear, Anita, I'll blow my brains out before I hit that kid." She tightened her embrace.

"So intense, he is," she whispered. "Don't say that, because as surely as you do we'll have ourselves a little mischievous brat who'll need a few good spankings." He turned to her.

"No. No one, no kid, ever *needs* a spanking. I just . . . hell, I don't know." He fell back on the bed, staring up at the ceiling. After a long pause, Anita joined him.

"Are you upset about your mother?"

"I love her, I do, hon, but . . ."

"But what?"

"I wish she'd hurry up and die."

There.

He'd said it, it was out, done, over with.

He heard Anita softly gasp.

"Corbin! What a terrible—"

"No, it's not," he said, looking at the small patch of burned flesh on his elbow. He'd messed up the soup that night, and Mom *did* like her soup to be just so . . .

"I wish I could blame her," he said. "But I can't, not really. Her old man used to pound the piss out of her when she was younger. She told me once about this leather strap he'd take to her whenever he got the notion, a strap as wide as the palm of my hand. She even showed me a scar on her shoulder he gave her. I guess he wasn't such a happy fellow."

"Sounds charming."

"Grandpa was a real sweetheart. He came to live with us for a while after my dad left. Mom took him right in, no questions, no fights, no nothing. He used to tell me that he knew Mom had forgiven him for being such a bad father. 'Time heals all wounds,' he said. 'Even them ones that nobody ever sees.'"

"Did she? Forgive him, I mean."

"She hated his guts, and hated herself for feeling that way. She took him in out of pity, that's all. He was dying and didn't have much money and had no place to go . . . God, it was so weird. You could . . . you could almost *see* the anger in the air whenever they were in the same room. I always tried to keep things happy. I tried to be a happy kid—"

—wipe that goddamn smile off your face, boy, or I'll do it for—

"—and keep things civil around the house. I loved them both."

Anita snuggled in closer to him, her fingers gently rubbing his chest.

"Then what's the matter? I know you had it pretty rough with her when you were a kid, but at least you forgave. Doesn't that count for something?"

"It should."

"At least you still love her." Corbin was scratching his leg, his fingers brushing against the garbage gash. He remembered all those nights of coming downstairs for a drink of water and finding his mother at the kitchen table, quietly drinking, quietly sitting, quietly allowing herself to die inside with every blink of her eyes. He tried to hate her, but never could. There was something in her that hurt so badly she had to get it out, had to express it, and that hurt was the only thing she could express or share, and—

—he blinked back something in his eyes—

—and that even *sounded* like bullshit. Maybe the temper flare-ups could be explained that way, but there were the other things: the not cooking his dinner, or breakfast, and screw lunch you little hog-jowls; the clothes that she never washed, acting like she didn't care if all the kids thought he was dirty and poor; the late nights on the weekends when he was sick and she sent him to his room, maybe buying him a few comic books or something to pass the time with, but never once getting him any medicine she couldn't buy at the grocery store, never calling up to ask how he was feeling, never coming in to kiss him on the forehead and tell him things would be all right.

Now she was sick and dying.

And he'd left her alone. All alone.

"I love her," he said, "but I wish I didn't." He rolled over and pressed his face into Anita's chest, trying to breathe away the uncertainty and anger.

So much anger.

He felt the baby kick again, but said nothing.

Christ, he thought, *am I starting to ignore the kid already?*

Maybe it was all supposed to be a game, like that grade-school game where you all took your seats before teacher came in and the guy at the back of the row slapped the neck of the person in front of him and said, "Pass it on," so that person slapped the one in front of them and so on up the row.

Corbin closed his eyes.

Pass—

—poor Grandma died giving birth to his mother, so Grandpa soothed his loneliness by beating the shit out of Mom because she'd killed his wife, maybe that had something to do with—

—it—

—didn't make sense, so Mom pounds on him because that's supposed to balance the scales, carry on the family tradition or something like that, a tradition that now had another generation coming—

—on.

So now the old wounds were coming back, huh? Like time-lapse photography: see the sun rise and set, see the flower bloom, see the scars resurfacing?

It ended now.

It ended with their child, the moment it was born.

Feeling a little better about things, Corbin soon fell asleep.

He awoke a few hours later and rose to take a shower. Anita was deep in slumber, so he moved carefully. She was due any day now, and she'd need her strength. He kissed her gently on the forehead before going into the bathroom.

He looked in the mirror and nearly screamed.

The bruise on his neck had spread out in every direction; it now reached up to the top of his cheekbone and down past his shoulder—

—he turned to see how far—

—the middle of his back. From the top of his cheekbone to the middle of his back. An obscene crescent that ached at the very touch of his fingers. His side felt weighted down. He looked hideous. The cuts on his palm had spread out, also, now halfway up the length of his arm. The garbage gash now ran all the way down his leg to the ankle.

He looked in the mirror.

An abomination stared back.

After a few more moments, it all became quite clear to him.

"One last time, huh, Mom? You gotta let me have it one last time."

God, please, make her die quickly!

He took his shower—which was almost impossible because of the pain—then put on his robe and lay back down.

He just prayed she died before there was more wound than him.

Anita woke him shortly after midnight, her face flushed and streaked with tears.

"My water broke!"

He was surprised how quickly and efficiently he moved; he grabbed the already-packed bag and loaded it into the car, came back up and carried Anita out, placed her in the car, called the hospital, locked the house, climbed in, and drove away. Once at the hospital they were met by the usual small army of nurses and an orderly with a wheelchair, out of the car Anita went, into the wheelchair, through the doors, into the elevator, doors closed—whoosh!—and awaaaaaaaaay we go.

Thirty minutes later Corbin sat in the waiting room, the ultimate cliché of the nervous first father; smoking cigarette after cigarette, pacing back and forth, looking up at every person in a white coat who breezed by. Anita had gone into labor almost at once, and the suddenness of everything worried him to no end, but the doctors here were pretty good and the one had said everything was looking normal, maybe happening a little fast, but normal, nonetheless, all the time asking Corbin about the horrible condition of his face, was it some recent accident, have you had it looked at yet, why don't you go down to emergency and have them check it out?

Eventually they left him alone.

After an hour and ten minutes he decided to go down to I.C.U. and check on his mother.

But first he went into the men's room.

The bruise had spread so much now it looked like a case of sunburn gone out of control; his face looked almost leathery.

He tried not to imagine what the rest of his body looked like.

The cuts on his arm were starting to seep slightly; a few paper towels tucked up the sleeves took care of that, though.

He looked once more in the mirror, decided he resembled a human being as much as he could, and took the elevator down two floors, to I.C.U. where his mother was waiting for him.

The nurses kept staring at him, giving each other cautious but concerned glances as he made his way past the beds filled with the diseased and dying to locate his mother at the end of the row.

For a moment he looked down to where the row of beds began, half-expecting to see the man at the end slap the woman next to him and then whisper his further instructions.

There were no movements, save that of the pumps next to each bed.

No passing it on here.

He looked down at the ruined shell that held his mother inside. Her breathing was strained and weak; there were so many tubes running out of her he almost couldn't tell what holes she'd been born with and which ones had been made over the last ten days.

He supposed it didn't really matter a damn.

God, how his body ached! So . . . damn . . . deep.

He leaned close to his mother's ear and whispered to her.

"Your grandchild is being born right now," he said. "You may not believe this, but I hope you live to see it."

Her eyelids fluttered a few times, then opened.

He could tell she wanted to smile, but couldn't.

She was staring at his face and its terrible discolorations.

"Little League, remember? That goddamned uniform I had to beg them for? Remember that Saturday, Mom?"

Her eyes grew wide and frightened.

He reached out and took her hand.

"I'm not mad, Mom, really I'm not. You know why? Because I don't think you realize you're doing it. I think it's all a question of just letting it . . . pass along. I think it might have been easier this way. Maybe you just made a wish sometime in the last few days that you could have done all the beating at once and just gotten it over with. You've got your wish now, Mom. This is what it would have done. Impressive, isn't it?"

Her eyes were filling with tears as she shook her head.

"Tell me that's what happened, Mom, please? Tell me you wished that you'd done it all at once and not prolonged things, please? Tell me!"

She gave a slow, frightened nod of her head, the tears sliding down her cheeks.

Corbin couldn't help but smile at the fear in her eyes, despite his better and more merciful instincts.

He squeezed her hand.

"You know what I think, Mom? I think after a while, after so many years and generations, it takes on a life of its own and none of us can control it." He was leaning very close now, whispering to her.

"I'm going to treat Anita and our baby better than Grandpa ever treated you, I promise, Mom. And I'll treat the kid better than you treated me. I know you'd want me to do that, wouldn't you?"

She tried to answer him, tried to open her mouth to form words, but the tube stuck down her throat caused her instead to sputter out a long and pathetic wheezing noise.

"It's better this way, just to get it all over with at once," he whispered to her.

She squeezed his hand.

The time was near and she needed to know.

"Yes, I love you, Mom, but I wish I didn't. I wish there was something I could've done for both of us when there was still a chance, but . . ."

Her eyes blinked, closed, stilled.

A buzzer went off.

As the nurses came scuttling out of their station Corbin made his way out into the hall, into the men's room.

Reaching up under his sleeve he removed the paper towels he'd stuffed earlier; they were gummy and drenched. His face looked even worse than before, like a mummy whose bandages had somehow become flesh but still were tightly wrapped. The cuts on his palm reached almost to his shoulder, as if struggling to join the crescent-bruise to use his body as the base for some hideous portrait. Staring at his eyes—the only place he could still recognize something of his old self in—he realized that he very much wanted to weep for his mother, but could not. Sometimes as a child he'd wept very late at night, but ever so quietly, wishing that his tears would reach out to her somehow, reach out and jostle her, tell her that it had to stop if either of them were to survive, and after a while—

—he blinked, remembering his words to her just a few moments—

—after a while it takes on a life of its own and none of us can control it.

He stared unblinking into his reflection.

So then where was responsibility? Who was to blame, were that the case? Could there *be* anyone to blame?

He felt his arms shaking.

. . . then if there could be no one to blame, why was the anger always present? Why did there have to be—

—fists. His hands were clenched into fists. He raised them toward his face, looked at them, and knew something, something that did make him weep, but just a little: an idea must have a catalyst in order to be made tangible, a principle must have an advocate in order to become known, and pain, cruelty, what-have-you, must have an inflictor in order to become real, because if it did take on a life of its own and found no way to make its way into a life, then it was simply left to its own devices, alone, stumbling around like a newborn child in the darkness, where it would remain stumbling forever.

He took a deep breath and unclenched his fists.

"I forgive you, Mom, for everything," he whispered low.

He started for the floor where his wife and child awaited him.

• • •

His mother had died at one twenty-nine A.M.

His daughter had been born at one-thirty.

And his wife had died at one thirty-one.

Corbin found himself to weep for Anita's death. He kept expecting the artificially sympathetic doctor to slap him upside the head and say, "Pass it on!" He sat alone for a very long time, but when he raised his head he saw that it was still night outside.

He stared at his hands for a very, very long time.

The emptiness was total and complete.

A little later he asked to see the baby. There was some quick and quiet discussion among the nurses on duty, one trying to get him to see a doctor about his condition, another making a call on the phone within the nursery, but, finally, they gave a nod and gestured for him to come to the viewing window.

The complications which had snatched away Anita's life were a blur to him now, like the lights, the hallway, the voice of the doctor who'd given him the news, everything seemed hazy, far away, not necessarily real, passing on, all except the smooth, cool window he was pressing his cheek against.

A nurse rolled one of the incubators over to the window, but he did not look down at that moment. He looked at his hands, the only part of him that seemed to be looking better, healthier, more capable.

An orderly rolled a covered cart up behind Corbin, then left it there while going into another room.

Corbin thought of the way his mother had looked so frightened and alone during those last few moments.

He wondered if Anita had seen their daughter before she died.

God, how he loved all of them.

But he could still feel his mother's whip hand.

. . . or was it hers after all?

He made a wish, a wish that came from a certain measure of knowledge given him over the last few hours—

—and looked down at his daughter.

The wide, ugly bruise on the side of her neck seemed to be growing darker, like the gash on her knee, the cuts on the palm of her hand—

—he nearly cried out, but as he took a step closer he saw that there was something odd about the cuts and the bruise, something soft, almost alluring, something—

He blinked his eyes. His heart skipped a beat.

They weren't cuts.

And it was no bruise.

They were birthmarks.

Dear God, he thought, the symbol of the family heritage.

He smiled as best he could at his daughter, then gestured for the nurse to place the baby back in its incubator.

He turned around and saw that the orderly had not yet come back for the cart. He stepped over, checked to see that no one was watching him, and pulled back the cover.

He selected a small scalpel from the rows of surgical instruments, slipped it into his pocket, and made his way out of the hospital, quickly into the night. The night. Filled with its shadows and stumbling children.

As he walked through the blackness he wept, a little harder than before, but not too loudly, for he knew there was a way out for both of them.

Time heals, he thought.

When it can.

And if it can't, then it's up to you. Because it's night.

And it's very dark.

And there are children stumbling through the shadows.

He slid the edge of the scalpel blade into a finger of his left hand and severed the tendon. Then another finger. Another. Another.

His left hand crippled now, he placed the scalpel handle between his teeth, bit down hard to steady it, and aimed for his right index finger, thinking how wonderful it would be to never again make a fist.

Corbin wished his daughter love, for she would receive all he had left to give.

As he sliced into his right hand, one thought kept echoing in his mind, a thought about time, about children, about heritage.

Heal me, he thought. *Heal me, heal me, heal me*. . . .

DAVID'S WORM

Brian Lumley

Brian takes delight in the Adam's-apple gulping-effect which his crop-haired military-policeman appearance has on those who meet him for the first time. But in fact he's a pussycat, and one of the most charming and creative horror authors working in Britain today. An unashamed enthusiast for the Cthulhu creations of H. P. Lovecraft, he taught himself to write (as well as a few natty card tricks) during the weary hours of night duty when he was a redcap in Berlin. Originally from Newcastle-upon-Tyne, he now lives with his wife and agent Dorothy in Brixham, in Devon. His latest novel *Vamphyri!* was recently published by Tor Books.

Professor Lees—chief radio-biologist at the Kendall nuclear research and power station—was showing his son some slides he had prepared weeks earlier from pond and sea water in irradiated test tubes. David was only seven, but already he could understand much of what his famous father said.

"Look," the professor explained as the boy peered eagerly into the microscope. "That's an *amoeba,* quite dead, killed off by radiation. Just like a little jelly-fish, isn't it? And this . . ." he swapped slides, ". . . is a tiny-wee plant called a *diatom*. It's dead too—they all are—that's what hard radiation does to living things . . ."

''What's this one?'' David asked, changing the slides himself.

''That's a young flatworm, David. It's a tiny fresh-water animal. Lives in pools and streams. Funny little thing. That one's a type with very strange abilities. D'you know, when one *planarian* (that's what they're called) eats another—" David looked up sharply at his father, who smiled at the boy's expression. ''Oh, no! They're not cannibals—at least I don't think so—but if a dead worm is chopped up and fed to another, why! The live worm 'inherits' the knowledge of the one it's eaten!''

''Knowledge?'' David looked puzzled. ''Are they clever, then?''

''Noooo—not strictly *clever,* but they can be taught simple things: like how a drop in temperature means it's feeding time; stuff like that, as I've said, when one of them is dead and chopped up, whatever he knew before he died is passed on to the planarian who eats him.''

''And they're not cannibals?'' David still looked puzzled.

''Why, no,'' the professor patiently explained. ''I don't suppose for one minute they'd eat each other if they *knew* what they were eating—we do chop them up first!'' He frowned. ''I'm not absolutely sure though . . . you could, I suppose, call them *unwilling* cannibals if you wished. Is it important?''

But David was not listening. Suddenly his attention seemed riveted on the tiny creature beneath the microscope.

''He moved—!''

''No he didn't, David—that's just your imagination. He *couldn't* move, he's dead.'' Nonetheless the scientist pulled his son gently to one side to have a look himself. It wasn't possible—no, of course not. He had been studying the specimens for three weeks, since the experiment, watching them all die off; and since then there had not been a sign of returning life in any of them. Certainly there could be none now. Even if the sustained blast of hard radiation had not killed them off proper (which of course it had), then colouring them and fixing them to the slides certainly must have. No, they were dead, all of them, merely tiny lumps of useless gelatin . . .

. . .

The next day was Saturday and David was not at school. He quit the house early saying he was going fishing at the pool. Shortly after he left, his father cleaned off his many slides, hardly missing the one with the tiny planarian worm—the one in David's pocket!

David *knew* he had seen the worm move under the microscope; a stiff, jerky movement, rather like the slug he had pinned to the garden with a twig through its middle one evening a few weeks earlier . . .

David's pool was his own. It lay in the grounds of the house, set far back from the road, in the copse that marked the boundary of his father's land. In fact it was a run-off from the river, filled nine months of the year by high waters flooding the creek running to it. There were fish, but David had never caught any of the big ones, not with his bent pin. He had seen them often enough in the reeds—even a great pike—but his catches were never any bigger than the occasional newt or minnow. That Saturday it was not even his intention to fish; that had only been an excuse to his mother to allow him to get down to the pool.

The truth was that David was a very humane boy really and the idea that the flatworm had been *alive* on that slide, no matter how, was abhorrent to him. His father had said the creature was a fresh-water dweller; well, if it *was* alive, David believed it should be given another chance. Immersion in water, its natural habitat, might just do the trick!

He put the slide down on a stone in a part of the pool not quite so shaded by the surrounding trees, so that the creature upon it might benefit from what was left of the late summer sun. There he could see it just beneath the surface of the water. He kept up a watch on the tiny speck on the slide for almost an hour before growing tired of the game. Then he went home to spend the rest of the day in the library—boning up on planarian worms . . .

. . .

In defiance of everything the books said, "Planny" (as David christened the creature the day after he saw it detach itself from the slide and swim almost aimlessly away) grew up very strangely indeed. Instead of adopting a worm-shape as it developed, with a lobey, spade-shaped head, it took on one more like an amoeba. It was simply a shapeless blob—or, at best, a roundish blob.

Now one might ask: "Just how did David manage, in such a large pool, to follow the comings and goings of such a small animal?" And the answer would be that Planny did not stay small for very long. Indeed no, for even on that morning when he got loose from the slide he trebled his size: that is, he *converted* many times his own weight in less wily, even smaller denizens of David's pool. In just a day or two he was as big as a Ping-Pong ball; and David had taken to getting up very early, before school, so that he could go down to the copse to check the creature's rate of growth.

Two weeks later there was not a single minnow left in the pool, nor a stickleback, and even the numbers of the youngest of the larger fish were on a rapid decline.

David never discovered just how Planny swam. He could see that there were no fins or anything, no legs, yet somehow the animal managed quite nimbly in the water without such extensions—and especially after dining on the first of the larger fish. It had been noticeable, certainly, how much the freakish flatworm ''learned'' from the minnows: how to hunt and hide in the reeds, how to sink slowly to the bottom if ever anything big came near, things like that. Not that Planny really *needed* to hide, but he was not aware of that yet; he only had the experience ("inherited'' of course) of the minnows and other fish he had eaten. Minnows, being small, have got to be careful . . . so David's worm was careful too! Nor did he get much from the bigger fish; though they did help his self-assurance somewhat and his speed in the water; for naturally, they had the bustling attitude of most aquatic adults.

Then, when Planny was quite a bit bigger, something truly memorable happened!

He was all of five weeks reborn when he took the pike. David was lucky enough to see the whole bit. That old pike had been stalking Planny for a week, but the radiation-transformed worm had successfully managed to avoid him right until the best possible moment: that is, until their sizes were more or less equal . . . in mass if not in shape.

David was standing at the pool-side, admiring Planny as he gently undulated through the water, when the ugly fish came sliding out of the reed-patch; its wicked eyes fixed firmly on the vaguely globular, greyish-white thing in the water. David's worm had eyes too, two of them, and they were fixed equally firmly on the pike.

The boy gawked at the way it happened. The fish circled once, making a tight turn about his revolving ''prey,'' then flashed in to the attack at a speed which left David breathless. The boy knew all about this vicious species of fish, especially about the powerful jaws and great teeth; but the pike in question might never have had any teeth at all—might well have been a caviar sandwich—for all Planny worried! He simply *opened up,* seeming to split down the middle and around his circumference until David, still watching from the pool-side, thought he must tear himself in two. But he did not. David saw a flash of rapidly sawing rows of rasp-like teeth marching in columns along Planny's insides—and then the creature's two almost-halves ground shut on the amazed pike.

Planny seemed to go mad then, almost lifting himself (or being lifted) out of the water as the fish inside him thrashed about. But not for long. In a few seconds his now somewhat *elongated* shape became very still, then wobbled tiredly out of sight into deeper water to sleep it off . . .

. . .

For a full four days after this awesome display David's worm was absent from its rebirth-place. There had been some rain and the creek was again swollen; which was as well for the oddly mutated flatworm, for there were no fish left in the pool. In fact, there was not much of *anything* left in the pool—at least, not until the afternoon of the pike's vanquishment, when heavy rain brought the river waters to restock the Planny-depleted place. For that ugly, sadly vulnerable fish had been the pool's last natural inhabitant, and until the rain came it would have been perfectly true to say of David's pool that it was the most sterile stretch of open water in the whole world!

Now it is probably just as well that the majority of tales told by fishermen are usually recognized for what they usually are, for certainly a few strange stories wafted up from the riverside during that four-day period, and not *all* of them from rod-and-liners. Who can say what the result might have been had anyone really tried to check those stories out?

For Planny was coming along nicely, thank you, and in no time at all he had accumulated all the nastiness of quite a large number of easily devoured pike of all sizes. He had developed a taste for them. Also, he had picked up something of the unreasonable antagonism of a particularly unfriendly, yappy little dog whose master called for him in vain from the river bank until late into the fourth night.

On the fifth morning, having almost given up hope of ever seeing the curious creature again, David went down to the pool as usual. Planny was back, and much bigger! Not only had he put on a lot of weight but his capacity for learning had picked up too. The little dog had gone down (or rather *in*!) almost without a burp, and Planny's very efficient digestive system had proved only slightly superior to his ''natural'' talent for, well, *picking* brains . . .

But while the animal's hidden abilities were not so obvious, his growth assuredly was!

David gaped at the creature's size—almost two feet in diameter now—as it came sliding out of the reed-patch with the top three inches of its spongy, greyish-white bulk sticking up out of the water. The eyes were just below the surface, peering out liquidly at the boy on the bank. It is not difficult to guess what was going on in Planny's composite knowledge-cells . . . or brain . . . or ganglia . . . or whatever! The way he had been hiding in the reeds and the way he carefully came out of them undoubtedly highlighted a left-over characteristic from his earlier, minnow period; the gleam in his peculiar eyes (of which David was innocently unaware) was suspiciously like that glassiness, intense and snide, seen in the eyes of doggies as they creep up on the backsides of postmen; and there was also something of a very real and greedy *intent* in there somewhere. Need we mention the pike?

Up into the shallows Planny came, flattening a little as his body edged up out of the water, losing something of its buoyancy; and David—innocent David—mistakenly saw the creature's approach as nothing if not natural. After all, had he not saved the poor thing's life?—and might he not therefore expect Planny to display friendship and even loyalty and gratitude? Instinctively he reached out his hand . . .

Now dogs are usually loyal only to their rightful masters—and minnows are rarely loyal at all, except perhaps to other minnows. But pike? Why the pike is a notoriously unfriendly fish, showing never a trace of gratitude or loyalty to anyone . . .

• • •

Approximately one hundred and thirty yards away and half an hour later, Professor Lees and his wife rose up from their bed and proceeded to the kitchen where they always had breakfast. A rather pungent, stale-water smell had seemingly invaded the house; so that the scientist's wife, preceding her husband, sniffed suspiciously at the air, dabbing at her nose with the hem of her dressing gown as she opened the kitchen door and went in.

Her throbbing scream of horror and disbelief brought her husband in at the run through the open kitchen door a few seconds later. There was his wife, crouched defensively in a corner, fending off a hideously wobbly *something* with her bleeding, oddly dissolved and pulpy hands.

David's father did not stop to ponder what or why, fortunately he was a man of action. Having seen at a glance the destructive properties of Planny's weird acid make-up, he jumped forward, snatching the patterned cloth from the table as he went. Flinging the table-cloth over the bobbing, roughly globular thing on the floor, he hoisted it bodily into the air. Fortunately for the professor, Planny had lost much of his bulk in moisture-seepage during his journey from the pool, but even so the creature was heavy. Three quick steps took the scientist to the kitchen's great, old-fashioned all-night fire. Already feeling the acid's sting through the thin linen, he kicked open the heavy iron fire-door and bundled his wobbly, madly pulsating armful—table-cloth and all—straight in atop the glowing coals, slamming the door shut on it. Behind him his wife screamed out something ridiculous and fainted, and almost immediately—even though he had put his slippered foot against it—the door burst open and an awfully wounded Planny leapt forth in a hissing cloud of poisonous steam. Slimy and dripping, shrunken and mephitic, the creature wobbled drunkenly, dementedly about the floor; only to be bundled up again in the space of a few seconds, this time in the scientist's sacrificed dressing gown, and hurled once more to the fire. And this time, so as to be absolutely sure, David's father put his hands to the hot iron door, holding it firmly shut. He threw all his weight into the job, staying his ground until his fingers and palms, already blistered through contact with Planny's singular juices, blackened and cracked. Only then, and when the pressures from within ceased, did he snatch his steaming, monstrously damaged hands away . . .

It was only in some kind of blurred daze that Professor Lees managed to set the wheels of action in motion from that time onwards. Once the immediate panic had subsided a sort of shocked lethargy crept over him; but in spite of this he cleaned up his unconscious wife's bubbly hands as best he could, and his own—though that proved so painful he almost fainted himself—and then, somehow, he phoned for the doctor and the police.

Then, after a further minute or so, still dazed but remembering something of the strange things his wife had screamed before she fainted, David's father went upstairs to look for his son. When he found the boy's room empty he became once more galvanised into frantic activity. He began rushing about the house calling David's name before remembering his son's odd habit of the last month or so—how he would get up early in the morning and go off down to the pool before school.

As he left the house a police car was just pulling up on the drive outside. He shouted out to the two constables, telling them they would find his wife in the house . . . would they look after her? Then, despite the fact that they called out after him for an explanation, he hurried off towards the copse.

At first the policemen were appalled by the loathsome stench issuing undiluted from the house; then, fighting back their nausea, they went in and began doing what they could to improve Mrs. Lees' lot. The doctor arrived only a moment later. He could see instantly what was wrong—there had been some sort of accident with acid. Relieved at the arrival of this sure-handed professional, the bewildered policemen followed the scientist's tracks to the pool.

There they found him sitting at the pool-side with his head in his tattily bandaged hands. He had seen the slide on the stone in the pool; and, in a dazed sort of fashion, he had noted the peculiar, flattened *track* in the grass between the house and the copse. And then, being clever, totalling up these fragile facts, he had finally arrived at the impossible solution . . .

It all hinged, of course, on those mad things his wife had screamed before fainting. Now, thinking back on those things, David's father could see the connections. He *remembered* now that there had been a slide missing from his set. He recalled the way in which David had declared the flatworm—the *planarian* worm—on a certain slide to be alive.

Quite suddenly he took one hand from his face and shoved it into his mouth right up to the bandaged knuckles. Just for a moment his eyes opened up very wide; and then he let both his hands fall and turned his face up to the patient policemen.

"God . . . God . . . *God-oh-God!*" he said then. "My wife! She said . . . she said . . ."

"Yes, sir—" one of the officers prompted him, "what did she say?"

Aimlessly the professor got to his feet. "She said that—that it was sitting at the breakfast table—sitting there in David's chair—*and she said it called her Mummy!*"

THE PET DOOR

Chris B. Lacher

Chris is twenty-five years old, married to Bonnie, and is a native Southern Californian, but tanless. He divides his time between editing *New Blood,* the horror-fiction magazine, and writing short stories and television scripts. His first novel is entitled *Digest the Flesh,* which may have something to do with his pre-literary employment as an ambulance attendant, morgue attendant, and tuxedo salesman. He looks like a rock star and his goals are decidedly material, but he still holds open doors for people who don't say thank you. Probably time he opened up "The Pet Door" for them . . .

Like the moon, this corpse had the same face as the one found last night.

The body lay in the gutter. Danny crouched before it. He retrieved his penlight from his jacket pocket, lit it, and shined the tiny circle of light into the face of the corpse. He sighed, fatigued and confused. This was the same guy who'd died yesterday, except he had clothes on now—a blue felt jogging outfit—when, yesterday, he had not.

Danny sat down in the street, cross-legged, and rested his arms on his knees. He sighed again, and stared at the dead face. Who are you this time? he wondered. A chill clawed him.

"Detective?"

Danny turned around. An abdominous uniformed officer leaned over him. His head eclipsed half of the full moon shining over his shoulder; the other half seemed to sit on his head like a leprous ear. Danny didn't reply.

"This isn't the guy we found across the street last night, though they sure do look alike. Must be his evil twin," the cop snickered.

Danny stood up. He wiped exhaustion from his eyes and said, "I'm dead on my feet, Reggie. Run this down for me."

The fat cop sighed crossly. "You weren't here last night?"

"No. I'm covering for Brudecker."

"Oh." The cop's tone softened. "The first one we found dead on the lawn over there." He pointed to the house across the street. "The second we found in the gutter tonight. Only difference is this one has clothes on."

Danny smelled sewer water and wet felt. He looked at the corpse. "It looks like he had a heart attack, or something."

"Lady next door said he was joggin' by and then stopped. He went up to that house"—again, he pointed across the street—"then he started runnin' and screamin'. His head's banged up, but I think that's from fallin' in the gutter." The cop waited for the detective's reply. There was none. The cop shook his head, slightly disgusted with the detective's indolence. "The house is abandoned, but maybe you want to check it out. Maybe the guy stumbled onto a drug deal, or somethin'."

"Yeah," Danny said. He crossed the street and approached the house. He moved as slowly as if he'd just risen from bed.

A small, colorless A-frame, the house had been abandoned for some time. Both the front door and the garage door were missing, and the windows were windowless sockets. A slight, cold wind indigenous only to the dark interior of the house whistled before Danny.

He heard a clicking noise. He looked down at his feet.

There was a small door, also doorless—a pet door, maybe—next to the front one, a shrunken twin. Danny bent to his knees, shined the penlight he still held into the hole, but saw nothing. He stood and stepped into the house. He felt the cold breeze. Danny pointed the light at the ground, searching out the pet door.

There was no door.

Stepping outside, he bent to his knees and put his hand into the black square. He felt the cold breeze lift the hairs on his hand, but that was all he felt. He pushed his hand in further, then reached in as far as he could. Nothing but cold air.

And the clicking noise, closer this time.

He pulled back his arm as if bitten. He stood as quickly as his fatigue would allow and peered inside the house again. There was no small door in there. Suddenly, he was afraid. He looked across the street, searching for the uniformed cop he'd spoken to a few minutes earlier. Danny saw him kneeling by the corpse. *''Reggie!''* he screamed in panic. The cop didn't acknowledge. Calm yourself, just calm yourself, he thought. His heart beat as noisily as a thousand marching soldiers. Danny called the cop again, was heard this time, and motioned for him to come across the street. As he walked, something on the cop's belt tinkled like ice cubes in a glass. When he was close, Danny kneeled and told him, ''Shine your flashlight inside the house, down by the door, and see if you see my hand.'' The clicking sounds hadn't stopped, but Danny put his hand inside the pet door, albeit slowly, nonetheless. ''See it?''

''No,'' the cop grumbled from inside the house.

Heart still marching, Danny reached all the way into the hole. ''Now?''

''No. You must be underneath, or something.''

''I'm not underneath. Okay, thanks.'' Danny retrieved his arm and stood. He brushed dirt off his sleeve, waiting for the cop to leave before he did anything else. He was utterly perplexed. He looked over to the corpse in the gutter across the street. Did this frighten you? Is this why you ran? He switched his gaze to the pet door. Blinking, he reached into his pants pocket, pulled out a quarter, knelt, and flicked it into the pet door. Then he went inside the house and pointed the flashlight at the ground.

He was almost in awe of whatever it was he had discovered.

Danny retrieved his quarter off the ground and hurried across the street.

. . .

In the dream, he saw the dog sniffing the pet door, then the dog crawled inside; something else crawled inside with it. He heard mating sounds, death sounds, clicking sounds . . .

He knew. It creates before it kills, it feeds.

When Danny woke up, he found himself staring at the phone. It was ringing. The words that were spoken to him seeped into his brain like mud. Cold air danced about him.

Another naked body had been found near the abandoned house. Danny was instantly afraid.

He began to hyperventilate. He lay flat on his bed, covered his mouth and nose with cupped hands, and tried to breathe regularly. He coughed, and then was able to inhale. He thought himself childish for frightening so easily; but then he realized that he didn't feel child*ish,* but child-like. A superstitious fear enveloped him. Simply, he was afraid of what was happening, much the way a child is afraid of spirits after a midnight chant. He stood before his front door. He didn't know if he could go any further.

The phone rang again. He hurried into the kitchen and answered it.

"Dan? Danny?" The voice sounded surprised.

"Yes. Who is this?"

No answer. The receiver on the opposite end was dropped. Danny heard muffled voices; someone screamed obscenities.

. . .

The naked body, dead, had the same face as Danny.

His ears started to ring; he was suddenly aware of nothing but the dead body at his feet. The night disappeared, the flashing red and blue lights stamped atop the police cars, the uniformed officers, the plain clothes, all were gone; except the house and the clicking noises . . .

Danny blinked. The world materialized slowly. No, no, he heard the clicking noises, but they were not the same as the noises he'd heard while near the pet door.

Something flashed in his eyes.

The police photographer was standing near him, clicking photographs of the dead body with Danny's face. From the middle of the driveway, Danny glanced at the pet door.

Clicking noises, like a camera . . .

He couldn't imagine, or believe, that something inside that house had photographed him. He did believe, however, that the dead thing with his face was not real. How could it be? He heard the clicking noises inside the pet door, summoning him, watching him. He turned, faced the house. Calling me . . . has part of me already . . . He started to sob. Slowly, he backed away from the photographer, the policemen, and drew his gun. He fired twice at the house, then charged the pet door. He dropped to his knees and fired wildly, spraying the remainder of his bullets into the hole, shrieking madly . . .

And then fell over dead. All the bullets that he had fired into the pet hole had hit him; two had lodged in his forehead, new eyes, and the others had hit him in the neck and chest.

. . .

He awoke in darkness. He knew.

He was with the many others, stuffed into a tight, black square that had no front, no rear. Souls; only souls, here, he thought, wondering why he still *could* think.

He saw a face.

A familiar face. He heard a familiar voice, but he knew no names, so he could yell no warning. The clicking sounds erupted around him, *from* him, loud as bombs, and then he was *speeding* toward the face. He stopped when he was close enough and clicked repeatedly. He heard the face's voice say, "I don't know. I hear clicking sounds."

The face disappears.

Hungry, he begins to create . . .

BY THE SEA

Charles L. Grant

When I asked Charlie to contribute to *Scare Care,* he made me a reciprocal offer to contribute to his *Shadows* series of horror-story anthologies. I could write what he like, but he insisted on one thing: no gross-out gore, no splatter-punkery. Charlie is the master of the quiet, cold, conclusive shudder. Born in 1942, he lives in Newton, New Jersey, where he has built himself over the years a formidable reputation with short stories like "A Crowd of Shadows" and novelettes like "A Glow of Candles, a Unicorn's Eye," both of which won Nebula awards, and numerous anthologies and novels, such as *The Hour of the Oxrun Dead.* This latest story has all of the subtle qualities that make Charles L. Grant one of our greatest creators of waking nightmares . . .

The day had finally cooled by the time Anne sat down, and she let the breeze chill her, take the sweat from her cheeks, loosen her shirt from the damp along her spine. The sun walked the gabled rooftops behind her, turning the sea to blood, the pebbled beach to slate, and her shadow reached formless for the incoming tide. Her knees were drawn to her chest, her hands wrapped about her shins. She rocked back and forth. She hummed. She watched the water. She stretched her neck and looked at the sky, looked for the clouds and saw only darkening blue.

Her cheeks puffed with gulps of air, and she could feel a faint headache stirring behind her brow. When she swallowed, she tasted nothing; when she shifted, her thighs ordered her to remain still.

Stupid, she thought; he'll be back. He has to come.

She wiped a slow hand over her face, then glanced up and down the beach, squinting as twilight deepened to dusk, wondering if someone would come along and rescue her, just the way they did in the movies and on television—someone dressed in tweed, with leather patches at the elbow, someone with a knobby walking stick and a playful dog that barked at the dark hovering birds.

Someone who knew what was going on.

But there was no one.

The beach was empty.

Just as her bed had been empty when she awakened this morning, when she woke up every morning, though she'd hoped and had been hoping since arriving in England that somehow her luck would change, that her appearance would be the object of a miracle, that one of the men she'd clumsily contrived to meet in pubs and in museums and in Underground stations would look at her, widen his eyes, and realize that she, Anne Marie Curtis, was the woman of his dreams.

Hoping always.

Dreaming sometimes.

And sighing less in self-pity than resignation when she dressed and ate and walked alone.

There was, of course, always Sam Edwards.

Sweet, gently persistent, and not at all what she wanted when she'd first and finally decided that living alone wasn't the way she wanted to spend the rest of her life. She'd had the career, the odd affair, the casual nights; she'd had the sting and burn of one man who'd left her for a woman he said was the old-fashioned type; she'd had the years, the decades, of being her own woman. Now she wanted more.

And a cat for company never quite filled the nights when she was alone. And lonely.

Sam. Who that morning had nearly frightened her to death.

. . .

She had swung out of bed at nine, was dressed and down in the crowded hotel dining room by ten. Her day, just another day until the day she left for home, was unplanned. Deliberately so, because she'd had a feeling while washing that she'd spent too much time planning, not enough time having fun.

"Hey," a voice had said quietly, just behind her left shoulder.

She had looked, and smiled, and nodded toward the chair on the other side of the small table, the only chair open as the other tourists, loners, and families and unabashed lovers filled all the rest and filled the room with chatter. "You look godawful," she'd said without malice.

Sam, pale blue eyes looking toward the ceiling, sighed loudly and snapped out his napkin, placed it just so on his lap. "It's the night life, don't you know. Keeps me up until dawn, and then they expect me to be bright and cheery for the fat ones and the little buggers who stick gum under the seats." He grabbed a piece of toast, winced at its color, and buried it in jam. "Y'know," he said, chewing, "if God had meant me to be a tour guide, I would've been born with a mike in my chubby little hand."

She gave him the laugh he wanted and sipped at her tea. "So quit."

"Can't do that, pet. Too busy getting rich."

"As a guide?"

"Here, now," he said in mock indignation, puffing his scrawny chest to show off the royal-blue jacket with the deep red piping. "Here, now, let's not demean the profession, shall we? We're a noble lot, we are, make no mistake about it. Just think about all those poor old ladies from Nebraska, wandering about town on their own, unable to speak the language, cowering on every corner because the traffic's going the wrong way. Can't you just see the havoc? Can't you taste the fear?" He shuddered as he straightened his black tie. "I couldn't do that, not quit. I'd never sleep again."

Another piece of toast, and a grin for the harried waitress who was trying to serve the room on her own.

"So," he'd said, leaning back and puffing his cheeks. "So, what's on for you today then? The Tower? The Gallery? Or is it the museum, to see all those mummies?''

''None,'' she told him. ''I've done that, thanks, and my feet are ready to curl up and die.''

''Ah.'' A cigarette from a black packet, a wooden match, and he squinted when a speck of sulphur flew at his face. ''Then would it be too much to hope for, that you'll take the day with yours truly?''

It was the same question he'd been asking since she arrived, fifteen days before, and he'd helped her up the winding stairs to her room on the third floor. It wasn't, he'd told her with the tone of one who knows, the most elegant bed-and-breakfast in the city, but it at least had the saving grace of having him around on a more or less permanent basis for the summer. Then he told her about the coach tours, gave her a sample of his spiel and one or two of his horrid jokes, and launched into his campaign to get her to come along.

''Yes,'' she said.

''You will?'' His eyes widened.

''I mean, yes, it's too much to hope for.''

''Damn.''

''No offense.''

''Ah well, none taken,'' he said lightly, though his eyes were disappointed. ''At least you take the suggestions. I suppose that's something.''

And it was, and for those suggestions—what tourist traps to avoid, what walking tours were the best—she was grateful.

London was confusing. Not the streets, but the people, the way the people lived. It was a foreign country, but she spoke the language; she spoke the language, but hadn't yet lost the feeling she was floundering in a place where no one understood her. Not even the men she hoped were the men of her dreams.

Sam had saved her more than once; he wanted to save her again.

A glance at her watch: ''You're going to be late.''

He stood with a flourish, tucking his cap under his arm. ''So I shall. Onward, then, to those dear Nebraska ladies.'' He winked. ''Dinner?''

She hesitated. ''Okay. If I'm back.''

With a delighted laugh he blew her a kiss, kissed the startled waitress on the cheek, and was gone before she knew he'd even left the table. Ten minutes later she rose herself, lingered for a while in the foyer reading the theater notices and museum discounts pinned to a corkboard on the wall, and went outside, down the steps, and stood at the curb.

All right, she thought to the businessmen, the students; all right, you lucky devils, throw yourselves into my arms.

They passed her.

She sighed.

She took a deep breath and looked up at the sky.

There were clouds white and puffed, there was a sun that drifted behind them, and there was a huge red and black coach parked at the curb, motor running, windows tinted, and Sam standing proudly by the door.

''I've decided to take on American traits,'' he said as he walked toward her. ''Today, I'm pushy. What do you think, does it suit me?''

A surge of anger, a glance up and down the street, and it occurred to her that he was taking a great chance, bringing the coach to her door. Concern, then, as he took her hand lightly and led her to the steps.

''Up you go, dear,'' he said, pushing her gently at the small of her back. ''Have a seat, the tour for the privileged begins in one minute.''

Four steps up, and she turned to nervously look over her shoulder. He was standing there, grinning foolishly, and her anger drained abruptly. With nothing else to do, why not do nothing? Let him show her all she'd already seen; let him get it out of his system and get him off her back so she could get back to dreaming.

She smiled.

He leapt onto the bottom stair, made a show of checking the street for further customers, then squeezed past her into the driver's seat.

''Can't go until you sit, pet,'' he told her, mildly chiding.

A shrug then, and she turned, and felt her mouth open.

There was no one else on the coach.

High, red-backed seats, the hum of air-conditioning, the smooth pull of the huge vehicle as it pulled away from the curb, so smoothly she didn't feel it, didn't know it until she saw the buildings sliding by; but there was no one else here, and she turned quickly, ready to demand an explanation.

But Sam was concentrating on the road, turning the corner and plunging into the traffic on Southampton Row without causing a ripple, his cap set upside down on the dashboard, his head tilted forward as if finding it difficult to see.

"Sam," she said, bracing herself in the aisle.

"Regulations," he said flatly without turning around, "require that the customers be seated whilst the contracted vehicle is in motion." And he laughed. "Have a seat, Anne. Have a seat."

"Sam, really . . ."

He looked around, and the pale eyes weren't pale, not by half. "Sit," he told her gently. "Sit. Don't get hurt. You wouldn't want to get hurt."

The door was closed. The coach was moving faster, slightly swaying, engine rumbling. She took the aisle seat across from him, looked out the window, looked back, and was afraid.

"Sam."

"Is it true, what I've heard? That American women are more promiscuous than anyone else?"

She blinked her confusion. "What?"

He reached over to a series of dials and switches on the dashboard, picked up a silver microphone, turned it on, and coughed to be sure it was working.

"Kings Way," he announced.

Her throat dried, and there was cold in her stomach.

"The Strand."

Traffic blared around her, pedestrians in and out of shops.

She closed her eyes and ordered herself not to scream.

"Regent Street."

"What?" She looked out again, and the pedestrians were gone. The streets were gone. The city had backed away from the road and there were overhead signs to Heathrow and the West Country. "Sam?"

The public address system sparked static.

"Windsor Castle on the right."

The coach rocked. Sam hummed.

Anne scrambled from her seat and made her way down the aisle, thinking there had to be an exit at the back. For an emergency. A fire. An accident. A way for those back here not to wait for those in front.

"Salisbury Cathedral."

As she moved she bent over, trying to see through the windows, but their tint had darkened as if the sun had set, and she could barely see more than a blur of green, a smear of brown.

Rocking.

Static.

"Is it true, Anne, that American women are so frustrated by their men that they have to come all the way over here just to get laid?"

She dropped heavily into the nearest seat and clasped her hands in her lap. Rape. Oh Jesus, she was going to be raped. He had put something in her breakfast tea, she was drugged, and he had kidnapped her. All the refusals, no matter how kindly and gently made, had finally grown too much for him, and now . . .

A tear she wiped angrily away.

Static.

She watched him—rocking in time to the rhythm of the racing coach, a finger tapping on the dashboard, bouncing a little when the road roughened for a stretch. From the back he could have been anyone, any one of the men she had met and lost already, until he turned around and grinned at her from the end of the aisle's tunnel.

The mike was at his lips.

"Don't worry, love," the speakers said, "I know just what you want."

She wanted to scream, and didn't; she wanted to race up the aisle and punch him, hurt him, and didn't; she wanted to know how they could be passing all the places he announced when less than fifteen minutes ago she was standing on the pavement and wondering what to do next.

She looked at her watch; it had stopped just at dawn.

Drugged. The bastard. The sonofabitch bastard had drugged her, and here she was, sitting like a helpless hapless female instead of doing something, making something happen, not behaving exactly like the sort of woman she'd despised all her life.

She stood.

"Customers," the speakers said, "will please be seated. No smoking."

She kept her gaze on his head, bobbing, sometimes jerking, and pulled herself along by the backs of the seats.

"Wembley Stadium."

"No," she said.

Sam looked around. "No?"

"It can't be." She kept on moving.

He grinned. "Mistress Curtis, you're living in a dream."

"No," she said firmly, midway along. "Let me out."

The steering wheel jerked and he looked back to the road, and when she looked as well, she saw nothing but a glare. The windshield was white and she couldn't see the road.

"Let me out."

"A woman," said the speakers, "who knows her own mind is a woman who knows that her mind isn't her own."

"Jesus Christ, Edwards, let me out!"

The coach stopped so abruptly that she was thrown into a seat, cracking her elbow on an armrest, making her gasp at the brief fire that lanced through her arm. Then she pushed herself to her feet again, swayed, held her forehead, and swore that she was going to tear his throat out.

He was gone.

The driver's seat was empty, the doors were open, and Sam was gone.

. . .

And she had walked all along an empty road, into an empty village whose doors and windows were locked, no cars at the curbs, no bicycles in their stands.

A sea breeze. The call of gulls. The smell of brine and damp stone.

Drugged.

She hugged her knees more tightly and watched the tide reach for her feet.

Someone will come, she thought; someone will come and tell me what's going on.

And she saw him as the sun danced on the chimneys and slid into the alleys, walking along the shore, kicking pebbles, throwing stones into the sea. He was whistling, skipping once or twice, looking up at the gliding birds and waving to them, waving to her, slipping his hands into his pockets after tossing his cap away.

No, she thought, and couldn't stand; her legs were too stiff, her ankles too weak, and she scoured the area around her frantically for something she could use to hold him off, to keep him from her.

He stopped directly in front of her, at water's edge, back turned. "Do you know," he said, arm extended, finger pointing, "that out there, so far out there you can't see it from here, is the marvelous and entire continent of Europe? Can you believe it, Anne? All of Europe and her capitals only a stone's throw away." He shook his head and turned around. "Amazing. Absolutely amazing."

Pale blue eyes, and a smile that made her shiver.

"You drugged me," she said, voice rasping, eyes burning.

"Oh no," he said. "Oh no, I wouldn't do that."

She found a rock and couldn't hold it.

She stood to run, and sat again with a rush of air from her lungs.

She couldn't find the tears, and she couldn't find the rage, and she already knew the answer before the question fought the wind: "Who are you, Sam? Who are you?"

"Me?" he said proudly. "Why, darling, you know me. I'm the man of your dreams."

CHANGELING

Graham Masterton

A former newspaper reporter and editor of *Penthouse,* I was inspired to write my first horror novel, *The Manitou,* when my wife Wiescka was expecting our first son, Roland. It concerned a Red Indian medicine-man who was reborn in the present day to take revenge on the palefaces, and became the last movie made by the late Bill *(Grizzly)* Girdler. Since then, I have written over a dozen more, including *Charnel House,* which won a special Edgar scroll; *Tengu,* awarded a Silver Medal by *The West Coast Review of Books;* and *Picture of Evil,* given the Prix Julia Verlanger in Paris. I live in Epsom, Surrey, with my wife, three sons, and a white Cadillac Fleetwood. My latest horror novel is *Walkers,* soon to be published by Tor Books.

The elevator door opened and there she was, looking directly into his eyes as if she had known that he was standing on the other side. Tall, beautiful, dressed utterly in white. He hesitated for a moment and then stepped back one half-shuffle to allow her to pass.

"Pardon mivrouw," he acknowledged. She smiled briefly but didn't reply. She passed him in a pungent swirl of Calvin Klein's

Obsession, and he turned around and watched her walk across the marble lobby and out through the revolving door. Her long brunette hair was lifted for a moment by the April wind out on the hotel steps. Then the doorman came forward to salute her and she was gone.

"You're going up?" asked an irritated American who was waiting for him in the elevator, his finger pressed on the Doors Open button.

"I'm sorry? Oh, no. I've changed my mind."

He heard the man growl, "For Chrissakes, some people . . ." and then he found himself hurrying across the lobby and out through the door, just in time to see her climbing into the back of a taxi.

The doorman approached him and touched his cap. "Taxi, sir?"

"No, no thank you." He stood holding his briefcase, the skirts of his raincoat flapping, watching the woman's taxi turn into Sarphatistraat, feeling abandoned and grainy and weird, like a character in a black-and-white art movie. The doorman stood beside him, smiling uneasily.

"Do you happen to know that lady's name?" he asked. His voice sounded blurry in the wind. The doorman shook his head.

"Is she a guest here?"

"I'm sorry, sir. It is not permissible for me to say."

Gil reached into his inside pocket and for one moment considered bribery; but there was something in the doorman's smile that warned him against it. He said, "Oh, okay, sure," and retreated awkwardly back through the revolving door. The two elderly hall porters beamed and nodded at him as he returned to the elevator. Stan and Ollie, one thin and one fat. They were obviously quite accustomed to irrational behavior.

Gil stood in the oak-paneled elevator as it took him up to the third floor and scrutinized himself in the brass-framed mirror with as much intensity as if he were a business partner whom he suspected of cracking up. He had never done anything in years as spontaneous as chasing after that woman. What the hell had come over him? He was married, with two children, he was right on top of his job. He had a six-bedroom house in Woking, a new Granada Scorpio, and he had been profiled in *Business Week* as one of the new breed of "totally committed" young entrepreneurs.

And yet he had hurried after that unknown woman as gauche and panicky as an adolescent autograph-hunter.

He closed the door of his suite behind him and stood for a long time in the middle of the room with his briefcase still in his hand, thinking. Then he set the briefcase down and slowly took off his coat. *''Pity about Gil, he's thrown a wobbly.''* He could almost hear them talking about him in the office. *''He was absolutely fine until that Amsterdam business. Probably suffering from overwork.''*

He went to the window and opened it. The hotel room overlooked the Amstel River, wide and gray, where it was crossed by the wide elevating bridge called the Hogesluis. Trams rumbled noisily over the sluis, their bells ringing, on their way to the suburbs. The wind blew so coldly through the window that the net curtains were lifted, shuddering, and Gil found that there were tears in his eyes.

He checked his pulse. It was slightly too fast, but nothing to take to the doctor. He didn't feel feverish, either. He had been working for four days, Tuesday to Friday, sixteen to eighteen hours a day, but he had been careful not to drink too much and to rest whenever he could. Of course, it was impossible to judge what effect this round of negotiations might have had on his brain. But he *felt* normal.

But he thought of her face and he thought of her hair and he thought of the way in which she had smiled at him; a smile that had dissolved as quickly as soluble aspirin; and then was gone. And against all the psychological and anthropological logic in the world, he knew that he had fallen in love with her. Well, maybe not in *love,* maybe not actually in *love,* not the way he loved Margaret. But she had looked into his eyes and smiled at him and wafted past in beguiling currents of Obsession, and in ten seconds he had experienced more excitement, more curiosity, more plain straightforward *desire* than he had in the last ten years of marriage.

It's ridiculous, he said to himself. It's just a moment of weakness. I'm tired, I'm suffering from stress. I'm lonely, too. Nobody ever understands how lonely it can be, traveling abroad on business. No wonder so many businessmen stay in their hotel rooms, drinking too much whiskey and watching television programmes they can't understand. There is no experience so friendless as walking the streets of a strange city, with nobody to talk to.

He closed the window and went to the mini-bar to find himself a beer. He switched on the television and watched the news in Dutch. Tomorrow morning, after he had collected the signed papers from the

Gemeentevervoerbedrijf, he would take a taxi straight to Schiphol and fly back to London. Against ferocious competition from Volvo and M.A.N. Diesel, he had won an order for twenty-eight new buses for Amsterdam's municipal transport system, all to be built in Oxford.

On the phone, Brian Taylor had called him "a bloody marvel." Margaret had squealed in delight, like she always did.

But the way the wind had lifted up that woman's hair kept running and re-running in his mind like a tiny scrap of film that had been looped to play over and over. The revolving door had turned, her hair had lifted. Shining and dark, the kind of hair that should be spread out over silk pillows.

It began to grow dark and the lights began to dip and sparkle in the river and the trams began to grind their way out to Oosterpark and the farther suburbs. Gil consulted the room-service menu to see what he could have for supper, but after he had called up to order the smoked eel and the veal schnitzel, with a half-bottle of white wine, he was taken with a sudden surge of panic about eating alone, and he called back and canceled his order.

"You don't *want* the dinner, sir?" The voice was flat, Dutch-accented, polite but curiously hostile.

"No thank you. I've . . . changed my mind."

He went to the bathroom and washed his face and hands. Then he straightened his necktie, shrugged on his coat, picked up his key, and went down to the hotel's riverside bar for a drink. The bar was crowded with Japanese and American businessmen. Only two women, and both of them were quite obviously senior executives, one lopsidedly beautiful, the other as hard-faced as a man. He sat up on a barstool and ordered a whiskey-and-soda.

"Cold wind today, hmh?" the barman asked him.

He drank his whiskey too quickly, and he was about to order another one when the woman came and sat just one stool away from him, still dressed in white, still fragrant with Obsession. She smiled to the barman and asked for a Bacardi, in English.

Gil felt as if he were unable to breathe. He had never experienced anything like it. It was a kind of panic, like claustrophobia, and yet it had an extraordinary quality of erotic compulsion, too. He could understand why people half-strangled themselves to intensify their sexual arousal. He stared at himself glassy-eyed in the mirror behind the Genever gin bottles, trying to detect any signs of emotional breakdown. But did it show, when you finally cracked? Did your face fall apart like a broken jug? Or was it all kept tightly inside of you? Did it snap in the back of your brain where nobody could see?

He glanced covertly sideways, first at the woman's thigh, then more boldly at her face. She was looking straight ahead, at the mirror. Her nose was classically straight, her eyes were cobalt-blue, slightly slanted, very European. Her lips were glossed with crimson. He noticed a bracelet of yellow-and-white gold, intertwined, that must have cost the equivalent of three months of his salary, including expenses, and a gold Ebel wristwatch. Her nails were long and crimson and perfect. She moved slightly sideways on her stool and he noticed the narrowness of her waist, and the full sway of her breasts. She's naked underneath that dress, he thought to himself, or practically naked. She's just too incredibly sexy to be true.

What could he say to her? Should he say anything? *Could* he say anything? He thought dutifully for a moment about Margaret, but he knew that he was only being dutiful. This woman existed on a different planet from Margaret, she was one of a different species. She was feminine, sexual, undomesticated, elegant, and probably dangerous, too.

The barman approached him. "Can I fix you another drink, sir?"

"I—unh—"

"Oh, go ahead," the woman smiled. "I can't bear to drink alone."

Gil flushed, and grinned, and shrugged, and said, "All right, then. Yes." He turned to the woman and asked, "How about you?"

"Thank you," she acknowledged, passing her glass to the barman, although there was a curious intonation in her voice which made it sound as if she were saying thank you for something else altogether.

The barman set up the drinks. They raised their glasses to each other and said, *"Prost!"*

"Are you staying here?" Gil asked the woman. He wished his words didn't sound so tight and high-pitched.

"In Amsterdam?"

"I mean here, at the Amstel Hotel."

''No, no,'' she said. ''I live by the sea, in Zandvoort. I only came here to meet a friend of mine.''

''You speak perfect English,'' he told her.

''Yes,'' she replied. Gil waited, expecting her to tell him what she did for a living, but she remained silent.

''I'm in transportation,'' he volunteered. ''Well, buses, actually.''

She focused her eyes on him narrowly but still she said nothing. Gil said, ''I go back to London tomorrow. Job's over.''

''Why did you come running after me?'' she asked. ''You know when—this afternoon, when I was leaving the hotel. You came running after me and you stood outside the hotel and watched me go.''

Gil opened and closed his mouth. Then he lifted both hands helplessly, and said, ''I don't know. I really don't know. It was—I don't know. I just did it.''

She kept her eyes focused on him as sharply as a camera. ''You desire me,'' she said.

Gil didn't reply, but uncomfortably sat back on his barstool.

Without hesitation, the woman leaned forward and laid her open hand on his thigh. She was very close now. Her lips were parted and he could see the tips of her front teeth. He could smell the Bacardi on her breath. Warm, soft, even breath.

''You desire me,'' she repeated.

She gave him one quick, hard squeeze, and then sat back. Her face was filled with silent triumph. Gil looked at her with a mixture of excitement and embarrassment and disbelief. She had actually reached over and touched him—not touched him, *caressed* him—this beautiful woman in the white dress, this beautiful woman whom every businessman in the bar would have given his Christmas bonus just to sit with.

''I don't even know your name,'' said Gil, growing bolder.

''Is that necessary?''

''I don't really suppose it is. But I'd like to. My name's Gil Batchelor.''

''Anna.''

''Is that all, just Anna?''

''It's a palindrome,'' she smiled. ''That means that it's the same backward as it is forward. I try to live up to it.''

''Could I buy you some dinner?''

"Is *that* necessary?"

Gil took three long heartbeats to reply. "Necessary in what sense?" he asked her.

"In the sense that you feel it necessary to court me somehow. To buy me dinner; to impress me with your taste in wine; to make witty small-talk. To tell me all those humorous anecdotes which I am sure your colleagues have heard one hundred times at least. Is all that necessary?"

Gil licked his lips. Then he said, "Maybe we should take a bottle of champagne upstairs."

Anna smiled. "I'm not a prostitute, you know. The barman thinks I'm a prostitute, but of course prostitutes are good for business, provided they are suitably dressed and behave according to the standards expected by the hotel. If you take me up to your room now, let me tell you truthfully that you will be only the second man I have ever slept with."

Gil gave Anna a complicated shrug with which he intended to convey the feeling that he was flattered by what she had said, but couldn't take her seriously. A woman with Anna's style and Anna's body and Anna's sexual directness had slept in the whole of her life with only one man?

Anna said, "You don't believe me."

"I don't have to believe you, do I? That's part of the game." Gil thought that response was quite clever and sophisticated.

But Anna reached out toward him and gently picked a single hair from the shoulder of his coat and said very quietly, "It's not a game, my love."

. . .

She undressed in silence, close to the window, so that her body was outlined by the cold glow of the streetlights outside, but her face remained in shadow. Her dress slipped to the floor with a sigh. Underneath, she was naked except for a tiny *cache-sexe* of white embroidered cotton. Her breasts were large, almost too large for a woman with such a narrow back, and her nipples were wide and pale as sugar frosting.

Gil watched her, unbuttoning his shirt. He could sense her smiling. She came over and buried the fingers of one hand into the curly brown hair on his chest, and tugged at it. She kissed his cheeks, then his lips. Then she reached down and started to unfasten his belt.

Gil thought: *This is morally wrong, damn it. I'm cheating the woman who gave me my children; the woman who's waiting for me to come home tomorrow. But how often does a man run into a sexual dream like this? Supposing I tell her to get dressed and leave. I'll spend the rest of my life wondering what it could have been like.*

Anna slid her hands into the back of his trousers. Her sharp fingernails traced the line of his buttocks, and he couldn't help shivering. "Lie down on the bed," she whispered. "Let me make love to you."

Gil sat on the edge of the bed, and struggled out of his trousers. Then Anna pushed him gently backward. He heard the softest plucking of elastic as she took off her *cache-sexe*. She climbed astride his chest, and sat in the semi-darkness smiling at him, her hair like a soft and mysterious veil. "Do you like to be kissed?" she asked him. "There are so many ways to be kissed."

She lifted herself up, and teasingly lowered her vulva so that it kissed his lips. Her pubic hair was silky and long, and rose up in a plume. Gil kissed her, hesitantly at first, then deeper, holding her open with his fingers.

She gave a deep, soft murmur of pleasure, and ran her fingers through his hair.

They made love four times that night. Anna seemed to be insatiable. When the first slate-gray light of morning began to strain into the room, and the trams began to boom over Hogesluis again, Gil lay back in bed watching her sleep, her hair tangled on the pillow. He cupped her breast in his hand, and then ran his fingers gently all the way down the flatness of her stomach to her dark-haired sex. She was more than a dream, she was irresistible. She was everything that anybody could desire. Gil kissed her lightly on the forehead, and when she opened her eyes and looked up at him and smiled, he knew that he was already falling in love with her.

"You have to go back to England today," she said, softly.

"I don't know. Maybe."

"You mean you could stay a little longer?"

Gil looked at her, but at the same time he made a conscious effort to picture Margaret, as if he were watching a movie with a split screen. He could imagine Margaret sitting on the sofa sewing and glancing at the clock every few minutes to see if it was time for him to be landing at Gatwick Airport. He could see her opening the front door and smiling and kissing him and telling him what Alan had been doing at playschool.

"Maybe another day," Gil heard himself saying, as if there were somebody else in the room who spoke just like him.

Anna drew his head down and kissed him. Her tongue slipped in between his teeth. Then she lay back and whispered, "What about two days? I could take you to Zandvoort. We could go to my house, and then we could spend all day and all night and all the next day making love."

"I'm not sure that I can manage two days."

"Call your office. Tell them you may be able to sell the good burghers of Amsterdam a few more of your buses. A day and a night and a day. You can go home on Sunday night. The plane won't be so crowded then."

Gil hesitated, and then kissed her. "All right then. What the hell. I'll call the airline after breakfast."

"And your wife? You have to call your wife."

"I'll call her."

Anna stretched out like a a beautiful sleek animal. "You are a very special gentleman, Mr. Gil Batchelor," she told him.

"Well, you're a very special lady."

• • •

Margaret had sniffled: that had made him feel so guilty that he nearly agreed to come back to England straightaway. She missed him, everything was ready for him at home, Alan kept saying, "Where's Daddy?" And *why* did he have to stay in Holland for another two days? Surely the Dutch people could telephone him, or send him a telex? And why *him*? George Kendall should have been selling those extra buses, not him.

In the end, it was her whining that gave him the strength to say, "I have to, that's all. I don't like it any more than you do, darling, believe me. I miss you too, and Alan. But it's only two more days. And then we'll all go to Brighton for the day, what about that? We'll have lunch at Wheeler's."

He put down the phone. Anna was watching him across the room.

She was sitting on a large white leather sofa, wearing only thin pajama trousers of crêpe silk. Between her bare breasts she held a heavy crystal glass of Bacardi. The coldness of the glass had made her nipples tighten. She was smiling at him in a way that he found oddly disturbing. She looked almost triumphant, as if by persuading him to lie to Margaret, she had somehow captured a little part of his soul.

Behind her, through the picture window that was framed with cheese-plants and ivy, he could see the concrete promenade, the wide gray beach, the gray overhanging clouds, and the restless horizon of the North Sea.

He came and sat down beside her. He touched her lips with his fingertip and she kissed it. His hand followed the warm heavy curve of her breast, and then he gently rolled her nipple between finger and thumb. She watched him, still smiling.

"Do you think you could ever fall in love with somebody like me?" she asked him, in a whisper.

"I don't think there is anybody like you. Only you."

"So could you fall in love with me?"

He dared to say it. "I think I already have."

She set her drink down on the glass and stainless-steel table next to her, and knelt up on the sofa. She tugged down her pajama trousers so that she was naked. She pushed Gil on to his back, and climbed on top of him. "You like kissing me, don't you?" she murmured. He didn't answer, but lifted his head slightly, and saw her looking at him with that same disturbing smile.

• • •

The house was always silent, except when they spoke, or when they played music. Anna liked Mozart symphonies, but she always played them in another room. The walls were white and bare, the carpets were gray. The inside of the house seemed to be a continuation of the bleak coastal scenery that Gil could see through the windows. Apart from the houseplants there were no ornaments. The few pictures on the walls were lean, spare drawings of naked men and women, faceless most of them. Gil had the feeling that the house didn't actually belong to Anna, that it had been occupied by dozens of different people, none of whom had left their mark on it. It was a house of no individuality whatsoever. An anxious house, at the very end of a cul-de-sac that fronted the beach. The gray brick sidewalks were always swirled with gritty gray sand. The wind blew like a constant headache.

They made love over and over again. They went for walks on the beach, the collars of their coats raised up against the stinging sand. They ate silent meals of cold meat and bread and cold white wine. They listened to Mozart in other rooms. On the third morning Gil woke up and saw that Anna was awake already, and watching him. He reached out and stroked her hair.

"This is the day I have to go home," he told her, his voice still thick from sleeping.

She took hold of his hand and squeezed it. "Can't you manage one more day? One more day and one more night?"

"I have to go home. I promised Margaret. And I have to be back behind my desk on Monday morning."

She lowered her head so that he couldn't see her face. "You know that—if you go—we will never be able to see each other any more."

Gil said nothing. It hurt too much to think that he might never sleep with Anna again in the whole of his life. He eased himself out from under the quilt, and walked through to the bathroom. He switched on the light over the basin and inspected himself. He looked tired. Well, anybody would be, after two days and three nights of orgiastic sex with a woman like Anna. But there was something else about his face which made him frown, a different look about it. He stared at himself for a long time but he couldn't decide what it was. He filled the basin with hot water and squirted a handful of shaving foam into his hand.

It was only when he lifted his hand toward his face that he realized he didn't need a shave.

He hesitated, then he rinsed off the foam and emptied the basin. He must have shaved last night, before he went to bed, and forgotten about it. After all, they had drunk quite a lot of wine. He went to the toilet, and sat down, and urinated in quick fits and starts. It was only when he got up and wiped himself by passing a piece of toilet paper between his legs that he realized what he had done. *I never sit down to pee. I'm not a woman.*

Anna was standing in the bathroom doorway watching him. He laughed. "I must be getting old, sitting down to pee."

She came up to him and put her arms around his neck and kissed him. It was a long, complicated, yearning kiss. When he opened his eyes again she was staring at him very close up. "Don't go," she whispered. "Not yet, I couldn't bear it. Give me one more day. Give me one more night."

"Anna . . . I can't. I have a family; a job."

With the same directness she had exhibited in the bar of the Amstel Hotel, she came up to him and put her arms around him, kissing his neck and his shoulders. His reaction was immediate. "Don't go," she repeated. "I've been waiting so long for somebody like you . . . I can't bear to lose you just yet. One more day, one more night. You can catch the evening flight on Monday and be back in England before nine."

He kissed her. He knew that he was going to give in.

That day, they walked right down to the edge of the ocean. A dog with wet bedraggled fur circled around and around, yapping at them. The wind from the North Sea was relentless. When they returned to the house, Gil felt inexplicably exhausted. Anna undressed him and helped him up to the bedroom. "I think I'm feeling the strain," he smiled at her. She leaned over and kissed him. He lay with his eyes open listening to Mozart playing in another room, and looking at the way the gray afternoon light crossed the ceiling and illuminated the pen-and-ink drawing of a man and a woman entwined together. The drawing was like a puzzle. It was impossible to tell where the man ended and where the woman began.

He fell asleep. It started to rain, salty rain from the sea. He slept all afternoon and all evening, and the wind rose and the rain lashed furiously against the windows.

He was still asleep at two o'clock in the morning, when the bedroom door opened and Anna came in, and softly slipped into bed beside him. "My darling," Anna murmured, and touched the smoothness of his cheek.

He dreamed that Anna was shaking him awake, and lifting his head so that he could sip a glass of water. He dreamed that she was caressing him and murmuring to him. He dreamed that he was trying to run across the beach, across the wide gray sands, but the sands turned to glue and clung around his ankles. He heard music, voices.

. . .

He opened his eyes. It was twilight. The house was silent. He turned to look at his watch on the bedside table. It was 7:17 in the evening. His head felt congested, as if he had a hangover, and when he licked his lips they felt swollen and dry. He lay back for a long time staring at the ceiling, his arms by his sides. He must have been ill, or maybe he had drunk too much. He had never felt like this in his life before.

It was only when he raised his hand to rub his eyes that he understood that something extraordinary had happened to him. His arm was obstructed by a huge soft growth on his chest. He felt a cold thrill of complete terror, and instantly yanked down the quilt. When he saw his naked body, he let out a high-pitched shout of fright.

He had breasts. Two heavy, well-rounded breasts, with fully developed nipples. He grasped them in his hands and realized they weren't tumorous growths, they weren't cancers, they were actual female breasts, and very big breasts, too. Just like Anna's.

Trembling, he ran his right hand down his sides, and felt a narrow waist, a flat stomach, and then silky pubic hair. He knew what he was going to feel between his legs, but he held himself back for minute after minute, his eyes closed, not daring to believe that it had gone, that he had been emasculated. At last, however, he slipped his fingers down between his hairless thighs, and felt the moist lips of his vulva. He hesitated, swallowed, and then slipped one finger into his vagina.

There was no question about it. His body was completely female, inside and out. In appearance at least, he was a woman.

"None of this is real," he told himself, but even his voice was feminine. He climbed slowly out of bed and his breasts swayed, just the way that Anna's had swayed. He walked across the room and confronted the full-length mirror beside the dressing-table. There was a woman looking back at him, a beautiful naked woman, and the woman was him.

"This isn't real," he repeated, cupping his breasts in his hands and staring intently at the face in the mirror. The eyes were his, the expression was his. He could see himself inside that face, his own personality, Gil Batchelor the bus salesman from Woking. But who else was going to be able to see what he saw? What was Brian Taylor going to see if he tried to turn up for work? And, God Almighty, it seemed absurd, but what was Margaret going to say if he came back home looking like this?

Without a sound, he collapsed on to the floor, and lay with his face against the gray carpet, in total shock. He lay there until it grew dark, feeling chilled, but unwilling or unable to move. He wasn't sure which and he wasn't going to find out.

At last, when the room was completely dark, the door opened, and a dim light fell across the floor. Gil heard a voice saying, "You're awake. I'm sorry. I should have come in earlier."

Gil lifted his head. Unconsciously, he drew his long tangled hair out of his eyes, and looked up. A man was silhouetted in the doorway, a man wearing a business suit and polished shoes.

"Who are you?" he asked, hoarsely. "What the hell has happened to me?"

The man said, "You've changed, that's all."

"For Christ's sake, look at me. What the hell is going on here? Did you do this with hormones, or what? I'm a man! I'm a *man,* for Christ's sake!" Gil began to weep. The tears slid down his cheeks and he tasted salt on his lips.

The man came forward and knelt down beside him and laid a comforting hand on his shoulder. "It wasn't hormones. If I knew how it happened, believe me, I'd tell you. But all I know is, it happens. One man to the next. The man who was Anna before me—the man who took the body that used to be mine—he told me everything about it, just as I'm telling you—and just as *you'll* tell the next man that you pick."

At that moment, the bedroom door swung a little wider, and the man's face was illuminated by the light from the hallway. With a surge of paralyzing fright, Gil saw that the man was him. His own face, his own hair, his own smile. His own wristwatch, his own suit. And outside in the hallway, his own suitcase, already packed.

"I don't understand," he whispered. He wiped the tears away from his face with his fingers.

"I don't think any of us ever will," the man told him. "There seems to be some kind of pattern to it; some kind of reason why it happens; but there's no way of finding out what it is."

"But you knew this was going to happen all along," said Gil. "Right from the very beginning. You *knew.*"

The man nodded. Gil should have been violent with rage. He should have seized the man by the throat and beaten his head against the wall. But the man was him, and for some inexplicable reason he was terrified of touching him.

The man said, quietly, "I'm sorry for you. Please believe me. But I'm just as sorry for myself. I used to be a man like you. My name was David Chilton. I was thirty-two years old, and I used to lease executive aircraft. I had a family, a wife and two daughters, and a house in Darien, Connecticut."

He paused, and then he said, "Four months ago I came to Amsterdam and met Anna. One thing led to another, and she took me back here. She used to make me make love to her, night after night. Then one morning I woke up and *I* was Anna, and Anna was gone."

Gil said, "I can't believe any of this. This is madness. I'm having a nightmare."

The man shook his head. "It's true; and it's been happening to one man after another, for years probably."

"How do you know that?"

"Because Anna took my passport and my luggage, and it seemed to me that there was only one place that she could go—*he* could go. Only one place where he could survive in my body and with my identity."

Gil stared at him. "You mean—your own home? He took your body and went to live in your own home?"

The man nodded. His face was grim. Gil had never seen himself look so grim before.

"I found Anna's passport and Anna's bank-books—don't worry, I've left them all for you. I flew to New York and then rented a car and drove up to Connecticut. I parked outside my own house and watched myself mowing my own lawn, playing with my own daughters, kissing my own wife."

He lowered his head, and then he said, "I could have killed him, I guess. Me, I mean—or at least the person who looked like me. But what would that have achieved? I would have made a widow out of my own wife, and orphans out of my own children. I loved them too much for that. I love them still."

"You left them alone?" Gil whispered.

"What else could I do? I flew back to Holland and here I am."

Gil said, "Couldn't you have *stayed* like Anna? Why couldn't you stay the way you were? Why did you have to take *my* body?"

"Because I'm a man," David Chilton told him. "Because I was brought up a man, and because I think like a man, and because it doesn't matter how beautiful a woman you are, how rich a woman you are . . . well, you're going to find out what it's like, believe me. Not even the poorest most downtrodden guy in the whole wide world has to endure what women have to endure. Supposing every time that a woman came up to a man, she stared at his crotch instead of his face, even when they were supposed to be having a serious conversation? You don't think that happens? You did it to me, when we met at the hotel. Eighty per cent of the time, your eyes were ogling my tits, and I know what you were thinking. Well, now it's going to happen to you. And, believe me, after a couple of months, you're going to go pick up some guy not because you want to live like a man again but because you want your revenge on all those jerkoffs who treat you like a sex object instead of a human being."

Gil knelt on the floor and said nothing. David Chilton checked Gil's wristwatch—the one that Margaret had given him on their last anniversary—and said, "I'd better go. I've booked a flight at eleven."

"You're not—" Gil began.

David Chilton made a face. "What else can I do? Your wife's expecting me home. A straight ordinary-looking man like me. Not a voluptuous brunette like you."

"You can't do this," Gil told him. "It's theft!"

"Theft? How can a man steal something which everybody in the whole world will agree is his?"

"Then it's murder, for God's sake! You've effectively killed me!"

"Murder?" David Chilton shook his head. "Come on, now, Anna, I really have to go."

"I'll kill you," Gil warned him.

"I don't think so," said David Chilton. "Maybe you'll think about it, the way that I thought about killing the guy who took my body. But there's a diary in the living room, a diary kept by most of the men who have changed into Anna. Read it, before you think of doing anything drastic."

He reached out and touched Gil's hair, almost regretfully. "You'll survive. You have clothes, you have a car, you have money in the bank. You even have an investment portfolio. You're not a poor woman. Fantasy women never are. If you want to stay as Anna, you can live quite comfortably for the rest of your life. Or . . . if you get tired of it, you know what to do.''

Gil sat on the floor incapable of doing anything at all to prevent David Chilton from leaving. He was too traumatized; too drained of feeling. David Chilton went to the end of the hallway and picked up his suitcase. He turned and smiled at Gil one last time, and then blew him a kiss.

''So long, honey. Be good.''

Gil was still sitting staring at the carpet when the front door closed, and the body he had been born with walked out of his life.

. . .

He slept for the rest of the night. He had no dreams that he could remember. When he woke up, he lay in bed for almost an hour, feeling his body with his hands. It was frightening but peculiarly erotic, to have the body of a woman, and yet to retain the mind of a man. Gil massaged his breasts, rolling his nipples between finger and thumb the way he had done with ''Anna.'' Then he reached down between his legs and gently stroked himself, exploring his sex with tension and curiosity.

He wondered what it would be like to have a man actually inside him; a man on top of him, thrusting into him.

He stopped himself from thinking that thought. *For God's sake, you're not a queer.*

He showered and washed his hair. He found the length of his hair difficult to manage, especially when it was wet, and it took four attempts before he was able to wind a towel around it in a satisfactory turban. Yet Margaret always did it without even looking in the mirror. He decided that at the first opportunity he got, he would have it cut short.

He went to the closet and inspected Anna's wardrobe. He had liked her in her navy-blue skirt and white loose-knit sweater. He found the sweater folded neatly in one of the drawers. He struggled awkwardly into it, but realized when he looked at himself in the mirror that he was going to need a bra. He didn't want to attract *that* much attention, not to begin with, anyway. He located a drawerful of bras, lacy and mysterious, and tried one on. His breasts kept dropping out of the cups before he could fasten it up at the back, but in the end he knelt down beside the bed and propped his breasts on the quilt. He stepped into one of Anna's lacy little G-strings. He found it irritating, the way the elastic went right up between the cheeks of his bottom, but he supposed he would get used to it.

Get used to it. The words stopped him like a cold bullet in the brain. He stared at himself in the mirror, that beautiful face, those eyes that were still his. He began to weep with rage. *You've started to accept it already. You've started to cope. You're fussing around in your bra and your panties and you're worrying which skirt to wear and you've already forgotten that you're not Anna, you're Gil. You're a husband. You're a father. You're a man, damn it!*

He began to hyperventilate, his anger rising up unstoppably like the scarlet line of alcohol rising up a thermometer. He picked up the dressing-stool, and heaved it at the mirror. The glass shattered explosively, all over the carpet. A thousand tiny Annas stared up at him in uncontrollable fury and frustration.

He stormed blindly through the house, yanking open drawers, strewing papers everywhere, clearing ornaments off table-tops with a sweep of his arm. He wrenched open the doors of the cocktail cabinet, and hurled the bottles of liquor one by one across the room, so that they smashed against the wall. Whiskey, gin, Campari, broken glass.

Eventually, exhausted, he sat down on the floor and sobbed. Then he was too tired even to cry.

In front of him, lying on the rug, were Anna's identity card, her social security papers, her passport, her credit cards. *Anna Huysmans.* The name which was now his.

On the far side of the room, halfway under the leather sofa, Gil saw a large diary bound in brown Morocco leather. He crept across the floor on his hands and knees and picked it up. This must be the diary that David Chilton had been talking about. He opened it up to the last page.

He read, through eyes blurry with tears, *"Gil has been marvelous . . . he has an enthusiastic, uncluttered personality . . . It won't be difficult to adapt to being him . . . I just hope that I like his wife, Margaret . . . she sounds a little immature, from what Gil says . . .*

and he complains that she needs a lot of persuading when it comes to sex . . . Still, that's probably Gil's fault . . . you couldn't call him the world's greatest lover.''

Gil flicked back through the diary's pages until he came to the very first entry. To his astonishment it was dated July 16, 1942. It was written in German, by a Reichswehr officer who appeared to have met Anna while driving out to Edam on military business. ''Her bicycle tire was punctured . . . she was so pretty that I told my driver to stop and to help her . . .''

There was no way of telling, however, whether this German Samaritan had been the first of Anna's victims, or simply the first to keep a diary. The entries went on page after page, year after year. There must have been more than seven hundred of them; and each one told a different story of temptation and tragedy. Some of the men had even essayed explanations of what Anna was, and why she took men's bodies.

''She has been sent to punish us by God Himself for thinking lustful thoughts about women and betraying the Holy Sacrament of marriage . . .''

''She does not actually exist. There is no 'Anna,' because she is always one of us. The only 'Anna' that exists is in the mind of the man who is seducing her, and that perhaps is the greatest condemnation of them all. We fall in love with our own illusions, rather than a real woman.''

''To me, Anna is a collector of weak souls. She gathers us up and hangs us on her charm-bracelet, little dangling victims of our own vicissitudes.''

''Anna is a ghost . . .''

''Anna is a vampire . . .''

''If I killed myself, would it break the chain? Would Anna die if I died? Supposing I tried to seduce the man who was Anna before me . . . could I reverse the changing process?''

Gil sat on the floor and read the diary from cover to cover. It was an extraordinary chorus of voices—real men who had been seduced into taking on the body of a beautiful woman, one after the other—and in their turn had desperately tried to escape. Business executives, policemen, soldiers, scientists, philosophers—even priests. Some had stayed as Anna for fewer than two days; others had managed to endure it for months. But to every single one of them, the body even of the plainest man had been preferable to Anna's body, regardless of how desirable she was.

By two o'clock, Gil was feeling hungry. The icebox was almost empty, so he drove into Amsterdam for lunch. The day was bright but chilly, and so he wore Anna's black belted raincoat, and a black beret to cover his head. He tried her high-heels, but he twisted his ankle in the hallway, and sat against the wall with tears in his eyes saying, "Shit, shit," over and over, as if he *ought* to have been able to walk in them quite naturally. He limped back to the bedroom and changed into black court shoes.

He managed to find a parking space for Anna's BMW on the edge of the Singel canal, close to the Muntplein, where the old mint-building stood, with its clock and its onion dome. There was an Indonesian restaurant on the first floor of the building on the corner: one of the executives of the Gemeentevervoerbedrijf had pointed it out to him. He went upstairs and a smiling Indonesian waiter showed him to a table for one, overlooking the square. He ordered rijstafel for one, and a beer. The waiter stared at him, and so he changed his order to a vodka and tonic.

The large restaurant was empty, except for a party of American businessmen over on the far side. As he ate his meal, Gil gradually became aware that one of the businessmen was watching him. Not only watching him, but every time he glanced up, *winking* at him.

Oh shit, he thought. *Just let me eat my lunch in peace.*

He ignored the winks and the unrelenting stares; but after the business lunch broke up, the man came across the restaurant, buttoning up his coat, and smiling. He was big and red-faced and sweaty, with wavy blond hair and three heavy gold rings on each hand.

"You'll pardon my boldness," he said. "My name's Fred Oscay. I'm in aluminum tubing, Pennsylvania Tubes. I just couldn't take my eyes off you all during lunch."

Gil looked up at him challengingly. "So?" he replied.

"Well," grinned Fred Oscay, "maybe you could take that as a compliment. You're some looker, I've got to tell you. I was wondering if you had any plans for dinner tonight. You know—maybe a show, maybe a meal."

Gil was trembling. Why the hell was he trembling? He was both angry and frightened. Angry at being stared at and winked at and chatted up by this crimson-faced idiot; frightened because social convention prevented him from being as rude as he really wanted to be—that, and his weaker physique.

It was a new insight—and to Gil it was hair-raising—that men used the threat of their greater physical strength against women not just in times of argument and stress—but *all the time*.

"Mr. Oscay," he said, and he was still trembling. "I'd really prefer it if you went back to your party and left me alone."

"Aw, come along now," Fred Oscay grinned. "You can't mean that."

Gil's mouth felt dry. "Will you please just leave me alone?"

Fred Oscay leaned over Gil's table. "There's a fine concert at the Kleine Zaal, if it's culture you're after."

Gil hesitated for a moment, and then picked up a small metal dish of Indonesian curried chicken and turned it upside down over Fred Oscay's left sleeve. Fred Oscay stared down at it for a very long time without saying anything, then stared at Gil with a hostility in his eyes that Gil had never seen from anybody before. Fred Oscay looked quite capable of killing him, then and there.

"You tramp," he said. "You stupid bitch."

"Go away," Gil told him. "All I'm asking you to do is go away."

Now Fred Oscay's voice became booming and theatrical, intended for all his business colleagues to hear. "You were coming on, lady. You were coming on. All through lunch you were giving me the glad-eye. So don't you start getting all tight-assed now. What is it, you want money? Is that it? You're a professional? Well, I'm sorry. I'm really truly sorry. But old Fred Oscay never paid for a woman in his life, and he ain't about to start just for some sorry old hooker like you."

He picked up a napkin and wiped the curry off his sleeve with a flourish, throwing the soiled napkin directly into Gil's plate. The other businessmen laughed and stared. One of them said, "Come on, Fred, we can't trust you for a minute."

Gil sat where he was and couldn't think what to do; how to retaliate; how to get his revenge. He felt so frustrated that in spite of himself he burst into tears. The Indonesian waiter came over and offered him a glass of water. ''Aroo okay?'' he kept asking. ''Aroo okay?''

''I'm all right,'' Gil insisted. ''Please—I'm all right.''

. . .

He was standing on the corner of the street as patient as a shadow as David Chilton emerged from his front door right on time and began walking his cocker spaniel along the grass verge. It was 10:35 at night. David and Margaret would have been watching *News at Ten* and then *South East News* just as Gil and Margaret had always done. Then David would have taken down Bondy's leash, and whistled, ''Come on, boy! Twice round the park!'' while Margaret went into the kitchen to tidy up and make them some cocoa.

He was wearing the same black belted raincoat and the same black beret that he had worn in Amsterdam; only now he had mastered Anna's high-heels. His hair was curly and well-brushed and he wore make-up now, carefully copied from an article in a Dutch magazine.

Under his raincoat he carried a stainless-steel butcher knife with a twelve-inch blade. He was quite calm. He was breathing evenly and his pulse was no faster than it had been when he first met Anna.

Bondy insisted on sniffing at every bush and every garden gatepost, so it took a long time for David to come within earshot. He had his hands in his pockets and he was whistling under his breath, a tune that Gil had never known. At last, Gil stepped out and said, ''David?''

David Chilton stood stock-still. ''Anna?'' he asked, hoarsely.

Gil took another step forward, into the flat orange illumination of the streetlight. ''Yes, David, it's Anna.''

David Chilton took his hands out of his pockets. ''I guess you had to come and take a look, didn't you? Well, I was the same.''

Gil glanced toward the house. ''Is he happy? Alan, I mean.''

''Alan's fine. He's a fine boy. He looks just like you. I mean me.''

''And Margaret?''

''Oh, Margaret's fine too. Just fine.''

''She doesn't notice any difference?'' said Gil, bitterly. ''In bed, perhaps? I know I wasn't the world's greatest lover.''

''Margaret's fine, really.''

Gil was silent for a while. Then he said, ''The job? How do you like the job?''

"Well, not too bad," grinned David Chilton. "But I have to admit that I'm looking around for something a little more demanding."

"But, apart from that, you've settled in well?"

"You could say that, yes. It's not Darien, but it's not Zandvoort, either."

Bondy had already disappeared into the darkness. David Chilton whistled a couple of times, and called, "Bondy! Bondy!" He turned to Gil and said, "Look—you know, I understand why you came. I really do. I sympathize. But I have to get after Bondy or Moo's going to give me hell."

For the very first time, Gil felt a sharp pang of genuine jealousy for Margaret. "You call her Moo?"

"Didn't you?" David Chilton asked him.

Gil remained where he was while David Chilton went jogging off after his dog. His eyes were wide with indecision. But David had only managed to run twenty or thirty yards before Gil suddenly drew out the butcher knife and went after him.

"David!" he called out, in his high, feminine voice. "David! Wait!"

David Chilton stopped and turned. Gil had been walking quickly so that he had almost reached him. Gil's arm went up. David Chilton obviously didn't understand what was happening at first, not until Gil stabbed him a second time, close to his neck.

David Chilton dropped, rolled away, then bobbed up on to his feet again. He looked as if he had been trained to fight. Gil came after him, his knife upraised, silent and angry beyond belief. *If I can't have my body, then nobody's going to. And perhaps if the man who took my body—if his spirit dies—perhaps I'll get my body back. There's no other hope, no other way. Not unless Anna goes on for generation after generation, taking one man after another.*

Gil screamed at David and stabbed at his face. But David seized Gil's wrist and twisted it around, skin tearing, so that Gil dropped the knife on to the pavement. Gil's high-heel snapped. He lost his balance and they both fell. Their hands scrabbled for the knife. David touched it, missed it, then managed to take hold of it.

The long triangular blade rose and fell five times. There was a sound of muscle chopping. The two rolled away from each other, and lay side by side, flat on their backs, panting.

Gil could feel the blood soaking his cotton blouse. The inside of his stomach felt cold and very liquid, as if his stomach had poured its contents into his whole abdominal cavity. He knew that he couldn't move. He had felt the knife slice sharply against his spine.

David knelt up on one elbow. His hands and his face were smeared in blood. *"Anna . . ."* he said, unsteadily. *"Anna . . ."*

Gil looked up at him. Already, he was finding it difficult to focus. "You've killed me," he said. "You've killed me. Don't you understand what you've done?"

David looked desperate. "You *know,* don't you? You *know.*"

Gil attempted to smile. "I don't know, not for sure. But I can feel it. I can feel you—you and all the rest of them—right inside my head. I can hear your voices. I can feel your pain. I took your souls. I took your spirits. That's what you gave me, in exchange for your lust."

He coughed blood, and then he said, "My God . . . I wish I'd understood this before. Because you know what's going to happen now, don't you? You know what's going to happen now?"

David stared at him in dread. "Anna, listen, you're not going to die. Anna, listen, you can't. Just hold on, I'll call for an ambulance. But hold on!"

But Gil could see nothing but darkness. Gil could hear nothing but the gray sea. Gil was gone; and Anna was gone, too.

. . .

David Chilton made it as far as the garden gate. He grasped the post, gripped at the privet-hedge. He cried out, "Moo! Help me! For Christ's sake help me!" He grasped at his throat as if he were choking. Then he collapsed into the freshly dug flower bed, and lay there shuddering, the way an insect shudders when it is mortally hurt. The way any creature shudders, when it has no soul.

All over the world that night, men quaked and died. Over seven hundred of them: in hotels, in houses, in restaurants, in the back of taxis. A one-time German officer collapsed during dinner, his face blue, his head lying in his salad plate, as if it were about to be served up with an apple in his mouth. An airline pilot flying over Nebraska clung to his collar and managed to gargle out the name *Anna!* before he pitched forward on to his controls.

A sixty-year-old Member of Parliament, making his way down the aisle in the House of Commons for the resumption of a late-night sitting, abruptly tumbled forward and lay between the Government and the Opposition benches, shuddering helplessly at the gradual onset of death.

On I-5 just south of San Clemente, California, a fifty-five-year-old executive for a swimming-pool maintenance company died at the wheel of his Lincoln sedan. The car swerved from one side of the highway to the other before colliding into the side of a 7-Eleven truck, overturning, and fiercely catching fire.

Helplessly, four or five Mexicans who had been clearing the verges stood beside the highway and watched the man burn inside his car, not realizing that he was already dead.

. . .

The civic authorities buried Anna Huysmans at Zandvoort, not far from the sea. Her will had specified a polished black marble headstone, without decoration. It reflected the slowly moving clouds as if it were a mirror. There were no relatives, no friends, no flowers. Only a single woman, dressed in black, watching from the cemetery boundary as if she had nothing to do with the funeral at all. She was very beautiful, this woman, even in black, with a veil over her face. A man who had come to lay flowers on the grave of his grandfather saw her standing alone, and watched her for a while.

She turned. He smiled.

She smiled back.

IN THE WEST WING

Roland Masterton

Our oldest son, Roland, was eleven when he presented me with his own contribution to *Scare Care.* He is boarding at Harrow School now, and is more sophisticated (and taller!) but he hasn't lost his interest in horror fiction (his new boys' project for the headmaster is a collection of his own horror stories, *Through the Eyes of a Child*)—nor has he lost his interest in helping children less fortunate. He likes Prince, frying his own bacon, fighting his brothers Daniel and Luke, and Harrow Football. In ten years' time, I expect to see him emerging as one of the next generation of horror writers . . .

Tom woke up. His radio-alarm glowed 2:15 A.M. He stared into the darkness of his room. The warmth came from his blond-haired wife, Martina.

He got up and stretched and ruffled his hair. He pulled on his well-worn jeans, then felt into the blackness for the door. He walked downstairs to the kitchen.

In the kitchen he shielded his eyes from the bright light when he opened the fridge. He picked out the orange-juice carton and gulped down the juice. Then he closed the fridge and sat himself in a comfortable chair in the living room and fell asleep.

. . .

In the morning he woke up to the smell of bacon and eggs. He greeted and kissed Martina, then he sat down to the great-smelling bacon.

"That's the post," said Martina. "I'll go and get it."

In a moment she was back, sorting through the letters.

"What's that?" asked Tom, looking up and chewing on a bacon rind.

"A postcard from Lady Bertha," replied Martina. "She wants us to go round and spend a couple of nights with her."

Tom shrugged, and dipped the last of his crispy bacon into the egg yolk.

After breakfast, they packed two nights' clothes, put them in the trunk of their car, and drove to Lady Bertha's manor-house.

It took an hour to get there, and Tom was glad to stretch his legs when he arrived. They rang the doorbell, and a butler answered them and showed them to Lady Bertha.

"Good day," Lady Bertha said. "I hope you had a pleasant drive. Do have a glass of sherry."

After a few glasses of sherry and a long chat, Tom noticed—behind a suit of armour—a padlocked door.

"What's behind there?" asked Tom.

Lady Bertha began to tremble, and say, "That's the—the west wing. It's too crumbly and broken-down to live in, so I closed it off."

Tom stared at the wall, puzzled.

. . .

That evening, after a hearty supper and another good chat, Tom and Martina went to their room.

It was almost midnight when Tom woke up. There was a thump coming from the west wing. *Thump, thump, thump*.

"Oh, go back to sleep," Tom told himself.

But the thumping went on and on. Tom got up and put on his jeans. He crept out of the room towards the west wing. He moved the suit of armour out of the way, and grabbed the sword from it. With great strength, he hit the padlock.

The sword broke, and clattered to the floor. But he had weakened the padlock. The *thump, thump, thump* carried on. With a poker from the fireplace, Tom hit the lock again, and it broke. He opened the door and went in.

Everything was dusty and covered with cobwebs. To his sides were doors, hundreds of doors. He turned to the left, and there was the *thump-thumping* behind one of the doors. He turned the key. The lock squeaked. The door burst open. Something black rushed out and hit him on the head with an axe. He felt the blood gush down his forehead. Everything began to fade . . .

. . .

He woke up to the smell of bacon and eggs. He greeted and kissed Martina, then he sat down to the great-smelling bacon.

"That's the post," said Martina. "I'll go and get it."

In a moment she was back, sorting through the letters.

"What's that?" asked Tom, looking up and chewing on a piece of bacon rind.

"A postcard from Lady Bertha," replied Martina. "She wants us to go round and spend a couple of nights with her."

Tom screamed.